They Also Serve

Darrell Wyatt

NEWMAN SPRINGS PUBLISHING
320 Broad Street
Red Bank, NJ 07701

First originally published by Newman Springs Publishing 2022

ISBN 978-1-68498-355-1 (Paperback)
ISBN 978-1-68498-356-8 (Digital)

Printed in the United States of America

This book is dedicated to the women of the greatest generation whose hard work and patriotism gave their menfolk the means to defeat their enemies.

It is also dedicated to the two hardworking, caring women I was privileged to love: my mother, Nina, herself a member of that generation, and my wife and partner of thirty years, Linda. I owe you both more than I ever deserved.

Contents

1

It was late 1944, and the second "war to end all wars" had dragged on for almost four long, miserable years. The Allies had finally turned the war in Europe around and had the Germans back on their heels. Many Americans thought it might be over by Christmas.

MacArthur was still slugging it out with Hirohito in the Pacific. As he had promised the Filipino people when the Japanese forced his retreat to Australia, he "had returned" to the Philippines. The American brass was planning the invasion of the Japanese Home Islands, which promised to be a major bloodbath on both sides. On the home front, young American women filled in the spaces left by the millions of departed men, working in the fields and the factories, keeping the "arsenal of democracy" going.

Two young women climbed well-worn wooden stairs up to their second-story apartment in the old brownstone section of St. Joseph, Missouri. The first girl unlocked the door and continued to ignore the pleas of the second girl. The first, June Taylor was a slim, blue-eyed, redheaded, twenty-two-year-old farm girl. She had graduated from DeKalb High School in northwestern Missouri and left her parents' tobacco farm to work in the big city of St. Joseph. June's hardy upbringing had instilled in her a sturdy independence. She found work at the Quaker Oats plant in the packing department. Quaker hired hundreds of women to replace the men who answered the call to arms. Quaker was one of the largest employers in St. Joseph, producing hot and cold cereals and pancake flour for both civilian and military consumption.

The second girl was her roommate, Betty Anderson, a feisty city girl from St. Joe. They met on the packing line and hit it off right away. Betty was eager to move out of her parents' house and

1

the supervision of her father, a Methodist minister. When Betty suggested sharing an apartment, June jumped at the chance. She was tired of living in the dormitory-style Young Women's Christian Association (YWCA).

Their apartment in a second-floor walk-up in a turn-of-the-century brownstone building had no elevators. Most of the time, the plumbing worked. The building had a super to fix it when it didn't, although it might take a while for him to get to it. The apartment had two bedrooms, a small living room, a bathroom, and a kitchenette with a two-person breakfast table. There was a tiny entry off the hallway. The hallway was oak, worn down by thousands of footsteps. Their apartment was clean and tidy, except for the occasional undergarment drying on the shower curtain rod in the bathroom. June and Betty hung their winter coats, purses, and hats on hooks in the entry. There was a good deadbolt lock on the door.

Betty was a leggy blond, with a figure that attracted the male of the species from blocks away. She liked their attention just fine and was rarely without dates on the weekend. Despite her outward appearance and love of fun, she was no airhead. Her suitors rarely got all they hoped for but usually had a good time. Having escaped the bounds of her parents' oversight, she was not about to get tied down by any young man. Her father was very displeased when Betty moved out. She kept his hands full growing up. He did not think a young single girl should be out gallivanting on her own and wanted her to go to college where she would find a suitable young man, get married, and have children. He was the pastor of a large well-heeled congregation. The church provided his family with a very comfortable two-story home.

June was more reserved and serious. Not that she was shy or lacked humor; she just wanted to get on with the business of saving her time and money toward nursing school. Sometimes, Betty dragged June into double dates with her date's buddies. Don was Betty's latest heartthrob. He was a tall, well-built, curly-haired guitar picker and a smooth talker. His band played the small nightclub circuit in towns like Oshkosh, Wisconsin, and Joplin, Missouri. The war broke up the band when Don and Mike entered service. And it was Mike and Don that Betty was pleading with June to double date.

"June, honey, you'll like Mike," Betty said. "He plays guitar in Don's band, and he's real cute."

Don was a talented guitar player but so-so as a lead singer. He could have made good money as a studio musician, backing up rising talent in recording studios, and maybe hooking up with one of them on lead guitar. But he wanted to go his own way and play his own music. None of his songs had caught on with wider audiences, and the one record his band made went nowhere.

Then the war caught up with him, and he enlisted in the Army Air Corps. They trained him as a navigator on B-17s and sent him to the Pacific theater to bomb the Japanese.

Betty met Don at a dance held for servicemen. Don was on leave from his squadron after their lengthy air campaign had supported the Army's bloody ground war on numerous Pacific islands and atolls.

His sideman, Mike, was on a three-week Christmas leave from Camp Crowder. Mike was a rangy, dark-haired young man, not a lady killer like Don but a personable sort. Mike twisted Don's arm to go to the dance and pick up girls. Don wanted to go nightclubbing instead but gave in when Mike said he had been told that a lot of girls went to these dances and were suckers for a uniform.

Betty's friend Wendy asked Betty and June to go to the dance with her. She said a lot of good-looking soldiers and airmen showed up, and anyway, it was their patriotic duty to entertain the troops.

They laughed, and Betty said, "Sure, I'll try it."

June declined. "Not me. Those guys are a little too grabby for me."

"Hey, girlfriend, that's half the fun." Betty laughed again.

"Well, you two go ahead and check it out, and if you don't get in too much trouble, maybe I'll go next time," June said.

"Spoilsport! You'll be sorry you missed it," Betty replied.

*****

The American Legion Hall was decked out in patriotic red, white, and blue streamers. A big "Welcome Servicemen" banner hung across the center rafters. There was a seven-foot Christmas tree decorated with multicolored lights and a variety of ornaments and tinsel. The American flag and the Army, Navy, and Marine Corps flags ringed the bandstand. There was a large crystal punchbowl and an assortment of homemade cookies on a table next to the bandstand. A three-piece trio played popular tunes. They were unpaid volunteers from the local American Legion. The guitar player wasn't bad. The bass player and drummer kept up with him, and they shared the vocals.

It hadn't taken long for the troops to spike the punch bowl. There was a section of folding tables and chairs facing the dance floor and another line of chairs along one wall for the wallflowers. There was a scattering of servicemen in uniform, mostly Army, but there were also airmen from Rosecrans Field and a pair of Marines. St. Joe was a long way from the nearest ocean; Betty and Wendy didn't see any sailors.

The two girls were getting cups of the spiked punch when Betty said, "Wow, get a load of that big hunk!"

"You mean the tall curly-haired soldier that just walked in with his buddy?"

"That would be the one," replied Betty. "I think I'll ask him to dance."

"Oh, Betty, you can't do that! Girls don't ask guys to dance," exclaimed Wendy, a little shocked by the idea.

"Just watch me," said Betty. "Come on!" And she started walking across the dance floor toward the two servicemen.

A reluctant Wendy trailed behind her.

"Hi, I'm Betty, and this is Wendy. We're greeters. Are you boys from a base around here?"

Don looked at Mike and said, "Greeters, huh? What a great idea." He turned back toward the sassy blond and said, "I'm Don, and this is Mike. Most recently I've been hanging out in the Pacific with a lot of Japanese while this rear echelon type has been hand-holding new recruits in southern Missouri."

4

"I'm sure Mike is making his own contribution to the war effort," Wendy objected. She thought the big guy was too egotistical by half.

"Hey, I like you. Let's dance," said Mike, holding out his arm.

The two of them joined the crowd dancing a spirited jitterbug. The November night was chilly, but the dancers worked up a good sweat with the swing dance.

Don looked at Betty and held out his arm.

"It took you long enough," said Betty as she accepted, and they joined the dancers on the floor.

At the end of the dance, Don spotted two couples leaving their table and urged Betty to grab it. The place had filled up, and the other tables were occupied. It looked like the two couples were leaving. The guys had on their service caps and overcoats.

Betty hustled over and narrowly beat another girl and her date to the table.

"Sorry, kids, but you snooze, you lose," Betty told them. "We'd invite you to join us, but our friends are on the way over from the dance floor. If you can find chairs somewhere, come on back!" she said cheerfully. "We'll make room for you."

"We might take you up on that," replied the guy.

But he must have found another table since the couple never returned.

Don and Betty had just sat down when Mike and Wendy joined them.

"What are those wings and colored ribbons on your uniform?" Betty asked, looking at Don's tunic.

"Well, the wings are navigator wings, and the ribbons are for going a full six months without once contracting a social disease."

Betty laughed and said, "Come on, what are they for, really?"

Don, like most combat veterans, was reluctant to talk to civilians about his decorations. But she did ask, and she sure was cute.

"The purple one is the 'I forgot to duck' medal. The others are 'I was there' medals for service in the Pacific." Don didn't mention the Air Medal he got for flying twenty-five bomber missions.

"The 'I forgot to duck' metal?" Betty challenged him.

"Yeah, it's for getting wounded."

"You mean you're a hero!" exclaimed Wendy.

"Nah, it just means we took some shrapnel from AA (antiaircraft) flack, and I was unlucky," Don said.

"Well, I think you're a hero," Wendy said.

"What do you do, Betty?" Don asked, steering the conversation away from the subject of heroes.

"That depends on the guy," Betty said and laughed.

Don laughed and waited for her to answer his question. She was a saucy one, all right.

"We both work at Quaker Oats," Betty said.

"You both make horse food, huh?" Don said.

When milling companies first started producing breakfast cereals from grains in the late1800s, the public was aghast. "They want to feed us horse food!" was the outcry. The pejorative label stuck.

"That old gag," Betty said.

"Can I get you girls some punch?" Mike asked quickly.

"Sure. Thanks," said Betty.

Wendy said, "I'll have a Coke."

Mike left the table to get the drinks.

The band started playing a slow number, and Don asked Betty to dance. Don held Betty close as they made their way around the floor. Betty put some distance back between them.

"You approached me first, remember?" Don whispered.

"This will do just fine," Betty said. "Horse food," she whispered in his ear.

"Touché!" Don said and pulled her in a little closer again.

The dance floor was getting crowded, and the wallflower wall was almost empty. Like Don, the other servicemen took advantage of the slow dance to get snug with their partners who didn't seem to mind.

Mike returned to the table with the drinks, pleased to see Wendy was alone. "So what brings a nice girl like you to a serviceman's dance?"

Wendy couldn't believe he was using the "what's a nice girl like you doing in a place like this?" line on her. "Betty asked me to come with her," she answered sharply.

There was an uncomfortable silence while Mike tried to think how he might regain his lost ground with Wendy.

"Oh, sure," he said. "I'm glad she did."

The rest of their evening went a little better, but Wendy declined the guys' invitation to continue the date with some night clubbing. Betty was clearly disappointed, but since she was Wendy's ride, she reluctantly said good night to Don after giving him her phone number.

Wendy was quiet on the ride back to her place.

Betty asked, "What's with you?"

"Mike didn't really do anything for me. I didn't want to encourage him."

"Well, I had a swell time with Don," Betty said.

"Sorry about that, but I'm sure he'll call you."

The atmosphere in Betty's Ford was a little chilly on the drive home.

2

The phone rang as Betty got home from work.

"Hello," she answered.

"Hello yourself, cutie," said Don. "Mike and I are playing a set on Friday night at the Frog Hop Ballroom, and we thought you girls might join us. What do you think?"

"Wow, you guys got booked at the Frog Hop? The Ink Spots played there," Betty said.

"There was a cancelation, and our manager got us in for a set," Don said.

"I'd love to go, but Wendy didn't hit it off with Mike," Betty said.

"What about your other friend June? You told me she was a good sport," Don suggested.

"Well, I can ask her, but I don't know if she'll go."

"If you can, meet us at the Frog Hop at 8:00 p.m."

"It depends on June."

"Are you okay for gas?" Don asked.

Gasoline was strictly rationed. You had a rationing sticker on the windshield of your car. Different stickers allowed different gallons/week allowances. The most common A sticker allowed four gallons per week. Betty had an A sticker, but an attendant at her gas station had a crush on her and usually let her have a little extra. It got charged to "spillage."

"Yes, I just got my week's ration," Betty said.

The gas rationing was primarily to ration tires. The tire rationing was the result of the Japanese cutting the US off from the rubber producing areas in the Far East, and the military needing almost all the synthetic tires US plants were producing. Limiting gasoline limited the miles driven and extended the life of the tires. The thirty-five miles/hour speed limit also limited tire wear, along with improving gas mileage. There was a limit of five tires per car for the duration of the war. There were scarcely any tires in the country whose inner tubes did not have patches on them. Drivers got adept at heat sealing patches on the rubber inner tubes. The inner tubes punctured easily when the tires got threadbare.

"Okay," Don said. "Hope you gals can make it. It'll be fun. I'll look forward to seeing you. I had a good time at the dance. Bye for now."

*****

When June got home after her shift at the plant, Betty was waiting to pounce on her about Friday night.

"Hey, girlfriend, guess what? We've been invited to a big shindig on Friday night."

"Is it okay if I take my coat off first?" grumbled June. "What kind of shindig?" she asked, hanging up her purse, coat, and hat.

"I told you about meeting that airman, Don, at the dance," Betty answered. "He's a real hero, with medals and everything. He called me this afternoon and invited you and me to come to a set his band is playing at the Frog Hop Ballroom."

"What do you mean, he invited you and me? He doesn't even know me," June said impatiently.

She sat down on the small loveseat in the living room opposite Betty, who was sitting in the overstuffed armchair.

"I told him about us being roommates," Betty said.

"Oh, yeah, what about Wendy? Why isn't she going?"

"Well, Wendy and Mike didn't hit it off very well."

"Who's Mike?" June asked.

"I told you, he's Don's friend! Boy, you never listen to me," Betty complained.

June got up and went to the kitchen and poured herself a glass of beer.

"Let me get this straight. You want me to go out with Wendy's reject so you can make time with the hero, right?" June observed. "You want a beer?"

"You really look on the bright side, don't you?" retorted Betty. "Just because Mike isn't Wendy's type doesn't mean you won't like him. He seemed like a nice guy to me."

"You'd say that if he was Jack the Ripper. You just need me to fill in for Wendy."

"Yeah, I'll have a beer," Betty said. "This conversation is making me thirsty."

June poured another glass and took both beers into the living room. She handed one to Betty.

"Oh, hell, I just thought you might like to get out of this apartment and have a little fun for a change. All you do is work and study for that exam. Give me one of your smokes. I just ran out."

"You're a lot of trouble, you know." She got her purse from the entry and took her cigarettes out. She shook one out of the opened pack and gave it to Betty. "For your information, I'm not spending my life on a packing line at Quaker Oats. High school is a long way back in the rear-view mirror, and I have a lot of stuff to relearn. But I'm going to pass my entrance exam and get into nursing school.

"It wouldn't kill you to have a little fun while you do, would it?"

"No, I suppose it wouldn't," replied June.

"Does that mean you'll go?" Betty exclaimed.

"I guess it does, but you'll have to lend me a pair of nylons. The last time you dragged me on one of these excursions, I ruined my only pair, and no, I won't tell you how they got the runners in them."

"I can take care of your nylon problem," Betty said.

*****

The girls arrived at the Frog Hop Ballroom Friday night in Betty's beat-up Ford Coupe. It had been in much better shape when her parents gave it to her at her high school graduation, but Betty's eyes often wandered away from the road, and she wasn't very good at parallel parking.

10

They wore their good coats over their party dresses and high heels. June had on the borrowed nylons. Betty had been to the beauty parlor to get her hair done. She wore a stylish hat atop the new hairdo.

Betty's stunning, June thought. *But then, I don't look too bad myself.*

The Frog Hop Ballroom was built by Frank Frogge, a widower with nine children. It boasted a 14,000-square-foot dance floor and a frog theme throughout. It was a step above a typical smoky, dark honky-tonk with small bandstands and cramped dance floors. On the right wall near the stage were three booths with padded green Naugahyde seats. They were usually reserved for VIPs. On the left wall was a very long bar. Later in the evening, a platoon of busy bartenders would man the bar. Only a few tended the bar when the girls came in. The huge dance floor was surrounded by tables with a frog logo in the center of the tabletops. The chair seats and backs were green Naugahyde. At the far end of the dance floor, tall red velvet show curtains enclosed the large raised stage.

"Great place, real classy, if you're a frog," June said sarcastically as they walked into the ballroom and looked around.

"Don't start!" Betty said. "Let's just have a good time."

They were met by a large man dressed in a black suit, a gleaming white shirt, and a black tie. He said to the girls, "Welcome, ladies, there's no cover charge for ladies tonight. Can I take your coats?"

The girls surrendered their coats, and he passed them on to the girl in the coat check booth. He gave the claim checks to Betty and June.

"We're meeting our dates. They're in the band playing the first set," Betty informed him.

"When does the entertainment start?" June asked.

"Usually around 9:00 p.m. Are you girls with Don and Mike?" he asked.

"Yes, we are," answered Betty. "Why?"

"They're in the last booth next to the stage. They told me to watch out for you. Can I escort you back?"

"We'll find them," Betty said as she took June's arm and walked back toward the stage.

Paintings of frogs adorned the walls of the ballroom. Every thirty feet or so, there was a shelf on the wall, holding a painted plaster frog. June shook her head as they walked past the frog displays.

"I think they're sort of cute," Betty said as they neared the back booth.

"Tacky is not cute," June said, stopping at the booth.

The guys sat across from each other in the last booth. They wore matching light-blue sports coats, dark-blue slacks, white shirts, and red ties.

Don saw the girls first and greeted them. "Wow, what a pair of dolls!"

"Don't overdo it, big boy. Shove over and make room for a lady," Betty said.

"I can do better than that," Don said as he got to his feet and ushered Betty into the booth.

Betty laughed and slid into the booth.

Mike imitated Don, vacating the booth to make room for June. "I'm Mike, and you must be June."

"Yeah, that's June, or a darned good copy," Betty interjected as June sat down and slid over to make room for Mike.

June studied Don. *My God*, she thought, *he really is a dreamboat.*

The stage curtains opened, and two men started setting up drums and sound equipment.

"What would you ladies like to drink?" Don asked.

"I'm going to have a sloe gin fizz," Betty replied.

"What would you like, June?" Mike asked.

"I'll have a glass of beer," June said. "Are those guys on the stage in your band?"

Don signaled to their waiter. The waiter approached wearing a short green jacket, a green bow tie with a frog on each side of the bow, and tan slacks.

June said to Betty, "They overdo the frog thing."

The waiter pretended he didn't hear June's remark.

"Don't listen to my friend," Betty told the waiter. "She got warts from a frog when she was little."

Don laughed, and the waiter smiled. Don gave the waiter the girls' order and said, "Give my friend and I another round, scotch on the rocks for me, and a Seven and Seven for my buddy." Don looked toward the stage, then said, "That's Dan and Sammy. Sammy always sets up the sound equipment. He's very good with it. They play drums and bass."

The two bandsmen wore the same light-blue jackets and dark-blue slacks worn by Don and Mike.

"The guy at the door said you go on at 9:00 p.m.?" Betty asked.

"Yes, we're up first," Don answered.

"The doorman wasn't wearing a frog tie. Maybe they drummed him out of the frog union," June said.

They all laughed. The tables near them started to fill up.

"What instrument do you play?" June asked Mike.

"I play the guitar. Don plays everything except drums and sax. He's playing lead guitar tonight."

"What do you mean, he plays everything?" asked June.

"He plays bass, steel guitar, the piano, the fiddle, and plays both electric and acoustic guitar."

"My, my, I'm impressed," June said.

"And I can walk and chew gum at the same time too," Don said with a grin.

"Good for you!" Betty said. She gave June a dirty look. "Aren't those drinks ever going to get here?"

"Here is our frog now," June said.

The waiter delivered their drinks and again ignored June's comment. He set two bowls of cashews on their table. "Compliments of the management," he said and walked away.

"It's the booth," Don said. "They do that for anyone in these booths. What should we drink to?"

"How about the end of the war?" said Mike, raising his glass.

"To the end of the war," Don said.

"Here, here," June said, clicking Mike's glass.

Everyone followed suit.

"The damned Krauts are on the run. The war's almost over in Europe," Mike said.

"But the Japs haven't given up yet," Don said.

"How about we talk about something else?" June said.

The war was a dark cloud hanging over her. June had two brothers fighting in Europe, and she worried every day she might get one of those dreaded telegrams.

"Girls at the plant get those War Department telegrams about their husbands or brothers almost every day," Betty said. "I agree, let's change the subject."

Betty sipped her drink, turned to Don, and asked, "When do you have to report back, Don?"

"I have three weeks of recuperative leave left," Don answered, checking the stage.

"Then you go back overseas?" Betty asked, taking a drink of her highball.

"Nah, I've been assigned to Rosecrans Field here in St. Joe," Don said. "I'm going to be training new navigators on trash haulers."

"That's great!" Betty said. "What are trash haulers?"

Don and Mike helped themselves to some of the cashews.

"C-47s, Gooney birds, we call them," Don said. "They're military versions of the Douglas DC-3. They're twin-engine transport planes. Combat flyers call them trash haulers."

June looked at Don and asked, "Isn't that disrespectful of the transport crews?"

"I've got plenty of respect for those guys," Don responded. "They can't shoot back."

The last band member joined the two onstage and took a saxophone out of its case.

"We better get up on the stage. We need to warm up and get the instruments tuned," Mike said, getting out of the booth.

"Yeah, it's almost time to wow the fans," Don agreed and followed Mike to the stage.

The three band members on the stage greeted Mike and Don and razzed them about their dates.

"Don't pay any attention to them, Mike. They're just jealous," Don said.

"You bet your ass we are," Danny said.

After the guys left, Betty looked at June a little sideways and said testily, "You seem to be paying a lot more attention to my date than you are to your date."

"What date? I'm just a fill in, remember," June said, taking another sip of her beer.

Betty searched through her purse and found her cigarettes. Taking one out of the pack, she lit up, blew a tidy smoke ring, and asked, "What do think of Don?"

"Kind of an arrogant SOB, isn't he?"

"Yeah, but he's dreamy," Betty said. "What did he mean 'recuperative leave'?"

"I think the Army gives leave to wounded soldiers," June answered.

"He said he had a Purple Heart medal. He wore the purple ribbon for it when I met him," Betty said. She watched as the band warmed up and took the last handful of cashews from the bowl in front of her.

"Did he say where he got wounded?" June asked.

Betty frowned and said, "Somewhere in the Pacific. He didn't say where exactly."

"No, I meant where was he hit with the shrapnel?"

"He never told me that!" Betty protested, taking a drink of her sloe gin fizz.

"Don't you want to know? What if it was someplace, you know, important!"

Betty paused midsip and stared at June, who laughed. Betty choked on her drink and laughed too.

"I never thought of that!" Betty said and kept giggling. "I have to have another drink on that. Hey, I need a refill. Are you ready for another beer?"

"Not yet. I still have plenty," June answered.

Betty waved down their waiter and ordered a refill. She took a last puff on her cigarette, put it out in the ashtray, and said, "You can't fly on one wing, you know."

"You know me, if I drink more than two beers, either I fall asleep or I run amok, you never know which. I'll just nurse this one along and have the second one when the guys come back."

Sounds of guitars and a bass tuning up came from the stage, along with a few drumrolls and the sweet sound of a saxophone.

"Looks like the boys are about ready to play," Betty said.

Several servicemen and their dates occupied three tables near their booth. The soldiers all seemed to know each other.

"This place is filling up," June observed.

"Yeah, and it's getting smokier and louder too."

"You're not helping the smoky part."

Betty blew another smoke ring at June and thumbed her nose.

The waiter arrived with Betty's drink, and she asked him, "How much is it?" She reached for her purse.

"Keep your money, doll. Your dates are running a tab. How about you, honey? Ready for a refill of your beer?" he asked June.

"Everybody's trying to get me drunk! No, I'll have one later," she said.

"Just signal the frog when you're ready," the waiter said and winked at June. He removed the empty cashew bowl and the empty drink glasses and left.

*****

"Testing, testing," came from the microphone on stage. Then Don said, "Merry Christmas! Welcome, everyone, to the world-famous Frog Hop Ballroom. We're the Jazz Tones. I'm Don Walker, that's Mike Thompson on the guitar, Sammy Chase on bass, Danny James on the drums, and Wild Willy Barton on the saxophone. We'd like to open with something y'all can dance to—"Paper Doll" by the Mills Brothers." Don rolled into a soft guitar riff and sang, "I'm going to buy a paper doll...I can call my own..."

"He's got a nice voice, doesn't he?" said Betty.

"Yes, he does, and I like that mellow saxophone, but the Jazz Tones?"

"What's wrong with the Jazz Tones? I like that name."

"You like it, you keep it," June said. "Of course, it's perfect for this place. Tacky all around."

Couples took to the dance floor, and two uniformed fellows approached their booth. The tall one had staff sergeant stripes on his sleeves.

He asked Betty, "How about a dance, doll?"

"We're taken, Buster. Our dates are up on the stage."

"Well, how about I ask permission. Which one is your date, honey?"

"He's the great big one singing into the microphone. Are you sure you still want to dance with me?" Betty said, arching her eyebrows at him.

The sergeant waved at the stage, getting Don's attention. Then he pointed at Betty and himself, and then at the dance floor and held up his arms to ask, "Okay with you?"

Don finished his verse, paused, and said into the microphone, "That's up to the lady," and continued the song.

The tables around their booth erupted in laughter and applause.

"See, it's okay with your date. Let's go."

"All right, Buster. But you better be a good dancer."

"Actually, my name is Manny, but you can call me Buster if you want."

"Let's go, Buster," Betty said, getting up and taking Manny's hand.

They whirled out on the floor and joined the other dancers.

His buddy said to June, "Should I ask your date for permission too?" He was short, stocky, and had corporal's stripes on his sleeves.

"That's a nice offer, but I'm just going to hold down the fort until our fellows finish their set. I'm not much of a dancer."

"Okay, have a nice evening. Your date is a lucky guy," he said, shaking his head and walking away.

As Betty and Manny danced past the stage, Betty stuck out her tongue at Don.

He gave her a thumbs-up and wrapped up his song.

"We're going to up the tempo with a song Al Dexter wrote for Bing Crosby and the Andrews Sisters," announced Don, and the band struck up "Pistol Packing Mama."

"Oh, let's swing!" exclaimed Betty and spun Manny around.

He caught up with her, and they started dancing the Eastern swing.

Don sang the lead, and the audience joined in the chorus. The saxophone player filled in between verses with some hot jazz notes. It was a hit with the crowd. The band played more top 40 hits, and one of their own songs.

After a few dances, Betty said to Manny, "Buster, I'm bushed," and she headed back to her seat.

"You are the biggest square!" Betty chided June. She turned her attention to Manny, who had followed her back to her booth, and said, "Manny, you're a dandy, but I better shape up and fly right! My date is finishing his set."

"It was my pleasure, little gal, and if that guy messes up with you, give me a ring," and he wrote his phone number on a cocktail napkin, blew her a kiss, and walked off.

Betty stuck the napkin in her purse and searched for her cigarette pack. She found it and a book of matches, shook out another Lucky, lit it, and asked June, "You want one?"

"No, I'm trying to quit."

"You're always trying to quit!"

"I know," June said. "But one of these times I might make it."

"Suit yourself," Betty said, blowing another smoke ring. "Hey, here come our dates!"

Don stopped at their booth and looked down at Betty.

"Well, are you through cheating on me?" Don asked, grinning.

"I don't know, another handsome guy may come along," Betty retorted.

"In that case, I'll sit with June. Mike, you sit with Miss Hot Pants here."

Mike grinned at Betty and raised his eyebrow.

"Works for me. Sit right here, Mike, and give me long, soulful looks," Betty said.

"June, how do you feel about switching dates?" Don asked.

"When you all get through working it out, let me know. I'm going to order my second beer now," June said, signaling their waiter.

Mike shrugged at Betty and sat down with June.

"Just to show you what a great guy I am, I'm going to forgive you for cheating, and I'll even buy you another gin fizz," Don said as he sat down next to Betty.

"Hey, that's a sloe gin fizz, not a gin fizz!" protested Betty.

"Make sure the bartender slows down her gin fizz, and bring another round for the rest of us," Don said to their waiter.

"That's a sloe gin fizz, a scotch on the rocks, a Seven and Seven, and a draft beer, right?" said the waiter.

"This guy's a keeper!" Betty said.

"You say that about all the boys," June said. "I'm glad you all straightened out the seating arrangement. I was about to move to another booth."

The next band had warmed up and been introduced. They swung into "Don't Fence Me In," another Bing Crosby hit.

"It must be Crosby night," said Betty. "Let's dance!" she said to Don, pushing him out of the booth.

"Now you're going to see some *real* dancing!" said Don.

Betty laughed as they took the floor.

"They make a nice couple," said Mike.

"Yes, they do," June agreed. "So you're on leave too?"

"Yeah, from Camp Crowder, down by Neosho."

Camp Crowder was a sprawling Army base carved out of the Ozark woods. It had grown willy-nilly as the wartime Signal Corps had expanded. It boasted six movie theaters, a fully staffed hospital, and three beauty salons for the WACs stationed there.

"What do you at Camp Crowder?"

"I'm a radio operator. Actually, I'm training new recruits on the SCR-300."

"The SC what?"

"It's a portable Army radio. Combat troops carry it in a back-pack on the battlefield."

"Is that all you do—teach recruits to use the SCR thing?"

"That's all I can talk about. Everything else is classified."

June wished her brothers were stationed in a camp in Missouri and not fighting in Europe.

"How did you get into the Signal Corps?' June asked.

"I was a ham radio operator in high school, and when I enlisted, the recruiting sergeant said I should go for the Signal Corps, so I did, and I got it."

"What's Camp Crowder like?"

"It's a pretty big base. Camps are supposed to be temporary facilities, not like forts that are permanent. But it grew like crazy early in the war.

"It sounds like a pretty good place to be a soldier," June said.

"Watch out for the bird shit though." Mike laughed.

"Okay, now you're joshing me!" June said.

"No, honest. The Signal Corps trains homing pigeons to carry messages, and we have a pigeon training unit at Crowder, and a hell of a lot of birds. Pigeons have been important in a lot of combat sit-uations where radio signals are not secure," Mike said. "We even had some hero pigeons."

Now he is pulling my leg, she thought. "Hero pigeons! Really?" June said. "What the heck is a hero pigeon?"

"No kidding. They were officially commended for 'heroic action against the enemy.'"

"What happens to them?" June asked.

"They are given to zoos."

"You learn something new every day," June said, shaking her head. She was warming up to Mike.

After a few minutes of watching the dancers, June asked, "Do you like what you're doing?"

Mike took a drink of his Seven and Seven and said, "It sure beats what Don was doing, flying combat missions over a godfor-saken piece of rock in the ocean with Jap Zeros and antiaircraft bursts everywhere. That's how he got wounded, shrapnel from AA, probably 40mm. But we're talking too much about me, what do you do?"

"It's not very exciting, I'm afraid. I work for Quaker Oats in the packing department. That's where I met Betty. But I want to be a nurse. I've applied to the nursing school at the University of Missouri."

"That's great! You must be pretty smart. I'll bet you got good grades in high school," Mike said. "Do you mind if I smoke?" He took a pack of Chesterfields out of his inside coat pocket.

"Go right ahead, I'm trying to quit, but other people's smoking doesn't bother me."

Mike put the cigarette pack back in his pocket and asked, "Would you like to dance?"

"I'm not much of a dancer, but I could dance a slow one if you want," June said.

"That's a slow one they just started. Shall we?" He slid out of the booth and waited for June.

She slid out after him. They waltzed to the music. Mike thought she felt as light as a feather. He liked holding her hand. June was surprised at how well they danced together. She didn't usually care for dancing, but she was enjoying herself. She put her head on his shoulder and moved in closer to him. They were both surprised when the music stopped. The band swung into a fast jazz number, and they returned to their booth.

"Do you have family in St. Joe?" Mike asked.

"Do I ever! But they're not in St. Joe. They live near DeKalb, a little town thirty miles south of here."

"You make it sound like there's something wrong with them. Are some of them in jail or something?"

June laughed. "Sometimes I wish my brothers are in jail. They love to torment me."

"You know, you still haven't answered my question," Mike said.

"I'm the fifth of six kids. I have two sisters and three brothers."

"Wow, did your folks finally figure out what caused that?" Mike asked.

June smiled and said, "It gets cold on the farm, and there wasn't much to do in the tobacco fields in the winter. Heat from those wood-burning stoves didn't get back to the bedrooms, and a lot went on under those heavy comforters. That's my theory anyway. Two of my brothers are in the army in Europe. They enlisted after Pearl Harbor. My brother John is 4F. He's a civilian employee of the Department of the Army in Washington, DC. He's in procurement administration, whatever that is." June picked up her glass of beer and took another drink.

"Two of those white stars on blue backgrounds are plenty for your mother to have in her window," Mike said.

June put her glass back down on the table and looked up at Mike.

"We worry about them all the time. My mother prays for them every night before she goes to sleep. How did we get on this topic anyway?" June asked. "What about your family?"

Mike's face clouded over. "I don't have a family. My father was killed in the trenches in France. My mother was never the same after that. She died two years ago."

"Mike, I'm sorry. Do you have any brothers or sisters?"

Mike sipped his cocktail. "No, I'm an only child."

Don and Betty walked back from the dance floor.

"You two look chummy," Betty said, sliding into the booth to make room for Don. "God, I need a drink!"

Don signaled to their waiter.

"I thought you guys got lost out in that mob," June said.

"We danced almost the whole set, didn't we, big guy?" Betty said to Don.

"We sure did, and I've got the blisters to prove it! I thought I'd never get off the dance floor," Don complained. He enjoyed every dance with her but liked to keep his dates off balance.

Betty wasn't going to let Don get away with that.

"It was fun, though I'm not sure Buster wasn't the better dancer. It's a close call," Betty said, poking Don in the ribs with her elbow.

"I wish you'd called him back halfway through the set, then he could have the sore feet," kidded Don. He slid into the booth and settled on the seat with Betty.

The waiter arrived and asked, "Another round?" He glanced at June to see if she had another zinger in store for him.

June just grinned back at him.

"No more fizzes for me. I'll have a gin and tonic and a big glass of ice water on the side. I'm parched!" Betty said.

"Another scotch on the rocks for me, and I'll second that request for the big glass of water. You don't have any foot cream, do you?" said Don.

"Oh, boo-hoo," said Betty. "I thought you soldiers were tough."

A guy at a nearby table snickered at Betty's remark.

"Knock it off, you two. I'll just have a Coke with ice," said June.

"The usual for me," said Mike.

The waiter left with their orders.

Betty focused her attention on the stage.

"Your band was cooking with gas. You're better than these guys," Betty said.

"We like to grandstand a little. I'm glad you liked us," Don said.

"What did you think of us, June?" Mike asked.

"Which one of you?" June quipped.

Don wasn't sure what she meant by that remark. He didn't ask her to elaborate.

Betty laughed and said, "That's what you get for asking June's opinion."

Out on the dance floor, a loud argument erupted over who had the next dance with a cute dark-haired elfin girl. The girl had a disgusted look and walked away from the uniformed disputants. A Frog Hop bouncer invited both to get some fresh air outside and cool off before they came back in.

"How about we change the seating for the ride home?" Don asked.

"What do you mean?" Betty asked.

"What if Mike takes June home, and you take me home in your car?"

"Works for me. Okay with you, June?" Betty asked.

June considered the idea for a moment. "No one asked Mike how he feels about it," June observed.

"I'd be pleased to take you home," Mike said.

"Then it's all settled. I'm ready to go if you guys are," Don said.

Don waved down their waiter and signaled for him to bring their check. The waiter went to the bar, asked for their tab, and brought back the check.

Don said, "I'll get it. We can settle up later, Mike."

*****

Betty asked Don to drive. She felt a little tipsy.

Don pulled Betty's Ford into the parking space in front of his cabin and shut off the engine.

"Slide over, honey. With the engine off, it's going to get chilly," Don said.

"And you're going to keep me warm, I suppose," Betty said, but she slid over next to him.

There was a loud party going on two cabins down from Don's. An airman and his date smooched on the walkway. This tourist camp was popular with the airmen from Rosecrans Field.

Don put his arm around Betty and leaned down to kiss her. She returned the kiss, broke away, and said, "Not bad for a first try."

Don kissed her again, a longer kiss than before.

"You're improving," Betty said.

Then Don rested his hand lightly on her right breast while he kissed her. Betty let him leave it there for a few seconds before she removed it gently with her right hand.

"It's definitely getting chilly. Let's go into the cabin. We can have a nightcap," Don said.

"As much fun as that sounds, I'd better be getting on home," Betty said.

"Okay then," Don said and gave her another kiss, a quick one. He opened the driver's door, got out, leaned his head back into the car, and said, "I had a great time, cutie."

"Me too, big guy," Betty said. *I better watch myself with this guy,* she thought. *He really rings my bell.*

Don closed the driver's door and walked up to his cabin. The party two doors down started to break up.

Betty slid over into the driver's position, started the car, and backed out of the parking space.

Don waved to her as she drove away.

You win some and you lose some, he thought. *But I like her. She's a livewire.*

*****

The apartment building was dark when Mike pulled up. Her neighbors were all in bed.

June leaned over, gave him a kiss on the cheek, and said, "I'm glad I came tonight. I feel like I made a new friend."

"I'm just a friend, huh? Sounds like a kiss-off to me."

"Do you always give up so easy? I meant what I said." June opened the car door, got out, and went into her building.

That was dumb of me, Mike thought as he drove off. *I'm already nuts about her.*

*****

I hope Betty held her own with Don, June thought as she waited for Betty to come home. She got a pen and paper and started a letter to her brother Ricky. She wrote to both her brothers in Europe every week. June knew he would laugh when he read about the Frog Hop. She put the letter in a stamped envelope, sealed and addressed it, and planned to drop it in a mailbox the next day.

Betty came strolling in and said, "Are you still up? I thought you'd be in bed."

"So what happened with you and Mr. Wonderful?"

"Well, I dropped him off at his place. He and Mike are sharing a tourist cabin near the river. It ain't the Ritz, but it's okay." She hung up her things and went into the kitchen to get a Coke.

"What happened?" asked June.

"Nothing. He got out, went into his cabin, and I came home." Betty opened the icebox and saw there were no more Cokes. "We're out of Cokes. I'll go by the market tomorrow before work. We could use a few other things too.

June normally did the grocery shopping and was pleased to see Betty volunteer for the chore.

"I know you're kidding about Don. Let me know what my half of the groceries comes to tomorrow," June asked.

"Hell, yes, I'm kidding you. We made out in the car, and that got into a little petting."

"That sounds more like you. How was the kissing?"

"That's for me to know and you to find out," Betty said with a laugh. She chipped some ice from the block in the icebox and put it in a glass of water.

"I'll leave the finding out to you," June said.

"Then Don invited me in for a nightcap," Betty added.

"The plot thickens," June said.

"I said I should be getting home, and he took that with good grace. He gave me another kiss and got out of the car. That was it."

"Not much plot thickening there," June observed. "Did he say he would call you?"

"No, but he'll call, all right," Betty said, taking a big drink of her water.

"Well, I'm pooped. I'm going to bed," said June, heading for her bedroom.

"Wait a minute! What about you and Mike?"

June stopped in her tracks and struck a provocative pose.

"We had torrid sex on the sofa and topped it off with a romp in bed," June said with a straight face. "I'll tell you all about it in the morning. Good night." She went off to her room.

"Bullshit!" Betty yelled at her.

3

The next morning, Don McNeill's *Breakfast Club* was interrupted by a network news announcer on their Zenith radio.

"This just came in over the wires. The headquarters of the Allied Supreme Command has announced that the German Army has launched a new winter offensive in the Argonne Forrest in Belgium. There is heavy fighting involving several German armored divisions. American and Allied forces are scrambling to deal with this unexpected German offensive. More news will follow as the situation develops."

The radio station returned to the Breakfast Club broadcast.

"Shit, I guess the war isn't over yet," June said. She continued cooking eggs and making coffee.

Betty wandered in from her bedroom in her robe and slippers.

"It looks my brothers aren't coming home for Christmas after all," June said dejectedly.

"Where are they now?"

"They're probably in the middle of that fight. They're both in Europe. Ricky's in the 101st Airborne Division. Lloyd is in the Fourth Armored Division in General Patton's Third Army," June said with a catch in her voice. "Damn this war anyway!"

Betty hugged her. "This is really tough on you, honey."

June turned her attention back to the stove. "Do you want some eggs? Mine are about ready. The coffee will be done in a minute."

"No to the eggs, but I'll take a gallon of that coffee," Betty said. "I may have overdone the Frog Hop last night."

"You should eat something, you'll feel better."

The radio station continued to the *Breakfast Club* where Don McNeil was reassuring America that "we would still whip the Nazis."

27

"I'll fry some toast when you're done with the skillet," Betty said, getting two pieces of Wonder Bread from the pantry and buttering them.

"You're making holes in that bread, you know. You should let the butter melt a little first," advised June.

"Mind your own knitting. Was any part of that bullshit about you and Mike last night, true?" Betty asked.

"I like Mike as a chum. I hope we'll be friends," June replied.

"Yeah, well, your 'chum' wants to get in your drawers," Betty observed as she finished buttering her bread.

"He'll have to get over that if he wants to pal around with me," June said. "I have to pass that entrance exam for nursing school. I don't have time to get serious with a guy." She ladled her eggs onto a plate that held the toast she had made earlier. She set her plate on the small two-seated breakfast table and poured herself a cup of coffee.

"The skillet's all yours," she said to Betty, leaving the burner turned on.

Betty put her buttered bread in the skillet. "God, I hate to work on Saturday," she groaned.

"Well, at least we're on swing shift this week. We don't have to go in until 4:00 p.m.," said June. "I think I'll do some Christmas shopping today before work. I need some cheering up from that war news."

June enjoyed seeing store windows with their Christmas manger scenes and the colorful lights strung over the downtown streets. The department stores played Christmas carols, and shoppers wished each other a Merry Christmas. The Salvation Army Santa rang his bell as loose change clinked into the red Salvation Army bucket. June loved Christmas.

Betty finished browning her bread, put it on a plate, and set it on the breakfast table. She poured her coffee and sat down, facing June. She added cream and sugar to her coffee and said, "Who are you buying gifts for?"

"My family draws names out of a hat. This year I drew my sister Virginia Jane. There's a five-dollar limit, so it's easy on everybody, and no one goes overboard."

"Do all your sisters have that two-name thing? That's so Southern," Betty said, taking a bite of her toast.

"All of them except me," June answered.

"How come you didn't get two names?"

"They tried to stick me with it when I was a kid. But I threw a fit every time, and they finally gave up."

"Jeepers! Now I just have to know. What is your middle name?"

"No way, I'm taking that to my grave," June said and finished her breakfast. She washed and put away the breakfast dishes. "If I'm going shopping, I better leave now. It's a long trolley ride downtown."

"I can drive you," Betty offered.

"No, thanks, you're not dressed. Finish your toast and coffee. I'll see you at work."

"Okay, do you want me to pack you a dinner for swing shift?"

"No, I'll pick something up downtown." June put on her coat and hat. She noticed her letter to Ricky on the small stand in the entry. She put it in her coat pocket and said, "See you later."

"Yeah, later!" yelled Betty to the closing door.

June walked to the mailbox on the corner. She took the letter out of her pocket and looked at it. She thought about the latest war news and the danger it posed for her brothers. Ricky and Lloyd were probably involved in the heavy fighting.

She dropped the letter in the mail slot and walked on to the trolley stop.

*****

At 4:00 p.m., Betty hurried to clock in at work. When she got to the packing line, she saw June with Debby, another girl on their line. Debby was crying, and June had her arms around her.

"What's the problem, girlfriends?" Betty asked, walking up to them.

"Debby just got one of those damned telegrams," June said, releasing Debby.

Debby sobbed and said, "My husband's dead. I don't know what I'm going to do."

"You should go home or go to your parents," Betty said. "We'll tell the supervisor why you had to leave. Do you have a way to get home?"

Just then, the lead lady on their line walked up and said, "What's going on? You girls need to get to your stations."

June explained the situation to the lead lady, who said, "June, you and Betty go to your stations. I'll help Debby. This wouldn't happen if you girls would stop giving the War Department your work addresses to avoid getting the telegrams at your homes." She gently took Debby's arm and led her away.

June and Betty moved toward their workstations, but June stopped Betty and said, "I gave the War Department my address here at work too. At the time I was still living at the YWCA, and I didn't want one of those awful telegrams going there. I guess I better change that now."

Betty didn't know what to tell her friend.

June had been working an hour when a white shirt came up to her station. He wore a tie and had one of those cheesy pocket protectors in his shirt pocket.

What does the administration want with me? June wondered.

"The supervisor wants to see you at the break," he said.

"Great, that means I'll miss my break. Why does he want to see me?"

"I guess he'll tell you when he sees you," the white shirt snapped at her. "You do know where his office is, don't you?" He walked off without waiting for an answer.

"Jerk," said June under her breath.

When the break whistle sounded, June walked off the shop floor and went up the stairs to the supervisor's office. The office had a glass wall facing onto the shop floor so the supervisor could oversee his subordinates. June knocked on his door and heard him yell, "Come in!"

She opened the door and approached his desk. The supervisor had two battered guest chairs with metal legs and cracked vinyl seats. They matched the desk. He had a little nameplate on the desk that said Mr. Williams, Packing Supervisor.

I guess that's so he'll know who he is and what he does, thought June uncharitably. She was still sore at the fathead with the pocket protector.

"Have a seat, Miss Taylor," he said. "I have good news for you. The scheduling department has an opening for a packing line scheduler. You have a good record, and you're a high school graduate. I recommended you for the job. It's yours if you want it."

June sat down in one of the beat-up chairs and realized she wasn't in trouble.

"Thank you for recommending me, Mr. Williams. What does the job pay?" June asked.

Mr. Williams checked the notice and verified the salary. "Twenty cents an hour more than you make now, and it's an office job."

June wasn't sure she could handle a scheduler's job. But twenty cents an hour was a lot of money. She stood up and looked Mr. Williams in the eye.

"Thank you very much, Mr. Williams. When do I start?" she asked.

"You start on the day shift, Monday. You report to Mr. Jamieson."

"Where is Mr. Jamieson's office?"

He gave her directions and told her Mr. Jamieson would be expecting her. "Wear a dress, not dungarees."

"Thanks again," June said and left his office.

June was a little dazed at this turn of events, but then she started getting excited. A raise! Twenty cents an hour was an extra $8 a week or $32 a month!

And I bet there are opportunities for advancement after I catch on to the job, she thought. *Tuition and fees for nursing school had just got closer! Now I'm sorry for the things I thought about Mr. Williams.*

June returned to the shop floor just as the break ended. She waited for Betty to return from her break.

"What did the supervisor want with you?" Betty asked.

"It's kind of a long story, but it's all good. I'll tell you about it after work," June said. "We better get back to the line. Our crabby lead lady is staring daggers at us."

There were six girls in each packing line section. The first two girls took a flat carton from a pallet, unfolded it, and put the carton down on the conveyor. The next two girls taped the bottom of the box and turned it upright. Conveyors of products fed the following four stations, where the girls loaded the products into the cartons. At the final two stations, closers taped the top of the cartons and off-loaded them on a takeaway conveyor. Another line section palletized the cartons and a forklift carried them away to the warehouse. The large bay held dozens of hardworking women overseen by lead ladies.

*****

After her shift, June went to her locker and retrieved her purchases from her shopping trip. She went to the parking lot and waited for Betty, who showed up a few minutes later. June put her shopping bags in the back seat of Betty's Ford and got in the car.

Betty said, "Give already! What happened with the supervisor?"

"Like I said before, it's a long story. And I want your attention on the road, not looking over at me. This poor car has enough lumps and bruises as it is."

"Come on! At least give me a hint," Betty pleaded.

"I'll give you the whole story when we get home. Which I hope is in a jiffy. My feet hurt, and I want to take off my shoes and kick back. Let's go, please."

"Okay, okay," said Betty.

When they arrived, June went into their apartment, took off her shoes, and collapsed on the love seat.

Betty was right on her heels and sat next to her on the love seat. "Well?" she said. "Give!"

"If you'll make us some coffee, I'll tell all," June said.

"I'll start the coffee, but you tell me about the supervisor while it makes. Then I'm having a highball."

Betty put coffee and water in the percolator and turned on the stove. She made her gin and tonic, and June related the conversation in the supervisor's office.

"At first, I thought I might be getting laid off or issued some kind of warning," June said. "I was pretty worried, but I didn't let Mr. Williams see."

"Wow, I'd have peed my pants! Then what happened?"

"It was pennies from heaven, that's what happened."

"What do you mean?"

"He said I was getting a promotion."

"No shit! What kind of promotion?"

The percolator started bubbling over, and the coffee hissed on the stove. Betty jumped up and ran to the stove to turn off the burner, getting some hot coffee on her hand in the process.

"Shit, shit, shit!" Betty yelled.

"I'll get some ice. Run cold water on your hand," June said.

Betty turned on the sink faucet and put her hand under the cold water. June opened the icebox and chipped off some ice from the block with the ice pick. She wrapped the chipped ice in a dish towel and took it to Betty.

"We should get one of those fancy refrigerators with ice cube trays," Betty said.

"Yeah, we'll do that when a rich uncle dies. Those things are over $200," June said.

"Give me your hand," June said.

"You know something? You will be a great nurse," Betty said seriously.

June's blushed, and she looked down at Betty's hand. "I don't think it's too bad." June put the towel-wrapped ice on Betty's hand.

"It feels better," Betty said.

"Leave the ice on for a while. I'm going to get some salve to put on it," June said, walking to the bathroom. When June returned with the salve, she said, "You had the burner on too high under that coffee."

"What, you're going to lecture me while I stand here in pain?"

"You said it felt better. Take off the ice and let me put on this salve," June directed. She inspected Betty's hand and said, "It doesn't look too red, but we should put on the salve just to be sure."

As June applied the salve, Betty said, "Let's get back to the subject at hand—no pun intended. What's the promotion?"

"Mr. Williams said it was for a packing line scheduler in the scheduling department," June said and put the cap back on the salve and returned it to the bathroom cabinet. When she returned to the kitchen, she lifted the percolator with a dish towel, wiped it off, and turned her attention to the coffee spill.

"How much would that pay?" Betty asked.

"I'll get a raise of twenty cents an hour," June said. "And it's an office job."

"That's great!" Betty said. "But that means we won't be working together. What about our hours? What shift will you be on?"

June continued cleaning up the coffee spill. "It's a day-shift job," she answered.

"I'm on swing shift!" Betty protested. "How will you get to work?"

"I might have to ride the trolleys. Monthly passes are five dollars," June said.

Betty went back to the couch, sat down, and picked up her highball. Taking a sip, she said, "I think my hand's okay."

"Leave the salve on for a few minutes more," June said.

"Maybe I can request a permanent transfer to day shift," Betty said.

"That would solve the problem, but do you really think they'd give it to you?"

"I think the personnel person is a guy. If it is, I can give him a good sob story, show a little leg, and see what happens. Just leave it to me. I'll work something out. I have Monday off. When I drop you off, I'll go in and talk with personnel about my shift change."

Betty finished her highball, and June went back to the kitchen and checked the percolator. She poured herself a cup of still remaining coffee and said, "At least, you left enough in the pot for another cup or two. Do you want a cup?"

"Stop busting my chops about the coffee, and yes, I will have a cup."

"The usual with cream and sugar, right?"

"Two spoons," Betty said.

June made Betty's coffee and brought both cups into the living room.

"I don't know how you drink it black. It's too bitter without sugar," Betty said.

"Farmers always drink it black and strong. When the day starts before sunrise, you need an eye-opener."

"Farmers can keep that before sunrise stuff and the black coffee too."

*****

"Chums! She said she wanted to be 'chums' with me," Mike said over breakfast in the kitchenette in their tourist cabin.

Don looked up from his plate and nodded sympathetically. "Not good, pal."

"I'd like to ask June out again, but she doesn't seem too interested in me."

"Do you like this babe?" Don asked.

"Yeah, I really like her," Mike answered.

"Well, pal, sometimes you just have to suit up and show up and see what happens."

*****

The phone in the apartment rang, and Betty said, "I'll bet that's Don!" She got up, walked to the kitchen, and took the phone off the cradle. "Hi!" she answered breezily. She said nothing for a minute or so. Then she held her hand over the receiver and shouted, "June, it's for you!"

Coming to the phone, June asked Betty, "Who is it?"

Covering the mouthpiece with her hand, she whispered, "It's Mike."

Taking the phone, June said, "Hi, Mike. What's up?"

"I called early so I could catch you before you leave for work," Mike said.

"Good thinking, I'm on swing shift. If you'd waited to call tonight, I'd have been at work, up to my eyebrows in cardboard cartons and oatmeal boxes," June said. "So what can I do for the Signal Corps?"

"I thought maybe you'd like to go out to dinner with me Friday night?"

"I'll have to check my busy calendar, but I can probably squeeze it in."

"Great! Is 8:00 p.m. all right?"

"That's fine. We'll go Dutch," June said.

Betty was eavesdropping and shook her head frantically at June. "What the heck are you doing?" she whispered.

"Hey, I can afford dinner for both of us," Mike said indignantly.

"That's good to know. But we're buddies. Buddies share."

"We'll see about that. I'll pick you up at eight o'clock," Mike said.

Mike hung up the phone and looked baffled.

Don asked, "She said yes, didn't she?"

"She said she wants to go Dutch," Mike said.

Don never had a girl offer to pay for her dinner, but the idea had appeal.

"I hope that rubs off on Betty," Don said and grinned at Mike.

Mike ignored Don's remark and changed the subject. "You know, Betty will wonder when you're going to call her."

"I'll get around to it. I like to build a little suspense and not jump the gun like some people I know."

"June, honey, what am I going to do with you. What do you mean, go Dutch?" Betty protested.

"Guys pay because they have expectations when they do. It wouldn't be fair to Mike since he couldn't have those expectations with me," June said reasonably.

"You sure like to complicate everything, don't you?" Betty said. "Guys like to pay when they take girls out. It makes them feel like men. You're just going to hurt his feelings."

"Different strokes for different folks," June said.

"Well, at least your guy called you and asked you out to dinner. I haven't heard a word from Don. I must be losing my touch," Betty said. "Maybe I should take a leaf out of your book and play harder to get."

"It's only been one day. Give Don a chance. He'll call you. If you do lose your touch, lose some of it my way, okay?" June said.

"That's bad news about the German counterattack. I thought we had the bastards licked," Mike said to Don as they finished their second cup of coffee.

"Yeah, it sure is. It'll buck up the damn Japs too. I hope the fucking Air Corps doesn't change my assignment now," Don said. "What about you and the Signal Corps?"

"I guess we'll both just have to wait and see."

Mike cleared his breakfast dishes and put them in the sink.

"Maybe Eisenhower will get off the dime and get the Army out of low gear," Don said. "Back to the home front. Where are you going to take June?"

"The Pioneer Room at the Jesse James Hotel," Mike said and started washing the dishes.

"Whoa, that'll take a lot of clams, won't it?"

"Yeah, I was going to take her somewhere cheaper until she started that Dutch talk. She won't want to split the check at the Pioneer Room."

"What's wrong with splitting the check? I wish I could find a girl like that," Don said. He still liked the idea.

"I don't want to be her pal. I want to be her boyfriend. Splitting the check gets me off on the wrong foot with her," Mike said.

"It's your dough, but I think you're making a mistake."

"It won't be the first one."

Don cleared his breakfast dishes and put them in the sink.

"Hey, don't leave those for me to wash!" Mike exclaimed.

"Don't flip your lid," Don said. "I'll do them later."

Don always said the same thing but rarely got around to doing them.

"You're worse than a wife," Don said. "I'm going to take the trolley downtown and soak up some Christmas atmosphere. Do you want to go along?"

"Sure, I'll just change clothes while you do your dishes."

"Oh, crap. All right, I'll do the damn dishes!" Don said.

Mike came out of his room looking spiffy in a blue cotton shirt and tan khakis.

"I can drive us if you want," Mike said.

"You might need your gas ration if you're going to squire June around," Don said.

"No sweat. I got a C sticker when I had to report for duty at Crowder," Mike said.

"The tires on your old jalopy look pretty bald. You're lucky you made it up here from Crowder."

"I had to patch an inner tube to get here. But I don't have any threads showing yet."

"You better hope we don't get a snowstorm. On those baldies, you'll slide around like a cow on ice," Don said.

"Yeah, you're right, and I don't know where I'd get any more," Mike said.

"Yeah, they're rare as St. Louie virgins," Don said with a grin.

Mike laughed. But his tires were on their last legs.

"You'd have to try the black market, unless your uncle is a big politician or something."

"I don't have any uncles. If the Army got wind of me buying tires on the black market, they'd court martial me or transfer me to the infantry, or both. No, thanks," Mike said.

"It was just a thought. Don't snap your cap, pal," Don said.

"Let's go, roomie," Mike said, getting his winter coat and a cap with earflaps.

"You look silly in that cap," Don teased Mike.

There was no snow on the ground, but there was a chill in the air. Trolley cars didn't come with heaters.

"You'll wish you had this cap by the time we get downtown," Mike retorted.

"I'll find a honey on the trolley, and she can keep me warm," Don said, putting on his own winter coat and a woolen watch cap.

They walked the two blocks to the trolley stop and sat down on the bench to wait for the next trolley.

"How did you end up in the Air Corps?" Mike asked.

There was another trolley stop across the street, with three people waiting on the bench. Two young women strolled past it. Don studied them until they turned at the corner and walked away. Girl watching was one of his favorite pastimes.

"I wanted to be a pilot," Don replied, answering Mike's question.

Mike was surprised at Don's answer. Pilots were officers and officers were college graduates. He pointed this out to Don.

"Usually they are officers, but the Army was desperate for pilots. I'd been an aircraft mechanic since I got out of basic training and mechanic school. I was a tech sergeant. They offered me a chance to attend flight school as a cadet. They mixed some NCOs in with the college boys, kind of as an experiment," Don explained. "I passed the flight physical."

"What happened? How did you end up a navigator?" Mike asked.

There was an intermittent flow of delivery vans mixed with a few commuters on this main artery with the trolley tracks. Before the wartime restrictions, this street was crowded with automobile traffic. Crowded trolley cars and buses had replaced much of the private travel. Gasoline rationing kept the cars in their garages.

Don continued his narrative. "Long story short, I washed out in fighter training. It turns out I have mild vertigo and I got dizzy in snap turns and rolls."

"Wouldn't that stop you from being on a bomber?"

"No, I'm fine at altitude, and bombers mostly fly straight and level. Even when we're evading flack, there are no radical maneuvers in a bomber. I never told the Army about the vertigo anyway," Don said. "I just asked to withdraw from the program."

Instructors encouraged cadets to withdraw if the cadet didn't think he could cut it. The Army didn't want to waste the instructor's time on men who weren't going into fighter cockpits.

"Then they sent me to navigator's school. End of story."

A trolley car pulled up to the stop across the street and picked up the three passengers from the bench. It headed away from downtown. A few minutes later, a downtown trolley pulled up to their stop, and Mike and Don got on.

The trolley was only half full. The working stiffs were already at work, having ridden earlier trolleys. There were a few young women mixed in with the uniforms, heading downtown to do their Christmas shopping. Mike and Don found an empty seat and sat down.

"Are you sorry you aren't a fighter pilot?" Mike asked Don.

"Hell, no. I saw what happens to fighter pilots in the Pacific. They fly Buffalos or Wildcats against Zeros. Sometimes they face four to one odds."

The Zero was the first-line Japanese fighter and a very capable airplane, maybe a little better than the Wildcat. They completely outclassed the American Buffalos.

"My B-17 was a tough bird. It flew off muddy runways surrounded by jungle and sometimes under mortar and artillery fire. It took a lot of hits and kept flying. My 17 always got me home. If they send me back, I'll stick to B-17s. I got dinged a little, but I got back to the land of the Big PX. A lot of fighter pilots didn't."

"Yeah, I'm happy to stick to good old Camp Crowder myself," Mike said as the trolley came to their stop at Sixth and Felix.

Downtown was all decked out for Christmas. There were ropes of evergreen boughs and lights suspended over the streets. The founder of the city of St. Joseph, Joseph Robidoux, had named Felix Street and other downtown streets after his children.

The pony express rider in the square was lit up with strings of lights from the NOMA Lighting Company. Department stores were busy with holiday shoppers. The larger ones had Santa handing out candy and asking the kids if they had been naughty or nice. Santa encouraged them to tell him what they wanted for Christmas, which was usually an expensive toy the store sold. Poorer mothers listened to Santa and wondered how they could pay for it.

"I'm going to look for a Christmas present for June," Mike said.

"You really have it bad for that chick, don't you?" Don said.

"Now you can mind your own business," Mike said. "Let's meet at Maid-Rite for lunch."

"Okay. Just don't go overboard on that present," Don warned Mike.

"Yeah, yeah, see you later," Mike said and turned toward the Townsend and Wall Department store. He joined the flow of shoppers passing the Salvation Army Santa ringing a bell at the front entrance. He tossed some change into the red bucket as he passed and received a booming Merry Christmas in return.

*****

When Don arrived at the Maid-Rite a few minutes after noon, he was carrying a Hartman Store bag. The restaurant was crowded with shoppers and office workers taking their lunch break. He could smell the mouthwatering odor of the frying hamburger meat and chopped onions. He saw Mike holding a table and walked over to join him.

"What do you have in the bag?" Mike asked.

"The same thing you have in yours, a Christmas present," Don replied.

"What, for me? You shouldn't have!" Mike said.

"Never mind who it's for," Don said, sitting down across from Mike.

"It couldn't be for Betty, could it?"

"If you give June a present, Betty will expect one from me. This is your fault," Don said grumpily. "Let's order, I'm starved."

"Me too. I'm going to have at least three of those small burgers, fries, and a chocolate milkshake," Mike said, signaling to the waitress.

The brown-haired waitress wore a knee-length white dress with little red maids that showed off her nice legs. When she came over to the table, Mike gave her his order.

"Do that twice, honey," Don said.

The waitress smiled warmly at Don and put in their orders.

Mike looked jealously at Don. *This guy is a chick magnet*, he thought. "What did you get her?"

"Why should I get her anything? All she did was take my order," Don said with a blank expression.

"Wise ass. I meant Betty," Mike said.

"I got her a see-through sexy nightgown, of course. What did you get June, combat boots?" Don asked.

"Ha, ha, you should be on the Abbott and Costello show," Mike said. "I got her nylons."

"What a big spender! What did they cost, twenty cents?" Don scoffed.

"It's the thought that counts, haven't you heard?" Mike retorted. "What did you pay for the nightie? That's kind of a personal gift by the way."

"A gentleman never tells," Don said. "Here comes our lunch."

Their waitress delivered their food and gave Don the check. She winked at him and walked away. Don examined the check. The waitress had written her phone number on it.

Don handed it to Mike. "Hold on to that in case the thing with June doesn't work out," he said, and grinned.

When the two friends had finished lunch, they rode the trolley back to their cabin.

Mike asked Don, "When are you going to call Betty? The suspense is great and all, but that is one fine-looking girl, and you probably have plenty of competition."

"I'll call her Monday. We'll go to the movies. There's a Bogart movie showing downtown at the Robidoux," said Don. He hung up his coat and watch cap and walked over to the radio. He turned it on, waited for the tubes to warm up, and adjusted the knob until he found the news. Things were still looking dicey for the American Army in Belgium.

"She'll probably rather see a soppy romance movie," Mike said. "I think the Hickory Theater on Eleventh and Hickory is playing one of the Hope and Crosby Road movies. Maybe that'll work if she doesn't like Bogie."

"Who doesn't like Humphrey Bogart?" Don asked.

*****

On Monday morning, after dropping off June at the plant entrance, Betty went to the lobby. She asked the receptionist for the personnel department. The receptionist directed her to the first-floor personnel office. Betty went through the door into the office and found a young man wearing horn-rimmed glasses, dressed in a white shirt and tie, sitting at a desk.

"Do you have an appointment?" the young man asked Betty.

"No, I don't. My name is Betty Anderson, and I work in the packaging department. I need to see the personnel manager. It's very important," Betty said.

"Well, I'll tell Mrs. Johnson you're here. But without an appointment, you'll just have to wait until she has an opening for you. Have a seat," the assistant said.

The assistant left his desk, walked through a private office door, and closed the door behind him.

Betty just realized the assistant had said the personnel manager was a woman. *Darn*, thought Betty, *so much for showing my legs. I thought it would be a guy.*

Five minutes later, the assistant returned to his desk.

"Mrs. Johnson will see you now. She has a break in her schedule. She can only give you a few minutes."

When Betty entered the office, Mrs. Johnson was frowning over a file.

She looks like a toughie, Betty thought. *No sob stories for me. I better stick to the truth.*

Mrs. Johnson put down the file, looked up, and said, "What can I do for you, Miss Anderson?"

"Mrs. Johnson," Betty said, "I work in the packing department. My friend June works there, too, but she just got a promotion to the scheduling department."

"Good for her. What has that got to do with you?"

"We were both working swing shift, but now June will be on days."

"So?" Mrs. Johnson was looking impatiently at the paperwork on her desk.

"She rides to work with me. She doesn't have a car, and it's a long trolley ride for her. I hoped you could transfer me to permanent day shift so she could continue riding with me," Betty explained.

"I'm not really the person you should see about this," Mrs. Johnson said. "You will have to check with your supervisor. If he approves your request, he'll forward the paperwork to personnel. Now you will have to excuse me, I have another appointment shortly."

She sure shined me on, Betty thought and left the office.

*****

When June hung up her coat and hat in her plant locker room, she heard two girls talking about the news. One of them mentioned the 101st Airborne.

June stopped them and asked, "What did you say about the 101st Airborne?"

"The news said there was heavy fighting in a city called Bastogne that the 101st Airborne Division was defending," one girl answered.

"My brother Ricky is in the 101st," June said with a stunned look on her face.

"Oh, honey, I'm sorry about your brother. I hope he makes it through okay," the girl said.

"We didn't mean to give you bad news," her friend said.

"I know you didn't," June said. "We better get to work."

4

Corporal Richard Taylor peered over the lip of the foxhole he shared with Private First Class (Pfc.) Salvatore Moreno. They were manning an Observation Point (OP) near the edge of the city of Bastogne. His battered binoculars barely still worked, their fatigue uniforms were filthy, and they had three weeks of stubble on their faces. They had dug the foxhole by enlarging one of the shell craters dotting the open space around them. The rest of their squad was behind them in the trenches. Yesterday's battle had forced the 101st Airborne Division to pull back into the trenches the American divisions had dug as a last line of defense for the city. The Screaming Eagles were holding on by their fingernails.

Broken, pock-marked buildings lay to their rear. Ricky and Sal stayed away from them. The Germans liked to probe them with mortar rounds, believing the Americans were using the upper floors for OPs.

Pfc. Salvatore rested back against the SCR-300 radio he was carrying. The sound of small arms fire rattled in the distance.

"Probably a German probe or patrols running into each other," Ricky said.

Pfc. Salvatore said, "I could eat the ass out of a bull elephant."

Corporal Taylor snorted and said, "What are you bitching about? You had breakfast, I didn't."

"Hey, I saved that chocolate bar for a week. And the damn thing melted. I had to lick it off the paper."

They heard the whistling of an artillery round overhead. It landed a hundred yards behind them.

"Intermittent and harassing fire," Ricky said.

"Yeah, they're just fucking with us," Sal said.

The combat-weary pair didn't get excited about anything less than a serious artillery barrage.

Ricky put the binoculars to his eyes again.

"If the fucking weather would clear up, the fucking Air Corps could drop in some rations," Sal said.

"Yeah, more ammo wouldn't hurt either. What have you got left?"

"Three clips for the BAR and four hand grenades. What about you?"

"Six clips for my M1 and a couple of grenades," Ricky said.

"Well, they've got us surrounded, the poor bastards," Sal said and laughed.

Ricky smiled ruefully.

*****

Betty left the Quaker Oats main office building, got in her Ford, and pulled out of the lot. She turned left on Frederick Blvd and headed out of town toward her apartment.

That "interview" with Mrs. See-Your-Supervisor was sure a bust, Betty thought.

She drove through the factory district and saw the ordnance plant on her right.

They're always busy, she mused. *Maybe June isn't the only one who can get a better job.*

She made a U-turn and drove back to the ordnance plant administration parking lot. The lot was huge and packed with cars, but Betty saw an empty visitor space in front of the administration building and grabbed it.

The administration building was a four-story brick building divided in half with a central structure that housed the lobby, the elevators, and large hidden ducts that contained utility runs. The lobby was large but plain.

Betty saw a directory board, checked it for the personnel office, and waited for the elevator to the second floor. It was packed, but a gentleman wearing a nice gray suit made room for her. When she got off, the gentleman in the expensive gray suit followed. When she stopped to look around, the silver-haired gentleman bumped into her.

"Excuse me, please. Can I help you, miss?" the man asked.

"I'm looking for the personnel office," Betty said.

"It's down this way. That's where I'm going."

They walked down the hallway together.

"Thank you. My name is Betty Anderson."

"I'm pleased to meet you, Miss Anderson. My name is Winston Matthews."

"I'm here to apply for a job," Betty said.

Mr. Matthews stopped in front of the office door and faced Betty. "What sort of job? Why don't we sit down on this bench for a moment?"

There were oak benches in the hallway outside the office doors.

Betty sat down next to Mr. Matthews.

"I'm looking for a secretarial position," she said.

"Do you have any experience as a secretary?" Mr. Matthews asked.

"I took shorthand and typing in high school. My job is at Quaker Oats, but it's on the packing line. I'm looking for a better opportunity. I'm a hard worker and very reliable."

"I'm sure you are," said Mr. Matthews. *What an attractive girl and bright to boot*, he thought.

"Look at me! I'm treating you like you're the personnel manager."

"That is entirely appropriate, Miss Anderson, as I am the director of personnel. I don't usually conduct interviews in the hallway, but sometimes I make exceptions for bright young people," Mr. Matthews said with a smile. "I'll introduce you to my administrative assistant. She can help you." He got to his feet and offered Betty a hand up. Then he said, "Mr. Harding, one of our production managers, needs to replace his assistant, who left her job to get married. You're not engaged, are you?" Mr. Matthews asked, joking.

"Not me. I'm free as a bird," Betty said.

"Come with me."

Mr. Matthews stopped at a door with a half-glass window and gold leaf lettering that read director of personnel. He opened the door, held it for Betty, and followed her in. A nice-looking, middle-aged woman was typing at her desk. She stopped typing when Betty and Mr. Matthews entered.

"Mrs. Smythe, this is Miss Anderson," Mr. Matthews said, making the introductions. "She is applying for the opening in Mr. Harding's office. See if Mr. Harding can fit an interview into his schedule."

"Certainly, Mr. Matthews. 'Ave a seat, Miss Anderson," Mrs. Smythe said, raising an eyebrow at Mr. Matthews. *She's a smasher, isn't she?* Mrs. Smythe thought.

"Good luck with your interview with Mr. Harding. I think he will find you satisfactory. It was a pleasure meeting you," Mr. Matthews said to Betty.

"It was a pleasure meeting you too. Thank you for taking your time helping me," Betty said, smiling at him.

Mr. Matthews smiled back, opened the inner door to his office, and went to work on the documents piled up on his desk.

Betty turned to Mrs. Smythe. "What does this position pay?"

"The starting salary is forty-five quid—I mean, dollars—per week," Mrs. Smythe answered.

Wow! Betty thought. *That's a lot of dough.* "What are the hours?"

"Work hours are 8:00 a.m. to 5:00 p.m. with an hour lunch break."

June and I can work with that, Betty thought.

"Wait out on the bench, love," Mrs. Smythe said.

When Betty had left, Mrs. Smythe called Mr. Matthew's extension and said, "Great gams, great figure."

"Don't be silly, Gladys. I ran into her in the hallway. She reminds me of my daughter. I felt sorry for her and decided to help her out."

"I believe you, but thousands wouldn't," Gladys said.

Mr. Matthews laughed and hung up.

Gladys picked up the telephone on her desk and dialed a number. She waited a moment, then said into the receiver, "Mr. Harding, it's Mrs. Smythe, in personnel. Do you 'ave 'alf a minute to speak

48

with a candidate? She's 'ere in my office now. 'Er name is Betty Anderson…I'll tell 'er." Gladys went out to the hall and told Betty, "Mr. Harding is sending a security guard to show you 'round to his office."

"A security guard?" Betty asked.

"The plant 'as its own security force. There are 450 of the blokes. We make munitions here, you know. The Boche would love to have a go at us."

"Of course, I've never worked in an ordnance plant before," Betty said.

"If you come to work 'ere, you'll be given an orientation to learn the regulations and procedures. Just wait 'ere. The guard will fetch you shortly," Gladys said and went back into her office.

Betty waited on the bench, pondering the opportunity. *Forty-five bucks a week! Mr. Matthews is certainly a nice gentleman. I hope the man I'm seeing is as nice as Mr. Matthews. I wonder if there really are German spies trying to blow this place up.* She shuddered. *Oh well, it's been going gang busters for almost four years, and nobody has blown it up yet. I'm sure I'll be okay.*

A man wearing a security guard uniform and a holster with a .38 caliber pistol approached her and asked, "Are you Miss Anderson?"

"That's me," said Betty.

"I'm here to escort you to Mr. Harding's office. Come with me, please," the guard said.

The guard escorted Betty out to the parking lot and seated her in a jeep. He drove her to one of the huge plant buildings. The building was divided into three large bays, housing the three main departments: stamping, loading, and packing. There were dozens of production workers in gray overalls tending workstations and machines.

Inside, the pandemonium of the heavy-metalworking machines was staggering. She jumped the first time a round went off.

"What are those gunshot sounds?" asked Betty, yelling to be heard above the din.

"They are testing cartridges. They take samples from production runs and test fire them," the guard yelled back. "Testing is in the building next to us. You should hear the noise in there."

It was too loud to talk, so Betty swallowed all the questions she wanted to ask. Going through a door from the plant floor, they entered a corridor. The guard turned left and walked to the end of the corridor to a connecting corridor.

"The stairs are just down here," he said.

The noise level had fallen to a dull roar, making it easier to hear him. Betty and the guard took the stairs to the second floor. The walls of the hallway were painted gray and bare of decoration. The floor was worn gray linoleum. It felt like a prison.

"Mr. Harding's office is just down this hall," the guard told Betty.

"That's better. You can actually hear yourself think up here," Betty observed.

There was still a hum in the background. And she could hear the muted sounds of the cartridges being test fired.

"You get used to the noise. The machine operators wear ear protection. The management is supposed to wear them when there're on the floor, but a lot of them don't bother. Mr. Harding's office is in here," he said when they reached the end of the corridor.

She walked into a large open room filled with small cubicles. The women inside them were busy at their desks. She followed the guard through the maze of office workers until they came to a wooden door. There was a sign protruding from the wall over the door that said, "Production Manager."

I guess here you don't get your name on your door, Betty thought. *Maybe they come and go too fast. I better find out about that.*

The guard knocked on the door and entered.

It had the same setup as the personnel office: a reception area and an inner office.

The receptionist had a desk, a typewriter, a phone with several buttons, and an intercom. She was buried under a sea of paper. She had an in-basket and an out-basket on her desktop. The in-basket was overflowing. There were three papers in the out-basket.

The harried secretary looked up and saw Betty and the guard. She pushed back a loose strand of hair hanging into one eye.

"Please tell Mr. Harding his appointment is here," the guard said to the woman.

The woman pressed a button on the intercom and said, "The guard is here with Miss Anderson."

"Send her in," said a gruff voice on the other end.

"Go on in," the receptionist told Betty.

The guard left to return to his duties.

Upon entering the office, June saw a stocky, muscular man with a crew cut sitting behind a utilitarian desk. He wore a white shirt with the sleeves rolled up and a tie pulled down from his collar. His ID badge had two red stripes running diagonally from the top right corner to the bottom left corner. His photo interrupted the stripes. He was glaring at her.

"I already don't like you. You're too young and pretty. My last assistant was young and pretty. Just when she finally learned her job, she married some soldier and went off to have babies," he said. "I don't have the time to keep breaking in assistants. What do you have to say to that?" He continued to glare.

Betty sized him up and decided he was testing her.

Well, we'll see about that, she thought. "I *am* young—too young to get married. I date guys occasionally, but I have married none of them, and I definitely don't want to have any babies yet," Betty said.

"That aside, why should I hire you?" he asked.

"You need to hire someone. That poor girl out there is laying an egg," Betty said.

"She's on loan from the quality control department. She's just filling in until I can find the right replacement. What would you do better if you had the job?"

"First, I'd sort through that mess on the desk. I'd sort it into three piles. First pile is the stuff that can wait. Second pile is the stuff that shouldn't wait. And the third is the stuff that absolutely can't wait. I'd go to work on the third pile. The second pile goes into the in basket. The first pile goes into the desk drawer until I get to it," Betty said.

"How would you know which paper to put in which pile?" Mr. Harding asked.

"I'd make sure you trained me to know. Besides, I'm sure a lot of it will be common sense after I catch on," Betty said.

"I'll say this, you've got moxie. What are you doing now? As hard as help is to find, I know you're working somewhere," Mr. Harding asked. "Sit down and take a load off."

Betty sat down and crossed her legs. "I'm working at Quaker Oats on a packing line. But I need to get an office job."

"Why do you need an office job?"

"My best friend, my roommate, is going into an office job at Quaker. I'm on swing shift. We only have one car, and she rides to work with me. It's a long trolley ride to the job for her if she can't ride with me."

So she's changing jobs to keep her friend from having to ride the trolley, Joe thought skeptically. "And that's the reason you're talking to me about a job?" he asked.

"That's not the only reason. I've wanted to move up, but nothing better has been posted on the job posting boards in the plant. I knew the ordnance plant is busy, so I thought I would check here."

"I can see that you have gumption. But do you have any office skills?"

"I can type fifty words a minute and take shorthand. I'm good on the phone. I can screen your calls," Betty said.

"How would you know how to screen my calls? Oh, right, you'd make sure I trained you!" He laughed.

Betty smiled.

"You'll have to go out on the factory floor sometimes. What about that?" Mr. Harding challenged her.

"I work on a factory floor now. I know how to get my hands dirty," Betty responded.

Quality control was hounding him to give back their girl, and she was struggling with his paperwork. This girl seemed bright enough.

"Well, hell, let's try it. When can you start?"

"I need to give notice at Quaker Oats, so would next Monday be okay?" Betty asked.

"If you're working on a packing line, they wouldn't give you any notice. They'd just lay you off," Mr. Harding said.

"That's them. I'm me."

"Okay, next Monday it is."

"I'll be here," Betty said.

Joe stood up, indicating the interview was over. He said, "Don't report here. Report to the personnel office at eight o'clock. They'll process you. That'll take all morning. Welcome aboard, Miss Anderson. I'll see you next Monday."

"Thank you very much, Mr. Harding. I'm excited about the job. See you Monday," Betty said.

5

"Boy, do I have a bulletin for you!" Betty told June when she picked her up in the Ford later that day.

"You got permanent day shift!" June said.

"Better than that, I got a new job."

"They gave you a new job? What will you be doing?" June asked.

Betty pulled out of the parking lot into traffic. During shift changes, the Quaker Oats lot got busy, and she narrowly missed sideswiping a Model A Ford.

"It's not at Quaker. I got a new job at the ordnance plant."

"Watch the road! What do you mean? How did that happen?"

Betty turned her attention back to the road. She had just missed a Chevrolet sedan with an old woman driving and yelled at her, "Watch where you're going, Granny!"

"Maybe we should hold this discussion when we get home," June said.

"Yeah, it's kind of a long story," Betty said. "How's your new job?"

"I think it's going to be fine. Not much happens on your first day."

June kept quiet the rest of the way home so Betty could concentrate on her driving. It all went well until Betty scraped the back fender on a lamppost as she was parallel parking.

"Don't say a word," Betty admonished June as they got out and went up to their apartment.

The girls hung up their coats and hats.

Betty said, "I'm ready for a highball to celebrate our new jobs. How about you?"

June rarely drank hard liquor. But she had an occasional gin and tonic with Betty.

"Sure, after your driving, I think I need one," June said.

Betty ignored June's remark, made the drinks, and handed June hers.

"Here's to climbing the old ladder of success."

"Cheers," June responded. "All right, what is all this about a job at the ordnance plant?"

"I went to the personnel office at Quaker and asked about the shift change. I explained about your change of hours and all. They blew me off. Mrs. Johnson passed the buck off to our supervisor. She said I had to get his permission first. I was kind of frosted when I got to the parking lot, and I saw the ordnance plant when I drove through the factory district." Betty sipped her highball and said, "So I took a flyer and drove into their parking lot."

"Go on. This is getting interesting," June said. She drank her gin and tonic.

"I applied for a job there. I thought about you moving up in the world, and I thought, why not me too? So I went into their main office and looked up the personnel department on the second floor. There were three elevators, and all were crowded. A man made space for me, so I rode to the second floor next to him, but then he got off with me!"

"Were you scared he was following you?" June asked.

"No, he was a nice-looking man wearing an expensive suit and tie. I just thought he worked on that floor. I asked him for directions to the personnel office, and we got to chatting. I told him I was going to apply for a job." Betty took her drink and sat on the love seat in the living room.

June followed her. "Why would you tell a stranger you were going to apply for a job?"

"Well, it's just as well I did since he was the director of personnel. His name is Mr. Matthews."

"You're jiving me!" June exclaimed.

"I kid you not. How lucky was that?" Betty told June the rest of the story.

"Stranger and stranger. You are amazing," June said. "Did you ask how much the job pays?"

"Forty-five bucks a week!" Betty said.

"What is Mr. Harding like?" June asked.

"I'm going to get a refill," Betty said. "Do you want one?"

June shook her head.

"At first he wasn't very nice. He said he didn't like me because I reminded him of his other young, pretty assistant who married a soldier and left her job just as she was getting good at it."

"What did you say?" June asked.

Betty returned with her drink and sat back. "I said I had plenty of chances to get married and I'm still single."

"This sounds like a very weird job interview. Is this guy a kook?"

"No, I don't think so. He's just a very busy guy and really needs a good assistant. The girl he has now is on loan from the quality control department, and she hasn't got a clue. I told him I saw her desk and could tell she was overwhelmed. He asked me what I would do if I had the job."

"Wow, what did you tell him?" June asked. *I'd have no idea how to answer such a question in an interview*, June thought.

"I told him how I would sort out the mess on the desk and how I would screen his calls."

"When do you start?"

Betty took a drink of her highball. "I start next Monday. I have to go into Quaker tomorrow and give notice."

"They'll probably fire you if you do. But I think they give you pay in lieu of notice," June said.

"Great, a week's paid vacation," Betty said. "Are you sure you don't want another drink?"

"After that story, I'd love another one. But then you'd have to put me to bed. You know I can't hold my liquor. But you go ahead. So you're going to be working days, and we can still ride together?" June asked.

"We may have to juggle things a little if one of us has to work late. You know what those salaried jobs can be like."

"That's all right. We can work it out. Say, congratulations on your new job. I'm really proud of you," June said emotionally.

"Thanks, girlfriend. I'm kind of proud of me too." Then Betty jumped up and said, "We need to celebrate!"

"You got it! Let's go to the steakhouse and live it up."

The phone rang as the girls were putting on their winter gear.

"I'll get it," June said. She was closest to the phone.

"Hello, this is Don. Can I speak to Betty?"

"Sure, hold on, and I'll get her," June told him.

"It's for you. It's Don," June said, holding out the phone to Betty.

Betty took the phone and whispered to June, "See, I told you he'd call." To Don, she said, "Hi, big guy. What's up?"

"There's a new Bogie movie at the Robidoux. I thought maybe you'd like to go with me Friday night."

"I don't know, Buster might want to take me dancing Friday night," Betty said, teasing him.

"I'll pick you up at seven thirty, okay?" Don said.

"With what? Mike is taking June out to dinner on Friday night. I thought he was the one with the car, not you."

"See you Friday night, cutie," Don said and hung up.

He's not much for explaining himself, Betty thought. *But I do like a man with self-confidence.*

"Let's go get those steaks. I'm got two things to celebrate now," Betty said.

In the car driving to the steakhouse, Betty told June about her date with Don. At the steakhouse, they discussed how to manage work transportation next Monday, with Betty going to the ordinance plant for in-processing.

"Don't worry about me. I can take the trolley," June said.

Steaks were hard to get and rarely available in the grocery store, and the only option was often a pricey restaurant. The two girls made the most of it, eating their steaks and talking about how it would be working at office jobs. June laughed at Betty's descriptions of the people she'd met that day.

*****

On Monday, Betty pulled into the main office parking lot at the ordnance plant at 7:50 a.m. and made her way to Mr. Matthew's office. She knocked on the door first and entered.

Mrs. Smythe looked up and said, "What can I do for you, dearie?"

"Mr. Harding told me to report to personnel this morning at eight," Betty said.

"I see. It's a natural mistake. The intake office is on the first floor." Mrs. Smythe gave Betty directions and said, "Go in and see the lady at the counter. She can 'elp you."

"Thank you, Mrs. Smythe. Please thank Mr. Matthews for his kindness to me. I'd better run, or I'll be late!" Betty said.

She rushed down to the intake office a minute after 8:00 a.m. and said to the gray-haired lady at the counter, "I went to the wrong office. I'm sorry to be late."

"What is your name, young woman?" the lady asked.

"I'm Betty Anderson. Mr. Harding told me to report here, Mrs. Murphy," Betty said, reading the lady's name on her ID badge.

"I'll notify intake that you're here," said Mrs. Murphy. "The rest of your group is already back in orientation."

Well, I'm off to a flying start, Betty thought.

Five minutes later, a young man came in and said to Betty, "Follow me, please." He wore a badge with his photo. A blue stripe ran diagonally from corner to corner on the badge.

The young man opened the third door down the hallway and entered a large room with high school desks lined up in rows. Most of the desks were filled with men and women who were writing on a form. The young man took a form off a stack on a desk at the front of the room and handed it to Betty.

"Fill out this application form and leave it on the desk," he said. "A trainer will take you to orientation."

Betty struggled with the application form. It was very comprehensive, including her academic history, work history, and any affiliation with German national groups or other subversive organizations. There were also questions about any arrests or convictions.

Betty thought about her driving citations. *Should I list those?* she wondered. They weren't really arrests. She looked at the last page where there was a paragraph warning that any false information on the form could lead to penalties for perjury or federal prosecution for making a false statement on a government form. She decided she had better list everything. They even wanted the make, model, and year of her car as well as the license number. She checked in her purse and found the copy of her registration she kept in it. Betty completed and signed the form apprehensively.

Next, she was photographed and given an order for a physical. Her intake group was escorted to an auditorium where they joined other groups for an orientation lecture. A speaker said the plant was the largest producer of .30 caliber and .50 caliber cartridges in the world, making 250 million cartridges per month, with 300 buildings spread over 291 acres and a workforce of 35,000 employees, half of them women. The plant operated twenty-four hours a day, seven days a week, and shop floor employees rode cartridge plant buses to their work sites.

Betty was overwhelmed. *What am I getting into?*

A presentation on regulations and procedures followed the orientation lecture. A slightly built, unhealthy-looking young trainer held up an employee handbook. He said, "The health and safety rules and regulations are in the handbook. Read it carefully when you get home tonight. Your supervisor will have you sign a form, verifying that you have read and understood the handbook. We are an ordnance plant. We handle dangerous materials. Keep that in mind."

A guy next to Betty whispered, "I guess he didn't follow the health rules."

There was some snickering and giggling.

Betty didn't join in. She was already on thin ice by being late.

A tall, middle-aged woman replaced the young man. Her name badge identified her as Mrs. Scott.

With no introduction or preamble, she began. "In the production buildings, we allow no ignition devices of any kind. No matches, no cigarette lighters."

"No two sticks to rub together," said the young man next to Betty.

There was more giggling. Betty edged away from the jokester.

Mrs. Scott stared sternly at the young man and said forcefully, "Any violation of this rule will lead to instant termination. Leave all such materials at home or locked up in your automobile."

The young man dropped his eyes, and Mrs. Scott continued her lecture.

"In the production areas, there are no cigarettes, cigars, or smoking materials of any kind. The penalty for possession of such materials in a production area is termination. No warnings. The only smoking areas are the cafeterias. At the breaks and lunch, those wishing to smoke will go to their assigned locker, remove their cigarette package, and take it to the cafeteria where they may smoke. Before returning to work, the cigarette packages must be returned to your locker and locked up. Are there any questions?"

Several hands went up, and a man asked loudly, "How do we light the damn things?"

The hands came down, and the woman said, "There are lighters permanently installed at several locations in the cafeterias. You'll see how to use them."

The woman stepped back from the podium, and a middle-aged, overweight man in a shirt and tie appeared who introduced himself as Mr. Wood. His discussion covered clothing and personal items.

"Except for undergarments, no personal clothing or jewelry is worn in production areas. Nothing except one personal handkerchief may be on your person. Everyone is issued cotton undershirts, coveralls, shoes, and socks. You will be assigned a personal locker and given a key to it. There are men's and women's changing rooms. When you have changed into what we call powder clothes, you will hang and or store your personal clothing and all personal effects in your locker. Are there any questions?"

Several hands went up. A young man asked, "Where do we get these powder clothes?"

"The plant will supply them. Clothing procedures are explained in the handbook."

Mrs. Scott returned to the podium.

"After lunch, please return to this auditorium for temporary badges and parking lot passes. You will receive locker assignments and keys as well. At the end of your first week, your B gas ration stickers are distributed. As military industry workers you are entitled to the B sticker."

Several of the new employees applauded or whistled.

"Welcome to the St. Joseph ordinance plant," she finished.

Mr. Wood escorted the new employees to the administration cafeteria.

"Your first lunch is free. There are twenty-two in-house cafeterias on the premises," the trainer said. "You will sign chits for your meals, and the cost will be deducted from your next paycheck. No cash or coins are allowed outside the locker rooms."

The mountain of information had dazed Betty, so she chatted little with her table mates at lunch. Even the smart-aleck young man seemed intimidated, and everyone was subdued.

After lunch, Betty's group returned to the auditorium where they were issued temporary badges, parking passes, and another lecture on movement around and in the plant.

I guess this is what it's like to work for the government, Betty thought.

She felt like she had just worked a double shift at Quaker Oats.

*****

"Well, how was your first day?" June asked as she shed her coat and hat at the front door.

"It was an ass-kicker," Betty answered. She was working on her second highball.

"Why, what happened?" June asked.

"I don't think I can explain it to you. You had to be there," Betty said. "I've never had so much crap thrown at me at one time before. Do you want a drink?"

"I'll have a beer. Does that mean you don't want to work there now?"

"No, I think the job will be interesting, but what an ordeal it was, getting inducted."

Betty got a beer out of the icebox, popped the cap with a church key, and took it to June with a glass. She retrieved her gin and tonic and brought it into the living room and joined June on the love seat.

"On the trolley, I was thinking I would call Mike and invite him to join me for lunch tomorrow," June said. "We can straighten out who pays the check at our dinner Friday night."

"You're still hung up on that?" Betty said. "Well, it's your brainchild, not mine. The day some guy wants me to pick up the check is the day all he'll see of me is my keister going away."

"I'm thinking of asking him to go to DeKalb to my family's Christmas party. He doesn't have any family of his own. I thought we could talk about it tomorrow. Christmas is next Monday," June said.

"Is this one of those 'pal' things?" Betty asked.

June ignored her question. "Do you want to come along with us? My family would love to see you," June asked Betty.

"No, my folks are expecting me. My dad is a pain sometimes, but I don't want to hurt his feelings. He's counting on me to come," Betty said.

"Are you going to invite Don?" June asked.

"Lord, no. My dad would have a fit," Betty said. "A nightclub musician?"

June set down her beer and opened her purse. She got out Mike's number, picked up the phone, and dialed.

"Hello," Mike answered on the third ring. He and Don had been fooling around with some melodies Don might use in a new song. He sat his guitar down on the chair next to the phone.

"Hello, yourself," June said. "I started a new job on Monday. Would you like to have lunch with me tomorrow and I'll tell you about it?"

"Sure, you bet," Mike said. "Where and when?"

"I only have an hour for lunch. Meet me at the Quaker Oats main lobby at twelve o'clock. We can have lunch in the cafeteria."

"Okay, I'll be there. Thanks for the invite," Mike said.

When June had got off the phone, Betty asked, "Are you getting a thing for Mike now?"

"He's growing on me," June said. She drank her beer.

"He's still just a pal, right?"

"We'll see," June said. She started having second thoughts about her growing interest in Mike. *I can't let him sidetrack me from studying for my entrance exam*, she thought. *I still have to brush up on math and science. I'm okay on English and geography, but history needs work, too. Those As I got in high school aren't helping me much now.*

"Does that mean you're giving up that harebrained idea about splitting the check?"

"We'll see," June repeated.

"I'm not very hungry after that ordeal today. I'm just going to make a ham sandwich for dinner, unless you want to cook something," Betty said.

"No, that's fine with me. I'll make them. You just relax."

"Great. Keep that up, and I'll consider marrying you," Betty joked.

The girls listened to the radio while they ate the sandwiches.

"Turn up that radio. It's almost time for *The Phantom* show," Betty asked.

June got up and went to the Zenith radio.

"I hope there's no more war news. I'm very worried about my brothers, especially Ricky," June said and tuned the radio, adjusting the dial to the right station.

She found it just as Orson Welles said, "*Who knows? The phantom knows!*" and the volume of creepy background music increased. June was relieved there were no interruptions about the war. Lamont Cranston, the Shadow, caught the killer by the end of the radio show.

*****

June spent the next morning at work learning line schedules and the sources of information that drove them. She shared a cubicle with Cheryl, her trainer. The cubicle was one of several in the scheduling office, which adjoined the planning office.

"What does planning do?" June asked Cheryl.

Cheryl explained that the planners take the sales forecasts from the sales department and break them down into product orders with delivery dates. Then the schedulers take the product orders and create the weekly schedules.

"Then we break the weekly schedules down into daily schedules and shift schedules."

"How do we know how many boxes of a product a shift can produce?"

"That's an excellent question," Cheryl said. "We have information from the production manager's office that helps us, reports that show the eight-hour capacities of each line. We get those updated every week."

"It sounds complicated."

"Don't worry. It isn't that tough. You're a bright girl. You'll pick it up, trust me," Cheryl reassured her.

This is a lot more interesting than packing boxes of Aunt Jemima pancake mix into cardboard cartons. I'm lucky to have Cheryl as my trainer. She really seems to know her stuff, and she's easy to get along with, June thought.

*****

At the lunch break, June waited in the lobby of the main office. Mike arrived at twelve o'clock, and they went to the cafeteria. It was packed with white-collar workers, but the lines at the food counters moved swiftly. They got trays, selected their food and drinks, and carried the trays to one of the cashier stations. The cashier rang up their selections.

"This is on me," June said. She took a bill out of her purse and handed it to the cashier and got the change. June carried her tray to an empty table, put her food and her drink on the table, and waited while Mike did the same.

Mike took their used trays back to the stand and then rejoined June at the table.

"So tell me about your new job," Mike said and took a bite of his hamburger.

"I think I'm going to like it. They put me with Cheryl, who has been a scheduler for two years. She's helping me get up to speed. Then I'll have three cereal packing lines to schedule on my own. Our boss seems okay, but I haven't had much contact with him," June said and tried a bite of her egg-salad sandwich and a drink of her milk.

"I've picked a very expensive restaurant for dinner on Friday," Mike said. "You may not want to split the check."

"Of course, I'm not splitting the check. I bought lunch today. Friday's your turn."

Mike stopped eating his hamburger in midbite, looked at June, and said, "Aren't you the one! I sure admire how you worked that out." He finished his bite of hamburger. *Now I wish I hadn't gone overboard on the restaurant Friday night*, he thought.

"What are you doing for Christmas?" June asked. "Do you have any plans?"

"Not really. I thought about going to the movies."

That's a sad way to spend Christmas, June thought.

"I'm going to get a piece of pie and some coffee. The pie looked good," June said.

Mike finished his hamburger and said, "I'm right behind you."

They returned to their table with their pie and coffee.

June said, "My family always has a family reunion at the farm on the holidays. Sometimes it's Thanksgiving. This year it's Christmas."

"That's very nice. I hope you have a good time," Mike said.

"It's a smaller group since two of my brothers went off to war. But my brother John will be home from Washington, DC. My sisters Emma Dee and Virginia Jane will be there along with my mom and dad, of course."

"They sound like a great family. I envy you," Mike said, eating his last bite of pie.

June made up her mind. She couldn't let Mike spend his Christmas alone.

"I'd like you to join us, if you want to."

"Are you sure I won't be intruding?" Mike asked.

"Not with us. It's the more the merrier with our bunch."

"I'd very much like to go," Mike said.

"We can talk about it some more on Friday," June said, finishing her pie. "I've got to run. I'm due back to work in two minutes." She got up, blew him a kiss, and took off. *I'm glad I invited him.*

Mike drank his coffee and thought about meeting June's family. He decided June must be starting to like him if she had wanted him to meet them. He hoped her family would share her feeling.

*****

That night Don and Mike were playing gin rummy and having a beer in their cabin. Mike told Don about June's invitation to her family's Christmas reunion at their tobacco farm.

"You're moving kind of fast, aren't you? Meeting a girl's family is serious business," Don said, and he discarded the ten of clubs.

"She's just being considerate since I don't have any family here, and I have no plans for Christmas," Mike said as he picked up Don's ten of clubs and discarded a seven of diamonds.

"So she's just feeling sorry for you?" Don suggested. He drew a card from the deck and discarded the queen of hearts.

"I didn't say that! I think I'm getting somewhere with her," Mike snapped back.

"Okay, don't get your panties in a bunch. You're probably right," Don conceded.

Mike drew from the deck and discarded the queen of spades.

Don picked up the queen of spades from the discard pile. He used his elbow to push it into his hand neatly between two other cards. Then he laid down the ten, jack, and queen of spades, four kings, a small club run, and discarded his eleventh card face down.

"Gin!" he exclaimed triumphantly. "I baited you with the queen of hearts," he crowed.

Mike was annoyed with Don's little trick of sliding the gin card into his hand with his elbow. It was Don's way of rubbing it in when he got his gin card.

"How far is it to this tobacco plantation?" Don asked.

"She said it's near DeKalb, about thirty miles south of St. Joe," Mike said. "Do you always have to do the elbow thing?" Mike sipped his beer, laid his hand face up on the table, and counted his losing points.

"Your tires will probably make it that far. Do you have enough gas ration?" Don asked.

"Yeah, I'm okay. I'm thinking of storing my car here in St. Joe and taking the train back to Joplin."

"How many points did I get on that hand?" Don asked, pencil poised over the score sheet.

"You got twenty-five points for gin and thirty-five points from me, so that makes sixty."

Don wrote it on the scorecard. Don put Mike's cards back in the deck and shuffled them.

"Why would you store your car here? I get it, you're coming back to see June, and you want your car available, right?" asked Don. He finished shuffling the deck and gave it to Mike to cut.

"What's wrong with that?" Mike asked. "With the thirty-five mile an hour speed limit, it's too far to drive from Crowder on a weekend pass. I can take the train and have Friday night and all-day Saturday and Saturday night with June. Then I can take the train back on Sunday.

"Wow, you've really worked this out, haven't you? But what if June doesn't like your plan?"

Mike cut the deck. "If she doesn't, she doesn't. That's up to her."

Don dealt the new hands, put the deck on the table, and turned the top card up to start the discard pile. It was the ace of diamonds.

"Listen, I have an idea. I'll keep the car at Rosecrans Field, and you can use it whenever you're here. Of course, I'd like to use it myself to see Betty," Don said.

Mike picked up the ace and discarded the jack of spades. "Thanks for the ace. That takes nine points out of my hand. I like your idea.

It'll save me paying storage, and it would be safer. Sometimes you get ripped off at those storage yards. You pick up your car, and the radio's gone," Mike said.

"I'll see if I can scrounge up better tires somewhere," Don said. "Well, it looks like we have a deal." Don picked up the jack of spades and slid it in between two cards in his hand with his elbow.

"You have to be shitting me," Mike said. "One lousy discard!"

"Gin!" Don yelled, laying down his hand. "You owe me five clams, sucker."

*****

Betty followed the directions given at her intake yesterday. She drove to the lot for Building 23 and parked in her assigned space, near the center of the lot. Betty walked to the employee entrance marked on her diagram of the building. There were six employee entrances. One was for salaried employees. Using that entrance, she was surprised to see timecard racks.

At Quaker Oats, only hourly employees punched in on time-cards. Salaried employees did not clock in. They wrote their hours on a time report that their supervisor signed. She went to the rack marked A-F and saw her name on a timecard. She punched in and put the card back in the rack. The racket coming from the production areas was as tumultuous as she remembered.

She made her way to Mr. Harding's office and entered. The quality control girl was at her desk.

Betty checked her watch. She was five minutes early.

The girl may be inept, but she was dependable, Betty thought. "Hi, I'm Betty Anderson. I'm reporting to work for Mr. Harding."

The girl looked up from the pile of papers she was holding.

"I'm Marlene and thrilled you're here. I can't wait to get back to my real job. Mr. Harding is at a meeting. He told me to show you what to do. He'll see you when he gets out of his meeting," the girl said.

"Thank you for helping me get started," Betty said.

"This is an organization chart for this building and a separate chart for the production department in this building. It shows the names, job titles, and who reports to whom."

"What do you do with them?" Betty asked.

"You use them to see who is sending memos to Mr. Harding. You'll learn who to pay attention to and who can be put off until later. Some of them don't like being put off and might complain to Mr. Harding. You'll learn which complaints he listens to and which ones he doesn't."

"Is all this stuff on your desk memos from people?" Betty asked. She sifted through some of the paper in the in-basket.

"No, reports are a lot of it. Pay attention to those. The Army is very fussy about reports, so Mr. Harding is fussy about them too," Marlene said.

"You seem to know what you're doing. Why aren't you caught up?" Betty asked.

"It's really too much for one person. A lot of this stuff could probably be ignored, and the important stuff caught up. But it isn't my job to discriminate, and I don't stick my neck out, so I just take everything as it comes," Marlene said.

"Could you teach me how to tell the important stuff from the rest?" Betty asked.

"Sure. But don't start changing things until I'm back in quality control."

Betty continued looking through the in-basket. Marlene put a paper in the out-basket.

"When will that be?" Betty asked.

"As soon as you're trained, I guess."

"Who decides if I'm trained?"

"Mr. Harding."

"Then let's get started training me," Betty said.

Two hours later, Mr. Harding returned from his meeting and saw Betty and Marlene seated behind the desk with their heads together.

Hum, he thought, *I think that pile of paper has gone down a little.*

"Is Marlene showing you the ropes?" he asked Betty.

"She's a whiz. I bet they miss her in QC," Betty said truthfully.

Last week she thought Marlene couldn't find her butt with both hands, and now she's a whiz. That's some change of attitude, he thought. *I wonder what's going on here.* "Well, stick with it. After lunch, I'll give you a tour of the building. Change into your powder clothes when you finish your lunch," he said. Mr. Harding went into his office and closed the door.

Marlene and Betty slowly worked their way through the pile in the in-basket. They heard the buzzer announcing the lunch break. Marlene accompanied Betty to the women's locker room and helped her locate her locker. She waited while Betty changed into her powder clothes and hung up her street clothes. Betty took her cigarette pack out of her purse and put her purse back in the locker.

"I'm glad you brought your locker key in with you. A lot of rookies forget them on their first day," Marlene said.

"My instruction sheet was quite clear about that. It made a point of it," Betty said.

"Yeah, they all do, but people still forget. I guess you're more careful than most."

"I need this job. I quit my old job."

"Burned your bridges, did you?" Marlene said. "I think you'll do fine. Mr. Harding comes across grumpy, but if you do a good job, he'll treat you fairly."

Marlene led the way to the cafeteria. It looked like most cafeterias, except people were dressed in gray powder clothes and it was smoky. Betty saw a man putting a cigarette up against a metal box mounted on the wall. He puffed on the cigarette until it was lit. When he moved away, Betty could see that the metal box had a cigarette lighter coil in the middle of it, like the lighters in cars.

The food counters were crowded with people in powder clothes. The noise level was high, with all the conversations at the tables and in the food lines.

Marlene took a metal tray at the start of one of the food lines and handed another tray to Betty. As they moved along, servers dished up their selections. The last station on the food line was for drinks. There was a cashier station at the end of the line. The cashier rang up Marlene's food and Marlene wrote her badge number on the receipt and signed it. The receipt went into a box next to the cashier. Betty followed Marlene's lead with signing her chit, and they went to find an empty table.

When they were settled at their table, Marlene said, "If you're going to smoke, we better eat fast. The rest of the lunch hour goes by quickly."

Betty tried her meatloaf and mashed potatoes. "That's not bad."

"The food's good. You don't get a lot of choices, but it's good."

Betty asked Marlene questions about some documents they had processed. Marlene told Betty funny stories about the people who sent the memos to Mr. Harding.

When they finished their food, Marlene picked up both trays and said, "Have your smoke. I'm going to the little girls' room." She dropped off the trays and went through the door to their locker room. The ladies' room was next to the locker room.

Betty took a cigarette out of her pack and went to the nearest one of the wall lighters. She put the cigarette up against the lighter. Nothing happened.

"You have to push the button."

Betty looked around to see who was speaking to her. It was a gray-haired Negro man sitting at a table with three other Negro men. Betty hadn't noticed the men, even though they were at the table near hers.

"Thank you, sir," Betty said to the Negro man. She followed his instructions and soon had her Lucky Strike lit and going.

"You're very welcome, miss," said the Negro man solemnly as Betty turned to go back to her table.

When Betty finished her smoke, she crushed out the cigarette in her food tray on the table. She got up to leave when the Negro man spoke again.

"Pardon me, I can see it's your first day. There are red butt cans on the walls. The cigarette butts go in them, miss."

Betty picked her butt out of the food tray and carried it to one of the red cans. She passed the table with the four Negro men, stopped, and said to the gray-haired Negro man, "Thank you again, sir." As she walked on, she thought, *That's the first conversation I've ever had with a Negro.*

*****

Betty stood at Mr. Harding's office door at 12:55 p.m. She knocked and heard him yell, "Come!"

Mr. Harding appraised her. She had on her powder clothes and shoes. She was wearing her temporary ID badge. There were no bulges in the pockets of her coveralls.

"Are you a smoker?" he asked.

"I had my smoke in the cafeteria," Betty said.

"Empty your pockets," he said.

Betty reached into the pockets of her coveralls and pulled them out. They were empty like they were supposed to be.

She just might work out, Mr. Harding thought. He opened the door of a small closet, reached in and took out what appeared to be a long gray lab coat on a hanger. He put on the coat, attaching his red striped badge to an upper pocket on the coat. Then he brought out two pairs of safety glasses and two small cases and gave one set to Betty.

"We're going to take a tour of the plant. I just gave you a pair of earplugs, the same earplugs basic trainees use on rifle ranges. Take them out of the case and put them in your ears. Leave the case on my desk. You can pick it up when we get back from the tour. Always wear the earplugs and safety glasses in the plant. Noise levels on the production floors exceed one hundred decibels. That will damage your hearing over time."

Mr. Harding waited until Betty put in her earplugs and put the case on his desk. "We won't be able to talk, so pay attention to what you see. If there's something I want you to see, I'll stop walking. When I think you've seen enough, I'll start walking again. Do what I do. Speak to no one. Do you have any questions?"

Betty shook her head.

When they entered the plant, Mr. Harding stopped in the first department. Machines were stamping cartridge casings from brass sheets. The casings collected in boxes, and a conveyor system moved the boxes to the next department. Betty studied the machines and marveled at how many casings they were producing.

Mr. Harding resumed his walk, and Betty followed him. They walked down an aisle, following the conveyors to the next bay. The boxes of casings went on the conveyors to automatic loading machines. The automatic loading machines installed primers and rammed powder and slugs into the casings. Overhead, flexible conduits fed the powder into the hoppers on the machines. Other conveyors brought boxes of primers and projectiles in to feed them. Powder-clothed men fed the components into the machines' hoppers. They wore face masks, earplugs, and safety glasses.

Small amounts of the gunpowder escaped into the air from the loading machines. Negro janitors swept up the powder on the floors, put it in rolling bins, and moved the bins out of the bay. The machines fed thousands of completed cartridges into boxes. The boxes moved down the conveyor system. Betty looked for the Negro men she saw in the cafeteria, but she didn't see any of them.

Other black men in gray coveralls were scattered among the white production workers. This was a new development, Betty learned later. Previously, the black workers had worked their own production lines. Only the black janitors worked the white production lines. Last week, the government had ordered the plant to fully integrate. Over objections from some white workers, the electrical, radio, and machine workers' union leaders passed a resolution to support the change. At a meeting of the union, the workers voted to overturn the resolution. But the government prevailed, and the plant was now integrated.

Even with the earplugs, Betty found the clamor daunting. The machines put out a steady roar, which was punctuated by the cracks of cartridges being test fired next door. Mr. Harding resumed his walk. They left the cartridge loading department and entered the packing department. Workers took the boxes of cartridges from the conveyor and moved them onto pack stations. The cartridges were packed into various containers on the pack lines. One line was backed up with cartridge boxes. That line had stopped their feed conveyor. Mr. Harding paused for several minutes. Then he exited the production floor and led Betty back to his office.

He said, "Have a seat." After she was seated in the guest chair, he asked, "What did you see?"

"I saw a lot of heavy, noisy machines; a lot of very busy people; and a lot of ammunition being made for our boys to shoot," Betty said.

Mr. Harding sat in his chair. "Anything else?" he asked.

"I wondered why one of the packaging lines was backed up, Mr. Harding."

"I wondered the same thing myself," he said. "From now on, call me Joe."

"Okay, Joe," Betty said. *If this had been a test*, she thought she passed it.

"Change out of your powder clothes, take your break, and get back to work," Joe said. "Keep your safety glasses and your earplugs in your locker."

Betty went to the ladies' locker room to put away the glasses and earplugs as Joe directed.

Joe returned to the plant to check out the stoppage at the packing line. He found the packing line lead man and asked him what was going on with the line.

"The quality control inspector found reject cartridges and stopped the line," the lead man told Joe.

The line employees were removing the boxes of cartridges from the feed conveyor and loading them on pallets. Forklifts took the pallets to an inspection area for inspection and sorting. The lead man told Joe that the packing supervisor had gone to the loading department to talk with the loading supervisor. When Joe arrived in the loading department, he saw maintenance mechanics checking out the automatic loading machines producing cartridges for this packing line. Mr. Harding went back to his office, happy the problem was being properly handled.

6

Sgt. Richard Taylor walked down the aisle between two crowded rows of hospital beds in the amputee ward. He was dressed in dirty, torn fatigues and wore a helmet over his helmet liner. It had a camouflage cover. The obviously new three stripes on his sleeves stood out on his worn fatigues. The makeshift hospital was in the center of Bastogne. It was bedlam. Doctors and nurses scrambled, trying to deal with the flood of casualties. Corpsmen were doing triage. The nurses were too busy for that. Patients cried out for attention and cursed the staff. The sounds of battle were incessant.

Ricky stopped at a bed halfway down the aisle.

"How are you doing?" he asked the patient with bloody bandages on his arm and the stump of his left leg.

The patient had gauze wrapped around his head. He had a transfusion rack next to his bed. Two plastic bags hung from the rack and fed plastic tubes into his arm. One bag was blood or plasma.

Sal looked like shit, Ricky thought. *I should have been with him. Maybe he wouldn't have got hit.*

Sal said, "I'm just fucking peachy. I'm only a BTK."

"I'm afraid to ask. What's a BTK?" Ricky said.

"Below the knee. That's a lot better than an ATK. We have some ATKs in here, the poor bastards. They don't have knees to work with artificial legs."

"I thought I taught you to duck," Ricky said.

"I was ducking, then the fucking building fell on me when an 88-round hit it," Sal said. "When did you get the extra stripe?"

"They gave it to me when they pulled me out of our squad and put me in charge of Third squad," Ricky said. "Sergeant Murphy got hit trying to stop a Kraut tank with a bazooka. The .30 gunner on

75

the Kraut tank got him. We were out of sergeants, so they picked me to replace him."

"How did you get here to the hospital?" Sal asked.

"They pulled the battalion back into reserve to regroup and refit, so I thought I would see if you'd been evacuated yet," Ricky said.

Sal grimaced and let out a small groan. "My leg hurts like hell and it ain't even there. Ain't that a bitch?"

Ricky said, "I talked to the doctor. He said the patients on this ward might be evacuated tomorrow. The weather is finally cleared up enough to get some planes in here."

"I guess I got one of those million-dollar wounds, huh?" Sal said bitterly.

A nurse tapped Ricky on the shoulder and said, "He needs another pain shot and to get some sleep."

Ricky moved out of her way. "Good luck, pal. I'll see you after the war," Ricky said.

"You're the one who needs the luck. Didn't you hear what General McAuliffe said when the Kraut general asked him to surrender today?" Sal said.

"Yeah, he said, '*Nuts!*'"

"You better hope Patton's Third Army gets here soon," Sal said as the nurse gave him his shot of morphine. Sal drifted off to sleep.

Sergeant Taylor walked out of the ward and back to the war.

*****

Friday night, Betty and June were getting ready for their dates. They had fought over who would shower first, and Betty won. Betty had her shower while June shaved her legs using a bowl of water in her bedroom.

"This would be a lot easier if you would hurry up with your shower and give me the bathroom back," June yelled.

Betty ignored June as she dried her hair. When she finished toweling off, she wrapped the towel around her hair, put on a well-worn terrycloth robe and slippers. She came out of the bathroom and said, "It's all yours now." She went to her room to put on her makeup.

June took her turn in the shower.

Betty finished her makeup and came into the living room in her bra and panties. She held two dresses on hangers. She said loudly, "Come out here for a second."

June came out of the bathroom dressed in her bathrobe.

Betty held the dresses out for June's inspection and said, "Which one?"

"The dressy one," June said without looking at the dresses.

"They're both dressy," Betty protested.

"I know," June said.

"You're a big help."

"I know," June said. "Next time you'll give me the shower first." She went to her room and selected a new fawn-colored cocktail dress to set off her red hair.

Betty took the dresses back to her room and selected the blue dress with the white collar.

The black cocktail dress is too much for a movie, she thought. *The blue dress matches my eyes. Phooey on June.* She started blow drying and brushing her hair. Then she put on the blue dress and looked at herself critically in her full-length mirror. *That'll warm up Don's engine.*

In the other bedroom, June pulled on the nylons Betty had loaned her. Fortunately, they had survived the Frog Hop. She secured them with garters and put on the cocktail dress. June ran a few brush strokes through her thick hair, and it soon fell into place in a short pageboy hairstyle. She picked her white high heels over the black pair. June's closet was Spartan compared to Betty's. She was saving every dime for nursing school.

The doorbell rang.

"I'll get it!" June yelled.

She put on the white high heels and went to answer the door.

"Hi, Don," she said when she opened the door and saw him standing in the hallway. "Come on in and sit down anywhere. Let me take your coat."

He took off his lined winter coat and handed it to her. She hung his coat in the entry. He was dressed casually in jeans and a blue buttoned-down collar shirt. He wore a white cable-knit sweater over the shirt.

He looks great, June thought. She glanced at her watch. It was seven thirty on the money. *Well, he is a soldier. He's used to being on time.* "Betty's dressing. She'll be out soon," she said.

Don sat down on the loveseat and said, "That's okay, I always allow extra time for girls to dress."

Aren't you the smug one? she thought, but she said, "Can I get you something to drink? We've got Cokes and 7-Up."

"Sure, I'll have a Coke. Thanks."

June went into the kitchen and opened a Coke bottle. She poured it in a glass and added chipped ice. She delivered it to Don and sat on the upholstered chair.

"Nice place you girls have here. It's cozy," Don said, sipping his Coke.

Hurry up, Betty, June thought. *Take this guy off my hands.* "I'm glad you like it," June said.

Hurry up, Betty, Don thought.

"Hello, big guy. Welcome to our digs," Betty said, entering the living room.

Thank God, thought June.

Thank God, thought Don. "You look sensational," Don said. *She really is a knockout*, he thought.

"You're not bad, yourself," Betty responded. *I love that cable-knit sweater on him.*

"We better go. We'll be late for the movie," Don urged.

"Just let me get my things," Betty said and went back into her room. She reappeared a few minutes later wearing a dressy heavy coat, gloves, and hat, and carrying her purse. "Let's get this show on the road."

"Have a good time!" June said as they left.

Something about that guy rubs me the wrong way, she thought.
He probably feels the same about me. He better treat Betty right.

*****

When Don and Betty came down the steps of the brownstone, Don steered her to a large black four-door sedan and opened the passenger door for her. She got in the car and studied the interior. It was not new, but it was clean. The seat was soft and comfortable.

Don got in his side and turned to June and said, "Pretty snazzy, huh?"

"It's a nice car. What is it and where did it come from? Did you steal it from a gangster?" Betty asked.

"It's a 1939 Oldsmobile sedan. I got it from an Oldsmobile dealer out on the Belt Highway," Don said.

"You bought this car?" Betty asked, looking at all the fancy gauges on the dash.

"No, I rented it for the night," Don said. "I have to take it back tomorrow."

"This must be expensive. We could have taken a taxi," Betty said.

"Nah, it was very reasonable."

Don explained that Oldsmobile, General Motors, stopped producing Oldsmobiles in 1943 when they changed over to war production. The dealer's lot had several 1937–'41 cars, mostly former trade-ins and mostly Oldsmobiles. He rented them out because he couldn't sell them thanks to the government restriction on selling cars. He wouldn't sell them anyway since they would go for as much as a new car when the war was over.

"He gives a discount to servicemen," Don explained.

Betty leaned back and relaxed against the velour seat while Don turned on the heater. "That's cold air," Betty protested.

"It'll warm up in a minute," Don said. He pulled away from the curb and joined the stream of traffic. "How did you like the Frog Hop?" Don asked, watching the traffic light turn green ahead.

He sped up to make the light. The powerful eight-cylinder engine responded briskly. *This car is peppy*, Don thought.

"I thought it was fun. June thought it was tacky," Betty frowned.

"Speaking of June, I don't think she approves of me," Don said, glancing at the side street as he crossed the intersection.

"Why do you think she doesn't approve of you?" Betty asked, looking out her window.

They were passing older brownstones. Most of the windows in the apartments had Christmas wreaths or Christmas lights decorating them. Betty enjoyed the holiday look of them.

"She was kind of sarcastic with me at the Frog Hop. Tonight, while I was waiting for you, she hardly said ten words to me. Don't get me wrong, she was polite, but that was all," Don said.

"Don't worry about it, I still like you," Betty said, elbowing him in the ribs.

"It's starting to snow. I better pay attention to my driving," Don said. He let up on the gas pedal.

*****

Back at the apartment, June had just decided on a hat to wear when the doorbell rang again.

She answered the door and invited Mike in. Under a lined topcoat, he was wearing the sport coat, shirt, and dark-blue pants he wore with his band. He had changed his tie. He was carrying a gaily wrapped package.

She took his coat and hat and hung them up. "What's this?" June asked, pointing at the package.

"Merry Christmas," Mike said and handed her the gift.

"Can I open it now?" she asked.

"Absolutely," Mike answered.

"Sit with me on the loveseat," June said.

When they were seated, June started peeling away the tape and unfolding the colorful paper, taking care not to rip or tear it.

"You're making me crazy. Just rip it open," Mike protested.

"We always save the paper in my family," June said as she got to the last fold and took out two pairs of nylon stockings. "Perfect!" she squealed and grabbed Mike and kissed him.

Mike was caught off guard and didn't have time to kiss her back, but he sure liked her kiss.

June held up one of the nylons and said, "How did you know my size?"

"I described you to the saleslady, and she picked the size and shade," Mike said.

"They will do just fine. Thank you very much," June said and squeezed Mike's hand.

"We should go. Our reservations are for nine o'clock," Mike said.

"Just let me get my coat," June said. She jumped up and went into her bedroom with the nylons and the paper, folding the paper and putting it on a shelf in her closet. She put the nylons in a dresser drawer.

I don't know about that frog waiter, but I'm beginning to think Mike is a keeper.

When they left the brownstone, it was snowing lightly, but it wasn't sticking.

Mike opened the Chevy's door for June and closed it after she was in.

"If it starts snowing harder and accumulating, I'll pull over and park. We can take taxis. My tires are not very good, and I wouldn't want to get in a wreck with you in the car."

"I'm not worried. You'll take care of us," June said.

Mike drove carefully and left plenty of room between his Chevy and the other cars.

"Now it looks like Christmas," June said cheerfully.

*****

"Maybe we'll have an old-fashioned white Christmas," Betty said as she watched the snowflakes fall on Don's windshield.

Don found a parking space a half block from the theater.

The theater lobby was arrayed in Christmas decorations. There was a Salvation Army Santa Claus ringing a bell outside the entry. Don searched his pocket and came up with some change and dropped it in the bucket.

"Ho! Ho! Ho! Merry Christmas," Santa bellowed at them.

Don got in line to purchase their tickets while Betty went to buy popcorn. The smell of fresh, hot buttery popcorn filled the air.

Don joined Betty in line, holding their tickets. They reached the counter, and Betty told the counterman, "I'll have the medium box of popcorn and a medium Coke."

Don amended the order. "Change that to a large box of popcorn, extra butter, and make it two medium Cokes." He turned to Betty with a smile. "We'll share."

They walked up the runway to a purple curtain blocking the aisle. Don handed their tickets to the usher, who tore them in half and handed them their ticket stubs.

Don followed Betty into the auditorium. As they walked down the aisle, Don whispered in Betty's ear, "Darn, the back row seats are all gone. I guess other couples had the same idea."

Betty stopped walking, turned around, and gave him a stern look and then broke down and giggled. "What about the balcony?" she suggested.

"All the teenagers are up there. I'm not interested in going back to high school," Don said.

"And when you leave, your shoe soles are covered in bubble-gum." Betty laughed.

They found two seats on the aisle halfway down the runway.

"I get the aisle, unless you want to keep jumping up and down to let me go to the little girls' room."

"It's fine with me. It's a perfect strategic location," Don said and sat down.

Betty sat in her seat on the aisle and whispered, "What do you mean?"

"For an assault on the objective," he said in a soft voice. "Have some popcorn. The movie's about to start." He handed her the bag of popcorn.

The Robidoux Theater interior was lavish with golden statues and gold-painted trim and seated three hundred people. The walls had exotic hardwood accents, and the aisles were carpeted and adorned with Robidoux logos. Plush velvet chairs and spring-loaded seats dotted the auditorium. They folded back up when vacated, making entry and exit easy. The arms of the chairs had cup holders built into them. Heavy maroon velvet stage curtains were trimmed in gold and were closed over the movie screen. When the house lights dimmed, the stage curtains opened and revealed a huge screen.

The title page appeared on screen, *Casablanca*, starring Humphrey Bogart, Ingrid Bergman, and Claude Rains.

Don placed his Coke into the cup holder and put his arm around Betty's shoulder. The credits scrolled down the screen.

Betty leaned toward Don and whispered, "Now I see what you meant about the strategic location. When does the assault on the objective begin?"

"It already has," he said; and he leaned toward her, pulled her a little closer, and gave her a kiss.

She kissed him back. She whispered, "You'll spill our popcorn if you're not careful."

A fat woman and her bald husband sat in the seats behind them. The woman was scowling at them. Her husband was mesmerized by Betty and plainly jealous of Don. Betty smiled at the husband and took a drink of her Coke and put it in the drink holder. The fat lady's scowl deepened. Don looked at her and shrugged. He looked back at Betty and grinned. Then he kissed her again.

The opening scene of the movie started playing on the screen. Betty watched the movie and ate a handful of popcorn. She held the bag out to Don.

Casablanca was a rerelease of a 1942 movie. It was set in the *neutral* open city of Casablanca, Morocco, and involved a jaded café owner and a French underground couple evading Nazi capture. Neither Betty nor Don had seen it.

Don finished his popcorn and put his arm back around Betty's shoulder. She leaned into his embrace, partly blocking the fat lady's view of the screen.

"Young woman, I can't see through you," the fat lady complained.

Betty glanced over her shoulder and suggested, "Try leaning the other way."

Don laughed. Betty kept her head on Don's shoulder.

They both got caught up in the movie.

Betty liked the tangled love story between Bogart and Bergman. Don liked Bogart outfoxing the Nazis. The fat lady's husband liked looking at Betty. The fat lady didn't like anything.

*****

Mike pulled his Chevy up to the valet stand in front of the Jessie James Hotel. It was still snowing, and Mike was glad to get the car under the portico. The hotel had a parking garage for guests of the hotel and the restaurant. The valet opened June's door. She slid out and stood next to the car while the valet went around and opened Mike's door. Mike got out and handed the valet his keys. The valet handed Mike a claim check.

Mike took June's arm and escorted her into the hotel. The lobby resembled a rich stockman's hotel in the 1890s. Even the lamps looked like gaslight fixtures. The check-in counter was made of massive hardwood. All the place was missing was Bat Masterson and Wyatt Earp. It was named, however, after an outlaw, not a lawman.

The cloakroom accepted their coats and hats.

To the left of the lobby was the entry to the Pioneer Room, newly remodeled to bring in the carriage trade.

The maître d' greeted them and said, "Welcome to the Pioneer Room. May I please have the name on your reservation?"

Mike answered, "Thompson."

The maître d' checked a large book on his stand. "We have a nice table for you, folks." He snapped his fingers, and a host rushed over. "Take Mr. and Mrs. Thompson to table seven."

The host wore a black tuxedo jacket, a white shirt, and a formal black tie. He led Mike and June to a secluded table. He pulled out June's chair and seated her.

"If there's anything we can do to add to your evening, please us know."

He bowed and left.

"Well, I'm certainly impressed, Mr. Thompson," June said solemnly.

"Snazzy joint, isn't it, Mrs. Thompson," Mike said with a grin.

The roaring nineties theme carried into the dining room. The tables had glistening white tablecloths, heavy silverware, and crystal glassware. The soft chair seats were dark-blue velvet.

"I don't know why he called us Mr. And Mrs. Thompson," June said.

"I guess we looked married. I kind of liked the sound of it though," Mike said with a smile.

"Is that a proposal?" June asked, kidding him.

"You'll know when it's a proposal," Mike said.

A waiter, wearing a blue jacket and a blue bow tie, approached their table. He gave them both menus with heavy purple covers.

"May I take your drink orders?" he asked.

June said, "I'll have a Tanqueray gin and tonic, please."

"I'll have a scotch and soda," Mike said.

"We have Dewar's, sir, or Cutty Sark," said the waiter.

"Dewar's, please," Mike said.

The waiter left to get their drinks.

"I'd like to ask you a question, but I don't want to offend you," June said.

"Ask away," Mike said. *I wonder if I'm dressed okay for this joint,* he worried.

"What kind of guy is Don?"

"He's all right. A little conceited, I guess," Mike said. "But that's because women fall all over him."

A server came up to their table carrying a tray with water glasses. She wore a short black dress, a white apron, and a white coronet. She served their water and left.

"Will he hurt Betty?" June asked Mike.

"Only if she gets too serious about him. Don isn't the settling-down type."

"Okay, thanks for being honest. Betty's my best friend."

The waiter returned with their drinks and set them on the table.

"Your waiter will be here soon to take your food order," he said.

"I thought you were our waiter," June said.

"I'm the drink waiter, but your table waiter will help you with your food order," he said and left the table.

"I'm glad he cleared that up," Mike said.

"There's sure a passel of them," June said. "I hope you brought a lot of cash, or we're doing dishes."

"I'm flush. When Don and I went shopping, I stopped here and looked at a menu. I came prepared, so order anything you want."

Mike and June were studying their menus when another waiter arrived at their table.

"My name is Claude. I'll be your waiter tonight," he said.

"Are you sure?" June asked playfully. "You're about the fifteenth waiter so far."

"Madame jests. How droll," Claude said. "We have two specials tonight. We have a Chateaubriand with Cognac sauce, and we have roast duck à l'orange. Our soup choices are classic French onion soup or Champagne squash soup."

"What would you recommend, Claude?" June asked.

"Both are excellent," Claude replied.

"We'll have the Chateaubriand," Mike said. He looked questioningly at June, and she smiled and nodded.

"Very good, sir," Claude said. "Would Madame prefer soup or salad?"

"The French onion soup, please," June answered.

Mike said, "I'll have the salad. What's the house dressing, Claude?"

"It's a very nice oil and vinegar, sir," Claude said.

"Let's go with that," Mike said.

Claude handed them both wine lists. "Our chef recommends the French Bordeaux with the Chateaubriand."

June looked at the prices on the list and said, "Do we look like the Rockefellers, Claude?"

"The California burgundy is also nice."

Mike said, "That's fine, Claude. Bring us a bottle, please."

"Very good, Monsieur. Your appetizers will be up shortly." Claude bowed and left the table.

"I wonder where they found Claude," June said. "He doesn't look like a cowboy, does he?"

"He's not what you think of when someone says Pioneer Room," Mike agreed.

"Did you notice he thinks we're married too? He keeps calling me madame, not mademoiselle," June said.

"Maybe it's an omen," Mike said.

Claude appeared back at their table with their wine. He presented the bottle to Mike, then opened it and poured a splash of the wine into Mike's wine glass.

Mike took a drink and said, "That's fine."

Claude served the wine.

June tasted her wine and said, "That's good. Who needs France when you've got California?"

After they had been served soup and salad, Mike asked, "What time do you want me to pick you up on Christmas day?"

"If we leave about noon, that'll be fine. We usually carve the turkey midafternoon and then open presents after dessert. It depends on when we can break up the pitch games. My family are nuts about pitch."

"I take it pitch is a card game?" Mike asked.

"Oh yeah, it's several card games—there's four-point pitch, there's seven-point pitch, and my favorite is ten-point pitch. Don't worry, we'll teach you the game," June assured him.

Mike was happy to see June having a swell time.

*****

Don and Betty exited the movie theater holding hands and walked down the snowy sidewalk to the Oldsmobile. Don opened Betty's door, and she got in. Don started the car and turned on the heater. The snow had stopped, and the street was damp but clear of snow.

"That was a great movie! Humphrey Bogart was cool," Don said, adjusting the heater.

"But he had to let her go at the end. That was so sad," Betty said. She had a tear in her eye.

"Are you going to cry again?" Don asked. "You got our popcorn soggy."

"I always cry at sad movies," Betty said.

"That lady behind us wanted to give you something to cry about," Don said.

Betty giggled and said, "I was tempted to slip her husband my phone number, just in case you don't work out."

Don laughed and said, "It's good to have a backup plan, honey."

Betty searched in her purse for her cigarettes. She found her pack of Luckies and took one out.

"Do you want one?" she asked Don.

"No, I better concentrate on driving. Do you want to stop for a nightcap?" Don asked and pushed in the car lighter.

"Do you suppose I could get a nightcap out by the river somewhere?" Betty asked disingenuously. She put the cigarette pack back in her purse.

"I know a place that just stocked up on Tanqueray and tonic," Don said, going along with her. The car lighter popped out, and Don held it up to light Betty's cigarette.

"Let's try that place," Betty said, taking a puff of her cigarette.

*****

"The chef prefers the cut of tenderloin to be carved in the kitchen rather than have the waiter carve it properly at your table. Oh, well, this is the Pioneer Room, after all," Claude said dismissively.

He deftly replaced their appetizer plates with the plates of tenderloin, browned new potatoes, and asparagus with a white sauce.

"The serving style is rustic, I'm afraid, but the meal is excellent. *Bon appétit*," Claude said and stalked off.

"I don't think Claude is very long for the Pioneer Room," Mike said.

"Probably not. But I get a kick out of him," June said. "This looks delicious. Let's eat!"

Claude was right. The meal was excellent.

*****

Don pulled into a space in front of his tourist cabin, turned off the engine and headlights.

"Are you ready for your nightcap?" Don asked.

"Absolutely," Betty said as she opened her door and got out. When they entered the cabin, Betty said, "Who's the neat freak? This is too clean for two single guys."

"It ain't me, doll. If you're looking for neat, wait for Mike to get home," Don said and laughed.

"I didn't come here for neat." She threw her coat on the faded couch and laid her hat and purse on a battered end table. She turned to Don, who was right behind her, grabbed him, and planted a kiss on his startled lips.

He hugged her and returned the kiss. When they came up for air, Don said, "Do you want your cocktail before or after?"

"There is a bedroom in this joint, isn't there?" Betty asked.

"Right this way, honey," Don said. He picked her up and carried her into the bedroom.

Mike and June finished their dinner.

"Would you like some more wine?" Mike asked, holding up the bottle.

"Okay, but you may have to carry me out of here," June said, holding out her glass.

Two white-coated young men came up to their table and cleared away their dinner dishes and silverware.

"Do you have a girlfriend down there in Neosho?" June asked.

"I go to Joplin occasionally to play a gig with a pickup band and dance with the girls who show up. I don't have a steady girl if that's what you're asking."

Claude reappeared, seemingly out of nowhere, with dessert menus. He handed them each a dessert menu and said, "The crème brûlée is nice."

Mike said, "Sounds good. I'll go with that and a cup of coffee."

"Make that two," June said.

"Very good," Claude said and left to put in their order.

"What the heck is crème brûlée?" June asked Mike.

"Whatever it is, it's over my pay grade," Mike said.

Betty played lazily with the hair on Don's chest. He played with the pert pink tip of her flawless pale breast. They were lying side by side, facing each other on the bed in the only bedroom of the tourist cabin. They were naked under the sheet.

"I knew you would be fun in bed," Betty said.

"Fun, as opposed to good," he protested.

"The Swedish judge deducted two points for the dismount," Betty said solemnly.

Don laughed and said, "I'll work on that." He kissed the perfect breast.

"Style points count," Betty said and laughed. She raised his head off her breast and kissed him. "Where's that nightcap you promised me?" she asked.

"I'm having a great time," June said. "But my head is spinning, so no more wine for me."

"The coffee will help that," Mike said. "I hope you don't mind, but I like you a lot."

"I don't mind, but my legion of admirers might," June said and giggled.

"Have any of your legion asked you out for New Year's yet?" Mike asked.

"Why, do you have a better offer?" June giggled again.

"I'll take you to the biggest New Year's blowout in St. Joseph, Missouri," Mike said.

"Which blowout is that?" June asked. "Thank God, here comes Claude with the coffee."

Claude served their crème brûlées and their coffees.

"I don't know which blowout yet, but I will before I pick you up, say at eight o'clock?" Mike took a taste of his dessert and said, "That's not bad for pudding."

June tried her dessert and said, "I thought it would be something fancier with whipped cream and a cherry on top or something. It tastes good though." She sipped her coffee.

"I think there's an offer on the table," Mike reminded her.

"I've taken it under consideration," June said formally, and then she giggled again. She drank the last of her coffee.

"My offer is good any time until Christmas," Mike said.

*****

Betty sat on the couch in Don's cabin. She was fully dressed except for her shoes and nylons. The nylons were in her purse, and her shoes were lying on the carpet in front of the couch. Her legs were tucked under her on the sofa. She took a drag on her cigarette.

Don was at the kitchen counter, mixing a gin and tonic for Betty and a scotch on the rocks for himself. He was smoking a Camel. He brought the drinks into the living room and handed Betty her gin and tonic.

"Cheers," he said, raising his glass.

"The things a girl has to do to get a nightcap around here. Cheers," Betty said.

"But you do them so well," Don said with a smile and sat down next to her.

"That was fun, wasn't it?" she said. "Thanks for being prepared." She leaned over and kissed him on the cheek.

"Safety first is my motto," he said, taking a drink of his scotch.

"I should probably get home soon," she said. She took a final puff of her cigarette and put it out in the ashtray on the end table.

"Let's finish our nightcap and then we'll go," Don said.

He was surprised to realize he didn't want her to go. Usually, he couldn't get girls out the door quick enough when playtime was over.

Better watch yourself with this one, Sergeant Walker, he thought.

*****

Betty was listening to the radio when she heard the front door open.

"Hi, roomie," she shouted over the radio.

"I'll be in in a minute," June shouted back and turned to Mike in the hallway.

"I had a wonderful time, Mike," she said.

Mike put his arms around her and leaned down to kiss her. The kiss lingered for what seemed like a very long time.

When it was over, June looked at Mike and said, "There is definitely more to you than meets the eye. Good night," June said.

"Good night, doll," Mike said.

June went in and closed the door behind her.

"How was your date?" Betty asked, turning down the volume on the radio.

June hung up her things and went into the living room.

"I'm not sure about my date," June said. "How was yours?"

"Didn't you have a good time? My date was great," Betty said.

"Yes, I did. I had a very good time."

"If you had a good time, what are you not sure about?" Betty asked.

"I'm not sure how I feel about Mike," June said.

"Ah-hah! He's not just a pal anymore, right?"

"You're right. Mike's not just a pal. But I can't get serious about him. A little fun is one thing, serious is another."

"As long as we're talking about fun, Don turned out to be a whiz in that department," Betty said with a smile.

"You didn't have sex with him!?" June exclaimed.

"You want to bet?" Betty said.

"You went to bed with him for fun?" June asked.

"June, honey, I don't know what experience you've had. But if sex isn't fun, what's the point?" Betty asked.

"I guess I'm going to have to think about that," June said. "But what if you got pregnant?"

"Don was prepared. I don't take chances."

"Let me get this straight," June said. "You go to bed with guys for entertainment?"

"I have to like the guy first. I don't have sex with strangers," Betty remonstrated.

June drank her tea. *I must love the guy first*, she thought. But I can't hurt Betty's feelings. She's my best friend. *Mind your own business, June.*

"Mike asked me to go out with him on New Year's Eve," June said.

"What did you tell him?" Betty asked.

"I said I'd think about it."

"Where does he want to take you? Someplace fancy again?"

"That is to be determined. He asked me on the spur of the moment," June said.

"Why didn't you tell him yes since you now officially like him?" Betty asked and finished her cup of tea.

"I'm just not big on New Year's parties, with drunks pawing at me and planting drunken kisses on me," June said. She got up from the loveseat and said, "I'm going to bed. Good night."

"Good night," Betty said. *Don didn't mention New Year's*, she mused.

*****

Next morning, June was studying an American history textbook when the phone rang.

June answered it. "Hello."

"Hi, it's Mike."

"I still haven't made up my mind about New Year's," she said. June covered the mouthpiece and said to Betty. "It's Mike."

Betty gave her thumbs up. She moved up next to June and listened in.

June shoved her away, but she moved right back.

"That's okay. That's not why I'm calling. How would you like to go to the Holiday Park today, if you don't have other plans?" Mike asked.

"What Holiday Park?" June said.

"Krug Park," Betty whispered to June.

June pushed her away again.

"Krug Park has a Holiday Park now until New Year's," Mike said. "Don told me about it. He said it's all lit up and decorated for Christmas."

"That sounds like fun. I love Christmas," June said, turning her back on Betty, who gave up and sat on the upholstered chair.

"I'll pick you up at 11:00 a.m. We can have lunch at Benny Magoon's and then go to the park," Mike said.

"See you then," June said and hung up. She frowned in disapproval at Betty.

"You made me miss the good part," Betty said. "What's up with you and Mike?"

"Mike's picking me up at eleven o'clock. We're having lunch at Benny Magoon's and then going to the park," June said. "Do you want to go with us?"

"Nah, two's company, three's a crowd. I'm going to do my hair and my laundry. I'll just hand around here and catch up on things," Betty said.

June picked up the history book and opened it to the page she had left off reading.

Don and Mike were rehearsing one of their original songs.

Don stopped playing and said, "I don't like the chord change here. Let's try a B minor."

Mike strummed a B minor chord. "Like that?" he asked.

"Yeah, I think so. Let's take it from the top and see how it fits," Don said.

They ran through the melody and put in the chord change.

"I like it better that way," Mike said.

"I think so too," Don agreed. "What time do you have to leave for your date?"

"I'm picking June up at eleven. I better get ready," Mike said. "What are you doing today?"

"I've got an idea for a new song. I'm going to work on it this afternoon," Don said.

"How was the movie last night?" Mike asked as he put his guitar back in its case.

"It was great. Bogie stuck it to the Nazis in the end." Don strummed the B minor chord again.

"And how was the part after the movie?" Mike asked.

"I told you, a gentleman never tells. However, she really is a humdinger."

"I'm happy to hear it. I'm going to get ready for my date. Good luck with the new song."

Yesterday's front passed through, and the day was crisp and bright. There was snow on yards and hillsides. It looked like winter, but it felt like fall. The snow was the perfect accent to the Christmas trees in home windows. Even the old brownstones were dressed for the holidays. Kids made snow men and had snowball fights. Mike drove carefully on the slippery streets.

It looks like Ebenezer Scrooge might live here, Mike thought as he parked in front of June's apartment house.

June opened the door to Mike's knock. She wore her winter coat and hat and had a red and green muffler around her neck.

"Merry Christmas," June said. "Let's go. I skipped breakfast and I'm starving." She breezed past Mike and yelled, "Bye!" to Betty.

"Have fun!" Betty yelled back.

June stepped out into the bright sunshine. She marveled at the sun glistening off the snow.

"It's like a scene on a Christmas card," she said to Mike.

She scooped snow off the railing on the steps and made a snowball.

Mike had gone ahead to unlock the car. When he bent down to put the key in the lock, June threw the snowball at him. June had played girls' softball in high school, and the snowball knocked off Mike's hat.

He looked at her in amazement. "I can't believe you did that," he said and stooped down to grab a handful of snow.

June already had another one. This one hit him in the back of his head. She had been the third baseman and had a good arm. She laughed out loud and looked for more snow.

When she bent down to make another snowball, Mike rushed her. He tackled her, and they both went down into the snow berm next to the sidewalk. He pushed a handful of snow in her face. They were both laughing.

"You should see your face," he said.

She shoved her handful of snow into Mike's face. She was laughing so hard she fell on her back on the snow berm. Mike bent down and wiped the snow off her face. He kissed her cold, flushed lips. She put her hand behind his head, pulled him closer, and kissed him back.

An elderly woman had stopped on the sidewalk and watched the show.

"Merry Christmas," she said when they finished their kiss. *That sure takes me back a lot of years*, she thought.

"Merry Christmas," they both yelled back and laughed some more.

The old woman smiled and walked on. *I think I'll surprise Herb with a big kiss when I get home from my walk.*

Krug Park had a big banner across its stone gateway that read, "Holiday Park, Merry Christmas." The entrance was festooned with strings of lights and boughs of evergreen. Santa's face smiled down on the crowd from the gateway arch. Mike found a place to park just down the street, and they walked back, holding hands. They entered the park and joined the crowd. The park was busy with young mothers and children, some accompanied by servicemen. Couples mixed with single servicemen and civilians. Even in civilian clothes, but Mike could tell the servicemen at a glance by the way they carried themselves. Everyone, except the mothers with crying children, was in a festive mood.

"Everything is decorated with Christmas lights," June said. "I'll bet this place is a fairyland after dark."

They wandered the pathways that surrounded a central fountain and two statues. The walks were embellished with small shrubs dotted around them. There was extensive landscaping and flower gardens everywhere, although most of them were dormant at this time of year.

"This is a very grand park," Mike said.

"I've been here in the summer with my sisters, but this is the first time I've seen it dressed up for Christmas," June said. "This is the oldest and largest public park in St. Joseph. The Krug family donated the land for the park to the city. They made their money in the meat-packing business."

They passed a lagoon with ducks and geese.

"In the summer, there are small boats for rent on the pond," June said.

"Hey, I think I see a castle up ahead!" Mike exclaimed.

"There's a five-mile walking trail beyond the castle," June said.

"No, thanks. The Army gives me all the walking I need."

There was a refreshment stand off to their left, next to a picnic area.

"Do you want to stop and get something from the stand?" Mike asked June.

"I'm still full of Benny Magoon's lunch. But I wouldn't mind a coffee," June answered.

They got their coffee and sat at one of the picnic tables. There was a playground next to the picnic area, and a noisy group of young children were taking advantage of it. Mothers kept watch from the picnic tables.

"Do you like kids?" Mike asked.

"Sure, I grew up surrounded by them," June said. "But it's going to be a long time until I want any of my own, if that's what you're asking. I have a lot of things to do first."

Mike drank his coffee and watched the kids playing.

"Do you want kids?" she asked Mike.

"I'd like to have a son someday to take fishing and play ball with, stuff like that."

One of the little boys in the playground was pushing a girl on the swings. She squealed and told him, "Higher!"

"What if you got a girl instead?" June asked.

"I'd want her to be like you," Mike answered.

June drank her coffee and looked at Mike for several seconds. "What if your wife wanted to do a lot of other things first?"

"I'd want her to be happy," Mike said. "Besides, there are a lot of things I want to do too. It's hard to do those things when you have kids. I think you can work things like that out if you love each other." Mike blushed and looked back at the playground.

The little girl stopped swinging and ran over to the slippery slide. The boy followed her.

June jumped up and said, "Let's go see the conservatory. There's a pond in front that used to have alligators in it. There are also Italian Renaissance structures."

They put their paper cups in the trash bin and headed off to the conservatory.

They spent the rest of the afternoon walking the grounds and talking. June forgot about the war and her brothers for a while.

7

S/Sgt. Lloyd Taylor looked at the burned, shattered trees of the Ardennes Forest as he passed by in his M4A3 Sherman tank. The tall, gaunt sergeant stood in the open turret, holding the handles of the mounted .50-caliber machine gun. He could hardly feel his gloved hands.

He wore drab olive-colored wool trousers, a woolen cap under his tanker's helmet, and a wool scarf around his neck. He had his tanker's jacket zipped up tightly around his throat. A Colt Model 1911A1 .45 caliber automatic pistol hung from his web belt.

S/Sgt. Taylor was the tank commander of a Sherman tank that was part of the spearhead of the Thirty-Seventh Tank Battalion, Fourth Armored Division of General Patton's Third Army Group. S/Sgt. Taylor had not slept or had a hot meal in thirty-six hours. It had snowed during the road march, and he was cold and exhausted. It was one of the coldest and wettest winters in recent history in the Ardennes Forrest. Patton's Third Army was racing to relieve the 101st Airborne Division the Germans had surrounded in the Belgium city of Bastogne.

"It could be worse, boys," S/Sgt. Taylor said into the intercom, connecting him to his tank crew. "We could be the infantry. Those poor bastards had to walk most of the 150 miles. They have more casualties from frostbite than from the Krauts."

Sherman crews loved their tanks. There were a lot more ways to be killed in the infantry than in their tank. The tankers' armored cocoon kept them safe from small arms fire, artillery fragments, and mortar fire. Of course, that didn't hold true for S/Sgt. Taylor when he was standing exposed in the open turret. That's why the tank commander had the most dangerous job in the crew.

"I'm not sure my little brother's worth all this effort," S/Sgt. Taylor joked on the intercom. "His 101st Airborne buddies, who jump out of perfectly good airplanes, aren't playing with a full deck."

"We'd laugh, Sarge, but we're too damn cold," Corporal Hendricks, his tank gunner, said. He could see his breath inside the tank.

"It's almost Christmas," said the greenhorn, Private Sanchez.

"*Feliz Navidad*, Sanchez," Hendricks said sarcastically, pulling his field jacket collar up again and slapping his gloved hands together.

"Do you think old Blood and Guts will have turkeys for us when we get to Bastogne?" the tank driver, Corporal Nowak, asked facetiously.

"Absolutely! Don't you guys know the Army loves you?" S/Sgt. Taylor said.

They passed the hulk of a US Army APC on the side of the muddy road. It was still smoking. German resistance had been light because General Patton's move had caught them with their pants down. But there were still occasional ambushes.

*****

Betty and June finished Christmas Eve dinner in their apartment. They had peanut butter sandwiches and hot rum toddies. Betty was working on her second toddy when June got up and went into her room.

"Something I said?" Betty yelled from the loveseat.

June returned with a small package wrapped in red-and-green wrapping paper. On the paper were reindeer, pulling Santa in his sleigh.

"Merry Christmas, roomie," June said and handed the package to Betty.

Betty set the package on the loveseat and said, "It's my turn." She went to her room and returned with a green package with a gold bow. "Merry Christmas, yourself," she said and gave the package to June. "Okay, on three," Betty said. "One, two, three!" Betty ripped her package apart and found a pair of costume pearl earrings. "These are really nice. Thank you, roomie."

"Well, you keep borrowing mine," June said as she carefully unwrapped her package. "You didn't!"

"I saw how much you loved them, so I just had to get you one," Betty said and laughed.

June hugged the plush green frog and said, "I'm going to name you Betty."

Betty laughed and sat back down on the loveseat with June.

June looked more closely at Betty, the frog, and saw a label sewn on one foot. The label said, "Frog Hop Ballroom." She set Betty the frog on the end table. "I didn't see you get this thing when we were at the Frog Hop," June said.

"I saw them at the back of the bar while Don and I were dancing. I had him get one and hide it with his band," Betty said.

June carefully folded the green paper and noticed a logo on it that read, "Frog Hop Ballroom." She set the folded paper aside, picked up her toddy, and held it up. "And a Merry Christmas to us all, my dear," she said, stealing Scrooge's line from the movie.

Betty touched glasses with her and said, "And a Happy New Year, roomie."

*****

"I've got to leave by eight o'clock. My parents like to open gifts early on Christmas morning," Betty shouted through June's bedroom door.

Christmas morning was another sunny day, and Betty was already dressed and putting on her makeup. She had a bag with gifts in it, ready to take with her.

"Can you drop me off downtown if it's not too far out of your way?" June asked, standing in the door to Betty's room.

"Isn't Mike picking you up here?" Betty asked. She put the cap on her lipstick and put it away in her purse. She squeezed past June and went to the front door.

"Yes, but I have to get a gift for him. I can take the trolley home. He won't be here until eleven o'clock."

Betty put on her coat and hat. "Shake your fanny then. I've got to go."

June dashed to her room, grabbed her hat, coat, and purse. She put them on hurriedly and joined Betty.

"I really appreciate this," June said.

"Who am I to stand in the way of romance?" Betty said as they headed to her Ford.

June asked Betty to drop her off at North Fifth Street at the Sears Roebuck store. The store was busy with last-minute Christmas shoppers. She went in and asked a clerk for the men's department. It was on the ground floor, just past the ladies' department. She found a salesclerk whose name tag said, "Bob."

"I'm looking for a gift for my boyfriend," she said to Bob.

Bob looked her over and asked, "Do you know his sizes?"

"I'm afraid not."

"In that case, a tie is always nice. Does he wear ties?"

"He's in a band. They wear ties with their band outfits," June said.

"Do they all wear the same tie or different ones?"

"They pick their own."

"Come with me," Bob said and led June to a walnut display counter with silk socks and ties.

The ties hung from small display racks on the countertop and the socks were behind glass on the shelves.

"What color is his jacket and slacks?" Bob asked as he went behind the counter.

"The jacket is light blue, and the slacks are dark blue. He wears a white shirt."

Bob looked through the selection of ties on the top of the counter.

"How about this one?' he asked, showing her a deep-blue silk tie with subtle red figures.

"That's good-looking," she said.

Bob reached into the cabinet under the counter and came up with a pair of silk socks.

"These should go well with the tie," he said.

"How much are they?" June asked. She fingered the tie and socks. They felt luxurious.

"The tie is ninety-five cents, and the sox are sixty-five cents," Bob said.

"Sold," June said. "Can you wrap them in Christmas paper?"

"Wrapped together or separately?" Bob asked.

"Together, please," June said. *That's about what Mike spent on the fancy hose he got me*, she thought. She didn't want to overspend and embarrass him. *I think he'll like what I got.*

*****

The drive south through the snow-covered hills to the Taylor's tobacco farm was spectacular. Fortunately, the roads had dried up, even the gravel road back to the property, but Mike still drove carefully on his worn tires. June's Christmas packages were on the back seat.

Mike was worried he wasn't bringing any gifts for her family.

"You already gave me my Christmas present," June reminded him.

"Well, at least I brought a bottle of white wine to go with the turkey. Does your family drink wine?" Mike asked as he steered around a pothole in the gravel road.

"Some of them do. Stop worrying, everything will be fine," June said.

"I don't have any experience with family get-togethers, that's why I'm asking."

"Turn left in the next driveway. You'll see the house up the hill. There's a fruit orchard behind the house."

The hillsides they passed were rocky and steep. Mike picked his way along, dodging the rocks in the roadbed. He came to the left turn and looked up the hill as he made the turn. The house sat near the top of a rounded knoll that was smoother and grassier than the rocky hills they had gone through. As he got closer, he saw gentle hills on the far side of the knoll behind the house. A grove of white sycamores stood out on one of them. The four-bedroom ranch house looked almost new.

"The house looks nice," Mike said and pulled in next to several cars and trucks parked in an open area in front of the house.

"Looks like everyone's here," June said.

The front door of the house opened, and people spilled out of it.

"Merry Christmas!" they shouted.

Several women came down to meet them. There was a lot of hugging and kissing. Mike stood back from the commotion and waited for things to settle down. The women were in floral print dresses. No one wore coats.

A gray-haired, middle-aged man in overalls shouted from the front door, "Get in the house before you freeze."

The throng broke up and headed to the house. June had her arm around Mike and said as they walked up to the house, "We're not big on formal introductions. You'll learn everyone's name as we go along."

"Should I get the stuff out of the car?" Mike asked as they walked.

"No, we can do that later. We don't open presents until after dinner."

When Mike entered the living room, he saw a tall, lavishly decorated Christmas tree next to the fireplace. Stockings with the owners' names hung from the mantle. They were bulging with inexpensive stocking stuffers. The house was warm and welcoming, and Mike smelled turkey cooking in an oven.

"I'm Emma Dee," a tall, slim redhead said after they came into the living room.

"This is Mike, my boyfriend," June said to her sister.

She called me her boyfriend, Mike thought. *I guess I'm making some headway.*

"Welcome to the Taylor madhouse, June's boyfriend. You'll get used to us," Emma Dee said and hugged Mike.

A short, plump woman with a nice smile joined Emma Dee's welcoming committee.

"I'm June's other sister, Virginia Jane. Merry Christmas," she said and hugged Mike.

He was getting used to Taylor hospitality. "I'm very happy to meet you both. Merry Christmas."

Emma Dee took their coats and hats and put them on the bed in the first bedroom down the hall.

"Let's go in and meet the rest of the clan," June said.

The gray-haired man who had shouted at them stepped forward and asked, "Who are you?"

June said, "This is Mike. He's my guest."

I just went from being a boyfriend to being a guest, Mike thought.

"Mike, this is my dad, Dee," June said.

"I'm pleased to meet you, sir," Mike said.

"Do you play pitch?" her father asked.

"I'm afraid not, sir," Mike said.

"Oh well, no one's perfect."

June's father wandered back to the card game he left in the living room. Two players sat at a folding card table on folding chairs and were waiting for Dee and Emma Dee to rejoin the game.

"Emma Dee, I better get back in the kitchen and help Mom," Virginia Jane said, clearly a very practical young woman.

Emma Dee joined her father at the card table, and Virginia Jane went to the kitchen.

June walked over to the card table, and Mike followed her.

"Hey, everyone," June said to the card players.

The card players looked up from their hands at June, except for her father, who snuck an ace from the deck and slipped it into his hand. He tried to slip another card back into the deck.

"Dad's cheating again," said a dark-haired woman with horn-rimmed glasses.

"Mike, this is my brother John and his wife, Marge," June said. "This is my friend, Mike."

John looked like the bureaucrat he was. He had the start of a paunch and thinning hair.

"Pleased to meet you, Mike," John said.

"I'm happy to meet you, Mike," said Marge. "He always cheats. Put the ace back, Dad. I saw you slip the ace of hearts into your hand from the bottom of the deck."

"I'm very happy to meet you all," Mike said. "Merry Christmas, everyone."

"It's a misdeal now," Marge said, throwing in her cards.

That started a big discussion at the table. Emma Dee threw in her hand, and June steered Mike away from the argument.

"Come on," June said. "I want you to meet Mother."

In the kitchen, her mother and her sister were hard at work on a Christmas feast. A dessert table held three pies and a chocolate cake. Virginia Jane prepared the green beans. An older woman, obviously June's mother, kept checking the turkey in the oven. The kitchen smelled wonderful. Mike wanted to eat everything.

"Mom, this is my friend, Mike," June said when she got her mother's attention. "Mike, this is my mom, Bess."

Bess was a tall, slim middle-aged woman with dark-red hair streaked with gray. She gave Mike a warm smile.

Now I see where June and Emma Dee get their good looks, Mike thought.

"I'm very pleased to meet you, Mrs. Taylor," Mike said.

"Call me Mom, everyone does," Mrs. Taylor said. "Or you can call me Bess if you like."

"Thank you, Bess," Mike said. He couldn't bring himself to call her mom.

"We'll eat about three o'clock," Bess said. "Why don't you show Mike around the farm?"

"That's Mom telling us we're getting in the way. Come on," June said and led Mike to the bedroom to get their coats and hats.

"Leaving so soon?" John said when they walked through the living room.

June said, "I'm giving Mike the grand tour, wise guy."

Outside, June took Mike on a path up the knoll. The bright sunshine made for a pleasant walk. When they reached the top, Mike saw an old two-story house on the next hill.

"That's the old farmhouse. My folks built the new one three years ago. I grew up in the old one you see there," June said.

The path led to the old house.

June moved a rock near the back door and found the key. She unlocked the door and opened it.

Mike said, "What is this?" and pointed to a metal stand with a metal arm and wooden handle. There was a spout on the opposite side.

"That's the cistern. It connects to the well where we got our water. You pump the handle for the water to come out."

"You didn't have water in the house?" Mike asked.

"Sure, when you carried it in," June said.

"What about the toilets?" Mike asked.

June closed the door and said, "Follow me." She walked around the corner of the house and pointed at the three-hole outhouse.

"Wasn't that kind of nippy in the winter, like now?"

"This is nothing. Try it in a blizzard," she said.

Mike shook his head. He couldn't imagine it. He shifted his gaze from the outhouse and saw another building behind the old house.

"What's that building back there?"

"That's the henhouse. Mom has a big flock of chickens, both fryers and layers. One of my chores was to gather the eggs every morning and feed the chickens. She has another henhouse behind the new house."

June led him back to the landing and through the door into a large kitchen. There was an old-fashioned wood-burning cookstove with six cast-iron burners. A long counter ran along the back wall under two kitchen windows. There were sinks under each window. The sink drains emptied into drain fields in the backyard. The floors in the kitchen were worn linoleum. There was a long homemade wooden table with wooden benches.

"This was our breakfast table and usually our lunch table as well," June said.

She walked through a doorway into the living room. Mike followed her. Two large stone fireplaces graced each end of the room.

The floor was stained oak boards, showing the wear of decades of family boots.

June walked to a window near the front door. "Look out there."

Mike joined her at the window. The road to the house wound up a rocky draw and ended in the front yard. There were several outbuildings, including one very large three-story barn. They were all in good repair.

"What's that big barn for?" Mike asked.

"That's the tobacco barn. When the tobacco leaves are harvested, tobacco sticks are punched through them, and the sticks with the leaves are hung on rails in the tobacco barn," June explained. "Let's walk down, and I'll show you the barn."

"Why are the leaves hung in the barn?" Mike asked.

A rabbit dashed off around the corner of the barn.

"They're nuisances. It's a chore trying to keep them out of the vegetable garden," June said when she saw what had drawn his gaze.

"Yeah, but they're cute," Mike said.

June shook her head and said, "City folks."

June answered Mike's question. "We dry out the leaves to the right moisture level. Then we take them down and bundle them to sell to tobacco brokers." She opened the man door next to the main barn doors.

Mike followed her into the barn. "What's that wonderful smell?" he exclaimed.

"You should be here when the barn is full of tobacco leaves. It's like a tropical rainforest in here. The humidity level is 99 percent. It feels like it's almost raining."

They walked further into the barn, and Mike looked up at rows of wooden rafters. They were spaced one above the other, all the way to the very high ceiling.

"How high is that roof?" Mike asked.

"The building is three stories high and 150 feet long," June said. "It holds most of the crop for the year."

"You should sell the fragrance to a perfume company. It's getting me excited," Mike said, teasing her.

"Let's see," June said. She wrapped her arms around his neck and kissed him.

Now he was getting light-headed, and it wasn't the tobacco.

June finally broke away, but her arms stayed around his neck.

Mike looked into her eyes and said, "I have a confession to make. I've loved you since you were giving our frog waiter a hard time."

"At the Frog Hop?" June said skeptically. "I don't believe in love at first sight."

"Nobody does, until it happens to them," Mike said.

"We better go back," June said hastily. But she held his hand on the walk back.

The pitch game was going on hot and heavy in the living room.

"We just bid and made three!" Emma Dee crowed to Mike and June.

"You two probably cheated again," Marge said.

"Where did you go?" John asked June.

"I took Mike on a tour of the old place. He'd never seen a tobacco barn before," June said and winked at Mike.

"What did you think of the fancy bathroom?" Emma Dee asked with a grin. She finished shuffling the deck and started dealing the cards.

"It looked pretty cold to me," Mike said.

"She told you all about putting your freezing fanny on the seat in a blizzard, didn't she?" Emma Dee said. She set the deck down and picked up her hand.

"Well, she didn't go into detail," Mike said.

"She skipped the part about the kerosene heater, I bet," Emma Dee said, and John laughed.

The players studied their cards.

"How many cards do you want?" Emma Dee asked Marge.

There was the sound of a bell ringing, and Bess announced, "Dinner's on the table."

"Just when we took the lead, darn it!" Emma Dee said, throwing down her cards.

"Break it up! You can finish the game after we eat," Virginia Jane said from the dining room.

The dining table was decked out with their good white linen cloth and groaning under the dishes of food. There was a baked bean casserole, green beans, two kinds of potato salad, coleslaw, a big bowl of mashed potatoes, tureens of white turkey gravy to go on the mashed potatoes, and stuffing from the turkey. There was also oyster stuffing and cranberry sauce in true Taylor tradition. The star of the show was a large beautifully browned turkey at the head of the table. Dee took his seat there.

"Mike, you're our guest, you sit at the foot of the table. June, you sit next to Mike. I'll sit next to Dad. The rest of you are on your own," Bess said.

When everyone was seated, Dee said, "Who wants to say grace?"

"I'll say grace," June volunteered. "Thank you, Lord, for the bounty we are about to receive. Bless everyone at our table and watch over those of our family who are still fighting in this awful war. Please help them defeat the evil of our enemies and return home safe to us. Amen."

"Amen!" everyone echoed.

"Hurry up and carve that turkey, Dad. We're all starving," Virginia Jane said.

It was another Taylor tradition that Dee carves the turkey at the table.

Each place setting had a glass of ice water, and there was iced tea in a pitcher on a side table.

Mike whispered to June, "I didn't bring in the wine. Should I go get it?"

She shook her head. "No."

Food dishes were passed around the table. Bess passed a platter of turkey. Virginia Jane excused herself and went into the kitchen. She returned with a plate of perfectly browned biscuits fresh from the oven. They went fast.

"There's more baking," she said.

When she brought out the next batch, they went fast too.

There was the hum of conversation, punctuated with laughter all around the table.

John and Marge were seated next to Mike. They asked him about Camp Crowder and the Signal Corps. His end of the table laughed when he told them about the pigeon poop. They avoided talk of the war.

When everyone had finished with the feast, June and her sisters cleared away the dirty dishes and brought in the pies and the cake.

"If anyone wants coffee, there's some ready on the stove," Bess said.

"I'll get it," Mike said. He went to the kitchen and got the pot of coffee and brought it to the table.

"You hang on to that one, Junie," Emma Dee said.

After the dessert, Dee and John went into the living room. The women went into the kitchen. Mike looked at June and shrugged his shoulders. She signaled for him to follow the men. She went into the kitchen and started helping the women do the dishes and put away the leftovers.

Dee took the easy chair while John and Mike sat on the sofa. John took a cigar out of his pocket and offered it to Mike. He used his cigar tool and clipped off the end, then handed the tool to Mike to do the same.

June won't begrudge me one cigar, Mike temporized.

"Don't you smoke?" Mike asked Dee.

"Never have. Never will," said Dee.

John took his cigarette lighter out of his pocket and lit Mike's cigar, then he lit his own. When both cigars were going properly, Mike said to Dee, "That's a funny attitude for a man who grows tobacco."

John laughed and said, "We've been telling Dad that for years."

"Growing tobacco put food on the table for my grandfather, my father, and for me. Smoking it just costs money," Dee said. "But you two go ahead. You're both putting money in my pocket right now."

Mike looked quizzically at John.

"What he means is there is a special type of tobacco used as the outer wrap on cigars. Cigarette tobacco and the tobacco inside cigars don't work. Our family grows the special kind, so you and I may be smoking Dad's tobacco.

In the kitchen, the women were busy.

"Where did you meet Mike?" Bess asked as she and June dried the dishes.

"At the Frog Hop Ballroom," June said and laughed.

"What on earth is the Frog Hop Ballroom?" Bess asked.

Emma Dee looked up from the sink and the soapsuds and said, "It's a great big dance hall in St. Joe. Count Basie played there."

"Jim and I went there once before the war," Virginia Jane said. "It was very loud and smoky."

"I don't understand. What were you doing in this dance hall?" Bess asked. She started putting away the dishes she and June had washed to make room on the counter for more.

"I went there with Betty, my roommate. She had a date with a bandleader and needed a date for his friend, Mike.

Bess finished up the last of the dishes and said, "I think Mike is a nice young man, but now I need to visit the ladies' room." She left the kitchen.

"Where did Marge go?" Virginia Jane asked, looking around the kitchen.

"I bet I know where she is," June said. "Follow me and don't say anything."

June led the way to the stairs down to the basement, tiptoeing with her finger to her lips. Emma Dee followed her. Marge was standing next to the furnace, smoking a cigarette.

"Hiding out, huh?" June said as she reached the bottom of the steps.

Marge was startled and said, "Be quiet. I don't want Dad to hear us and come down here." She took a quick drag on her cigarette.

Emma Dee said, "Give me a puff and I'll be quiet." Marge handed the cigarette to Emma Dee, who sucked in deeply.

"I usually go behind the henhouse to sneak a smoke," Emma Dee said. She handed the smoke back to Marge.

"Do you want a puff?" Marge asked June.

"I'm trying to quit, but I'll take one," June said. She took the cigarette from Marge and took a small puff.

"You all look ridiculous hiding out in the basement to smoke because you don't want Dad to catch you. What are you, thirteen years old?" Virginia Jane asked, coming down the steps to the basement.

"You know he's old-fashioned about women smoking. I don't want to hurt his feelings," Marge said.

Virginia Jane shook her head and went back up the steps.

Marge started to put the cigarette out in a tin can when Emma Dee said, "Let me have the last drag." She took the smoke from Marge, took a long drag, and put it out in the can.

"We better get back up, it's time to do presents," she said.

When June returned to the living room, Mike came over to her and said, "I got your presents out of the car. They're on the bed in the first bedroom."

"Thanks," she said and kissed him on the cheek.

"Everyone, bring your gifts in here," Dee said, holding a hat with pieces of paper in it.

They fetched their gifts and found seats in the living room.

Dee reached in his hat and took out a piece of paper and unfolded it.

"Bess," he said. "You're up first, honey."

Bess handed a colorfully wrapped gift to John. He unwrapped it and said, "Just what I wanted, Mom." He put the pipe in his mouth and posed for the room.

"That makes you next, son," Dee said.

John handed his gift to Virginia Jane.

She tore the paper open and said, "John, how did you know I wanted a scarf? Thank you."

The succession of gifts continued and came around to June. Dee had drawn her name and gave her a russet-colored soft woolen muffler. June handed her gift to Emma Dee, who grabbed it and ripped open the wrapping paper.

"My Sin perfume," she squealed. "You know me too well, but what about Mike?"

"I'll take care of Mike," June said. She reached into her gift bag and took out a professionally wrapped package and handed it to Mike.

Mike took the package and thanked June. "You have a wonderful family, and I'm glad you included me in your get together," he said to the gathering.

"Open the present already!" Emma Dee said. "I want to get to the punch."

Mike opened the wrapping paper and took out the tie and matching socks.

"Wow!" Mike exclaimed. "I'll be the belle of the ball in these."

"Punch is served," Virginia Jane said.

The group retired to the dining room for the traditional Taylor punch in a huge crystal punch bowl. There was a smaller bowl beside it.

"Mike, that's eggnog if you prefer it," Bess said.

There were crystal cups next to the punch bowl.

"If Lloyd was here, the punch would be spiked," Emma Dee told Mike.

When everyone had a cup of punch, Dee said, "Merry Christmas to all of us here, and God watch over those of us who aren't."

"Merry Christmas!" they all said and drank the toast.

Each of the women hugged the man or woman next to them. June hugged Mike.

All this hugging isn't that bad, Mike thought. *I could get used to it.*

The pitch game soon resumed. Mike looked at his watch and signaled to June.

"Hey, everyone!" June said, "We have to go before it gets dark."

Mike approached Dee and said, "Thank you so much for having me and sharing your family with a stranger."

"I don't see any strangers," Dee said. He shook Mike's hand. "You're always welcome here, son."

Bess hugged Mike and said, "Come back soon."

That started another hug fest at the door. Mike stood outside, waiting for June and the other women to say their goodbyes. Just when it looked like they were winding down, one of them would say something, and that started them up again.

John came up to Mike and said, "There's no way on this earth to hurry these women. You might as well get accustomed to it."

June finally broke free and got in the car with Mike. As they pulled away, the group was still shouting and waving. June waved back through the open window. She scooted over on the seat and rested her head on Mike's shoulder. She had a sad look.

"What's wrong?" Mike said. "I hope I didn't make some terrible mistake back there."

"Nothing's wrong. They all loved you. I just miss my brothers, and I'm sorry they weren't there with us."

"I'm sorry they missed it too. I'd like to meet them," Mike said.

"I know I should be happy and grateful for what I have, and most of the time, I am. But it's awful to live with this fear I have for them."

"I think you just described all the women in America," Mike said and put his right arm around her. It stayed there until they were back at her apartment.

*****

"How was your family reunion? Did they like Mike? Did he like them? Give!" Betty asked June in their apartment Christmas evening.

"The reunion was great. They liked Mike, and he liked them. Mike gets turned on in tobacco barns. End of story," June said. The tobacco barn lingered in June's memory.

"What was that about a tobacco barn?" Betty asked. She sat at the kitchen table with June.

"Never mind. How did it go with your parents?" June asked. She poured Betty a cup of tea.

"Actually, they were okay. Dad made it through dinner without lecturing me about anything," Betty said.

June sipped her tea and said, "I like your sweater. Is it new?"

"It was a Christmas present from my dad. Mom gave me this scarf. What kind of loot did you get?"

"My dad drew my name and gave me that nice muffler hanging in the entry."

The doorbell rang. Betty had a date with Don. He called her that morning at her parent's house.

Betty sat her cup down and went to the door. She saw that Don had a gift in his hand.

She said, "I didn't get you anything."

"Are you going to invite me in or what?" Don asked.

Betty stepped back and Don came in.

"Merry Christmas," June yelled from the kitchen.

"Merry Christmas," Don yelled back and handed Betty the gift.

Betty went to the loveseat and sat down.

Don sat down next to her. "Well, are you going to open it?" he asked.

Betty's face lit up, and she tore off the wrapping paper. It was a pretty cotton nightgown with bunnies on it.

"I love it," she said. She held it up to herself. It looked like her size.

June came in from the kitchen and sat in the chair. "The sales-girl picked that out for you, didn't she?" June asked.

"Heck, yeah," Don said. "I was going to get her something slinky."

"I don't care who picked it out. I love it. Thank you, Don," Betty said and leaned over and kissed him.

"Can I get you something to drink, Don? I made some tea," June asked.

"Put some ice and sugar in it, and you've got a sale," Don said.

June got up to make his drink.

Don said, "I think I might get the band a gig at a New Year's Eve party. Would you girls like to go? I know you and Mike have a date."

"Mike hasn't told me where he wants to take me," June said. "If it's okay with him, it's okay with me."

"This party will be at a private club and the upper crust will be there. It won't be as rowdy as most New Year's parties, but it should be fun."

"The fewer drunks, the better for me," June said.

8

On the day after Christmas, newly promoted M/Sgt. Lloyd Taylor hastily ducked down into his Sherman tank when .30-caliber machine-gun rounds ricocheted off his turret. He peered over the lip of the turret and spotted the machine-gun nest in a shell-pocked building near the road. The tank's 76mm main battery fired at the machine gun position in the remnants of a two-story apartment house in Bastogne. The HE (high explosive) shell collapsed the building. M/Sgt. Taylor manned his .50-caliber gun and studied the cloud of dust and debris. As it settled, he saw two dust-covered men in German helmets emerge with their hands up. It had become a common sight in Bastogne. Germans were surrendering all over the city.

"Nice shot, Hendricks," M/Sgt. Taylor said to his gunner, Corporal Hendricks.

The Thirty-Seventh Tank Battalion, Fourth Armored Division, had broken through the German perimeter and trapped the Krauts against the besieged 101st Airborne. Allied air forces had capitalized on the clearing skies and had been pounding German concentrations and supply lines for two days. Meanwhile, the Second Armored "Hell on Wheels" Division had stalled the main thrust of the German offensive toward Antwerp.

M/Sgt. Taylor's D Company was mopping up scattered pockets of German resistance. After this last skirmish, D Company rolled on into downtown Bastogne.

*****

"Have you figured out where you're taking June on New Year's Eve?" Don asked Mike.

The day after the Taylor Christmas party, Don and Mike sat in their tourist cabin surrounded by amps and speakers. They were fooling around with the melody for another of Don's new songs. He had the lyrics almost worked out. Don tried another key on his guitar and sang a verse. It still didn't sound right to him.

"No, I haven't. Do you have any ideas?" Mike asked.

"I sure do," Don said. "I called our manager and asked him if he had heard of any last-minute gigs on New Year's Eve."

"How did you get ahold of Herb on Christmas day?" Mike asked.

"Easy, that's the only day he's ever home. His wife Sherry was a little pissed at my interruption."

Don tried a guitar run and sang another verse. Mike put down his guitar and got a cup of coffee.

"Let me know when you have something to play," Mike said.

Don laid his guitar aside and said, "It'll come to me." He got his own cup of coffee.

"Anyway, Herb said he might know of something, a private party maybe," Don said. "He's going to call me today."

"I don't know if June and Betty want to sit around and watch us play on New Year's Eve. They already did that once," Mike said. "Remember the Frog Hop?"

"They're good with it. I asked them about it last night when I gave Betty her Christmas present. I'll call Herb now."

Don called Herb's home number, and they spoke for several minutes.

"Go ahead and book us in," he told Herb. And then he said to Mike, "It's all set. The Friars Club is having a private party for their members. The trio they booked canceled."

"What about the rest of the band?" Mike asked. He unplugged his guitar from his amp and put it away in the case.

"Danny and Sammy are good to go. Willy has other plans. But we don't need a sax for this." Don pulled the lead from his guitar and put it away.

"Sounds good," Mike said. "What time do we go on?"

"Nine o'clock. The friars are having dinner at eight o'clock. Herb said we have dinner if we want."

"That's a good idea. We'll have a hard time getting dinner reservations anywhere this close to New Year's," Mike said.

They put away the amplifiers and speakers.

"We'll pick the girls up at 7:00 p.m.," Don said.

*****

Sgt. Richard Taylor sat at a small table outside what was left of a sidewalk café. His Third squad loitered on the sidewalk, reclining against the remains of the wall. Corporal Samuel Dawson sat in the only other chair at the table. He had scavenged a bottle of wine from the rubble inside the café. Sergeant Taylor took a drink and passed the bottle on to Pfc. Jankowski. Replacements had arrived in the city, and third squad had been relieved along with the rest of the battalion.

Sergeant Taylor heard the distinctive squeak of tank treads. "Shermans," he said to Corporal Dawson.

They were very familiar with the sound of Sherman tank treads. A jeep with a lieutenant in the front seat and a private first class driver appeared around a corner up the street. Three tanks followed the jeep and headed their way. As they got nearer, Sergeant Taylor read the unit markings on the bumpers of the jeep—Third Army, Fourth armored division, Thirty-Seventh tank battalion.

"Holy shit, it's my brother's outfit," Ricky said to Sam.

They stood up and watched the lead tank approach. There was a tall, skinny soldier standing in the turret wearing a tanker's helmet. He had the stripes of a master sergeant on his sleeves and the triangular three-colored patch of an armored division at his shoulder seam. There was a 4 and a thunderbolt in the center of the patch. Unlike other armored divisions, there was no yellow motto strip under the patch.

When the lead tank reached them, the master sergeant put up his arm and signaled the following tanks to stop. He issued the same order to his crew. The jeep ahead slowed and stopped. The lieutenant

119

in the jeep stood up and looked back to see what was holding up his column. He got out of his jeep and walked back to the lead tank.

The master sergeant climbed down from the turret of his tank and walked across the road. He embraced Sergeant Taylor in a ferocious hug and said, "I thought for sure the Krauts had killed you."

"They gave it a hell of a try, bro," Ricky said. "It's nice of you guys to do a little mopping up after us."

The lieutenant walked up to the two sergeants.

"Hey, boss, this is my little brother, Ricky," Lloyd said to the officer.

"Let me shake your hand, Sergeant. You guys put up a hell of a fight," the lieutenant said.

"It's my pleasure, sir," Ricky said. "Your Shermans are a beautiful sight. You pulled off some impressive shit getting here yourselves."

M/Sgt. Taylor got his lieutenant's permission to spend the night with the paratroopers.

The Taylor brothers got drunk together on a case of wine the Third squad had *liberated* from a derelict building. M/Sgt. Taylor left the bourbon in his tank for his crew to have their own celebration. It was common practice with tankers to stash a bottle of "medicinal" booze in their tanks.

*****

On Friday, Betty was nearing the end of her second week at the ordnance plant. She got to her desk with a few minutes to spare before the start of the shift. Marlene was already there, as usual.

She had just sat down when the phone rang.

"Mr. Harding's office, Betty speaking," she answered.

When she first started work, she had said, "Miss Anderson speaking," but most of the callers were production people who said things like, "I need to talk to Joe. Is he putting on airs now?" or similar remarks. As a result, she started answering with her first name, and they knocked off the snide remarks. One line was a direct line to Joe's boss. She answered that one more formally.

"This is Mark from Stamping. Is Joe in his office yet?" the caller said.

Stamping machines pounded in the background.

"Hold for a moment, Mark. I'll check." Betty put the line on hold, pushed the intercom button, and said, "There's a call for you on line one, Joe."

There was no answer. She pushed the button for line one.

"He's not in his office yet, Mark. Maybe he's out in the plant. Can I take a message?"

"Just tell him to call me when he comes in. Thanks, Betty."

Marlene was sorting through mail that had arrived just before quitting time the day before. Betty wrote a note to call Mark and went into Joe's office and put it in the center of his desk. She smiled when she saw the overflowing in-tray. Now that Betty had caught up with the backlog on her desk, Joe wasn't keeping up with his. She left the message because Joe didn't like to be stopped as he was passing through reception to his office. Betty was learning how he liked things done. She had ideas about helping him deal with his in-tray, but she was waiting for him to release Marlene back to QC and declare herself trained.

"Did you find anything interesting in the mail?" Betty asked Marlene.

"Maybe this one," Marlene said, and handed her a memo.

It was from Beatty Wilson in the automatic loading room asking Joe for guidance on a personnel issue. Some of his black janitors were asking for transfers to production jobs. Beatty was passing a hot potato on to Joe. He could have referred the janitors to the personnel department, but he clearly didn't want personnel to get mad at him. Rather, he'd have them mad at Joe. Since the government had forced the whole plant to integrate, everyone was scared stiff of any issues involving race.

"What should we do with that one?" Marlene asked Betty, deferring to her.

Betty had some experience with Beatty Wilson and knew he was a cover-your-ass type of supervisor.

"I'm going to put an 'urgent' note on it and put it on Joe's chair for his action," Betty said.

This was a device she invented to make sure Joe looked at important papers. She'd only done it once so far, when Joe had tossed an urgent memo back in his in-tray without reading it. His boss had called him about that memo, and Joe was embarrassed he hadn't read it. Betty put the memo on Joe's chair and went back to her desk. She started going through the rest of the mail.

Joe came in and went through to his office and closed his door. He came back out two minutes later and said, "I told you I would read the urgents immediately. You don't have to put them on my chair."

"That's good to know, boss," Betty said.

"Marlene, you are going back to QC on Monday. Your boss is very happy to hear it."

"Yippee," Marlene said.

"Does this mean I am officially trained now?" Betty asked.

"Don't push your luck," Joe said. "Come into my office." He turned and went back into his office.

Betty followed him.

"Close the door and have a seat," Joe said. "I'm very pleased with your work. You've added a pile to mine though." He pointed at his in-tray. "I'm just kidding. You're working out great. I'm sending your notice of permanent status to personnel today. You're on full benefits starting Monday. Congratulations."

"Thanks, Joe. I like my job, and I like working for you. I can offer some suggestions about that in-tray if you like," Betty said.

"We can talk about that later. What did you think of Beattie Wilson's memo?"

"I think he's sticking it to you. I'd watch that guy," Betty said.

"What do think I should do about the janitors?"

"I think you should have Mr. Wilson interview them and determine which ones are qualified for production jobs and send you another memo with his recommendations."

Joe considered Betty's suggestions and slapped his desk with his hand.

"Hit the ball back into his court! That's exactly what I'm going to do. Send a memo to him with those directives."

*****

At Quaker Oats, Cheryl handed June the completed production orders from Thursday.

Each day the lines reported their output against the production order for that day.

"What you are looking for are shortages from the production order quantities."

June studied the first production order Cheryl handed her. It was from line four, one of the three lines June was scheduling.

"Line item eight is short six units," June said.

"Add six units to the quantity on that item on today's schedule."

"What if the pack line is missing a lot of units?" June asked.

"That doesn't happen very often. The packing line supervisors' performance reviews are mostly based upon their conformance to schedule."

June thought about her experience on the pack line.

"Sometimes, when I was working on my pack line, we ran out of cartons and once we had several people off sick. We didn't pack our normal amount those days," June said. "We didn't get them added the next day."

"If one of the lines has a serious problem that makes them 20 percent or more short of any item, we don't get that completed production order. It goes to Tim, and he works out a new line schedule with the production manager," Cheryl said.

Tim was the pack line scheduling supervisor and Cheryl and June's boss.

"I still have a lot to learn," June said. *Maybe I bit off more than I can chew. I'm still unprepared for the nursing school exam, and now I have to learn all this stuff too.*

"Don't worry, it'll be easy after you've done it a few times," Cheryl said.

"I sure hope you're right."

*****

The Friars Club New Year's Eve dinner and dance was in one of the large conference rooms at the Robideaux Hotel.

Sammy and Danny went in early on Sunday afternoon to set up the instruments and equipment. A lot of New Year's parties were scheduled on Saturday since New Year's Eve fell on Sunday this year. The Friars Club stuck with tradition and held theirs on Sunday.

Mike rang the apartment doorbell at 7:00 p.m., and Betty opened the door. She wore her dressiest gown with matching high heels, nylon hose, and had been to her hairdresser.

"You look sensational, honey. Where's Don's date?" Mike kidded her.

"I heard that. I'm Don's date. Where is the big hunk?" June said, coming to the door.

Don followed Mike into the apartment and said, "You look sensational, Betty. Sorry, Mike, I'm stealing your date," Don said and hugged Betty.

Mike examined June. She wore a simple but elegant black cocktail dress with a white collar, black high heels, and a pair of the hose Mike gave her for Christmas. She had been to Betty's hairdresser, and her red hair looked stunning against the white collar of her dress.

"I'm sorry, miss, but have you seen my date? She's a farm girl who hangs around tobacco barns," Mike said. "I didn't know Betty had a friend who is a movie star.'

"Oh, hush, a girl's got to spruce up once in a while. You look spiffy yourself," June said.

Mike wore his band outfit. He pulled up one leg of his slacks to show off a silk sock that matched his dark-blue silk tie.

"I'm going to steal that tie and those socks when Mike's not looking," Don said.

Betty and June got their coats and hats.

"Let's go," said Betty. "I've never been inside the Robideaux Hotel."

They took two cars. June rode with Mike, and Don drove Betty in her car.

The Robideaux Hotel lobby was ornate with marble floors and fluted marble columns. Walnut panels lined the walls below gold flocked wallpaper. The countertop on the walnut reception desk was marble. They checked their coats and hats in a cloakroom across the lobby from the reception desk.

There was a small stylish sign atop a brass stand at the base of marble stairs that said, "Friars Club Dinner, Meeting Room 3."

"I knew the place was ritzy, but I didn't expect all of this. This is a palace," Betty said.

They went up the stairs and looked for meeting room 3. They saw several people in dinner clothes going into a room down the carpeted hallway.

A man dressed in hotel livery checked invitations at the door. He checked their invitations and said, "Your party is at table 32."

There were table numbers on short stands in the center of dazzling white-linen-covered tables. Victorian-style chairs sported a monogrammed *R* on the padded seat backs. Guests in formal wear filled the room. Most of them were older couples. They found table 32. It was a table for eight, against the wall farthest from the stage. There was an intimidating array of glasses and silverware at each setting.

"This table is obviously where they put the hired help," Don said.

"It's just fine. I'm going to have a great time tonight," Betty said.

Don and Mike seated the girls. Sammy, Danny, and their dates appeared at the table, carrying drink glasses.

"You guys missed the cocktail hour," Sammy said. "This is Doris."

Doris was an overweight red-faced bleached blond in a low-cut dress that was straining to keep all of her in it.

"Hi everyone," she said.

Don made the introductions.

"Hi, Doris," they said.

Doris and Sammy sat down across from Don and Betty.

"What a swanky joint, huh?" Danny said.

He was with his wife, Ann, who greeted the table shyly. She was a short, brown-haired bashful young woman who rarely attended gigs the band played. She knew everyone at the table except June and Betty. Danny and Ann sat across from Mike and June.

Don read the one-page menu on the table. There was a choice of salad with Caesar dressing or New England clam chowder. The entrée choices were beef Bourguignon or chicken ala king. Dessert was a chocolate brownie with ice cream or pineapple upside down cake.

"Did you hear the war news today on the radio?" Danny asked as he studied his menu.

"I'm afraid to listen to it," June said.

"No, it's great news. Patton's Fourth Division broke through and relieved the 101st Airborne Division at Bastogne. The German offensive is stalled and starting to break up," Danny said.

"Maybe your brothers are okay," Mike said. "If your family hasn't heard from the War Department, they're probably all right."

"I pray you're right. Let's change the subject," June said and picked up her menu.

The beef looks good to me. What is that Bor-gug-non all about?" Danny asked, attempting to pronounce the word.

Don laughed and said, "It's a burgundy wine sauce. Try it, it's good."

"How do you know so much about it?" Doris challenged Don.

"I had it in Australia at a restaurant in Sydney when I was on leave," Don explained. He hoped Doris lightened up on the booze. He had seen her in action before.

Mike said, "I'm going to have it. What about you, June?"

"I'll try the chicken," June answered.

Don signaled to one of the waiters, who sent someone over to them.

"Can I help you, sir?" the waiter asked. His gold name tag said Larry.

"We are the band tonight. We should probably order soon," Don said.

"Would anyone care for a cocktail?' Larry asked.

Everyone ordered a cocktail except June, who ordered tonic water.

Larry took their food orders.

Don said, "Everyone is having the beef except June and Ann. How about we order a bottle of red wine and glasses of white wine for June and Ann?"

Everyone agreed with the plan.

Larry returned with their cocktails, and a server appeared with a crystal pitcher of water. A sommelier arrived just after Larry left. He handed them all wine menus.

"What do you recommend?" Don asked him.

"The Californian pinot noir is nice with the beef, and we have a house Chablis that goes well with the chicken," he said. The sommelier was an experienced waiter who knew his patrons. Band members did not order expensive wines.

Don looked around the table. There were nods of approval.

"We'll have a bottle of the pinot noir and two glasses of the Chablis," Don said.

The sommelier hesitated and said, "May I suggest a small carafe of the Chablis and a second bottle of the pinot noir?" He gestured at the table, calling Don's attention to the size of the group.

"That's fine," Don said.

"What do you say the guys split the booze tab?" Sammy asked. The friars were covering the dinners, but the alcohol was on them.

Mike thought about that for a few seconds. He and June were the lightest drinkers in the group. Sammy and his date would probably be the heaviest drinkers. She had that look.

"I'm in for splitting the wine. To save you from doing long division, Sammy, let's have separate checks on the booze," Mike said.

"Yeah, last time we split a tab with you, my check doubled," Danny said to Sammy.

"What do you girls do for a living?" Doris asked, turning to Betty and June.

"I work at the ordnance plant as an administrative assistant," Betty said. She sipped her cocktail.

"Is that like a secretary?" Doris asked.

Betty gave Doris a dirty look and said, "Yeah, it's like a secretary."

June saw Betty's expression and hastily intervened. "I work at Quaker Oats. I'm a scheduler."

"Is that like a secretary?" Mike asked innocently. He tried to keep a straight face, but he started laughing.

Don laughed, and June couldn't help herself. That did it for Betty, and she really broke up. Danny laughed next. Ann looked embarrassed.

"What's so funny?" Sammy asked.

That brought another round of laughter.

Doris said, "You're just a bunch of comics, ain't you?"

"I work part-time at the five-and-dime store," Ann interjected.

Larry and a server reappeared and served the chowders and salads. When they left, everyone started on their appetizers. There was no more discussion of secretaries.

"How's your new song coming along?" Danny asked Don.

Don put down his salad fork and said, "The lyrics are almost there. I'm still working on the melody. I think I need it to be jazzier. It sounds too much like a ballad."

Still trying to pour oil on troubled waters, Ann asked Doris, "What do you do, Doris?"

Doris had been focusing on her clam chowder and ignoring the table. "I'm a secretary," she said automatically.

The table froze, and the forks and spoons stopped in midair. Betty was the first to laugh. It was bedlam, and they all broke into laughter, even Ann and Sammy.

Doris looked furious. The laughter continued. When it threatened to die down, someone would giggle and start it off again.

Doris's expression changed. She grinned, and then she laughed out loud. "Okay. The joke's on me," she said, and they laughed with her.

They were finishing their appetizers when the sommelier arrived with their wine and set the carafe on the table. He showed Don the bottle of wine. Don nodded his acceptance, and the sommelier opened the bottle with his corkscrew. He poured a sample of the wine into Don's wine glass.

Don tasted the wine and said, "That's fine."

Larry poured the red wine for everyone except Ann and June, then set the bottle on the table. He poured a taste of the Chablis in Ann and June's glasses and filled them when the girls nodded their approval.

"This stuff is sour," Doris said. "I like sweet wine." She set down her wineglass and took a drink of water.

"Yeah, it doesn't taste very good," Sammy agreed.

Don flagged down a passing waiter and told him to get the sommelier.

The sommelier stopped at Don's chair and asked, "Is there a problem, sir?"

"Some of our group expected their wine to be sweeter," Don said politely.

"Perhaps we can exchange your other bottle, unless everyone is unhappy with the pinot noir?"

"That would be fine. What would you suggest?" Don asked.

"We have a Roscato sweet red. Why don't you let me bring you a bottle?" He left to get it.

"What do we do with the wine we just tasted?" Sammy asked Don.

"Let's wait and see what the sommelier brings," Don said.

The sommelier brought a tray with a bottle of wine and four wine glasses to the table.

"Which guests would like the sweeter wine?" he asked.

Sammy and Doris held up their hands, and the sommelier placed new wine glasses in front of them. He opened the Roscato with his corkscrew and poured a sample for Sammy.

Sammy tasted it and said, "I like that."

The sommelier poured a sample into Doris's glass.

She drank it and said, "That's better."

He filled both their glasses and put the bottle on the table in front of Sammy.

Don looked at the sommelier's name tag and said, "Thanks, Pierre."

"You're welcome, sir. Enjoy your meal."

Larry and a server arrived with their entrees.

June took a bite of her chicken ala king. "That's very good," she said.

Don tried his beef and said, "This is as good as the beef I had in Australia, maybe better."

Everyone concentrated on eating their dinner. They were obviously enjoying the food and the wine.

"I wonder how much that Roscato will cost us," Mike whispered to Don.

"Probably nothing beyond what the pinot noir would have cost us," Don whispered back. "Pierre will take care of it." Don looked at his watch. It was nearing 9:00 p.m. "Finish up, guys. We need to get to the bandstand," he said.

"What about dessert?" Doris asked.

"You girls go ahead and order your desserts. Tell Larry we'll order ours at the first break," Don said.

He and Mike got up and headed for the dark bandstand. Sammy and Danny gulped down their last bites and followed them. While the band was warming up, Larry delivered the girls' desserts.

All the girls had ordered coffee with their desserts, except Doris, who opted for more of the Roscato. Sammy had two glasses of the Roscato with his dinner. No one else drank it except Doris, so she still had part of the bottle.

"This sweet wine ish really good," she said. She was showing the effects of the three glasses of wine, the two cocktails she drank at the cocktail party, and the one she drank before the meal. She had gotten more exuberant with each glass.

Ann was sitting next to her and looked worried. It wouldn't be the first time one of Sammy's dates threw up her dinner before the night was over.

"How about having some coffee with your dessert?" Betty asked Doris. "It's a long night yet. Maybe we should pace ourselves."

"Pace myself, you say! Are you calling me a horse?" Doris demanded. "What kind of crap is that!"

Betty had finished her dessert and was having a cigarette with her coffee. She blew a smoke ring at Doris.

Doris screamed, "You bitch!" She lurched out of her chair, caught her high heel on a leg of the chair, and fell to the carpet.

Doris's scream caught Sammy's attention. He rushed off the bandstand, grabbing Don, and they hurried to the band table. They tried to assist Doris to her feet. She screamed obscenities at them and pushed away their hands.

Sammy finally got Doris to her feet and said, "Sorry, Don, I'll have to take her home. I'll be back as soon as I can."

"Don't worry about it. I'll play bass, and Mike can play lead guitar. Just take care of Doris," Don said.

Sammy led Doris away. She was protesting she wanted to stay at the party. Don followed to make sure she left all right. June came along to bring Doris's coat and hat.

When June returned, Ann was seated next to Betty. June sat down on the other side of Betty and said, "They got her in Sammy's car, after she threw up on the curb."

"We're off to a flying start in the new year," Betty said and laughed.

"You didn't have to provoke her, you know. What was that bit with the smoke ring?" June asked.

"She provoked me first. I was just trying to get her to slow down," Betty said.

"It's water under the bridge. Let's forget it and have a good time," Ann said.

June looked around at the other tables. They had gotten their show and were back to whatever they were doing before Doris's pratfall.

"Well, I guess that's what happens when you have a table full of secretaries," Betty said and laughed.

June tried to give Betty a stern look, but she couldn't help it. She laughed too.

Don was on the bandstand, warming up on Sammy's bass and tuning it to his liking.

The master of ceremonies, dressed in a tuxedo, approached Don and asked, "Is the band ready to play? It's already ten minutes past nine and people are getting a little restless." He wanted to head off any more unfortunate scenes at the band table.

Don looked at Danny and Mike. They signaled okay.

"Yes, we're ready," Don said.

The relieved MC stepped to the microphone and said, "Here to entertain us this New Year's Eve are the Jazz Tones. Please welcome them with your applause."

There was polite applause mixed in with catcalls.

"Your girlfriends already gave us a show."

Don turned to Danny and Mike and said, "'Pistol Packing Mama,'" which was always a crowd favorite. Mike led straight into the song on lead guitar, and after the intro, Don started the lyrics. By the time they got to the second stanza, the crowd was singing the chorus with them.

"The guys handled that well," Betty said.

"Yes, the crowd is back on their side. I'm surprised this highbrow bunch goes for a rowdy song like that one," June said.

"It was on the hit parade for several weeks," Ann observed. "It must have general appeal."

Don finished the last chorus to enthusiastic applause. The band continued with an upbeat jazz number, and people started to dance. There were several versions of the jitterbug displayed, and even the older dancers gave it a go.

"The crowd is definitely warming up," June said.

"Wait until they get more booze in them. Then you'll see warming up. Doris won't be the only broad heaving her cookies, hopefully in the ladies' room," Betty said.

June and Ann finished their dessert and had refills on their coffee. Betty hardly touched her dessert.

Larry refilled their coffee, asked them if they would like a digestif.

June asked, "What do you have?" June didn't want to admit she had no clue what a digestif was.

"Tonight, we have a special selection for the occasion. We have a Grasshopper, Brandy Alexander, a white Russian, and a caramel apple martini," Larry recited.

June said, "Which one has the least amount of alcohol?"

"We can make you a white Russian with a light touch of vodka that tastes very nice."

"I'll have one of those," June said.

"I'll have one too," Ann said.

"I'll just have the coffee," Betty said.

Larry left with their orders.

From the stage, Don announced the next song. "Let's slow it down and give all you lovers a chance to dance a little closer."

There was laughter and a few cheers from the dance floor as the band struck up the "Tennessee Waltz."

"Are you feeling okay, Betty? You usually like dessert drinks," June said.

"I feel a little light-headed. The wine got to me, I guess.

A nice-looking middle-aged man in a tuxedo approached their table and said, "My wife doesn't dance, but she gives me her permission if I can find a partner. Would one of you lovely ladies do me the favor of a waltz?"

Betty said, "I'm your huckleberry."

"My name is John, and who are you ladies?"

Betty got up and said, "I'm Betty, and these are my friends, June and Ann."

"Charmed, ladies," John said. He held out his arms and swept Betty into a classic waltz whirl. They were both good dancers and enjoyed dancing with a skilled partner.

After a turn around the floor, Betty asked, "Which one is your wife?"

John pointed to a table and said, "She's the beautiful jealous lady in the pink-and-white evening gown."

"I thought you said she gave you permission to dance with someone else," Betty said as they whirled away from the table where his wife was sitting.

"She did, and she's a good sport about it. But she still gets a little jealous when I'm lucky enough to snare a beautiful young dance partner."

They danced another round and Betty kidded, "I wouldn't want to jeopardize anyone's marriage, John."

"It's lasted twenty-five years. It'll probably last the night," John said and laughed.

The waltz ended, and the band announced a break. John escorted Betty back to her table just as Don and Mike arrived from the bandstand.

"Cheating on me again," Don said to Betty. "And he's a handsome bugger too."

"Very kind of you to say so, sir. You're a very lucky man. My name is John."

Don laughed and said, "I'm Don, and these rascals are Mike and Danny. Please sit down and join us."

"I appreciate the invitation, but I'm afraid I better be getting back to my wife before she finds another handsome bugger," John said. "It was very nice to have met you all. Thank you for the waltz, Betty. You're a wonderful dancer. Happy New Year to everyone."

"Happy New Year," they all responded as John left.

"Nice fellow," Mike said.

Don signaled to Larry, who came over to the table. "Who wants drinks?" Don asked.

Mike said, "I'll have a beer, Budweiser, if you have it. It's hot on that bandstand."

"I'll have the same," Danny said.

Don ordered a Dewar's scotch on the rocks. "Aren't you girls having a drink?" he asked.

June said, "I'm still working on my white Russian."

"Me too," Ann said.

"What about you, Betty?" Don asked.

"I think I'll stick with water. I'm pooped from the dancing and the wine," Betty said.

June was surprised. Betty was usually the last one standing at parties.

The noise level in the room grew as the evening progressed. Ties on the men's tuxedos had come undone, and others had disappeared entirely once collars were opened. Larry and the other waiters hustled to keep up with the drink orders. During the band's break, a Bing Crosby record played on the speaker system.

"I'm really enjoying your music, and the crowd is having a good time," June said.

"Remember the last time we played a New Year's Eve party?" Danny asked.

"It was that nightclub on the river south of Joplin," Mike said.

"Now that was a rowdy crowd. There were fights breaking out from 11:00 p.m. onward," Don said.

"And beer bottles flying at the bandstand," Danny said.

June looked dubiously at Mike and said, "There weren't really beer bottles thrown at you?"

Don said, "That was nothing. It's a good thing we carry black jacks in the guitar cases. A few soused patrons made their displeasure with our song selection known by storming the bandstand."

"Yeah, knots on a few heads sorted that out," Danny said.

"But that wasn't the worst of it. About 2:00 a.m., as we were packing up our instruments and gear, Don went to get our money from the club owner," Mike said.

At that moment, Larry showed up with their drinks, and Mike paused.

Don took a drink of his scotch and continued the story. "The owner was drunk. He said we stunk, and he wouldn't pay us."

"The nightclub was a two-story building, with a ballroom on the second floor with a balcony overlooking the river," Mike explained. "Don dragged the owner to the balcony and hung him out over the river by his feet."

"He changed his mind about paying us," Don finished.

"Did that really happen, or are you all jiving us?" Betty asked.

Danny took a drink of his beer and said, "Some of those out-of-town joints get pretty rough. It happened all right. And it wasn't the first time we had to remind a club owner what he owed us."

Don turned to Betty and suggested, "Let's dance."

"Let's wait for a slow one," Betty said.

She's not herself tonight, June thought.

Danny stood up and held out his hand to Ann. She smiled, got up, and they went out on the dance floor to join the other dancers.

"My leave is up tomorrow," Mike said. "Don is dropping me off at the train station in the morning."

"You're not driving back to Crowder? What about your car?" June asked.

"I'm leaving it here with Don," Mike said.

"Why are you doing that?" June asked.

Don looked at Mike and raised his eyebrows. Obviously, Mike had not shared his plan with June.

"So I'll have it here when I come back," Mike said, looking intently at June.

June blushed. She was surprised how pleased she was that Mike was coming back to St. Joe to see her. But then she frowned, worried that time with Mike would sidetrack her from getting to nursing school. She had to take her entrance exam in three months, and it was over three years since high school. She needed to cram for all the subjects that were a distant memory. And she had to keep her new job. She needed the money for her school fees and tuition.

Don raised his glass to the table. "Happy New Year," he said.

Everyone raised their glasses and said, "Happy New Year."

"Why don't you go with me to drop Mike off tomorrow, June?" Don asked.

Mike looked pleadingly at June, who glanced at Don and said, "Okay, what time?"

"We'll pick you up at nine thirty. Mike has to get on the train at ten thirty," Don said.

"I already have my ticket," Mike said.

Don asked Betty, "Do you want to go with us?"

"I'm sleeping in tomorrow. You guys go without me," Betty said. She was tired and looked forward to staying in bed in the morning.

The record player changed to a slow ballad.

"Shall we?" Mike asked June. Mike held her close while they danced. He felt her thighs pressing against his, and his body reacted the way a healthy male body does, so he pulled away from her a little.

June said, "I was worried I was losing my sex appeal," and pulled him back to her.

They danced cheek to cheek, and Mike was lost in the warm feel and scent of her.

"The song is over," June said.

"That's too bad," he said.

When they got back to their table, Don said, "Breaks over. Back to the salt mines."

By midnight, the room was loud and smoky. At 11:58 p.m., the MC returned to the stage and began the countdown to the New Year. When he got to the last ten seconds, the room counted with him. At the stroke of midnight, everyone shouted, "Happy New Year!" and Don and the band started singing "Auld Lang Syne." When they finished, Don announced a short break, and they joined the girls at the table. The guys gave their dates a New Year's kiss.

"We have to play until 1:00 a.m.," Don said to the table.

The band returned to the bandstand, and Don announced, "For those of you who are still standing, we'll start our last set with a Mills Brothers tune, 'You Always Hurt the One You Love.'"

By the time the band finished their set at 1:00 a.m., only a few stragglers were left, and the guys made quick work of putting away their gear.

9

Don retrieved Betty's car from the hotel garage and picked her up at the entrance. He headed for his cabin. When they were halfway there, Betty leaned against the car door and went to sleep.

Mike and June left for the apartment. Mike had to dodge a drunk driver at an intersection but made it through unscathed. June leaned against him all the way home. Mike parked at her brownstone, and they went up to her apartment. They kissed in the hallway, then June let them in.

"Do you want a nightcap?" she asked.

Mike hung up his coat and hat and sat on the loveseat. "Come sit with me."

When they were both seated, he looked into her eyes and said, "I realize we haven't known each other very long. And if I weren't going back to Camp Crowder tomorrow, I'd not rush things. But I love you, and I don't want to take a chance you thinking this was just a fling for me. When a guy finds the right girl, he's a fool to let her get away. Will you marry me?"

She looked at something he was holding in his right hand. It was a diamond ring.

She was stunned. Then she said, "Oh, Mike, I just can't—I have to go to nursing school!" She started to cry.

Mike put his arms around her.

"If you have to go to nursing school, that's fine. When I get out of the Army, I'll work while you go to school."

June stopped crying and looked at him. Mike released her.

"But, what about you? Don't you have your own plans?" June asked.

"Sure, I do. I want to go to school too. I want to take electrical engineering."

"How can you do that if you're working to support a wife?"

"Lots of ways. There are night classes, and after you graduate, you can support us while I finish my schooling. We'll just have to do things our way, not the conventional way."

June was having trouble taking all this in. She had not thought about being married. Her plans stopped at becoming a nurse.

"I love you. Do you love me?" Mike asked.

"Maybe...I don't know..." June jumped up and went into the kitchen.

Mike pondered his situation. You ask a girl to marry you and she says yes or no. What do you do when she says maybe? He followed her into the kitchen.

"I'm crazy about you. My proposal stands. But take all the time you need to think it over."

There was a knock on the front door.

Don opened the door and yelled, "Is everybody decent? We're coming in." He carried Betty into the living room and said, "She went to sleep in the car, so I brought her home."

"Is she okay?" June asked, coming into the living room.

Betty mumbled something and went back to sleep.

"She's fine. I think the wine didn't agree with her," Don said. "Is this her room?"

"That's it," June said and opened the door for Don so he could lay her on her bed.

"I'll undress her and get her under the covers," June told him.

Don went back to the living room and sat in the easy chair.

"Sorry to ruin your evening with June, Mike," he said.

"I asked her to marry me," Mike said.

Don jumped up and grabbed Mike's hand and shook it. "Congratulations, you dog, you! You never told me you were going to propose to her."

"She didn't say yes." Mike took back his hand.

Don sat back down and said, "I'm sorry, pal."

"She didn't exactly say no either. It's complicated. We should probably go."

"Damn, Mike, you're leaving in the morning," Don said.

June came out of Betty's room and said to Don, "She's fine. She just had too much to drink." She didn't look at Mike.

Mike stood up and nodded for Don to do the same.

"We'll be by in the morning to pick you up," Don said and ushered Mike to the door.

June didn't respond as they left.

*****

June left a note for Betty, who was still asleep when Don and Mike returned in the morning to pick her up. Mike and June rode in the back seat while Don drove.

Don groused. "I never thought I'd end up being a chauffeur. I might have to give you back your car."

"Just keep your eyes on the road, James," Mike said and looked inquiringly at June.

"Do you still have that ring?" June asked him.

Mike's face lit up with a huge smile, and he reached into his pocket. He took the ring out of its box and put it on her finger.

"It was my mother's ring," he said. "She gave it to me shortly before she died. She said she wanted her new daughter to wear it when I found her."

June's eyes teared, and she said, "It fits just fine. I'll be proud to wear it."

Don watched them in the rear-view mirror as they hugged and kissed.

"Now that you two are practically an old married couple, you should stop scandalizing the help." Don turned into the train station and stopped in a loading/unloading zone.

A redcap hurried to get the luggage. He opened the trunk and took out the suitcase and the duffle bag. The olive-green duffle bag had white stencil markings, "Sgt. Michael Thompson, RA

16574562." Mike got out of the car while the redcap opened June's door for her.

Don stayed in the car.

Mike walked up to the driver's window and said, "You're my best man, you know."

"Congratulations, buddy. I'm happy for you," Don said. "I've never been a best man before."

"I'll see you in a week or two. Thanks for the lift and take good care of my car, pal." Mike went around the front of the car and hugged June. "I'll call you tomorrow night. By then, I should know when I can get a weekend pass."

June kissed him. "Have a good trip, fiancé, and don't be picking up any loose women. You have your limit already."

Mike showed his ticket to the redcap, who said, "Track six. Follow me, sir."

June waved at him as he went into the train station.

June got back into the front seat of the car.

"Congratulations to you too, honey," Don said. He started the car, put it in gear, and pulled away from the station.

"Thank you for taking good care of Betty last night." June said. "I'm glad you're going to be Mike's best man."

"How's Betty this morning?" Don asked as he drove back toward the apartment.

June looked at Don and said, "She was still asleep when I left. I'm getting worried about her. I'm afraid she might have caught a bug."

Don made a left-hand turn and glanced at June. "I'll call her this afternoon," he said.

When he pulled up in front of her building, he said, "I think it's great about you and Mike. You two will be good for each other."

June leaned over and kissed Don on the cheek. "You keep this up, and I might start really liking you," she said.

When she entered the apartment, Betty was sitting at the breakfast table, having coffee and toast.

"Hi, I feel like shit. I think I'm getting a cold," she said.

June walked over and felt Betty's forehead. "It doesn't feel hot. I don't think you have a fever, but I'll get the thermometer." When she returned and gave Betty the thermometer, Betty saw the ring on her finger.

"Oh my God, when did you get this?" she asked. "Does that mean what I think it does?"

June said, "Put the thermometer under your tongue and close your mouth. Mike asked me to marry him last night when he brought me home. I said yes this morning."

Betty put the thermometer in her mouth, dying to ask June questions about Mike and her engagement. June checked her watch. When time had elapsed, she took the thermometer out of Betty's mouth and studied it.

"You don't have a fever," she told Betty.

"Tell me all about your engagement," Betty said. "Where was I when this was going on?"

"Mike brought me home from the New Year's party. You went with Don in your car, but you fell asleep, so he brought you home." June took two plates down from the cupboard, went to the icebox, and took out ham and cheese. She started slicing the ham and putting it on her plate.

"Do you want me to make you a sandwich?" she asked Betty.

"No, I'm having toast. I'm not very hungry. What happened next?"

June cut a slice of cheese from the cheese loaf and put it on the plate. She put the ham and cheese back in the icebox.

"When Mike and I got home, he asked me to marry him. I never thought about getting married and didn't know what to say to him." June got bread and mayonnaise from the pantry and finished making her sandwich. She poured a glass of milk and carried her lunch to the breakfast table.

"So what *did* you say to him?"

"I said I couldn't marry him. I had to go to nursing school."

Betty had a puzzled expression on her face. "Then how did you get the ring?"

"I tossed and turned all night thinking about it, when I finally realized that I love the big lug. So this morning in the car I said yes."

Betty still couldn't picture her sensible friend being swept off her feet like this.

"But what about nursing school? I thought that was your dream?"

June ate a bite of her sandwich and took a drink of milk. "It still is my dream. Mike and I talked, and he supports my going to nursing school."

"Well, hell—congratulations then, roomie. Mike's a great guy."

June finished her sandwich and milk and got up to wash her plate and glass.

"So when's the wedding? Are you going to move to Neosho?" Betty asked. She got up to get more coffee. She was feeling better.

"We haven't had time to talk about any of that," June said.

"Is Mike coming over later?" She poured her coffee and brought it back to the table.

"Don and I took Mike to the train station. His leave is up today. He's leaving his car here with Don. He's going to get a weekend pass as soon as he can."

"What about your job? Have you told your family?" Betty asked.

"I like my job, and we will need the money."

"What about your family?"

"When Mike gets his pass, we'll go out to the farm and tell my family. Mike doesn't know that yet, but he will."

*****

"I thought we were supposed to be relieved," Sgt. Richard Taylor said to Lt. Bryan Wilson, his new platoon leader.

They were standing on a beat-up highway north of Bastogne where the new lieutenant got their orders from battalion.

Lieutenant Wilson had a shiny gold bar on each shoulder of his brand-new fatigue jacket. He was one of the replacements added to what was left of the 101st Airborne Division.

"Sergeant, I go where the Army tells me, just like you," Lieutenant Wilson said.

With these replacements added, the Allied command decided not to relieve the 101st, but to use them to pursue elements of the retreating German army. Ricky's regiment, the 506th, saddled up and attacked north toward the town of Recogne. There were other towns before Recogne, and they were defended. The battered 506th suffered some of the worst shelling of their war when German 88s fired tree bursts into the forests where they were holding the front line. Then they had to attack the towns the 88s were defending. Many companies in the regiment had less than half the men they had brought to Bastogne.

*****

The train in St. Joe was jammed with soldiers returning, like Mike, from Christmas leave. The redcap found Mike a seat and stowed his bags in the overhead compartment. This was a good arrangement until they got to Kansas City, where Mike changed trains.

When Mike boarded the Missouri Pacific train to Joplin, he took the opportunity to relieve his bladder, which had been nagging him for the past forty miles. He left his bags on his seat. When he exited the restroom, the train car had filled up. He pushed past soldiers standing in the aisle and found his seat taken by a two-hundred-pound muscular master sergeant.

"That's my seat," he said to the master sergeant.

The master sergeant looked up at Mike and laughed. "I don't see your name on it, buddy."

"I left my bags on that seat," Mike said.

The master sergeant said, "Tell someone who gives a shit. I didn't see any bags."

Mike saw his bags in the overhead compartment. *Great*, Mike thought. *Now I get to fight this asshole for my seat.*

Mike saw a conductor squeezing his way down the aisle and checking tickets. When the conductor got to him, Mike showed him his ticket and said, "This guy is in my seat."

The conductor looked at his ticket and said, "This ticket gets you in this car. Seats are not reserved."

The master sergeant smirked at Mike and leaned his head back and closed his eyes. There were no other empty seats, and there were men standing in the aisle.

"The railroad overbooks the seats," a lean, well-dressed blond-headed man said. The man was sitting in the seat across the aisle from the master sergeant. "They claim they are helping the troops. Do you feel helped?"

What Mike felt like was wrestling the master sergeant for his seat, but he studied the affable civilian who just spoke to him.

"If that's your duffle bag in the overhead, I'd get it down and sit on it. It beats standing all the way to Joplin," the fellow suggested.

Mike got his duffle bag down, knocking off the master sergeant's overseas cap. The master sergeant glared at Mike and picked up his cap. Then he went back to sleep.

"My name is Warren Nelson, but my friends call me Slats," the blond man said.

"I'm Mike Thompson." Mike shook Slats's hand and sat down on his duffle bag.

There was just enough space for people to squeeze by him if he stood up and moved to one end of the bag.

"How did you get a seat? You got on here in Kansas City, didn't you?" Mike asked Slats.

"I tipped the conductor, and he let me on first. This isn't my first train ride," Slats said. "Actually, I usually get a compartment, but this was a last-minute thing, and they were all gone," Slats continued. "Now I get to see how the other half lives." He laughed.

"You look like you're well-off. Why didn't you take a plane?" Mike asked.

"Scared to death of the bloody things, don't you know," Slats said with a phony British accent.

"Why are you going to Joplin?" Mike asked. He had to get up and let a young, attractive lady get by him.

"I hope she has a big boyfriend to save her a seat," Slats said. "Chivalry is dead on the Missouri Pacific. I'm going to a funeral actually."

"I'm sorry. Is it someone close to you?" Mike asked.

"It's my brother. His body was returned from Hawaii. He was an Army officer."

"I'm sorry about your brother, Slats. Are you in the service?" Mike asked. He got up to let the attractive lady go back to her seat. The train jostled her into him, and he felt her breast against his arm.

She gently pushed away from him and said, "Excuse me, please, sir." She moved on before he could respond.

He watched her very fetching rear end go down the aisle and take the seat near the end of the car being held for her by her large boyfriend.

"I share your appreciation for a tidy derriere," Slats said. "In answer to your inquiry, no, I am not in the service of our country. When I answered the call of my friends and neighbors to the flag, I was found wanting. It seems they do not have a pressing need for asthmatics, even mild cases."

"It must be rough on you, losing your brother in the war," Mike said.

Slats turned his head to face Mike. "That's quite perceptive of you, Mike. I assume your friends and neighbors found you satisfactory?"

Mike was in civvies. "I'm in the Signal Corps. I'm going off Christmas leave to Camp Crowder."

"So did you see a girl or two in the wicked city of St. Joseph on your leave?" Slats asked.

"I met a girl and asked her to marry me," Mike said.

"On the first date? That was a little impetuous, don't you think?" Slats asked with a smile. "What did she say?"

"She said yes, but it wasn't on the first date. I spent my leave going out with her. I went to meet her family on Christmas day. She has a big family. They're tobacco farmers."

"Still, that's pretty fast work. Marriage is a big commitment. Are you sure about this? I ask you as a friend, taking the liberty of considering you my new friend, of course."

"I loved her from the first time I met her. I know people think love at first sight is a crock. So did I, until it happened to me," Mike said.

Slats studied Mike for a few moments. "You seem a pretty level-headed sort. I believe what you're telling me, and frankly, I'm jealous of you. Nothing like that has happened to me. I'd love to meet this enchantress."

"You'd like her, Slats, and she'd like you," Mike said.

Slats stood up and said, "Take my seat. I'm going to the club car to spend some of my family's ill-gotten money. It's hurting my back to see you squatting on that duffle bag."

Slats stepped aside far enough for Mike to take his seat. Mike put his bag in the overhead, taking care not to disturb the sleeping master sergeant. When Mike sat down, Slats reached in his coat pocket and took out a business card.

He handed it to Mike and said, "I may spend the rest of our trip in the club car. Call me sometime. I want to hear how this romance works out." He laughed and walked up the aisle.

"Hey, thanks, Slats," Mike said. *I'll never see that guy again,* Mike thought.

It was almost 10:00 p.m. when the train got into Joplin. Mike had to report in before midnight, or he would be AWOL (absent without leave).

Mike saw three Signal Corps troops getting off the train ahead of him at the Joplin station. He hurried up to them and asked if they were going to Camp Crowder.

One of them, a tech sergeant, saw Mike's duffle bag and asked, "Do you need a lift?"

"Yeah, thanks, I'm with the 800th. My name is Mike."

"Tom left his car in the parking lot when we went up to Kansas City for a New Year's party. I hope he still has tires on it," the tech sergeant said. "I'm Jim. The corporal there is Dave, and Tom is the private first class. Every time he gets a few stripes, he gets drunk, starts a bar fight, takes a swing at an MP, and ends up losing a couple of stripes. There's his jalopy, and it still has tires."

"I told you, the railroad patrols that lot. See all the fancy cars, the railroad doesn't want to piss off their owners by letting their cars get robbed," Tom said.

Tom's car was a beat-up Ford Fordor sedan. The three friends had small AWOL bags, so there was room in the trunk for Mike's bags. He got in the back with Dave.

"I have to report in by midnight," Mike said.

"Join the club. We're all in the same boat," Jim said.

Tom turned his head and said, "No sweat. We'll be at the main gate at eleven thirty at the latest. We can all sign in off our passes at the MP station."

"I'm on leave. I have to sign in at the 800th orderly room," Mike said.

"We'll drop you at your orderly room and go back to the gate to sign in," Tom said.

"I really appreciate this, boys," Mike said.

Tom neared the Camp Crowder main gate at 11:20 p.m. There was a long line of cars waiting to enter. They weren't the only soldiers coming off holiday passes and leaves.

"I'm screwed," Mike said. "You guys should be okay, but I'll never get through to my orderly room before midnight."

Jim looked closely at the gate and said, "There's a shorter line at the walk-through gate. Let's grab your gear and go. If we can get you through the walk-through gate, you can get a lift from a car that got through."

"What about you?" Mike said.

"I'll wait for the guys to pick me up," Jim said. "Let's go!"

Mike grabbed his duffle bag, and Jim got his suitcase. Mike was still in his civvies, but he had his leave orders in his coat pocket. That's all he would need to get through the MPs at the gate. The two of them hustled down the line of backed up cars.

"Get your orders and ID cards out, and be ready to show them!" an MP sergeant kept repeating to the line.

Mike and Jim were ready when they got to the gate. An MP corporal checked orders, and an MP private first class checked ID cards. They got through the checks quickly.

Jim flagged down a car just coming through the gate and said, "Can you take my friend to the 800th orderly room? He needs to sign in off leave." Jim hadn't noticed the blue sticker on the bumper of the car. When he leaned in the window, he saw the eagles on the epaulets of the driver. "I'm sorry, Colonel, I didn't see your bumper sticker," Jim said.

"Throw your bags in the back seat and get in, Sergeant."

Mike heard the exchange and did what the colonel directed. The colonel's car was a 1941 Ford Deluxe Fordor Sedan, one of the last cars Ford had made before converting to war production.

"You need to go to the 800th orderly room, son?" the colonel asked.

"Yes, sir. I'm checking in from Christmas leave. I really appreciate this, sir," Mike said.

"I hope you had a good leave, son," the colonel said.

"I'm T/Sgt. Thompson, sir. I got engaged this morning to a girl I met before Christmas. She lives in St. Joe."

The colonel made the turn toward the 800th Signal Training Regiment.

"You just came from St. Joseph today, Sergeant?" the colonel asked.

"Yes, sir. I came on the train," Mike said.

"No wonder you're cutting it close. Well, here we are," the colonel said and pulled up in front of the orderly room. "And with time to spare."

It was 11:55 p.m.

Mike jumped out of the car, opened the back door, and took out his bags. He closed the back door, leaned in and said, "Thank you again, sir."

"Congratulations, Sergeant. I'm sure she's a nice girl."

"Yes, sir, she is," Mike said and grabbed his bags and hurried into the orderly room.

*****

On Monday morning, June was making coffee and pancakes for breakfast when Betty appeared, dressed for work. She offered Betty pancakes as she turned down the burner under the percolator.

"I'm not really hungry, but I should eat something. Make me a couple, please," Betty said. She got a cup of coffee and sat at the table.

"How are you feeling this morning?" June asked. She put three pancakes on her plate and poured the batter for two more in the skillet.

"I think I may be getting a cold, but it could just be the late night and the drinking," Betty said.

"Why don't you call in sick?" June said. She turned over the pancakes and set her plate on the table. She got a plate and silverware for Betty.

"I don't want to miss work on my new job, especially not right after New Year's. My boss will think I'm a flake."

June ladled the pancakes on Betty's plate.

Betty dropped June off at Quaker Oats and went on to her parking space at the ordnance plant. Today was her first day on her own without Maureen, and she wished she felt more energetic. She was going through the mail when Joe came in. He stopped at her desk.

"How was your holiday?" he asked.

Betty put down the memo she was reading and said, "It was great. My roommate got engaged on New Year's Day. How was yours?"

"No one got engaged, but we had a pretty good party with my family and the neighbors. Is there anything interesting in the mail?"

"Just this, from Beattie Wilson," she said and handed him the memo.

He read it.

Date: December 29
To: Mr. Harding, production manager
From: Mr. Wilson, loading department supervisor
Subject: Interviews of applicants for production jobs
    Due to the sensitive nature of this situation,
I recommend the job applicants be referred to the
personnel department for interviews and action.

Beattie Wilson wouldn't give up on passing the buck without a fight, Joe thought. "If the spineless bastard didn't do such a good job running his department, I'd fire his ass!" Joe said. "Sorry about my language."

"I'd like to see you fire his ass too. Did you notice he didn't copy personnel?" Betty said.

"Of course, he didn't. He still wants me to be the bad guy with personnel," Joe said. "He knows they don't want to get within a mile of this. Call the SOB and tell him I want to see him, now!" Joe took the memo and went into his office.

Betty pushed the phone button that connected to the plant paging system. "Mr. Wilson, call the production office, Mr. Wilson call the production office."

A few minutes later, her phone rang.

"Mr. Harding's office, Miss Anderson speaking," she answered the phone.

"This is Mr. Wilson answering the page. What's up?"

"Mr. Harding wants to see you in his office now."

"I'm in the middle of something. Put me through to him."

Betty put the call on hold and pushed the intercom button. "Mr. Wilson is on line one."

"I told you to have him come to my office," Joe said.

"That's what I told him, Mr. Harding, but he insisted I put him through to you."

"Okay, I don't want to put you in the middle. Put him through."

June pushed down the button for line one and said, "Please hold for Mr. Harding." She pushed the intercom button. "He's on hold on line 1, sir."

Joe pushed the button for line 1 and said, "Get your ass up to my office, now." He hung up.

Beattie Wilson came into Betty's office and said, "I'm supposed to see Mr. Harding."

Beattie looked like a seven-year-old in trouble in the principal's office.

Betty pushed the intercom button and said, "Mr. Wilson is here."

"Send him in," Joe said on the intercom.

Beattie walked to the door of Joe's office and went in. Joe was looking down at a paper on his desk. He didn't look up when Beattie came in.

"You wanted to see me?" Beattie asked tentatively, standing in front of Joe's desk.

Joe continued studying the paper and ignoring Beattie. Beattie sat down in the guest chair.

Joe looked up and said, "I didn't tell you to sit."

Beattie jumped back to his feet, stammered an apology, and hung his head.

Joe put down the paper and looked up at Beattie.

"Who is in charge of the loading department?" Joe asked Beattie, glaring at him.

Beattie said, "I am, Mr. Harding." He gripped the chair back with a white-knuckled fist.

"Who is in charge of the janitors in the loading department?" Joe asked, continuing to glare at Beattie.

Beattie looked puzzled and then said, "I am."

Joe rubbed his chin and said, "Are you sure it's not me or the personnel department?"

Beattie thought carefully about his answer. He knew his job might be on the line. "No, sir, I'm in charge of the janitors in my department." He let go of the chair and stood up straight.

"You might remember that the next time you feel the urge to send me memos. You are dismissed. Get back to work."

Beattie turned and walked out of Joe's office. He left with more of Joe's respect than he came in with.

Betty slogged through the rest of the day. She was in and out of Joe's office frequently.

The holiday had stacked up work for the salaried staffs. The plant didn't stop working on holidays, and there were reports from the three shifts to catch up on. It was almost quitting time when Betty brought the last group of reports in to put in Joe's in-tray.

"You look a little peaked, Betty. Are you feeling okay?" Joe asked.

"I think I may be catching a cold," Betty said.

"Then stay home tomorrow. I don't want you here if you're sick," Joe said.

"There's too much to do, I can't stay home," Betty said.

"I can borrow Marlene for a couple of days. If you still feel sick in the morning, go to the doctor. Get over it and come back well. It won't help me if you spread germs in my office," he said gruffly.

Betty picked up June from work. On the way home, June told Betty about her day. Betty concentrated on driving and said little.

When they got home, Betty said, "I'm going to lie down a while. I'm bushed." She went into her room and took off her shoes and nylons. She got under the covers and went to sleep.

June started making some chicken broth for Betty and a fried egg sandwich for herself. The phone rang. June turned down the heat under the broth and answered the phone.

"Hello," she said.

"Hi, it's Don. Can I speak to Betty?"

"She's in bed. She wasn't feeling well when she came home. I'll tell her you called."

"Okay, I hope she isn't coming down with the flu or something," Don said.

"I hope not too. Bye."

"Goodbye," he said.

June went back to the kitchen and turned up the burner on the soup. She put mayonnaise on her bread and ladled the fried egg on the bread and made a sandwich.

After lunch, she poured the chicken broth into a bowl and set it on the table with a soup spoon. She went into Betty's room and gently shook her.

"Wake up, roomie. I made you some soup."

Betty opened her eyes and said, "I fell asleep." She sat up. "Let's go. I'll try your soup."

June followed Betty to the kitchen and asked, "Do you want some crackers?"

"No, I'll just have the soup." Betty tried a spoonful. She shrugged and said, "It's good. Could you make us some tea?"

June got down the teapot and filled it with water. She put it on the stove and turned on the burner. "What kind of tea do you want?"

"Give me a regular Lipton tea bag. I don't want that English stuff you drink."

"You sound better," June said. She got a Lipton tea bag and gave it to Betty. She took down her tin of Earl Grey tea. "It's not English tea. It's grown in Ceylon."

The water in the teapot was now bubbling, and June took down two teacups and saucers. She poured hot water in a cup and gave the cup and saucer to Betty. She put a scoop of her Earl Grey tea leaves in the pot to steep.

Betty put her Lipton bag in the hot water and left it for a few minutes.

"I feel a little better. I think the soup helped."

She stirred two lumps of sugar into her tea.

June turned off the burner after steeping her tea leaves for exactly three minutes. That was her formula for making Earl Grey tea. She strained the tea and poured herself a cup. She sat down with Betty and added two lumps of sugar as well.

"Do you plan on going to work tomorrow?" June asked.

Betty drank some more of her tea and said, "Yes, I feel better after my nap.

*****

Mike reported at the Radio Operations and Repair School at 8:00 a.m. Tuesday morning.

M/Sgt. Torres, the first sergeant of the school, was drinking coffee and studying a morning report at his desk when Mike arrived.

"You certainly look bright-eyed and bushy tailed this morning," M/Sgt. Torres said.

"It was after midnight when I got through signing in at the orderly room. And I was on a train all day. See how bright-eyed you are after that, Top."

"Your class of stumbling civilians are waiting for you in classroom seven to teach them the intricacies of the SCM-300," M/Sgt. Torres said.

Mike went to the coffeepot and got a cup of coffee. "It looks like the Germans are on the run again. Maybe we can finally get the damn war over with."

"We still have the Japs to deal with. Taking their home islands will be a bitch," M/Sgt. Torres said.

Mike took roll call at his 8:30 a.m. class and began "Introduction to the SCM-300 Field Radio." He lectured for the first hour and demonstrated the operation of the radio for the next hour. The final hour, he had the students make their own radio calls on the unit. Then he turned them over to their training sergeants for lunch, afternoon drills, and physical training. They were in their sixth week of basic training.

The 800th Signal Corps took enlistees and draftees directly into basic training and technical training. The raw recruits did not go through their eight weeks of basic training at Fort Leonard Wood like the infantry recruits. But even radiomen had to be converted from civilians into soldiers. So drill sergeants taught them to march, follow orders, and get yelled at and abused just like the infantry. In between, they got classes in technical subjects. After graduation, the brighter ones would be selected for advanced training and become specialists in subjects like radio security, intelligence, and high-frequency power station operation and repair. The others were assigned to one of the hundreds of signal units or to combat units as radiomen.

After his class, Mike went back to the school office and asked M/Sgt. Torres if he could see the commanding officer, Captain Benson. M/Sgt. Torres picked up the phone on his desk and pushed the button that connected him to the CO.

"Sir, Sergeant Thompson would like a word with you."

"Go on in," he said to Mike.

Mike went through the door to the CO's office and marched up to his desk. He stood at attention, keeping his eyes above the CO's head.

"Sir, Sgt. Thompson requests permission to speak to the commanding officer."

"At ease, Sergeant. What can I do for you?" Captain Benson asked.

"Sir, I got engaged to a girl in St. Joe on my leave," Mike said.

"Congratulations, Sergeant. Sit down. I see this may take a while."

Mike sat in the visitor's chair and continued, "It was sort of last minute and we didn't have time to discuss our future. I'd like to get a three-day pass to go see her as soon as the duty schedule allows."

Captain Benson leaned back in his chair and considered Mike's request.

"This is not official yet, but the colonel has been informed that this is our last class of recruits. The war is winding down in Europe. And the War Department is dropping Army recruiting quotas."

Mike leaned forward in his chair and asked, "Are they going to close Camp Crowder?"

"I heard nothing about closing the camp. But we are dialing back training activities. Back to your situation, I think we can spare you for a weekend. See First Sergeant Torres. Whatever he arranges is okay. You've done a good job for me."

Mike stood up, saluted, and said, "Thank you, Captain."

The captain returned his salute, and Mike pivoted and left the office. He stopped at M/Sgt. Torres's desk and said, "I'd like a word with you when you can fit me in, Top."

M/Sgt. Torres said, "See me after lunch at 1300."

"Okay, Top," Mike said and left the office.

*****

Don decided to report in on Tuesday, his last day of leave, and check out his new unit, rather than wait for the midnight rush. He drove Mike's Chevy up to the gate of Rosecrans Field at the French bottoms, as this area of St. Joseph had been called since the 1800s. Rosecrans Field was also designated St. Joseph Army Airfield. Don was in uniform and showed his orders to the MP at the gate. The MP waved him through after telling him he needed to get airfield bumper stickers for his car. He and Mike had anticipated this. Mike gave him the pink slip and registration and a power of attorney for the car.

Don followed the sign to the provost marshal's office and parked in front. He took his paperwork in and applied for the red (enlisted) bumper sticker. He paid $25 for the sticker and base registration. Then he cleaned the bumper and put on the sticker.

Don's unit, the 562nd Training Squadron, was a subordinate unit of the First Operational Training Unit at Rosecrans Field. The mission of the 562nd was training aircrews on transport aircraft. Mostly, they trained crews for the C-47 "Gooney Bird" transports. The C-47 was a Douglas Aircraft DC3 twin engine workhorse of the Transport Command. The 562nd had a version of the C-47 with structural modifications for navigation training.

Don found the 562nd orderly room and reported to the company clerk, Corporal Ericson.

The corporal looked at Don's orders and said, "You're still on leave, Sergeant. Are you bucking for general or something?"

"No, I'm just avoiding the midnight rush, and I had to get my car registered. My girl's working, so I thought I'd check out my new home."

The corporal got up and knocked on a door behind him.

"Come!" said a voice behind the door.

The corporal nodded at Don to follow him. "The sergeant's reporting in, Top," the corporal said and handed Don's orders to the first sergeant.

First Sergeant Calhoun looked at Don's orders. He laid them down and picked up a clipboard from his desk. "You're assigned as a navigator trainer. That means you're cadre. You get a private room." He checked the clipboard again and said, "Corporal, take Sergeant Walker to barracks five and issue him his key. You have parking space 17 assigned to you, Sergeant. You need to get a sticker for your POV (privately owned vehicle)."

"I just left the provost marshal, and it's on the car," Don said.

"Report here at 0800 tomorrow. The captain likes to meet his new men. Then the corporal will get you squared away with your assignment. Welcome to the 562nd."

Don followed the corporal to his desk.

The corporal unlocked a key cabinet and took out a room key. "It's $5 if you lose it," he said and handed the key to Don and a map of the airfield. "The orderly room is here. And barracks five is here. The NCO club has a decent mess hall and a bar.

*****

After lunch, Mike went back to the orderly room for his 1300 meeting with M/Sgt. Torres.

M/Sgt. Torres waved Mike into his office. "I hear congratulations are in order, Mike." He got up and shook Mike's hand. "You're the only cadre member who got himself engaged on Christmas leave."

"Thanks, Top. Did the captain mention my pass?"

"Yeah, I checked the schedule. You don't have duty this weekend, and things are slowing down. I guess the captain told you," M/Sgt. Torres said. "See Corporal Mendoza for your pass. Your classes are over at 11:00 a.m. Friday. We started your pass at eleven thirty. It's a hell of a long trip to St. Joe and back on a three-day pass."

"I really appreciate this, Top." Mike stopped at the company clerk's desk.

Corporal Mendoza looked up and said, "See me tomorrow and I'll have your pass ready, Sarge."

"Thanks, Juan."

Mike went back to his training office and wrote up his daily evaluation reports on his students' progress. He prepared his class plan for the next day. Those chores took most of the afternoon.

*****

On Tuesday morning, Betty was feeling better.

She dropped June off at work and went to her job at the ordnance plant. When Joe arrived, Betty said she would like to meet with him about some ideas she had.

Joe always checked the production floor first thing and made sure operations were running smoothly. When he returned to his office, he told her to come in. He still had an overflowing in-tray.

"What did you want to talk to me about, Betty?" he asked.

"That," she said, pointing to his in-tray. "I think I can help."

"How do you propose to do that?" Joe asked.

"A lot of that paperwork is daily production and QC reports. It's routine stuff."

"Not always. Sometimes there are problems in those reports that I need to see," Joe said.

"Yes, I know. But most of the time, it's just routine. I've been reading those reports, and if you can help me understand the important stuff that you need to see, I can sort them by priority. Then you'll only have to study the ones that need careful study. The rest you can just initial and toss them in the out tray. I could do the same thing with the memos. A lot of those are just CYAs and your name is on the distribution list."

"CYAs?" Joe asked.

"Cover your ass," Betty said.

Joe laughed. He looked at the overflowing tray and thought of the time he wasted on a lot of it. He stood up, picked up the pile in the tray, and handed it to Betty.

"Put your money where your mouth is," he said. "Do your sorting. Ask me for help if you're not sure which pile a paper should be in. I'll check on you until I'm satisfied nothing important is slipping through the cracks."

Betty picked up the pile of papers to carry them back to her desk. Part of the pile slipped as she went through the door. She bumped her arm on the door but caught the papers and put the pile on her desk. When she started working through them, she noticed she had bruised her arm on the door. *I didn't think I hit my arm that hard,* she thought. At the end of the day, she picked up June at Quaker Oats. She was very tired. *I'll take a nap when I get home,* she thought. *Maybe I do have a cold.*

*****

Tuesday night in his barracks room, Mike studied the train schedules he picked up in Kansas City. On Friday, the Southern Belle left Joplin for Kansas City at 2:00 p.m. The Southern Belle was the new streamliner between Kansas City and New Orleans and the fastest train around. It also had a good connection to St. Joe with only a forty-five-minute layover in Kansas City.

He checked with his fellow cadre and found a sergeant who had leave and was going into Joplin Friday morning. He agreed to drop Mike off at the train station, so Mike called the Kansas City Southern desk and reserved a seat on the Belle and the connecting line to St. Joseph. The Belle was pricey, but it was a luxury liner and seats were reserved. There would be no quarrels with master sergeants about his seat. It was nonstop service between Joplin and Kansas City, and he'd be in St. Joe by 8:00 p.m. Unfortunately he couldn't make connections with the Belle coming back to Joplin. This time he would make sure he kept his seat out of Kansas City.

He called Don's unit at Rosecrans and left a message for Don to pick him up at the train station at 2000 hours (8:00 p.m.) on Friday.

*****

Wednesday night, June was studying geography when Mike called.

"Hello," June answered.

"Hi, honey, I can't tie up this phone for too long, so please just listen. I'll be in St. Joe Friday night. Don's picking me up at the train station at eight o'clock. I'll drop him off at Rosecrans Field and head to your place. Do you think Betty would mind me sleeping on the couch? If that's a problem, maybe you could book me a room somewhere near you?"

"Oh, Mike, I can't believe you're getting back here so soon. I want to go to the farm and let my folks know about our engagement."

"That's great, honey, let's count on it. I need to get off this phone. There are three guys waiting to use it. I'll call you tomorrow night. I love you. Bye."

"Goodbye, I love you too," June said.

His barracks mates made smooching sounds, teasing him. He gave them the finger as he walked past. They laughed.

"Was that Mike on the phone?" Betty asked, coming out of her room.

"Yes, he got a pass for this weekend. He's coming in on the train Friday night, and Don is picking him up. How are you feeling?"

"The nap helped. But I've never run out of energy like this before. Maybe I should see a doctor. I'll ask my boss to let me take a sick day on Friday.

"That's a good idea," June said.

"What are you and Mike going to do this weekend?" Betty asked from the kitchen. She started making a toasted cheese sandwich. She hadn't eaten since she came home.

"We're going to the farm to tell my parents about our engagement. I'll call them from work tomorrow and let them know we're coming on Saturday. Oh, Mike asked if he could sleep on the couch Friday night."

"I won't ask the obvious question about your boudoir because I know how big a prude you are. Sure, he can sleep on the couch," Betty said.

On Thursday afternoon, Betty went through Joe's backlog of paperwork and sorted it. Afterward, he worked through it quickly. He only had to show Betty one report and one memo she should have put in the priority pile. His in-tray was now almost empty. He stopped at her desk on the way to a meeting with his boss.

"Thanks for helping me with that boondoggle," he said.

"Joe, I think I should go see my doctor tomorrow. I haven't felt like myself this week," Betty said.

"Absolutely, you do that. I can get Marlene to fill in tomorrow."

Betty and June stopped after work at a Chinese takeout restaurant they liked. Betty got egg drop soup. Her appetite had not returned. June got her usual order of chicken chow mein and egg rolls.

When they got home, June made tea from the tea leaves the restaurant sold. They ate their Chinese takeout meals at the kitchen table.

"I'm taking the day off tomorrow like we talked about. I'm going to see our family doctor," Betty said.

"Was your boss okay with that?" June asked. She had another mouthful of her chow mein.

"Yes, he's a good guy under his blustering," Betty said. "I'll call my mother and have her make the appointment. She's been going to Dr. Leyland for years. If she calls him, I know he will fit me in."

Betty finished her soup and one of June's egg rolls.

After dinner, she called her mother.

"Mom, it's Betty. I haven't been feeling well this week, and I think I should see Dr. Leyland. Could you call him and make an appointment for tomorrow?"

"What do you mean, you haven't been feeling well?" Kate asked.

"I've been tired and have no appetite. I think I may have a cold," Betty said.

"Do you have a temperature?"

"I don't think so. June keeps checking me."

"I'll call him right now. I have his home number," Kate said.

"Don't make it too early, I have to give June a ride to work," Betty said.

"I'll call you right back," Kate said and hung up.

"Hey, I can ride the trolley if you need to go early," June said when Betty had put the receiver down. She cleared away the remains of their meal and made them both another cup of tea.

"Let's see what Mom finds out," Betty said.

While they were having their tea, the phone rang.

"It's Mom," said Kate. "Dr. Leyland will see you at 10:00 a.m. tomorrow morning. I'm going in with you. Come over here after you drop June off at work."

"Okay, Mom. Thanks for getting the appointment. I'll see you in the morning." Betty hung up the phone.

"What's happening?" June asked.

"I have a 10:00 a.m. appointment with Dr. Leyland. Mom's going in with me. I'm going over there after I drop you off."

*****

On Friday morning, June worried about Betty's visit with her doctor. But she and Cheryl were meeting with the materials planner to coordinate the production schedules with the materials plan, and she needed to focus. Every week there was a joint planning meeting between the production planner (June) and the materials planner for her packing lines. The purpose was to ensure the production schedule was supported by the cartons and other packaging supplies the lines would need. The materials planner would alert her if there were any shortages that would affect her lines.

Material shortages were a constant problem. Food producers like Quaker had a high priority, but not as high as the defense contractors. If a supplier had to short one or the other, the food producer would be shorted. The materials planner alerted buyers to expedite shortage materials. It was a juggling act to keep the line schedules realistic, so the production managers and supervisors could run their lines efficiently.

June paid close attention to the discussion between Cheryl and the material planner. There weren't any serious shortages to deal with this week, so the meeting was brief.

*****

Betty and Kate sat in Dr. Leyland's waiting room at 10:00 a.m. Dr. Leyland's nurse called them into the examination room at 10:15 a.m. The nurse took Betty's vital signs and wrote them on her chart.

When Dr. Leyland appeared, he said, "Hello, Kate. What seems to be the trouble, Betty?" He studied her chart and waited for her answer.

"I'm always tired and don't feel like eating," Betty told the doctor.

"Come and sit on the exam table and I'll check you out," Dr. Leyland said. He examined her eyes, ears, and throat and listened to her chest with his stethoscope. "You have a mild fever today. Have you been running a fever?" he asked.

"I don't think so," Betty said.

"Do you have a cough, or a sore throat, or shortness of breath?"

"No, mostly I just feel tired and not myself," Betty said.

"You probably have an infection, possibly a cold or a bacterial infection. Usually in a healthy young person like you, the best treatment is to get a lot of rest, good nutrition, and let your immune system handle it. I'll give you aspirin for the fever and a course of vitamins to help your immune system. You need to stay in bed for a week or two. Rest is important. Do you have someone to take care of you? I understand you have your own place now?"

"I'll take care of her," Kate said.

"I want to see you in a week. Make an appointment with the receptionist. Call me if you develop a high fever or other serious symptoms. I wouldn't worry too much. This is the season for these kinds of infections. Just take care of yourself and you'll be over it soon."

When Betty and Kate left the surgery, Kate said, "Let's stop by your apartment and pack some of your things. You can stay with your father and I until you are well.

Betty pulled away from the curb and headed to her apartment. "My friends will want to see me. Is Dad going to be okay with that?"

"I'll make sure he is," Kate said.

"I have to pick June up from work today. What is she going to do for a ride next week?" Betty asked.

"Maybe you lend her your car?" Kate asked.

"Sure. What are you thinking?" Betty asked as she turned onto her street.

"Your father has nothing scheduled this afternoon. He can pick her up at work in your car today and come back home. Then she can keep your car for next week," Kate said.

Betty pulled up in front of her apartment. "That should work."

After gathering up her things at the apartment, Betty drove to her parents' house.

*****

Mike leaned back and relaxed against the soft, comfortable seat. The Southern Belle was a thoroughbred compared to the cart horse he rode on the trip down to Joplin. The Belle had stewards delivering coffee or soft drinks to his compartment. There was a deluxe dining car with a nice lunch buffet. He selected a roast beef sandwich and a tossed salad.

So this is how the other half lives, he thought.

He got a cup of coffee from a large shiny silver percolator. The cup and saucer were porcelain with the Southern Belle monogram. The tables had linen tablecloths and heavy silverware.

Too bad I change trains in KC, he thought as he enjoyed his lunch.

*****

Betty's father, Ray, was parked in a visitor space in front of the Quaker Oats main office building at 4:30 p.m. He hoped June would recognize Betty's Ford when she came out. He had only met June briefly when he dropped off some of Betty's things at their apartment shortly after the girls had moved in. He had wanted to see the neighborhood where she was living. He was happy to meet June, who seemed like a respectable, acquiesced young woman. He had been afraid Betty was moving in with a party girl. He was skeptical about giving her Betty's car to use, but Betty and Kate insisted on it. He was happy about Betty staying at home where her mother could see her through her illness, so he acquiesced to their plan about the car.

A crowd of young women came out the main door and headed for the parking lot. He recognized June about the time June saw the Ford and turned toward it. When she neared the car, she saw who was driving, and she stopped, a puzzled expression on her face. Ray leaned over and opened the passenger door for her.

She got in the car and closed her door. "Hello, Mr. Anderson. Where's Betty?" she asked him. She had recognized him but wondered why he was picking her up. She hoped this didn't mean Betty was worse.

"She's at home with her mother. They saw the doctor today, and he thinks she has some sort of infection. He advised Betty to rest up for a week and get someone to care for her. Since you have to work, her mother will care for her until she is over her illness."

That made sense to June, but she still wondered why he was there to pick her up.

"I could have taken the trolley if you had called me," she said.

He backed up and turned the car around. Then he pulled out of the lot and merged with the commuter traffic. "Betty wants you to have the car to get to work next week. I'll give you the car to drive back to the apartment."

June looked at Ray in surprise. "What did you say?" she asked.

"Betty was worried about you having transportation next week, so she wants you to use her car until she is better," Ray said.

"I don't feel right about taking her car," June said. "I can take the trolley."

Ray decided to wait until he got home to discuss this further with June. He slowed in front of his house and pulled into the driveway. The house was a two-story Tudor home with a full front porch. Tidy white columns supported the roof of the porch. Ray turned off the engine and appealed to June.

"Please reconsider. Betty will worry about you, and she doesn't need that while she's recovering. You'll be doing her a favor by using the car. You do know how to drive it, don't you?"

June laughed and said, "I started driving my dad's old Model A on the farm when I was ten. I can drive a Ford. Now I'd like to go in and see Betty."

Ray handed the car keys to her.

The interior of the house was warm and pleasant. Family photographs and a silver cross hung on the walls of the entry. An inviting living room sat off to the left of the entry, furnished with overstuffed seating and cherrywood tables. The walls were papered in a light, cheerful pattern that offset the darkness of the wood furnishings. A huge picture window let in a generous amount of light. The dining room and kitchen opened off to the right side of the hall. A walnut staircase ascended to the second-floor bedrooms and bath.

June had never been inside Betty's family home before, and she was surprised at how well a Methodist minister lived. Betty's mother, Kate, was in the kitchen preparing dinner.

"You have a lovely home, Mrs. Anderson," June told her.

"Thank you, dear. It is the parsonage for our church," Kate explained to June.

"Where's Betty?" Ray asked his wife.

"She's asleep. She wanted to take a nap before dinner," Kate said.

"I wanted to thank her for lending me her car. How is she feeling?"

"She just needs to rest for a few days. The doctor will see her again next Friday. She should be better by then," Kate said.

"Please thank her for the use of her car and tell her I will come by to see her after work on Monday. My fiancée and I are going to my parents' house this weekend," June said.

Kate stopped stirring a pot on the stove and said, "Betty didn't mention your engagement. That's wonderful news, dear."

"It just happened. He's a soldier stationed at Camp Crowder, and he's coming here tonight on the train. We're going to my parents' farm tomorrow to announce our engagement to my family."

"Congratulations to you both. It sounds very exciting," Kate said, taking June's hand.

"Yes, please accept my congratulations and best wishes as well," Ray said. "I wish Betty could find a suitable young man and settle down." Ray had to restrain himself from persistently tendering this advice to Betty. He knew it irked her.

"I better get going. I don't like to drive after dark if I can avoid it," June said.

"Be careful, dear. This time of day the roads are busy," Kate said.

She said goodbye to Ray at the door and went out to Betty's car. She was still nervous about using the Ford. What if someone ran into it or dinged it in a parking lot? Then she realized no one would ever notice the difference with all the damage Betty had already done to it.

Driving back to her apartment, June remembered Mike was coming tonight, and he didn't know Betty was staying with her parents. *This should be an interesting night,* she thought and smiled. She stopped at the market and picked out two nice porterhouse steaks, two potatoes, and the makings of a tossed salad. She was lucky finding the steaks; the market was usually out of them.

She picked up a dozen eggs, bacon, and a loaf of Wonder Bread. Finally, she selected a bottle of California cabernet wine.

That takes care of dinner tonight and breakfast tomorrow, she thought. *Mike can take care of dinner tomorrow night. I can't wait to tell my folks about our engagement. Emma Dee will be green with envy.* She smiled.

10

Don sat on a bench next to the platform at the St. Joseph train depot. He wore his uniform since he was going to have Mike drop him back at the Rosecrans Field gate, and the MPs rarely hassled NCOs in uniform. The eight o'clock train from Kansas City was a few minutes late. He had called June at 6:00 p.m. and discovered Betty was staying with her mother. June filled him in on Betty's doctor visit, and he decided to visit her on Sunday when he didn't have duty.

The train pulled into the station and stopped amid a cloud of steam, interrupting his thoughts. The locomotive was an old coal-burner, still in service for short runs. Passengers started disembarking down the steps of the passenger cars. Don saw Mike coming down from a middle car with his suitcase. He was dressed in blue jeans and a button-down collar shirt under his heavy coat. He wore his military low quarter shoes. They had a bright shine but were scuffed up from the trip. With his short haircut, he was the picture of a soldier on leave. He searched the platform for Don.

Don got up from the bench and met Mike as he came down the platform.

"Is my car still in one piece?" Mike asked Don as they shook hands.

"Yeah, except for the odd taillight and a ding here and there," Don said. "How was your train ride?"

"The first one to Kansas City was great. I rode the Southern Belle, and I felt like John D. Rockefeller. Talk about swank!" Mike answered. "Are you going with me to see June and Betty tonight?"

"Betty's got some kind of infection. She went to the doctor with her mother today. She's staying with her parents for a few days until she gets over it," Don said.

"I hope she's well soon," Mike said.

"I'm going to stop by her house on Sunday and check on her," Don said.

They walked out to the parking lot to Mike's Chevy, where Don pointed out the left front tire.

"Remember how bad this one was? One of my buddies found that one for me. You owe me five clams."

Mike gave him the money gratefully.

"You can drop me off at Rosecrans Field," Don said.

He directed Mike to the main gate at Rosecrans Field, where Mike thanked him for the pickup.

"Can you get away Sunday morning to drop me off at the train? I need to be at the station at 0900?" Mike said. "Then I can leave you the car again."

"Sure, just pick me up at the gate at 0800. Have a great time with June and her family," Don said. "I guess her father won't need a shotgun to make you marry his daughter."

"Very funny, chump."

Driving over, Mike thought about June being alone in the apartment. *This could turn into a great night*, he thought. *I better stop at a drugstore just in case.*

June tossed the salad and baked the potatoes. Then she seasoned the steaks and had them ready to broil in the oven. She opened the bottle of wine to breathe. It was a few minutes after nine o'clock, and Mike would be arriving soon. The table was set with dishes and silverware on a linen tablecloth. There was a small red candle, ready to light. June wore a cocktail dress and low-heeled shoes. She was bare-legged and wore a minimum of makeup, just a pink lipstick.

I'm engaged, and my guy is on his way here, she thought. A shiver of excitement ran down her spine. She felt like the prom queen on the night of the prom. June's only brush with sex was in high school with her steady boyfriend at the time. She wasn't even sure if she was still technically a virgin. She laughed when she thought about that night in his Olds convertible. The whole thing had lasted less than two minutes. They broke up shortly afterward.

Mike rang the bell to June's apartment.

I wish I had some flowers to give her, he thought. *At least, the drug store had some Whitman chocolates. I hope she likes chocolates. I don't know why I'm so nervous. We are engaged to be married after all.*

When June opened the door, Mike's nervousness vanished, and he said, "I forgot how pretty you are." He stepped forward and took her in his arms to kiss her.

The kiss lasted for a long time.

Finally, June broke away and said, "What's that you have in your hand?"

"I hope you like chocolates," he said and closed the door behind him. He handed her the box and hung up his hat and coat.

"We can try them later. Right now I need to put our steaks on to cook. How do you like yours?"

"Medium rare, pink in the middle," he said. "I'm starving. That cattle car I rode from Kansas City had nothing to eat."

She took the seasoned steaks off the platter and put them in the oven, along with the potatoes. June mixed in the salad dressing and sat the salad bowl on a small side table she brought in from the living room. Their kitchen table wasn't big enough to accommodate formal dining.

After two minutes, she opened the oven door and took out one steak and put it on the platter. She left the other one in the oven.

"Is that one mine?" Mike asked. He sat at the table and watched his fiancé cooking him a steak dinner. It was a sight he could easily get used to.

"No, it's mine," June said. After another couple of minutes, she took Mike's steak and their baked potatoes out of the oven and placed them on the table. She set a butter dish and a small bowl of sour cream on the side table.

"I have a bottle of cabernet opened. Would you like a glass, honey?" she asked.

"I'd love a glass, and I really like it when you call me honey," Mike said.

June blushed and said, "I could probably get used to doing it." She poured the wine into two wine glasses and set them at their places on the table.

171

Mike raised his glass and said, "To the prettiest girl west of the Mississippi River."

June touched his glass with hers and said, "To the biggest liar west of the Mississippi River."

They drank their toast and laughed.

"I really meant my toast," Mike said.

"So did I," June said.

She sat down and served the salad.

Mike tried the salad and cut a bite of his steak. It was done perfectly, just the way he liked it.

"A Kansas City Steakhouse couldn't do it any better, Mrs. Thompson."

"Thank you, Mr. Thompson, but I think you're jumping the gun a little," June said and smiled. "Speaking of that, when would you like to get married?"

"How about tomorrow?" he replied, semiseriously. He cut open his potato and added the butter and sour cream. "This is a great dinner," he said.

"You're just starved from your train ride. We can't get married tomorrow. Tomorrow we go to my parents' farm to tell them our news."

"I'm okay with any day you want. I hope this war will be over soon and I'll be out of the Army."

"What are you going to do then?"

"You mean besides marrying the prettiest girl west of the Mississippi? I'll get a job in electronics and go to school at night to be an electrical engineer."

They finished their dinner, and June cleared the table.

"Okay, partner, time to do the dishes," she said and looked at him for his reaction.

Mike leaned back in his chair and scratched his head. After a minute or so, he said, "You wash, and I'll dry."

When they finished the dishes, June poured them another glass of wine. They went into the living room and sat down to drink it.

"What are your plans after our wedding, honey?" Mike asked her.

June sipped her wine and contemplated his question.

"I have to pass my entrance exam at the end of March, if I can get up to speed on algebra and science by then."

Mike took another drink of his wine and said, "I'm pretty good with math and science, maybe I can help you."

"Give the man a big cigar. If you keep giving me all the right answers, what are we going to fight about?"

"With that red hair, honey, I'll bet you think of something," Mike said and laughed.

"That's enough wine for me," she said. "I think it's about my bedtime. Are you ready for bed, Mr. Thompson?"

"I don't have any pajamas, Mrs. Thompson," he said. "Soldiers don't get issued them."

"We'll just have to rough it," June said and led him into her bedroom.

June was naked as the day she was born. Mike looked her over from head to foot.

"I was wrong. You're the prettiest girl in the whole damn country," he said.

"You're not so bad yourself." June said to Mike, who was in the same condition.

They lay down together on the bed, and he took one of her nipples in his mouth. Then he raised his head and said, "I'll be gentle."

She reached down and took hold of him. "The heck you will!" she said. "But your friend needs to get dressed."

Mike jumped out of bed and got something out of his jeans pocket.

Things went well after that. Mike kept his word. He was gentle, the second time. He fell asleep with June's arm and leg draped over him. They never got around to trying the chocolates.

Now I know for sure, June thought. *For all practical purposes, I was a virgin.*

*****

The German ambush caught Ricky's squad off guard. They didn't think there was a German within miles of them. The lead platoon of his company was five miles up the road and almost to Rocogne. They had leapfrogged Ricky's platoon, who was the company reserve. Ricky's squad went into a small hamlet to rest. When they came into the town square, a machine gun opened up on them. Three of his squad members went down immediately. Ricky retreated with the rest of his squad into the village leather shop. Ricky peeked out of a window and saw that Corporal Washington and Private Collins were still moving. They had taken cover behind the well in the center of the square. Washington's left leg was dragging, and Collins had also been hit in the first burst of machine gunfire. But they were alive. Private Dawson wasn't moving at all. The machine gun nest was on the second floor of a wine shop across the square. The company had bypassed it when they went through on the main road.

Ricky sent three of his squad members to flank the machine gun nest, and he and the rest of the squad laid covering fire on the machine gun position. The three flankers came under fire from another German position and scrambled back to the leather shop. The only open retreat was to the rear.

"Did you guys mark that other German position?" Ricky asked one of the flankers, Pfc. Franklin.

"Yeah, they have our left flank covered, but they don't have direct fire on our guys in the square like that machine gun does," Franklin said.

Pfc. Franklin was a broad-shouldered black man from Detroit, Michigan, who had joined the squad in Bastogne.

Ricky got him promoted to private first class because he had proven himself in a firefight on the road from Bastogne.

"Okay, listen up, everyone. This is the plan," Ricky said. "Franklin and I will get Washington and Collins. The rest of you lay down covering fire on that machine gun."

"Sarge, that's what the bastards want you to do. That's why they haven't killed our guys yet," Pfc. Morgan said.

"Who still has smoke?" Ricky asked, ignoring Morgan's protest.

No one answered him. He pulled the one remaining smoke grenade from his web gear.

"When I throw this grenade, start the covering fire. Franklin, you get Collins, and I'll get Washington."

Washington was a slightly built black man who looked like he might be able to hobble on his uninjured leg. Collins was bigger and heavier and looked like he would need to be carried. Franklin could handle him better than Ricky.

"Okay, on three. One, two, three." Ricky threw the smoke grenade, and the squad opened up with covering fire.

He and Washington rushed out to the well. The smoke grenade initially shielded them from the view of the machine gunner. Franklin was faster. He grabbed Collins and lifted him on his shoulders in a fireman's carry. Ricky got to Washington and grabbed his arm and pulled him to his feet. So far, the suppressive fire from the squad had kept the machine gunner's head down. Then all hell broke loose. There was an explosion near Ricky, and he felt something hit him in the chest and side.

Hand grenade, he thought.

Franklin was through the door with Collins when the machine gun fired again. Ricky had held on to Washington's arm when the grenade went off. Ricky was dazed, but he dragged Washington back to the leather shop. The machine gun went silent.

Maybe the gunner got hit, Ricky thought.

He was almost through the door of the leather shop when he heard the report of a single rifle shot.

"Sniper," he registered.

His left arm went numb, and he fell through the doorway of the leather shop, pulling Washington in with him.

*****

Mike was in the shower, rinsing his hair when he felt a warm body press up against him. Two arms wrapped around him, and he heard a voice in his ear, "I'll wash yours, if you'll wash mine."

When both were washed, Mike said, "What do we do now? My little friend is out of clothes."

"And here I thought you were a Boy Scout," June said. "It's a good thing one of us is prepared." She handed him a foil envelope.

"There's something appealingly naughty about sex in the morning," he said.

They made love playfully.

Thank you, Mr. and Mrs. Anderson, for taking Betty for the night, Mike thought.

I've never been this at ease with a man, June thought.

June finished cooking their bacon and egg breakfasts, while Mike sat at the table drinking his coffee.

"When do you want to leave for your parents' farm?" he asked.

"Any time after breakfast is fine." She served the bacon on their plates with the eggs and toast. She poured a cup of coffee for herself and topped up Mike's cup.

"How do you want to announce our engagement?" he asked. He dipped his toast in an egg yolk and took a bite.

June ignored the egg dipping and ate her scrambled eggs with a bite of bacon.

Nobody's perfect, she thought. "Let's tell them together," June answered.

"Well, okay, but you go first," Mike said. "If your father goes for his shotgun, I'll have a head start."

"If anyone went for a shotgun, it would be Emma Dee," June said and laughed.

"Should I ask your father for your hand?" he asked and took another dip of his egg and a bite of bacon.

"It's a little late for that, don't you think." June laughed. "My mom will probably notice my ring right away."

They finished breakfast, and June put the dishes and skillet in the sink.

Mike followed her to the sink and said, "You cooked, I'll do the dishes."

"No, cooking is my job. Don't worry, you'll have your own jobs to do. You wash, and I'll dry this time," June said.

They were on the road to the farm when Mike looked over at June and said, "I quit smoking. Since you quit, I thought I shouldn't smoke around you. And since I plan to be around you a lot, I thought I might as well quit altogether."

June looked askance at Mike and said, "Now I have to actually quit too. Are you going to break me of all my bad habits?"

"Not sex."

They both laughed. Shortly after turning onto the gravel road from the state highway, there was a rumble from the rear of the car. Mike pulled over to the edge of the gravel road and stopped.

"Is this the old running-out-of-gas routine?" June asked.

"Nope, it's just a flat tire. Since we're equal partners and all and since I'm doing the driving, I guess you get to change the tire."

"Did you forget what I said this morning about each of us having our own chores? Well, this one is yours, partner," June retorted.

"I was just making sure you knew how. You might get stranded sometime," Mike observed.

"I grew up on a farm, and you think I don't know how to change a tire?"

Mike surrendered and got out of the car to change the tire.

Good thing Don got that new tire on the front, he thought. *That left me with an okay spare. I'll patch the flat when we get to the farm.*

When they pulled into the yard at the farm, they saw an olive-green sedan parked there.

They got out of the car and saw US Army stenciled on the door of the green sedan. When they neared the house, the front door opened and two men in uniform walked out. They were wearing dark-green tunics and pink trousers. One of them had the single stripe of a private first class, and the other had the railroad tracks (two silver bars) of a captain on his epaulets and silver crosses on his lapels.

The captain said politely, "Good afternoon," as he went to the sedan and got in the passenger seat.

The private nodded his head at them and got into the driver's seat.

As the sedan pulled out, June turned to Mike with a stricken look on her face.

He took her in his arms and said, "Hang in there, honey. We don't know how bad it is." But he recognized a notification team when he saw one. The captain was a chaplain, and the private was his driver. It had to be about one of her brothers.

June started to cry.

Mike held her tightly and said, "We have to hold ourselves together for your parents. Your mom and dad need you now."

June wiped her eyes with a handkerchief, and a determined expression took shape on her face.

"You're right. Let's go," she said.

Mike kept his arm around her waist, and they went into the house.

June's mother was sitting on the couch in the living room. She looked dazed. She held a Western Union telegram in her hand.

June's father was saying, "Mother, he'll be all right. He's going to be all right."

Bess came out of her funk when she saw June and Mike walking into the living room.

"Junie, Ricky's been hurt," she said.

June sat down next to her mother. She took the telegram out of her mother's hand, handed it to Mike, and hugged her mother.

Mike read it and said to June, "Your brother was wounded. He's in a hospital in Belgium. There's a number to call for more details." Mike handed the telegram to June's father and said, "You're right, sir. We need to stay positive about his chances to recover."

Bess took hazy notice of Mike and said, "Hello, Mike, Ricky's been hurt."

June recognized the signs of shock in her mother. "Do we have any brandy in the house?" she asked Dee.

"There's some sort of fancy bottle Lloyd brought home with him one time. It's never been opened," Dee said. "I'll go get it."

"Let's lay her down on the sofa and elevate her legs," June said to Mike.

Mike helped June get Bess in position and put a sofa pillow under her legs.

"This will do for now, but please get two or three pillows and a blanket from the bedroom. We may need to call her doctor." June checked her mother's breathing, which seemed okay. Her mother wasn't sweaty or clammy.

Mike rushed off to a bedroom and got a blanket and two pillows. June placed the pillows under Bess's legs and covered her with the blanket.

Dee returned with an unopened bottle of Courvoisier and a glass. Mike stripped off the foil wrap and pulled out the cork. He poured a couple of ounces into the glass.

June tilted her mother's head up so Mike could give her a drink.

When she drank the brandy, Bess opened her eyes and sat up. She looked around at everyone and said, "What happened?"

June said, "You fainted, Mom. I think you're all right now."

June helped her mother sit up on the sofa.

Bess was recovering. She threw off the blanket and pillow, looked at June and said, "Land sakes, I've never fainted before. Ricky's going to be okay, isn't he?"

"You bet he is. We'll call that telephone number and find out how he's doing," June told her mother.

"Why did you and Mike come all the way out here today?" Bess asked June. She looked from one to the other.

Dee returned to the living room and said, "The coffees on. How are you feeling, Bess?"

Mike answered Bess's question, "We can talk about that while we're having our coffee. You just rest for a minute and get your strength back."

"I'm fine now. I don't know what came over me to act so goofy. I was just asking Mike and June why they came out here today," Bess said to Dee.

He looked at June and asked, "Why did you come out here today?"

June said, "Why don't we go sit at the kitchen table and have our coffee, and we'll tell you."

June got down cups and saucers and went to the refrigerator to get the cream.

Dee checked the coffeepot and said, "It's ready."

While Dee served the coffee, June put the cream pitcher and sugar bowl on the table. She sat down next to her mother.

June pointed at Mike and said, "Mike is going to be your new son-in-law." She showed her mother her ring. "We got engaged yesterday."

"That's wonderful news!" Bess said.

"We came out here today to tell you both before we told anyone else," June said.

Dee looked at Mike and asked, "Do you love her?"

"I loved her the first time I met her. I want to spend the rest of my life with her."

Dee turned to June and asked her, "Do you love him?"

"Yes, for better or for worse. I've warned him he'll have his hands full with me," June said.

"Welcome to the family, son," Dee said.

Bess's head was spinning again. First, the news about Ricky, and now June is engaged to be married. She turned to June and asked the first question that came into her mind.

"When do you plan to get married?"

"I wanted to talk with you about that. I thought we could have the wedding in the church in DeKalb," June said.

Bess drank her coffee and took her time before answering. "I'll talk to the reverend, but when do you want to have the wedding?" Bess repeated.

"We wanted to have it as soon as we can," Mike said.

"Why the big rush?" Dee asked, looking at Mike suspiciously.

Mike looked at Dee and realized what he might be thinking.

"There's no need to rush or anything," he stammered.

June looked at his red face and laughed. "Everybody, just settle down. I'm not pregnant, for crying out loud. We have decisions to make about our future and not a lot of time to make them.

Bess said, "Ricky and Lloyd will want to be at your wedding if they are back from the Army.

Mike remembered the telegram about Ricky.

"Would you like me to call the number on the telegram and find out what details we can about Ricky? I'm used to dealing with the Army," Mike said.

"That's a good idea," Dee said.

Dee showed Mike where the telephone was in the living room. Mike sat on one of the living room chairs near the sofa. Bess and June brought their coffee into the living room and sat on the sofa to listen in.

Mike dialed the telephone number on the telegram.

"War Department, dependent information section, this is Corporal Riley speaking."

Corporal Riley's voice sounded like a young woman. She must be a WAC (Women's Army Corps), Mike thought.

"Corporal Riley, this is Sergeant Thompson. I'm calling on behalf of my fiancé and her family. They just received a WIA (wounded in action) telegram about a family member, Sgt. Richard Taylor, with the 101st Airborne. Can you give us more information about Sergeant Taylor's condition and status?"

"There is a number on the telegram below the date and time. Could you please read it to me, Sergeant?" Corporal Riley asked Mike.

Mike looked at the telegram and saw the date and time at the top of the telegram. Below the time was a long number. He read it to Corporal Riley.

"Please hold for a few minutes while I retrieve that file. Or I can call you back if you prefer?"

Mike gave Corporal Riley the Taylor's phone number and said he would wait for her call. He hung up the phone. He turned to June and her parents.

"A Corporal Riley answered the phone. She will call us back when she has the information about Ricky," he explained.

"Thank you for calling," Dee said.

Bess said, "Goodness, it's lunchtime. I'll get something started in the kitchen. June, do you want to help me?" She started for the kitchen, and June followed her.

"Do you know June wants to go to nursing school?" Dee asked Mike when the women had gone.

"We talked about that. Both of us want to complete higher educations. I'm going to study electrical engineering. Electronics is the coming thing, and I want to get in on it."

"What about June? How can you both go to school at the same time?" Dee asked.

"We have to work that out. I'm ready to do whatever it takes for both of us to have our dreams."

Dee was impressed with his new son-in-law. "Maybe Bess and I can help you kids out. We'll talk about that when you make your plans.

The phone rang. Dee indicated Mike should answer, so he picked it up and said, "Hello, this is the Taylor residence."

Bess and June heard the phone ring and returned to the living room as Mike answered the phone. He didn't speak for several minutes. Then he said, "What is the prognosis?" He listened for another minute. Then he said, "Thank you, Corporal Riley. I'll inform Sergeant Taylor's family." He hung up the phone.

"How is Ricky? How's my boy?" Bess asked.

"Why don't you and June sit down, and I'll fill you in on Ricky's condition," Mike said.

June took her mother's hand and sat with her on the couch.

"Go ahead, Mike," June said.

"First, Ricky's not in danger. His condition is serious, but not life-threatening," Mike said.

"Oh, thank God!" Bess said. She hugged June in relief.

"What does 'serious' mean?" June asked.

"He has severe wounds, including shrapnel wounds to his chest and side, and a bullet wound to his left arm. He is in stable condition, and they will transfer him back to Walter Reed Army Medical Center in Washington, DC. as soon as his doctors in Belgium say he is recovered enough to be transported by air," Mike said. "Walter Reed will do reconstructive surgery on his left arm."

"What's wrong with his arm?" June asked.

"The bullet shattered bones in his arm. Apparently, Walter Reed is the best facility for the surgery Ricky needs to save his arm. I hate to put it like that, but that's what the corporal said."

Bess started crying.

June put her arm around her mother and said, "He's alive and he's going to be coming home to us. That's what matters for now."

Bess wiped her eyes with the sleeve of her dress and said, "You're right, June." She got up from the couch and went back into the kitchen to finish making lunch.

June followed her back to the kitchen.

Mike said to Dee, "We had a flat tire on the way here. I'm going to go patch it, so we'll have a spare for the drive back."

"Do you need help with that? I've got inner tube patches in the garage."

"Thanks, but I always carry several of them."

"It'll be easier to work in the garage. I'll pull our car out," Dee continued.

"Thank you, sir. I'll go pull my car up to the garage and wait for you."

When Mike had the Chevy in the garage, he examined the flat tire. It had picked up a nail, but the tire body was okay. He patched the inner tube, changed the repaired tire, and put the spare back on the rear tire rack.

When Mike came back into the house, he joined Dee in the living room. Dee was sitting at the card table, playing solitaire.

"Do you play pitch?" he asked Mike.

"I'm afraid not. Just a little poker now and then in the barracks and gin rummy with my friend, Don."

Dee gave Mike a tutorial on the game of pitch, as played by the Taylor clan. Mike was hopelessly confused after the first five minutes.

In the kitchen, Bess made egg-salad sandwiches and chicken soup from leftover chicken in the refrigerator. June prepared a fresh pot of coffee.

When Mike came into the kitchen after his pitch lesson, Bess was saying to June, "There are so many unknowns right now with Mike in the service, Ricky in the hospital, and we haven't even told your sisters about your engagement. How are you and Mike going to set a date for your wedding?"

June turned to Mike and said, "We can allow a little time to work everything out. But I want to set our wedding date now today."

Mike looked at the calendar on the wall in the kitchen. "How about we make it the fifteenth of April? It's a Sunday, and that gives us three months to work things out. With luck, I will be out of the Army by then. If not, I'll get leave."

"April 15 is one month after Tax Day," June said. "I like it. You won't forget our anniversary because I'll remind you every March 15" (Tax Day was changed to April 15 in 1955).

Bess put the sandwiches on a serving tray on the table. She took soup bowls from the cabinet over the kitchen counter and set them on the table.

"You should call your sisters after lunch," Bess said to June.

"I'll call them both and I'll call John too," June said.

"Mike, please tell Dee that lunch is ready," said Bess.

Mike fetched Dee from the living room and sat down at the table. June served their coffee. Bess ladled the chicken soup into their bowels from the saucepan. June started the sandwich tray around the table.

June said to Dee, "Papa, we set the wedding date. We're getting married on April 15."

Dee took a bite of his sandwich and thought while he chewed it.

"Is that date okay with you, Bess? You're the mother of the bride. You and June have a lot of planning to do. And what about Lloyd and Ricky?"

"It's fine with me. We can't stop our lives for the war. Whoever can come to the wedding will be there," Bess said.

They ate lunch and talked about the wedding. Bess asked June if she wanted to wear Bess's wedding dress. It had been June's grandmother's dress, and Bess had it stored in her cedar chest in case one of her daughters wanted to wear it.

"I'd love to wear grandma's dress, Mom, if it will fit me."

"I think it will. I used to be about your size before you kids came along. I'll make adjustments and it'll fit perfectly," Bess said.

After lunch, June called her sister Emma Dee.

"Hello," Emma Dee answered. "Who is this? I'm just getting ready to go out."

"Well, you'll just have to wait. It's June, and I'm calling to tell you I'm getting married."

"Come on, June, stop fooling around. I have a date. He'll be here any minute. What do you want?"

"Hold on. I'm putting my fiancé on the phone," June said and handed the phone to Mike.

"Hello, Emma Dee, it's Mike. We met at the Christmas party," Mike said, looking askance at June for putting him on the spot.

June laughed and took back the phone.

"You're really getting married?" Emma Dee asked.

"I'm really getting married, sis."

"Well, hell, that's great! Mike is a catch. But what does he see in you?"

"I'd tell you, but the folks are listening." June laughed.

Emma Dee smiled. "I'm supposed to be the naughty one in this family, not you."

"It must have rubbed off on me. The wedding will be on April 15."

"Who's going to be your maid of honor?" Emma Dee asked.

"I thought you and Virginia Jane could mud wrestle for it," June said and giggled.

"Speaking of mud, just remember, I have more dirt on you than she does."

Bess said, "June, let me speak to her for a minute," and held out her hand for the phone.

"Emma Dee, Mom wants to talk to you for a minute," June said and gave Bess the phone.

"Honey, we had some bad news today. Ricky was hurt and is in a hospital in Belgium. I'm going to put Mike on the phone. He talked to the Army about Ricky." Bess handed the phone to Mike. She didn't feel up to reciting the details of Ricky's injuries and answering Emma Dee's questions. She hoped Mike wouldn't mind.

"Emma Dee, I'm sorry to have to give you this news," Mike said.

"What did Mom mean, hurt? Hurt how?" Emma Dee asked in a frightened voice.

"Your brother was wounded in action. He suffered shrapnel wounds to his chest and side and a bullet wound to his arm."

"Is he going to die?" Emma Dee was almost in terror.

"His wounds are not life-threatening. I should have said that in the beginning. That was stupid of me. I'm sorry," Mike said.

"How bad is he?" she asked and sat down in a chair in her living room.

"He has a broken arm. The Army plans to transfer him by air to the Walter Reed Army Medical Center in Washington, DC. They will do reconstructive surgery on his arm. The other wounds are apparently not too serious."

"Put my mom back on the phone, please, Mike."

Mike handed the phone to Bess. "She wants to talk to you."

"I'm back, honey," Bess said.

"How are you doing, Mom? You have had a lot going on there today."

There was a knock on Emma Dee's door.

"Shit!" she exclaimed. "Sorry, Mom. My date's at the door. Hold on a minute."

She put the phone down and went to the door. Her date, Ed Benson, was standing there, smiling.

"Ed, come in and sit down. I'm on the phone with my family."

He followed directions and sat down in an easy chair.

Emma Dee picked the phone back up and repeated, "How are you doing, Mom?"

"I'm okay now. It was a shock when the Army men came and told your dad and I about Ricky."

"What Army men?" Emma Dee asked.

"Two Army men came in an Army car and gave us the telegram about Ricky being hurt and in a hospital. Mike and June came shortly after the Army men left," Bess said.

"Put June back on the phone, Mom, please," Emma Dee said.

Bess handed the phone to June.

"Busy day for all of us, huh?" June said.

"Mom and Dad are okay?" Emma Dee asked June.

"We're all worried about Ricky, but they're handling it," June said.

"Have you given John and Virginia Jane all this news?" Emma Dee asked. She held her hand over the mouthpiece of the phone and told Ed to just take a load off while she talked to her family.

"You were my first call. I'm going to call them next," June said.

Ed relaxed against the sofa cushion and waited for Emma Dee to finish her call. There was no telling how long she might be on the phone.

"My date is waiting. Call John and Virginia Jane. Congratulations on your engagement. I'm thrilled for you both, honey." She hung up the phone.

"What was that all about?" Ed asked Emma Dee.

"Let's go. I'll tell you about it on the way to the matinee."

*****

June called her brother John and gave him the news about her engagement and Ricky's injuries. John was very happy for her and said he liked Mike when they met at the Christmas party. She gave him the telephone number on the telegram so he could follow Ricky's progress.

There was no need to listen to June repeat her news to her sisters, so Dee took Mike to the card table in the living room and continued explaining pitch to him.

"If you're going to be a member of this family, you have to be a pitch player," Dee told Mike.

Mike resigned himself to his fate and tried to understand the game.

Bess sat next to June on the couch while she made her calls.

"When you call Virginia Jane, I want you to let me tell her about Ricky. You give her your good news first, and the two of you talk about it all you want. Then turn her over to me, and I'll break the news about Ricky. I fear she will take it hard," Bess said to June.

"Sure, Mom. Whatever you think is best," June responded.

When June got Virginia Jane on the line, she told her about her engagement to Mike.

"Who's going to be your maid of honor?" Virginia Jane asked immediately.

"I told Emma Dee that the two of you could mud wrestle for it," June answered.

"You mean you called her first!" Virginia Jane complained.

"I wish I'd got a puppy instead of two sisters," June said. "He'd be a lot less trouble."

"Just remember, I know more about the skeletons in your closet than she does."

June laughed and said, "That's what she said."

"Well, you're getting a good man in Mike. I'm very happy for you. Congratulations, sister."

"Mom wants to talk to you, hold on," June said and handed the phone to Bess.

"Virginia Jane, honey, are you sitting down?" Bess asked her.

"No, I'm not. Why are you asking me that? What's wrong?"

"Please, honey, humor your mother and sit down. Tell me when you have."

Virginia Jane sat in an overstuffed chair next to the table, where she kept her phone. "Okay, I'm sitting," she said, dreading what might come next from her mother.

"Your brother Ricky has been injured. He's not in critical condition, but his wounds are serious. He's in a hospital in Belgium, but the Army says he will be flown to the Walter Reed Army Medical Center when he is well enough. They have to fix his arm there."

"What's wrong with his arm?" Virginia Jane asked.

Bess covered the receiver and asked Mike if he would mind telling Virginia Jane about Ricky.

He said, "Sure."

"I'll put Mike on the phone. He talked to the Army and can explain it better," Bess said. She handed the phone to Mike.

"It's Mike, Virginia Jane," Mike said as Bess sat back down on the couch with June.

"Hi, Mike, what's wrong with Ricky's arm?" Virginia Jane asked.

"A bullet struck his arm and shattered some of the bones. The Army is sending him to Walter Reed Hospital because they have the best reconstructive surgeons in the world."

"Thank you for telling me, Mike, and welcome to the family. Take good care of my little sister," she said.

*****

M/Sgt. Lloyd Taylor stopped his jeep at the entrance to the 107th Evacuation Hospital near Bastogne. The Evacuation Hospital was in a two-story building that was damaged, but still standing. He was on a three-day pass from his outfit, Company D, Thirty-Seventh Tank Battalion. The battalion was in reserve and being refitted for the push into Germany. The division chaplain notified him his brother was wounded and arranged the compassionate pass so Lloyd could visit his brother.

A tired, wan nurse's aide at reception said, "What can I do for you, Sergeant?"

"I'm here to see my brother, Sergeant Richard Taylor with the 101st."

The aide checked through a row of clipboards hanging behind her on hooks on the wall and found the one she was looking for.

"He's on the second floor in the heroes' ward," she told him.

"What the hell is the heroes' ward?" he asked.

"It's just a nickname the nurses gave to the ward where the soldiers who have been decorated for valor are treated," she said.

"You mean you have to get a medal to get on a ward here?" he asked in astonishment.

"Just that ward, and you have to have a good chance of recovery. We're overwhelmed with casualties. We save our efforts for the wounded who are the most likely to make it. It's called triage."

"What does medals have to do with that?" he asked. He looked around him. There were wounded in litters coming in and out of the hospital in waves.

"Look, Sergeant, just be happy your brother made the cut. He's scheduled to be air evac'd to England tomorrow and then on to the States.

"Okay, can I see him?" Lloyd asked.

She pointed toward the stairs and said, "Stand aside for the litter bearers."

He walked toward the stairs, dodging the medics bringing in wounded. The smell of blood and infection was pervasive, and many of the wounded had lost control of their bowels and bladders. The medical staff didn't have time for that. He worked his way up the stairs. Litter bearers were bringing a different kind of casualty down the steps covered with bloody sheets or blankets. The hospital had long since run out of body bags. These casualties would be turned over to the grave registration troops.

Lloyd had thought the war couldn't shock him anymore. He was wrong. When he got to the second floor, he walked into the open ward and stopped a nurse.

"I'm looking for my brother, Sgt. Richard Taylor," he said to the nurse.

"He's the third from the far end on the right-hand side. He's in a body cast," she told him.

"How's he doing?" M/Sgt. Taylor asked her.

"He's a lot better than most of our patients. He's up here on the second floor, and he's leaving here tomorrow or the next day," she said, snapping at him.

Like all the other doctors, nurses, and medical staff he'd seen, she was near exhaustion.

"Thank you, nurse. You all have a hell of a tough job to do," he said.

He walked down the center aisle of the ward until he got near the end. Ricky was supported by an apparatus with a harness to keep his arm in the proper position. There was an IV stand and tubes running down into his right arm. He had a half upper-body cast that extended down his left arm. There was an assortment of dressings on his chest and side. He was propped up in the bed with pillows behind his back and appeared to be sleeping or dozing. Lloyd walked up to the side of the bed and looked down at his brother.

A doctor stopped in the aisle and came over to Lloyd.

"Can I help you, Sergeant?" he asked.

Lloyd saw the captain's bars on his collar.

"He's my brother, Doctor. Is it okay to wake him up?" Lloyd asked.

"Sure, but don't stay too long. He needs all the rest he can get. He will be groggy. He had a shot of morphine an hour ago."

"What's in the IV bags?"

The doctor looked at the chart at the foot of the bed. "He's getting fluids and penicillin to fight infection. His blood loss has been stabilized."

"Why is he in all that plaster?" Lloyd watched Ricky's face, but he still had his eyes closed.

"He had a severe bullet wound to his left arm. It shattered bones in the upper arm. We're keeping it immobilized until he can be transferred back to the States, where we hope they can save his arm. Usually, it would have been amputated already, but he has priority status. He's been nominated for an award of the Silver Star Medal and a Purple Heart, of course." The doctor gently touched Ricky's cheek and said, "Wake up, Sergeant. You have a visitor."

Ricky opened his eyes and looked sleepily at Lloyd. "Hi, there, brother," he muttered.

"You look like King Tut," Lloyd said. "What's all this shit about you trying to be a fucking hero?"

"Where do you keep getting all the extra stripes, Master Sergeant?" Ricky asked.

"I get them at the PX for a quarter apiece. What the hell happened to you?" Lloyd asked.

"A sniper got me, probably a .50-caliber sniper round. It did too much damage for a .30 caliber," Ricky said.

"What about all the patches on your chest? You look like a quilt."

"Grenade fragments," Ricky said. "Most of them ended up in the side of a well, or I wouldn't still be alive." Ricky's eyes drooped.

The doctor said to Lloyd, "That's probably enough, Sergeant. He really needs to rest."

"You're going home, little brother. You pay attention to the doctors and nurses and no more hero crap, hear me?"

Ricky didn't respond.

"He's really going to be air evacuated back to the States, sir?" Lloyd asked the doctor.

"He and ten other decorated men are going. Your brother saved the life of one of his squad members after he got the grenade wounds. He was under fire from a machine gun at the time."

"Well, damn," Lloyd said and turned away so the doctor couldn't see the tears welling up in his eyes. *You're a better man than me, little brother*, he thought. Litter bearers were draping a sheet over one of the patients as he walked by. Being a hero hadn't helped that guy much.

11

It's a hell of a shame about Ricky, Mike thought as he drove to pick up Don at Rosecrans Field Sunday morning. The damn war in Europe will be over soon, and he got hit now after surviving all the fights the 101st has been in.

June tried to enjoy their dinner out after they got back to St. Joe from her parents' farm, but she had a hard time holding back her tears. She had held herself together for her parents and her siblings, but her worry caught up with her when she was alone with Mike.

After dinner, they went back to her apartment. Mike had to leave first thing in the morning to meet Don, so they went to bed early. June was emotionally exhausted, and Mike held her until she went to sleep. He soon followed her. It had been a long day for him too.

Mike got up early Sunday morning and gulped a cup of coffee and wolfed down the toast a sleepy June made for him while he was shaving, showering, and getting dressed. He kissed her and hurried out the door. He just made it to the main gate at Rosecrans field at 0800.

After he dropped Mike off at the train depot, Don drove to Betty's parents' house. Mike told him about June's brother on the drive to the depot.

Tough luck for him and his family, Don thought. But maybe he'll be okay. At least he's not coming home in one of those cheap boxes or body bags, like a lot of my buddies in the Pacific. It was a harsh thought, but prolonged combat sucked things like compassion out of you. It was slow to come back.

Don found the address and parked down the street in an open spot. Nice neighborhood. There's a big Methodist Church on the corner. He rang the bell.

Betty's father opened the door and looked inquiringly at Don. "Yes?" he said to the good-looking young man dressed in pressed jeans and a blue button-down collar shirt under his winter coat.

"Sir, my name is Don Walker. I'm a friend of Betty's. Her friend, June, told me about Betty's illness. And I came by to see her. I hope I'm not intruding."

"Who is at the door, Ray?" Kate asked and looked past him at Don.

Ray turned his head and said to Kate. "It's a young man who says he is a friend of Betty's."

"My name is Don Walker, and you must be Betty's mother?" Don said.

"My goodness! Why are we letting Mr. Walker stand out in the cold? Come in, young man," Kate said.

Ray stepped back to let Don come in the house.

"Come in and sit down in the living room, Mr. Walker. Would you like something to drink? I just made coffee," Kate said.

Ray and Don took their seats in the matching upholstered chairs in the living room opposite the large floral sofa. There was a carved walnut coffee table in front of the sofa and matching end tables next to the chairs.

"Please call me Don, Mrs. Anderson, and I'd love some coffee. With cream and sugar, please."

"Then you must call me Kate, Don, and this is Betty's father, Ray."

"I'm pleased to meet you both," Don said.

When Kate left to get the coffee, Don asked Ray, "How is Betty doing?"

"I've been better. What are you doing here?" Betty's voice came from the bottom of the stairs. She had heard voices downstairs when she woke up from a nap. She came into the living room just as Don asked about her.

"I'm here to see you. I just dropped Mike off at the train depot," Don said. "Come sit down on the sofa. You look unsteady on your feet."

Betty sat down next to him.

"You do look a little pale, honey," Ray said. "Maybe you shouldn't be out of bed."

"I'm tired of being in bed," Betty said. "I'm glad you came, Don."

"Here's the coffee," Kate said, bringing in a tray with a silver carafe of coffee, cups, spoons, and a cream pitcher and sugar bowl.

Don got up to help her with the tray.

"Just put it on the coffee table, Don. Everyone can help themselves," Kate said and then turned to her daughter. "Betty, should you be up?"

"I'm okay for a little while, Mom. I want to visit with Don. He came all the way from the airfield to see me."

"Ray, we should let the young people visit. Get your coffee and come into the kitchen with me," Kate said.

In the living room, Betty told Don what happened to her.

"I saw the doctor on Friday. He told me to rest for a week, so I came home with Mom," Betty told Don. "I'd kiss you, but I don't know if I'm contagious. I feel like crap, and I'm bored stiff."

"I should have brought my guitar and entertained you. Next time, I will," Don said.

"How's your new song going?" Betty asked.

"It's going pretty good. The lyrics are done. I'm still working on the melody."

"How did Mike and June's engagement announcement go over with her family?" Betty asked him.

"He said it went great," Don said. Don didn't tell her about Ricky. She was feeling bad enough without that.

They talked about Mike and June and their wedding plans and June's family. Don told her about his new job as cadre at the airfield, and Betty told him how she'd helped her boss with his paperwork. Soon, Betty started looking tired.

Don said, "I think we should let you get back to bed. I'll come again next weekend, and we can go out if you're feeling better. I'll call you Friday night."

"That sounds like a plan. Go say goodbye to my folks," Betty said.

Don went to the kitchen to tell her parents he was happy to meet them and that he would call Betty on Friday night to see how she was doing. Kate said he was welcome to come and see Betty and they all said their goodbyes.

Don went back to Betty and held her hand and kissed her forehead.

"Rest up and get well, babe," he said. "I'll talk to you on Friday."

*****

On Monday morning, Betty called the ordnance plant and asked to be transferred to Joe Harding's line.

"Mr. Harding's office, Marlene speaking," a voice answered.

"Marlene, hi. This is Betty. I need to talk with Joe," Betty said.

"Betty, how are you doing?" Marlene asked.

"Not too good. I've got an infection, and my doctor says I need to rest for a week. Can you put me through to Joe?"

"Sure, hold on."

Marlene put the line on hold and pushed the intercom button. "Joe, Betty's on line one for you," she said.

Joe put down the report he was reading. His in-tray was full again. "Betty, how are you? When are you coming back to work?"

"My doctor said I have an infection and need to rest and stay in bed this week. I see him again this Friday. Hopefully, I can return to work next Monday. I'll call you on Friday after I see my doctor."

"Take care of yourself. I need you back as soon as you're well. I'll notify personnel so they can put you on sick leave," Joe said.

"Thanks, Joe. You're a peach," Betty said and hung up.

Joe pushed the button on his intercom and said, "Come in for a minute please, Marlene."

Marlene came into Joe's office with a notepad and pencil.

"Fill out a sick leave form for Betty, and I'll sign it. Then send it up to personnel. Make it out from last Friday through this Friday."

*****

In Belgium, litter bearers were unloading Army Dodge ambulances lined up at a landing strip. Eighteen litter patients were being loaded on one of the Douglas C-47 Skytrain medical evacuation flights to London. This Skytrain was a two-engine transport configured for medical evacuations. It was the workhorse of the Medical Air Evacuation Transport Squadrons. It was used for shorter flights between forward landing strips and hospitals. Sgt. Richard Taylor was one of the eighteen litter patients on board. Fortunately, the Allies now controlled the skies over Belgium, and the German fighter threat was gone. When the last litter was loaded and secured, one of the medics closed and locked the entry door. Shortly afterward, the pilot got his takeoff clearance from the makeshift control tower and rumbled down the dirt runway. Ricky would be in London by that afternoon. His transfer orders entitled him to hook up with another medical evacuation flight at London Airport.

After the Douglas C-47 landed in London, the litter patients were unloaded and distributed to another line of Army ambulances. Most of the patients had been sedated. Sergeant Taylor's litter was placed in an Army ambulance and driven across the field to the taxiway for several Douglas C-54 Skymaster transports. The C-54 Skymaster was the four-engine long-range Douglas transport that the Army Transport Command used for transoceanic flights.

As Ricky was loaded on the C-54, he started to regain consciousness. The pain in his left arm was excruciating, and he screamed. The litter bearers put his litter down on the rack and secured it as quickly as they could. Then a medic on the flight administered a shot of morphine, and Ricky faded back into unconsciousness. Ricky wasn't the only litter case needing this relief. It took another two hours for all the assigned patients to show up and be loaded. Finally, the Skymaster was buttoned up and cleared to taxi. Despite the primitive accommodations (litters were stacked on metal racks, three high on each side of the fuselage with a narrow aisle down the middle), the medical flights lost very few lives in transport. The medical and nursing crews did a heroic job caring for their patients that were usually the most seriously wounded. Most of the deaths that did occur resulted from plane crashes or enemy action against the flights. Sergeant Taylor, after intermediate fueling stops, would be in Washington, DC, Tuesday night.

*****

When June got home from work at Quaker Oats, she made two phone calls. The first was to Betty; the second, to find out about Ricky. Betty had not improved. She had no appetite, and her mother said she was looking thinner. She had a low-grade fever most of the day. They were going back to her doctor on Friday.

On the second call, the night nurse on the desk at Walter Reed was reluctant to discuss a patient's status. She took down June's personal information and suggested June call next day to get authorization to speak to the night nursing desk.

At lunch break the next day, June called Walter Reed and finally got through to a patient relations person, a medical corps captain, Captain Swain. The captain called Ricky's ward on another line and got his status. Ricky was scheduled for surgery on his arm the next day. They had to stabilize him after his arduous flights before they could do the surgery. His shrapnel wounds were healing normally, with no infections.

June explained she worked days and needed to call after hours and asked who she could contact for further updates. Captain Swain said he would give June's name to the head of nursing to instruct the night desk to give her updates when she called. June thanked him.

"You don't have to thank me. Your brother is a hero. We'll do what we can for you and your family and, of course, your brother. If you need to add any other family members to our call lists, just give me their names."

"What do you mean, my brother is a hero?" June asked.

"He's going to get the Silver Star Medal for valor in combat. He saved the life of one of his squad members," Captain Swain said. "There will be an official presentation of his decorations when the doctors think he is up to it. He's getting the Purple Heart Medal too."

"You've been very kind, Captain. I'll pass on updates to my family. I'm sure you are all very busy."

"It's absolutely all right, Miss Taylor. Call as often as you like. Your brother couldn't get better care than our doctors and nursing staff."

"Goodbye, Captain," June said and hung up. She immediately called her mother and updated her on Ricky's condition.

"Captain Swain told me Ricky is a hero. They're giving him some medals for saving another soldier's life," June said.

"Just a minute, honey. I want you to tell your father about this. Dee, come to the phone!" Bess hollered.

Dee came into the living room from the den, where he had been paying bills.

"What is it?" Dee asked Bess.

"Talk to June. She has more news about Ricky," Bess said. She handed him the phone.

"Hi, honey, what's up?" he asked.

"Ricky's in the Walter Reed Army Medical Center. He's having surgery on his arm tomorrow."

"The Army got him back here pretty fast," Dee observed.

"Captain Swain at Walter Reed told me that Ricky is a hero and will get some medals."

"What did he do to get medals?" Dee asked. He sat down in one of the living room chairs. Bess sat on the sofa.

"All I know is he saved the life of one of his men," June said.

"What medal is he getting?" Dee asked.

"The Silver something and a Purple something," June said.

"A Silver Star and a Purple Heart?"

"Yes, I think that's what the captain said."

Dee looked at Bess and said, "Our son is getting the third highest award they give for valor in combat. They don't give that out with the Wheaties." He handed the phone back to Bess.

*****

Major Reston, the chief orthopedic surgeon at Walter Reed Hospital, studied the chart and X-rays of Sgt. Richard Taylor. He was discussing Sergeant Taylor's case with the head of surgery, Lieutenant Colonel Masters.

"Whoever immobilized his arm in Belgium gave us a fighting chance. That cast was hideously ugly, but it did the trick. I see very little secondary damage. And there's no sign of gangrene or infection," Major Reston said.

"Yes, but the humerus was almost severed, not to mention the other bone damage. And we haven't even talked about nerve damage," Lieutenant Colonel Masters said.

"You're right. He needs three surgeries to save his arm. And making the arm work will be a long process of physical therapy, if it ever does work. But God knows how many man hours and critical resources have gone into trying to let this guy keep his arm. I will not be the one who throws in the towel," Major Reston said.

"Don't you think we should ask the patient first and let him know what he will be in for?" Colonel Masters said.

"I did ask him, and I laid the pain and suffering on thick, if he goes ahead with it."

"And what did he say?"

"He looked me in the eye and told me he came into this hospital with two arms, and he expected to leave the same way, whatever it took. He's got the guts for this if I do."

"Okay, Doctor, he's your patient," the colonel said.

*****

The past week June had started working directly with the three line supervisors on her packing lines. She was amazed at how much the direct communication helped her scheduling process. Two of the supervisors were quick to see the value of helping June produce workable schedules and anticipate problems the line may be facing. They still had to meet their quotas but rearranging the sequence of product changeovers could often make that goal easier to obtain.

The third supervisor, Mr. Jennings, was another matter.

"I don't have time to spend sitting in an office and jawing with you," he said. "Just do your job and send down the production orders."

Cheryl told June to see the packing manager about him.

"I don't want to get a reputation as a snitch. I knew he wouldn't want anyone encroaching on his territory. I know him from when I was working the line next to his," June said. "The other two lines are doing better since we started working closer with each other. Maybe he'll come around."

"It is a good idea, and I'm going to tell our supervisor about it. I won't say anything about Mr. Jennings," Cheryl said.

After lunch, June was working at her desk when Cheryl came up to her and said, "Tim wants to see you."

"Tim Sullivan, our boss?" June asked.

"Yes, in his office," Cheryl said.

A few minutes later, June knocked on Tim Sullivan's office door and went in.

"You wanted to see me, Mr. Sullivan?" she asked.

Mr. Sullivan looked like her high school chemistry teacher. He was a lanky six-footer with a wild tangle of ginger-colored hair streaked with gray. He wore a bright-blue sleeveless wool sweater-vest over a rumpled white shirt. A gaudy bow tie completed the picture. He peered at her through black horn-rimmed glasses.

"Call me Tim," he said.

Tim Sullivan liked to be on a first name basis with his subordinates.

"Have a seat. Cheryl told me about your idea to coordinate with your packing line supervisors. How's that going?" Tim asked.

June sat down in the guest chair. "I think it's going well. It's helping me send down better sequenced production orders. The supervisors say it is helping them meet their quotas," June said.

"All the supervisors?" Tim asked knowingly.

"Most of them," June said vaguely.

"Well, anyway, I like the idea. And so does the packing department manager. We're going to meet with him and discuss it. Then you will write an SOP (standard operating procedure).

June was bowled over. "I wouldn't know where to begin," she objected.

Tim leaned back in his chair and appraised June's reaction. Then he tried to reassure her.

"It sounds a lot more complicated than it is. Really, all you'll be doing is saying who meets with whom, how often, and about what. That's it. I'll help you with the SOP format. All we're trying to do is improve the communication and coordination between the departments. You're already doing it."

"Should I keep on doing it?" June asked.

"You bet. You're the test case. Keep up the good work."

*****

Kate took Betty to see Dr. Leyland on Friday.

After his examination, he said, "The fever, the lack of appetite, and general malaise lead me to believe you may have influenza, Betty. I'm going to put you on a course of penicillin tablets. Continue taking aspirin for the fever. Kate, Betty must immediately be quarantined. No visitors. If you need help with nursing, call my office and we'll arrange it. If you or Ray develop symptoms, call me at once. I will come see her next Friday at home. So far, her fever has been relatively mild. If the fever gets worse, take her to the hospital.

"Betty, you must try harder to take in nourishment. Kate, give her lots of rich chicken soup and anything else she can keep down. If she doesn't improve next week, I'm going to have her go into the hospital for some tests."

"Are we going to have those quarantine labels stuck on our house?" Kate asked.

"No. Right now I'm ordering quarantine as a precaution. If we go ahead with tests and they come back positive for influenza, then I am required to notify the health department. First, let's see how you do on the penicillin, Betty. I'm going to give you an injection to give you the starting dose of penicillin."

Penicillin had proven effective against bacterial infections and would stop secondary infections if Betty's illness was viral.

When they got home, Betty asked her mother to call her boss, Joe Harding, at the ordnance plant and tell him she wouldn't be back at work next week either. Then she went to bed.

Kate called the ordnance plant number and told Mr. Harding's secretary about Betty's situation. The girl, Marlene, said she would inform Mr. Harding.

*****

Don was in his barracks at the end of his duty day, Friday. He changed into his civvies and got on the pay phone in the hall.

"Hello," Kate answered the phone.

"Hello, this is Don. Can I speak with Betty, please?"

"I'm sorry, but she's asleep right now. We just got back from the doctor's office," Kate said on the phone.

"What did the doctor say? How is she?" Don asked.

"Dr. Leyland thinks she might have the flu. If so, she is contagious. He's quarantined her," Kate said. "And she can't see anyone except me."

"For how long?" Don asked.

"Until he sees her next Friday. He's going to do a house call here and will decide then," Kate said.

"How's she feeling? Is she getting better?" Don asked.

"No, she's about the same. She has a low fever and is very tired all the time. I guess that is because of the flu. Dr. Leyland gave her a penicillin shot, and she has penicillin pills to take. We hope that will help her improve."

"Okay, please tell her I called, and I hope she feels better soon. I'll call again this weekend if that's okay?" Don said.

"That's fine. I'll tell her you called, Don," Kate said.

I'm worried, Don thought. *I never really worried about a girl before. What's that all about?*

June got the same story from Kate when she called on Saturday morning. Kate said Betty was in quarantine. She was staying in her room and couldn't come to the phone.

"I'll tell her you called, June, and I'll see if we can get a line in her room. I'm going to call the phone company on Monday. She needs to talk to her friends."

"Okay, I'll call back later in the week, or she can call me after I get home from work when she has a phone available," June said.

When Kate hung up, June called the nurses' station on Ricky's floor and talked to the nurse.

"Sergeant Taylor had his first surgery on his arm yesterday. He is back in his room and out of intensive care. He is scheduled to have his second surgery in two weeks when he has recovered from the first," the nurse said.

"How many surgeries is he having?" June snapped at her, distressed by this news.

"Miss Taylor, I can only tell you what is in his chart. It indicates he is scheduled for a second operation on his arm in two weeks. I'm sorry if I have upset you. But it looks like he's doing as well as could be expected at this stage. I'll make a note in his chart to have Captain Swain call you on Monday with a more complete update."

June gave the nurse her telephone numbers at home and work.

"I'm usually home by 6:00 p.m.," June said. "I'm sorry I was rude to you."

"I understand, Miss Taylor. You're just worried about your brother. I'm putting your contact information in his chart. You should hear from Captain Swain Monday."

"Thank you," June said.

On Monday, the nursing office notified Captain Swain about Miss Taylor's call. He caught up with Major Reston on the major's rounds.

"Sergeant Taylor's surgery went even better than I hoped. We repaired the humerus, and it looked like he has good circulation in his arm. We hope that enough nerves were undamaged to give him reasonable function. He still has damage to other bones in his arm that need to be addressed. We couldn't keep him under anesthesia any longer, but we knew that going in. He will need two more surgeries, but that hopefully will be it. They should not be as involved as the first one, and we are optimistic at this point, barring any complications," Major Reston said.

"Thank you, sir. I will communicate that to his family. They are very concerned. His sister seems to be the primary family contact, so I'll call her today," Captain Swain said. "Also, sir, the Awards Branch would like to arrange to present Sergeant Taylor with his decorations when he is up to it."

"Let's hold off on that until we see how he recovers," Major Reston said. "That probably means not this week."

"Yes, sir, I'll inform the awards people."

The phone rang at 6:00 p.m., shortly after June got home from work.

"Hello," she answered.

"Hello, this is Captain Swain with Walter Reed Army Medical Center. Can I please speak to Miss June Taylor?"

"This is June Taylor," June said. She sat down at the kitchen table with the phone.

"Miss Taylor, I am pleased to report that your brother came through his surgery very well. I spoke with Major Reston, his surgeon, who said the large bone in his arm, his humerus, was successfully repaired. Your brother's arm has good blood circulation and partial restoration of function is likely. There is still considerable damage to be repaired, so a second surgery is scheduled in two weeks if your brother is sufficiently recovered from this surgery. Are there other family members you would like me to call with this update?"

"No, thank you, Captain Swain. I am keeping them informed," June said. "Goodbye and thank you for your call."

June immediately called her brother, John in Washington, DC. John lived in a Virginia suburb across the Potomac River from Washington. His house was near the new Pentagon building.

John was in his office at home, eating a hasty dinner as he studied forecasted requirements for blood and plasma to support the upcoming Pacific campaign against the home islands of Japan.

War Department planners in the Pentagon building were expecting very heavy casualties in that campaign, which meant the need for a vastly increased supply chain of medical equipment and medical supplies of all kinds. John was working twelve-hour days alongside a G-4 brigadier general, a supply and logistics officer, and his staff.

"Hello, this is John Taylor," he answered his phone.

"John, this is June. I just spoke with Captain Swain at the Walter Reed Army Medical Center about Ricky. He had surgery on his arm last Friday. His surgeon, a Major Reston, said the surgery went well. But there is still a lot of damage to repair, so Ricky will have a second surgery in about two weeks."

"Can he have visitors?" John asked.

"I didn't ask Captain Swain about visitors, but I imagine he can. I have Captain Swain's telephone number and extension, so you can find out." June read off the numbers to John.

"How are you doing, sis?" John asked her.

"I feel better now Ricky is back here in the US, and his doctor is optimistic about his chances to recover use of his arm. I was very scared for a while there."

"I'll try to see him on Saturday if they allow visitors. I'll call you after I see him," John said.

"How are you doing, John? How's Marge?" June asked.

"I'm busy as hell. We're gearing up for the push in the Pacific. I'm very worried about the men who will have that fight. The casualty estimates are frightening. Marge is fine, except we rarely see each other. She volunteers at Red Cross blood drives, and I can hardly get out of that new five-sided monstrosity they opened last year. I still get lost in the maze of corridors in that place."

"Maybe the Japanese will surrender," June said.

"I'm afraid their emperor and generals don't know how to surrender. Anyway, I must get back to work. I'll call you Saturday, June."

*****

"Eyes right!" the class cadet sergeant commanded, and the guidon bearer dipped the unit flag in salute as the unit passed the reviewing stand. The officers and the NCOs in the stand returned the unit salute.

Sgt. Mike Taylor was in his class A uniform and stood at attention in the reviewing stand while his class of recruits paraded by.

"Eyes front!" the cadet sergeant commanded after they cleared the stand.

The class made a column left movement, another column left movement, and marched back in formation to the front of the reviewing stand.

"Column, halt! Left face!"

The class was now in three ranks, facing the reviewing stand.

Captain Benson, the school commander, shouted, "Attention to orders. Class number 568-Zulu has successfully completed course number 134–53 and course 245–22, basic infantry training and basic radioman training, and has graduated on this date. Congratulations, men. Dismissed!"

The class threw their caps in the air and roared, whooped, and hollered. It had been a tough ten weeks. There was a lot of rowdy hugging and backslapping.

"Well, that's it," Captain Benson said to Mike and the other cadre. "That's the last class of recruits."

"What do we do now, skipper?" one of the training sergeants asked.

"I'm going to have a beer. The rest of you can pick up your weekend passes in the orderly room from M/Sgt. Torres. Report to my office on Monday morning at 0900. Well done, all of you."

*****

Dr. Leyland completed his morning appointments on Friday and closed his office early after lunch, giving his staff a long weekend. He drove over to the Anderson home and parked in their driveway.

Kate opened the front door and greeted him.

"Thank you so much for making this house call. Betty hasn't gotten any better. I'm very worried."

"Well, let's have a look at her," he said.

He exchanged greetings with Ray and followed Kate up the stairs to Betty's room. His first impression was that she looked gaunt and listless. She was losing weight.

"Has she been eating?" he asked Kate. He sat on the edge of the bed and studied Betty.

She seemed to focus on him and said, "Hello, Dr. Leland. I'm not feeling very well."

Kate said, "She takes a little soup now and then, but I can't get her to eat much else. The pills don't seem to be helping."

Dr. Leland took her blood pressure and pulse and examined her eyes, nose, and throat. He listened to her heart and lungs, then he palpated her abdomen.

"Are you experiencing any pain?" he asked Betty.

"No, I just feel tired all the time, and I'm not hungry. I have to force myself to eat."

"Okay, you just rest. I'm going to talk with your mother."

Dr. Leyland took Kate out into the hall and closed the door.

"I don't like the way she looks. Except for the low-grade fever, she doesn't have a classic influenza presentation. If it was flu, she should be responding better by now. I want you to get her dressed. I'm going to admit her to St. Joseph Medical Center for some tests, and I want to get some nourishment in her. Pack a small bag with her toilet articles and underwear. She may be there for a few days. We must get control of whatever she has. I'll call the hospital and arrange for her to be admitted. Take her there this afternoon as soon as you can get her ready, or I can call an ambulance."

"No, Ray and I will take her. Do you think this is something serious, Doctor?" Kate asked.

"I don't want alarm you or Betty. But it's better to be safe than sorry. We'll know a lot more after we get back the tests I've ordered. In the meantime, they can get fluids and nourishment in her with an IV. She needs both. Let's go back in and talk with her."

Dr. Leyland explained to Betty, "Betty, I'm concerned about your lack of improvement. I need you to be tested so we can figure out what's happening and start getting you better."

Betty said, "What kind of tests?"

"Blood tests, primarily. We need you to go to the hospital for a few days until we get control of your illness," he said.

"I don't have the flu?"

"It's still possible that you do. The tests will tell us for sure. Once we know what's happening, we can do a better job of fighting whatever you have."

"Mom, do I have to go to the hospital?" Betty asked, frightened at the prospect.

"It's just a precaution, honey. We don't want you to get worse. The tests will help the doctor find out what's wrong with you. I'll pack you a bag, and your father and I will take you to the hospital. Come on, let's get you dressed," Kate told her.

"I'll be downstairs with Ray," Dr. Leyland said and left the room.

Ray and Kate checked Betty into the hospital for her tests later that day and stayed with her until she went to sleep. This was the first time any of their family had been in a hospital, as Kate had given birth to Betty in her home. Kate wept as they left the hospital.

On the way home, she said to Ray, "I need to call Betty's work and let them know what's going on with her."

*****

Franklin Delano Roosevelt was being inaugurated president of the United States of America. No previous holder of that office had been inaugurated more than twice, but it was Mr. Roosevelt's fourth time.

While John visited his brother, Ricky, in the Walter Reed Army Medical Center in Washington DC, a huge crowd of journalists,

VIPs, and the public spread out on the lawn in front of the portico of the White House. Only Mr. Roosevelt's wife, his doctors, and his closest advisors knew how fragile his health was on this day.

Sgt. Richard Taylor was in a semiprivate room with a T/Sgt. Randall, who was asleep when John arrived. T/ Sgt, Randall had a cast on his right leg. Ricky was awake and reading an outdated copy of the *Reader's Digest*.

"Improving your mind, I see," John said. He pulled a guest chair up to Ricky's bed and sat in it.

"Yeah, I'm reading the Humor in Uniform page. I needed a laugh," Ricky said and chuckled. He laid the magazine down next to him on the bed.

Ricky's arm was in a cast, but the chest section of the cast was gone. He thanked God when he woke up and found it missing. The itching under that cast had driven him nuts. He still itched under the arm cast, but he had talked a janitor into sneaking him a wire coat hanger. Once he unhooked and straightened it out, he could reach the itchy spots and scratch them. Sometimes he thought the relief was better than sex. Yesterday, the attending doctor had dialed down his pain medicine and Ricky was alert.

"I brought you some things," John said and handed Ricky a paper bag.

"I hope it's a pint of Jack Daniels," Ricky said. "Or a girly magazine."

"Maybe next time," John said. "I didn't know how much stimulation they let you have."

"Not very much, and my nurse looks like a Notre Dame linebacker," Ricky said with a laugh. He flinched at a pain in his side and said, "Don't make me laugh. The stitches are still there in a few places." Ricky opened the paper bag and took out a deck of playing cards and a small booklet entitled *101 Games of Solitaire*. "I'm going to have to learn how to shuffle one handed for a while. Hey thanks, brother. I'm really bored in here, at least until the radio programs come on at night. My roommate's wife brought him a radio. We listen to the Lone Ranger, Ozzie and Harriet, Sam Spade, the Phantom—all the good stuff."

Two soldiers in Class A dress uniforms appeared at the door to Ricky's room.

"May we break into your visit? We won't take long, I promise," the major said.

The other man was Staff Sergeant MacAfee, who had a chest full of decorations and badges. Sergeant MacAfee wore the four stripes of his rank and a Big Red One patch of the First Infantry Division on his right shoulder.

This guy has a CIB (Combat Infantry Badge) and a Silver Star mixed in with his "I was there" campaign ribbons. He's been there and done that, Ricky thought.

Ricky also noted the Purple Heart ribbon among the fruit salad decorations on his chest.

The major looked like a rear-echelon type. His decorations were of the "I was there" variety.

"What is your business with my brother?" John asked them, getting up from his chair. John resented the interruption and was concerned the Army may be changing its plans for Ricky's treatment.

"What is your name, sir?" the major asked John respectfully and stepped into the room along with Sergeant MacAfee.

"My name is John Taylor, Major. Again, what is your business here?"

"Would you please stand alongside your brother's bed?" the major said. He stood next to Sergeant MacAfee on the other side of the bed.

"Relax, John. I know why these men are here. Please make this short and sweet, Major," Ricky said.

The major read from a copy of orders.

"Attention to orders: Sergeant Richard D. Taylor, RA 16657392, then commanding 3rd squad of the 1st Platoon, 2nd Battalion. 506th Regiment, 101st Airborne Division engaged a German force estimated to be at least platoon size in the area near Recogne, Belgium. Sergeant Taylor's squad, then in Company reserve, was ambushed by the German force, taking casualties to three of Sergeant Taylor's squad. Ignoring a hail of machine gun and small arms fire, Sergeant Taylor left the building where his remaining squad had taken cover and ran to a well in the village center where his three squad members had gone down. In the process of lifting one of his men, Sergeant Taylor suffered wounds from a hand grenade. Ignoring his wounds and concussion from the explosion, Sergeant Taylor dragged his man toward the building sheltering his squad. Sergeant Taylor was again wounded by sniper fire, and ignoring this wound, Sergeant Taylor dragged his man into the shelter of the building and collapsed from his wounds. His actions saved the life of his squad member and inspired another member of his squad, who saved the second wounded man at the well.

"Sergeant Taylor's actions were above and beyond the call of duty. His heroism, valor, and leadership characteristics are in the finest tradition of the United States Army and reflect great credit upon him and upon the military service. Entered the military service from Missouri."

After the major read the citation, he said, "You are hereby awarded the Silver Star Medal, the Purple Heart Medal, and the Combat Infantry Badge. Congratulations, Sergeant Taylor."

Sergeant MacAfee pinned the decorations to the pillow next to Sergeant Taylor's head and said, "Well done, paratrooper." He put the medal boxes and ribbons on the night table next to Ricky's bed.

The major and Sergeant MacAfee saluted Ricky and left his room.

John's eyes watered, and he said, "Good job, little brother. I'm very proud of you."

"I earned the CIB and the Purple Heart. I'm not so sure about the Silver Star," Ricky said.

"Didn't you do what that citation said?" John asked.

"Yes and no. I went out with Franklin to get my guys. That's the only brave thing I did. Franklin should have got the medal. He didn't get shot because he was faster and stronger than me. He saved Collins's life. Everything happened so fast, I really don't remember very much after the grenade went off." Ricky turned his head to look at the medals and the CIB. "At least, I earned the CIB. That really means something."

"How's your arm?" John asked. He reached over and picked up the sealed deck of cards and started tearing off the cellophane wrap.

"It itches like crazy. Major Reston says it looked better than he thought it would when he opened it up," Ricky said.

John finished opening the deck of cards and took them out of the box. He separated out the two jokers and started shuffling the deck.

"Did they say how long you're going to be in here?"

He dealt cards to Ricky and himself on the tray table. He turned up the top card and set it down face up next to the deck on the table. It was the seven of diamonds.

"I'm afraid to ask. It's going to be at least a few weeks. They have one or two more surgeries, and then I'll have several weeks of physical therapy. What are you dealing?" Ricky asked.

"Gin rummy," John said. "I'm sorry you have such an ordeal to go through."

"Not me. I'm lucky I've still got the arm. Most guys wounded like me lost their arms in Belgium or France. That little piece of metal on the pillow got me home with my arm still attached. How do you expect me to hold and play my cards?" Ricky said.

"Look at them one at a time and arrange them on the table. Play them with your right hand. Suck it up, Sergeant," John said and laughed.

Ricky laughed too and flinched again. "I told you not to make me laugh," he said.

*****

John called June when he got home from Walter Reed.

"You won't believe what happened when I saw Ricky at Walter Reed."

"What happened? How was Ricky?" June asked.

"Ricky looked pretty good, considering. He came through his arm surgery okay. His surgeon thinks he has a good chance of recovering at least some function in his arm. Ricky's just happy he still has the arm. He said if he'd stayed in Belgium, he wouldn't have kept it."

"What was it I wouldn't believe?" June asked.

"While Ricky and I were talking, two soldiers came into his room. One of them was a major and the other one was a sergeant covered in ribbons and badges," John said.

"What did they want with Ricky?" June asked.

"That's what I asked them." John turned to Marge and said, sotto voce, "Make me a gin and tonic, honey."

"So what did they want?" June asked in exasperation.

"They were there to give Ricky some medals a Silver Star, a Purple Heart, and a Combat Infantry Badge."

"Captain Swain at Walter Reed told me Ricky would be awarded the medals. He said Ricky saved someone's life."

Marge handed John his drink. He took a big sip and said into the phone, "They read the citation that went with the Silver Star. It made Ricky sound like Audie Murphy. It choked me up."

"Why? What did he do?" June asked. "Wait a minute. I need to turn off the radio."

She set the phone on the table and went to turn off the Zenith. She returned to her chair and picked up the phone.

"I'm back," she said.

"June, it's long distance, for crying out loud!" John said. He looked at Marge and shrugged his shoulders.

"You're the one wasting time now. What did Ricky do?"

"The Germans ambushed his squad. Three men were hit by machine-gun fire and tried to hide behind a well in the village square. The rest of the squad took shelter in a building. Ricky and a guy named Franklin ran out of the building to try to rescue their men. Franklin got his guy and made it back to the building. When Ricky got to his guy, the Germans threw a hand grenade, which exploded and wounded Ricky. Ricky kept dragging the guy back to the build-ing. At the doorway, Ricky got shot in the arm by a sniper. Despite his wounds, Ricky got his guy inside. Both of the men they rescued recovered from their wounds."

"He saved a man's life and risked his own to do it," June said in wonder.

"Ricky said the only brave thing he did was going out of that building under the nose of a machine gun. I sure couldn't do something like that," John said.

"Me neither."

"I'll call Mom and Dad and tell them about my visit with Ricky at Walter Reed."

"I already mentioned Ricky's medals to Dad. But you can tell him about the write-up they read to you."

"It's called a citation," John said.

"You better hang up. The telephone company will get your next paycheck if you don't."

John said, "Okay, goodbye, sis."

12

On Monday, with the trainees gone, the Signal School at Camp Crowder looked deserted. Mike reported to the orderly room at 0900 as ordered.

M/Sgt. Torres directed Mike and another cadre sergeant to join their fellow cadre in the lecture room at the school. M/Sgt. Torres walked over with them and went in and sat down in the front row.

Captain Benson stood in front of the lectern and said, "The War Department is winding down the war footing we've been on. The Army will shrink as a result, and we are part of that. The Pentagon calls it a Reduction in Force, or RIF. At least for now, they're going to try to hold on to career NCOs. Each of you will meet with an S-1 (Personnel) sergeant who will explain your individual options to you. M/Sgt. Torres has the schedule of meetings. The meetings will be held at battalion headquarters from 1000 today through 1600 on Wednesday. Battalion will process your orders after these meetings. Until then, you are all confined to base, but at liberty until your meeting with S-1. Are there any questions?" Captain Benson asked.

"How do I stay in this chicken outfit?" one sergeant joked.

"You men have done an excellent job training a lot of men, many of whom are alive because of your training. I'm proud of the job we did here. I was privileged and honored to be your commanding officer. Good luck to you all," Captain Benson said.

"*Attent-hut!*" M/Sgt. Torres yelled.

The men came to their feet and stood at attention as Captain Benson walked out of the building. M/Sgt. Torres took his place at the front of the room.

"The meeting lists are posted in the orderly room. Well done all of you, and good luck. Dismissed," M/Sgt. Torres said.

There was a rush to the orderly room. There were four lists hanging on clipboards. Names were in alphabetical order. Mike waited until the T through Y clipboard was not in use. When he checked it, he discovered he was scheduled for his meeting with S-1 on Tuesday at 1300, which meant he had the rest of today and half of tomorrow with nothing to do.

I guess I'll go to the NCO club and shoot some pool. They've probably got it open now. They won't want all these guys wandering around the post. He perused the rest of the lists and found the names of the guys who had their meetings today. He'd catch up with them later and see what the deal was.

*****

Ray and Kate picked Betty up from the hospital. Her fever was gone. She was more alert and chatted with her parents in the car. Kate was glad they decided to put her into the hospital and anxious to get Betty's test results. The hospital said Dr. Leyland would call when he had the results.

Later in the day June telephoned; and Kate told her Betty was home from the hospital, awake, and could come downstairs to the phone.

"I'm feeling better, June," Betty said. "We are supposed to hear from Dr. Leyland when he gets the results of my tests."

"I'm glad you're home from the hospital and feeling better. I'll bring your car over to you after work tomorrow," June said.

"Oh, please don't do that. I'll be out sick from work all this week. Mom called my boss, and he extended my sick leave. The car would just be in the way here. Please keep it until I need it."

"Okay, I'll keep it, but you hurry up and get well. I miss you. Call me when the doctor gets your results," June said.

"Mom is signaling me to hang up and come to dinner. I miss you too, roomie."

"Okay, I'll come see you this weekend if you are still at your mom's house. Bye."

They both hung up. June didn't tell Betty about Rickie because Betty already had enough on her plate to deal with. She'd tell her when Betty was well.

*****

Monday afternoon, Mike checked with the cadre members that had met with S-1. The career guys were given new assignments. One of the noncareer sergeants told Mike he was given a choice of reenlisting or being discharged. He chose to be discharged.

"Even if I re-up, when the war is over, they're going to riff me. They'll have to riff lifers with a lot more time in service than me. They won't have any choice. I'm getting out now so I can get a good job before all the competition gets out and starts looking. You should do the same, Mike."

On Tuesday, Mike reported to battalion headquarters after he had lunch in the NCO mess hall. He was ten minutes early for his meeting at 1300 hours with the S-1 sergeant. He waited in the reception area.

The door to the S-1 office opened at 1305, and a sergeant came out. The battalion clerk told him to go in. He saw a master sergeant sitting behind the desk. There was a worktable set up next to the desk with piles of forms on it. There was a chair in front of the desk and one at the worktable. The rest of the office was bare. The flag stands were gone, along with the unit plaques on the walls. The desk and the credenza behind the desk were bare. The wind-down had already started.

"Come in and take a seat," the master sergeant said.

The white name tag above his right fatigue jacket pocket said Fenton. Mike didn't know him. M/Sgt. Fenton had a cloth representation of the Combat Infantry badge sewn above his left pocket. He had Signal Corps insignias on his collar points. That didn't make sense to Mike, as he knew the Signal Corps did not award CIBs. Mike wasn't about to ask M/Sgt. Fenton about the discrepancy. Instead, he sat down in front of M/Sgt. Fenton's desk.

"You are RA, Regular Army. Does that mean you are a career soldier?" M/Sgt. Fenton asked Mike.

"No, I enlisted after Pearl Harbor. I'm a civilian in uniform, Sergeant," Mike said.

"Okay. That makes everything simple for you. I have voluntary discharge papers for you to sign. You will be discharged for the convenience of the service. It's an honorable discharge. You'll be entitled to any veterans' benefits a grateful nation confers on veterans. Do you have any questions?" M/Sgt. Fenton asked.

"When will this happen? I'm engaged to be married," Mike asked.

"Congratulations on your engagement. You'll be out in the next week or two. It depends on how fast all this paperwork gets processed. In the meantime, you're assigned to temporary duty assisting POW administration."

"What the hell is POW administration?" Mike asked.

"As you probably already know, this camp is the happy home of two thousand or so German prisoners of war, mostly captured former tankers from Rommel's Corps in North Africa. Two thousand POWs need a lot of administration. You'll help with that until you get discharged to your home of record."

"Shit, Sergeant, I don't want to be a damned prison guard," Mike said.

"You've been in the Army four years, and you still don't know that the Army doesn't give a shit about what you do or do not want to do?" M/Sgt. Fenton said in mock amazement.

"Okay, okay. I can put up with anything for two weeks," Mike said.

"They won't make you a guard anyway. You need special training for that. You'll probably be pushing paper for two weeks. They're getting ready for the repatriation effort after the Krauts surrender. They're going to ship those prisoners back to the Fatherland as fast as possible and get them off Uncle Sam's books. Now do you have any other stupid questions?" M/Sgt. Fenton asked.

"What about pay?" Mike asked.

"You'll get a final pay for duty time spent after your last regular pay. And you'll get paid for any accrued leave you have left. You also get a travel allowance to your home of record. Spent this windfall wisely, my son," M/Sgt. Fenton joked. "Anything else before I lay the paperwork on you?"

"I don't want to offend you, but I'm curious about the CIB," Mike said.

"Yeah, it raises a lot of eyebrows. But I earned the son of a bitch, and I'm going to wear it. My Signal Company was attached to the Second Infantry Division just before the Normandy invasion. The division commanding general said, 'I don't give a shit what the fucking regulations say. Anyone who landed on Omaha beach with the Second Infantry Indianhead Division is getting a fucking CIB,' or so the story went. He issued the orders, and no one wanted to tell a major general he couldn't do it. There were some other awards like that with units or individuals attached to infantry units in battle."

"You were at Omaha beach, Sergeant?" Mike asked respectfully.

"Yeah, now let's get the paperwork done. I got a lot of guys to see today."

*****

"This is Dr. Leyland's nurse calling for Mrs. Anderson," the person on the other end said when Kate picked up the phone.

"This is Mrs. Anderson." Kate beckoned to Ray to come to the phone.

"Is that Dr. Leyland on the phone?" he asked Kate, but she motioned him to be still.

"Dr. Leyland would like to see you and your daughter, Betty, in the office at three this afternoon, if that would be convenient," the nurse said.

"Yes, we'll be in at 3:00 p.m." Kate said. "It's his nurse," she said to Ray when the call ended.

She went upstairs to Betty's room, where her daughter was napping after lunch.

"Betty, honey, wake up." Kate shook her shoulder gently.

"I'm awake, Mom," she said and turned her legs and sat up on the edge of the bed. "What's happening?

"The doctor's office called. We have an appointment at 3:00 p.m. to see him," Kate said.

Ray, Kate, and Betty arrived at Dr. Leyland's office at 2:45 p.m. They were anxious to hear the results of Betty's tests. There were two other patients in the waiting room, an elderly woman with her husband and a middle-aged man. The nurse called the man to a treatment room. Thirty minutes later, she called the Andersons into the doctor's office.

When they were all seated, Dr. Leyland stood up from his desk and went over to Kate.

"I'm afraid I don't have very good news. The blood tests indicate Betty has cancer."

Kate was hit like a ton of bricks. Betty turned white, and her hands clenched the arm of her chair.

"There must be some mistake. Betty's too young for something like that," Kate protested.

Betty was stunned and shook her head back and forth in denial. Ray looked at Kate and Betty and could think of nothing to say.

Betty finally got out of her chair and stood staring at Dr. Leyland. "What did you say?"

Kate put her arms around Betty and held her.

Ray stood up and repeated what Kate had said. "Betty can't have cancer. She's a young woman. Young women don't get cancer! How can you be sure that it's not something else?"

Betty's face grew paler, and she started to collapse. Ray and Kate caught her and helped her back into her chair.

Dr. Leyland opened his office door and shouted, "Nurse Peterson, come to my office, *stat!*"

She hurried into his office, responding to his urgent call.

"Let's get Betty into a treatment room and onto the table. Ray, help me get her to her feet."

With Ray's help, Dr. Leyland got Betty back into one of the treatment rooms and onto a padded examining table. Betty was stupefied.

Dr. Leland listened to her chest.

"Take her BP and pulse. Check her temperature," he told Nurse Peterson. "Then stay with her while I talk to her parents in my office. I'll be back shortly."

He ushered Ray and Kate back to his office.

Kate resisted. "I want to stay with Betty!"

"She will be all right with the nurse. I want to be sure you and Ray understand what we are dealing with," he said. "Please sit down, both of you. Getting hysterical won't help Betty."

Kate sat down reluctantly. Ray moved his chair close to Kate's chair and took her hand.

Dr. Leyland moved his office chair closer to them and sat down. He leaned forward and said, "The hospital test showed cancer in her white blood cells. People of all ages get this type of cancer. Sometimes this disease attacks children, often very young children. It is called chronic myeloid leukemia."

"Oh, my God! My little girl has leukemia!" Kate exclaimed.

"The test is almost always a clear diagnostic. I will order a bone marrow study to corroborate the blood tests."

"What is the cure for this, Doctor?" Ray asked. "Will she have to be in the hospital again?"

"I'm afraid that there is no cure at this time. There has been research going on to find a cure since the last century."

"Are you saying our daughter will die?" Ray asked with a catch in his voice.

Kate started to cry.

"There are treatments that have been tried, with mixed results. Sometimes there have been remissions for varying periods. And, as I said, there are very active research efforts going on all over this country and the world. A breakthrough could happen at any time."

"My God, Ray, what are we going to tell Betty?" Kate asked, drying her eyes.

Dr. Leyland said, "You two talk this over. I'm going to check on Betty." He left the office.

"She's not a child, honey," Ray said. "If she's going to fight this thing, she needs to know what she's up against. She's a strong girl."

Betty had recovered and was sitting up on the table.

Dr. Leyland checked Betty's vital signs with the nurse. He saw no reason to hospitalize her again, so he sent her home with her parents. He said he would call them the next day to discuss treatment options.

*****

Mike finished his first duty day with the POW administration. He had reported to the POW administration building at 0830 as directed. Mike saw two fellow cadre sergeants sitting in the lobby.

He asked them, "What's happening, guys?"

One said, "Go up to the desk and sign in with the private first class. I don't think they know what the hell to do with us."

Mike signed in with the private first class and was told to wait in the lobby. Someone would come and get him.

"You're right, Larry," he said to the cadre sergeant. "They don't know what to do with us."

Finally, a corporal came up to them and said, "We're getting a work area organized for you guys. Take off. Have lunch. Come back here at 1300."

Larry said, "I've got a car. Let's go to Neosho and look around a little. We can have lunch in town and then come back here at 1300."

"We're confined to camp," Mike said. "We don't have passes."

"We'll go out a side gate. There's only one MP, and he isn't checking anyone in uniform with a camp sticker on the car during duty hours in the middle of the week," Larry said. "Anyway, that corporal told us we were free until 1300. We won't be AWOL, and I doubt the POW administration cares what we do until 1300."

"I'm in," said the other cadre sergeant. "I'm not sitting around here with my thumb up my ass until 1300. Let's go. You coming, Mike?"

"Yeah, I'm in too," Mike said.

Neosho was a small town south of Joplin next to Camp Crowder. Now it was a small town whose main drag had swollen with hock shops, dry cleaners, and beer joints. It was hard to find the original town among all the clutter. It was too early for the bar girls, so they had little luck girl watching. They got lunch in a diner and reported back to the POW administration building.

The same corporal appeared and led them back into a large lecture hall that had been converted into a makeshift work area. There were three long tables with a row of ten chairs on each side. The table had two stacks of papers in each workspace. Most of the chairs were taken up by sergeants, with a few corporals thrown in. A podium was set up at the far end of the room.

"Just sit anywhere there's an empty seat," the corporal said. "The lieutenant will tell you what to do."

A first lieutenant walked up to the podium, and the corporal called, "*Ten-hut!*"

The chatter cut off, and everyone stood up roughly at attention and looked toward the podium.

"At ease. Take your seats, men," the lieutenant said. "My name is Lieutenant Parker, and I'm with the POW administration. First off, let me apologize to you NCOs for what you will be doing. You were basically dumped on us because the camp didn't know what else to do with you for the next week or two. So since you are NCOs, we can't make you police up cigarette butts or paint rocks." He paused while they all laughed. Those were the kind of make-work chores sergeants gave to privates to keep them busy. "But some of you may wish that's what we did with you after a few days."

The laughter was a little forced this time.

"On these tables in front of you are two stacks of forms. The left-hand stack has lists of the names and hometowns of POWs in Camp Crowder. The right-hand stack has Geneva Convention forms. I see by some of your expressions that you're way ahead of me."

He sipped water from a glass on the podium.

"Your task, gentlemen, is to take the information on the lists and write it in on the forms, one name to each form. The top form on the Geneva Convention pile has the appropriate information blocks highlighted."

There were groans and mumbles from the crowd.

"That's right, gentlemen, we're turning you all into clerks for however long we have you. And, being NCOs, I realize that most of you are skilled at dodging what I'm sure you regard as chickenshit. Let me caution you now. Your Battalion S-1 sections have been directed to add another two weeks to your service with us if we tell them you have been giving less than the cheerful and diligent cooperation they have come to expect from you." His expression got serious, and he looked around the room at all of them. "Are there any questions?"

"What are those fucking Geneva Convention forms?" a voice called out amidst laughter from the group.

"That's an excellent fucking question," Lieutenant Parker said, amidst more laughter. "Allow me to explain. The Geneva Convention folks are very concerned that prisoners of war receive the kind and generous treatment they have earned by virtue of sticking up their hands and dropping their weapons."

There was more laughter.

"And the United States Army and those kindhearted folks in the funny five-sided building in Washington, DC, share their concern and wish to reassure the Geneva Convention folks that we have done everything in our power to be good hosts to our Kraut guests. So before our guests leave, we ask them to sign this Geneva Convention form testifying to their good treatment."

"So why do we have to write in their names and addresses? Didn't they go to Kraut grade school?" one of the sergeants near the front asked.

"It turns out that some of our playful guests will write fictitious names on their forms or otherwise fuck them up," Lieutenant Parker said. "Also, German script is hard to read. So we, or in this case, you, do it for them."

There was no laughter.

"I will add this additional caution, in case some of you feel play-ful. Don't do it. It'll get you on your S-1's shit list. See the corporal if you have any questions about your assignment." He started walking away from the podium.

The corporal called, "*Ten-hut!*"

225

The men stood at attention until Lieutenant Parker was out of the room. The men looked at the piles of paper. "This is some shit," was the universal sentiment.

*****

Mike's neck was sore, and his hand was cramped. He had the beginning of a headache.

I really would rather police cigarette butts and paint rocks, he thought. He called June from the pay phone in his barracks, hoping her cheerful voice would improve his mood.

She answered, "Hello, this is June speaking."

"Sweetheart, I love hearing your voice," Mike said.

"Julio, I love hearing your voice too," June said dramatically.

"Who the hell is Julio?" Mike demanded gruffly. "I'll kill the bastard!" Mike threatened, joking back at her.

June laughed and said, "I love you too, Sergeant Thompson."

Mike laughed and said, "I needed a laugh. It's been a long damn day."

"Why, what happened?" June asked. She set aside the geometry text she was reading.

"It's not worth talking about. But I did get some great news yesterday."

"What was the great news yesterday?"

"The Army is discharging me. I'll be a civilian in a couple of weeks."

June squealed and jumped out of her chair.

"That's wonderful! But you didn't get into trouble or anything, did you?"

Mike almost choked on his drink. "No, no. It's nothing like that. They're discharging a bunch of guys here at Crowder. They call it a Reduction in Force. We just graduated our last class of recruits, and the Army is starting to wind down. They're only keeping the career NCOs who want to stay in. I'm just waiting for the orders to be cut, then I'm headed up to St. Joe to find some girl to marry me."

June sank back down in the chair. "Good luck with that. Oh, Mike, this is great news. What are you going to do in St. Joe, now that you're going to be a civilian?" she asked him.

"Look for a job with an electric or electronics company. I'm getting out ahead of the competition, so I don't think I'll have trouble finding a job. How's your job going?" Mike asked. "Just a minute, I have to put another quarter in this phone." He heard the coin drop, and the line was open again.

"It's going fine. My boss is giving me more responsibility. Are you sure you can afford me? How many quarters do you have?" she teased him.

"I'm fine. I borrowed some quarters from Julio," he teased in return.

June wanted to tell Mike about Ricky, but it was too involved over the phone. She'd tell him when he returned to St. Joe.

"You better save Julio's quarters. I want to talk to you Saturday morning when I'm off work," June said.

"Okay, Mrs. Thompson. I love you. Bye."

"I love you too, Mike. Bye," she said and hung up the phone.

*****

"Dr. Joel Friedman's office," the receptionist answered the phone.

"This is Dr. Leyland. I'd like to speak to Dr. Friedman, please."

"Hold the line, please," the receptionist said. She put the phone on hold and pushed the button for Dr. Friedman's line. "Doctor Leyland is on line one for you."

Dr. Friedman put down the file he was reading and said, "I'll take the call now, Wilma," and pushed the button down for line one. "Hello, Miles, what can I do for you today?" he asked his friend and longtime colleague.

"I have a patient, the daughter of a family I have treated for many years. She is twenty-three years old. I had some blood tests run at St. Joseph's Hospital after what I initially suspected was influenza. The tests came back positive for leukemia," Dr. Leyland said.

"My God, Miles, I'm sorry to hear that. Did you do a bone marrow study?"

"No, her symptoms match the white blood cell results. I'm holding off on the bone marrow study. It's an option, of course."

"What do you want from me, Miles?" Joel asked.

"This is way out of my league, Joel. You're the best internal medicine doc I know. Would you accept a referral?" Dr. Leyland leaned back in his chair and frowned. He knew what he was asking of his colleague.

"There's no cure, Miles. You know that, of course."

"Yes, I do know that. But there have been remissions. And researchers all over the planet are working on treatments. This is an otherwise healthy, strong young woman with her life ahead of her. Her father is a minister, and her mother is a wonderful woman. These are very good people that I am powerless to help."

"Miles, we Jews invented guilt. Don't try it on me, my friend. But I'll tell you what I will do. I have a friend at Johns Hopkins Hospital who is an oncologist. I'll call him and discuss the case with him. Can you send me a copy of her file?"

"I'll drop it off at your office today. Her test results are in the file," Miles said.

"I'm not making any promises, Miles. I'll get back to you after I talk with my colleague," Joel said.

Dr. Leyland called the Anderson home. Kate answered the phone.

"Kate, this is Dr. Leyland. Can I speak to Ray, please?"

"You found out it was all a mistake, didn't you?" Kate said.

"Kate, is Ray home?"

"No, he's working. Tell me why you're calling!" Kate demanded.

"Kate, you need to calm down, and I'll talk to you about why I called."

Betty came into the living room and asked, "Who are you yelling at, Mom?"

Kate forced herself to calm down and said to Betty, "It's Dr. Leyland, honey." She motioned Betty to come closer so she could hear the conversation. "I'm calm, Doctor. Why are you calling?" Kate asked.

"I am not the best doctor to help Betty. I am looking into other resources. I expect to have a recommendation for you early next week. In the meantime, there is no reason to treat Betty like an invalid. She needs to get fresh air and exercise whether she feels like it or not. And she must eat! Also, she needs to drink plenty of water. If she develops any pain or high fever, take her to the hospital."

Betty pushed her mouth up to the phone and said, "Can I go to work?"

"Yes, if you feel up to it. But come home if you get too tired. Now let me speak to your mother again."

"Do you really think she should go to work, Dr. Leyland?" Kate asked.

"Until we can develop a treatment plan, we need to keep her as healthy as we can. A big part of that is her mental attitude. The more normal her life is, the better. We can't do any harm, and we might be doing a lot of good. You and Ray need to switch gears. Just treat her normally. I know that's asking a lot, but that's the best thing for her right now."

"Okay, Doctor. I'll tell Ray. Please call as soon as you know more. Thank you," Kate said.

"What did Dr. Leyland say to you, Mom?" Betty asked.

"He said you and I need to go for a walk. So let's go," Kate said.

*****

Dr. Friedman called Dr. Leyland Friday afternoon. "Miles, I talked to my friend at Johns Hopkins. He said the same thing I did. There's no cure. But there are therapeutic treatments that have sometimes produced remissions. He said I could do them for the patient here as easily as he could there. I read her file, and it's a heartbreaking situation. I'm willing to supervise her treatments in the hospital if you follow up with supportive treatment afterward. I think we're both in for a rough time though."

"Of course, I'll do the follow-ups. I don't want to look a gift horse in the mouth, but why are you doing this, Joel?"

"I have very little experience with cancer in general and leukemia in particular. Any cancer patients generally end up in St. Louis or one of the big research hospitals back east. This is my chance to learn all I can about it in a treatment setting. I will not treat our patient as a guinea pig, but that is my reason."

"There's nothing wrong with that. And I guarantee you that you couldn't treat this patient like a guinea pig, even if you wanted to. Wait until you meet her and her family," Miles said. "What's our next step?"

"I've ordered the treatment materials and supplies for the first treatment regimen. They will be at St. Joe's Hospital Monday. Have her parents check her in Tuesday morning. We'll begin treatment then," Joel said.

"What is the treatment regimen?" Miles asked.

"It's an arsenic compound. I know how that sounds, but it's sometimes effective in producing a remission," Joel said. "In the meantime, my friend will try to get another treatment released to us. It's for the military, and Hopkins is running trials with it."

"I'll tell the Andersons to take Betty in early Tuesday morning," Miles said.

*****

Saturday, the apartment felt empty to June without Betty's boisterous presence. After she had her breakfast, June called Betty's parents.

Ray answered the phone. "Hello, this is the Anderson residence, Reverend Anderson speaking."

"Hi, Reverend Anderson, this is June Taylor. Can I speak to Betty, please?"

"Just a moment, June, I'll call her to the phone," he said. "Betty, June's on the phone for you."

Betty was having coffee with her mother in the kitchen. They had just finished breakfast. Betty had managed to eat a bowl of oatmeal. She got up and went to answer the phone. She didn't know how to break the bad news to June, not over the phone for sure.

"Hi, June," she said when she took the phone from her father. "Can you come and see me today?"

"Sure, what time do you want me to come? How are you doing?" June asked.

"Come whenever you want to. We'll talk when you get here," Betty said.

"I'll come right now," June said. "See you in a little while."

Betty sounded strained on the phone, so June got bundled up and went out and got into Betty's Ford. She wondered if Betty might need her car back. She stopped at a gas station on the way.

June parked in the Anderson's driveway and went to the door. When she rang their doorbell, Betty answered the door. She was dressed to go out in her heavy coat, hat, and muffler.

"Let's go for a ride," she said to June.

"Okay, let's go. Do you want to drive? It's your car."

Betty didn't answer. She got in the passenger side and closed her door.

June got in the driver's side and started the engine. "Where do you want to go?" she asked Betty.

"Let's go to Krug Park," Betty said. "It's a nice day."

When they got to the park, June found a parking space near the stone main entrance. Since it was a weekend, the nice weather had brought families and couples to the park. They walked a little way past the pond. Betty looked tired, so June stopped at the same picnic area where she and Mike had talked before Christmas. The concrete tables had small fire pits burning on the tabletops. The girls found a warm spot to sit near one of them.

"I'm going to get a hot dog and a cup of coffee from the vendor," June said. "What would you like?"

"Get me the same, cream and sugar in the coffee." Betty started searching for money in her purse.

"This is my treat, hon," June said and walked over to the vendor's window.

She returned with a tray holding their food and coffee. She gave Betty her hot dog and coffee and said, "Okay, what's going on?"

Betty looked into June's eyes and said with tears running down her face, "I've got cancer."

June hugged Betty fiercely and held her while she cried. June's eyes were wet as well.

"I'm so scared, June," she said between sobs.

"I know you are, honey," June said. A million questions went through her mind. She didn't ask any of them. She just held Betty until Betty stopped crying. Betty dried her eyes on a handkerchief she took from her coat pocket.

"Our coffee's getting cold," Betty said. "Eat your hot dog."

June took a bite of her hot dog and a drink of her coffee. Betty took a small bite of her hot dog and sipped her coffee.

"I'm going into the hospital for treatment next Tuesday," Betty said.

"Good, the sooner the better. We have to get you over this thing," June said. "You're my maid of honor."

Betty said, "I wouldn't miss it for anything, June. I love you."

"I love you too, roomie," June said.

Returning from the park, Betty was ready for a nap. She hugged June and went up to her room.

Kate asked June to join her in the kitchen for some hot tea. "Did Betty tell you what is happening?" Kate asked.

"She told me she has cancer, and she is going into the hospital next Tuesday for treatment," June said.

"She has leukemia. There is no cure. There are treatments that might produce a remission. That's what we are hopeful for." Kate paused and gathered herself together. "This is a nightmare for her father and me. I'm trying to keep up a positive front for Betty."

June reached out and patted Kate's hand. "What can I do to help?" June asked Kate.

"Just be her friend. Our doctor said not to treat Betty like an invalid. So please treat her normally. I know how hard that can be to do. I'm struggling with it myself. But that's the best thing we can do for her. The more activity she engages in, the better. When she gets tired, she can rest."

They both sat and drank their tea in silence.

"Has anybody told her friend Don?" June asked after a few minutes.

"We haven't told anyone yet, not even Ray's congregation. Betty wanted to tell you herself, so we waited for you to talk to her."

"She should be the one to tell Don," June said. "But I don't know what I'll say if he asks me how she is doing."

"If that happens, tell him to call me, and I'll handle it," Kate said.

"Okay. What do you want me to do with her car?" June asked.

"Please just keep it for now. I don't think she should be driving."

"I'm going to leave now. Is it okay to call tomorrow?" June asked.

"Betty is going to church with us tomorrow. I imagine she'll be tired out and want to nap after the service, but please call her later in the day."

"My offer to help extends to you as well. Anything I can do, please tell me," June said, getting up from her chair.

"Bless you, dear. You go on. I'm going to sit and finish my tea."

*****

Saturday night, June was listening to the Jack Benny show on her radio when her phone rang. It was Mike. June turned off her radio.

"I'm using up Julio's quarters. I don't want him calling you," Mike joked when she answered.

"Mike, I got some terrible news today," she said.

"Is it one of your brothers?"

"No, it's Betty. She's very ill. She got some tests done at the hospital, and they found out she has leukemia."

"My God! Leukemia! That's bad, isn't it?"

"Yes, there's no cure. But there are treatments that might put her into what they call remission. That's when the disease is dormant. She's going to start one of the treatments on Tuesday."

"I'm so sorry, honey. Is there anything I can do for her or for you?"

"You're doing it right now. Have you heard any more about your discharge?"

"No, but I hope it's soon. It may be next week. They're running out of makeshift work to keep us busy. Has anyone told Don about Betty?"

"No, Betty's mother and I talked about that. Betty wants to tell him herself. Betty only told me today. She and I went for a ride to Krug Park, and she told me at that same picnic table where you and I sat. I asked her to be my maid of honor."

"Okay, just don't tell Emma Dee or Virginia Jane," he joked. "I'm sorry to be joking at a time like this."

"No, no. Don't be sorry. We need all the laughs we can get. Betty's mom said to treat Betty normally, not like a sick person. Let's treat each other the same way."

"It's a deal. Well, I'm almost out of Julio's quarters. Are you going to be okay?"

"Yes, I have to be for Betty's sake, and I'm going to be a wife soon," June said.

"Good night, honey. I love you."

"Good night, Mike. I love you too."

*****

Next week, Don flew one of the modified C-47s with navigation training gear to Hatbox Army Airfield in Muskogee, Oklahoma, with three navigator trainees and a flight crew. It was not a long flight, but it followed a tortuous route. They did an RON (remain overnight) and flew back to Rosecrans Field Saturday. On each flight, he had a trainee demonstrate his skill (or lack thereof) with the navigation equipment. Pilots hated this part. They had to turn control of the plane over to green navigation students. Part of the learning process was making mistakes and seeing what the consequences were. Pilots liked to know where their plane was at all times. When the navigator didn't know where he has directed the plane, the pilot didn't know either. Don's job was to stay on top of these errors and correct the flight path when he thought the trainee had learned enough from his errors.

His current crop of three trainees weren't too bad. Two of them would make good navigators once they were fully trained. The third one was iffy. He spent a lot of the flight time working with the third guy, which did not please the pilot. On the return trip, the guy was improving. Maybe he'd be worth the time and effort Don spent on him. The trainees and the flight crew regarded Don with awe. He was a combat veteran with twenty-five bomber missions in the Pacific. They were flying a Gooney Bird transport back and forth between Missouri and Oklahoma.

Don got back from his training flight on Saturday afternoon and called Betty's parents' number.

Kate answered the phone.

"Can I speak with Betty, Mrs. Anderson?" Don asked.

"Yes, just hold on a minute while I call her to the phone," Kate said.

"Betty, it's Don for you," she said.

Betty was working on a jigsaw puzzle with her father on a folding card table. They had most of the border pieces in place for what would be a picture of a castle on a lake in Austria. Betty and her father had done jigsaw puzzles together since she was in grade school.

Betty got up from the couch and went to the phone.

"Hi, Don. I'm glad you called. Could you come over to my parents' house tomorrow afternoon? I have something to tell you, and I'd like to tell you face-to-face, not on the phone," Betty said.

"That sounds like bad news. Are you giving me the brush-off?"

Betty laughed and said, "It's not that bad. What about tomorrow?"

"Sure, what time?" Don asked.

"We're going to church. Mom and I will be home afterward, but I'll probably take a nap. How about around three o'clock?" Betty asked. "We can go out for coffee or something."

"Okay. I'll pick you up at three."

Betty told her mom about her date with Don on Sunday after church.

"Are you sure you don't want to tell him here when your dad and I are here to help?'

"Yes, I'm sure, but thank you for offering, Mom," Betty said.

*****

Reverend Anderson had just wrapped up his sermon on the power of prayer. "My friends, I picked today's topic for a very special reason. My family had some bad news this week. My daughter, Betty, is ill. After undergoing tests at St. Joseph's Hospital, we were told she has leukemia."

There were gasps and exclamations from the congregation. The women who were close friends of Kate were surprised and upset. Some started to cry.

"This is a grave illness, but there are treatments for it. Betty is going into St. Joseph's Hospital next Tuesday to begin treatment. Please check with the hospital before trying to visit her. The treatments may prevent visits. If any of you want to send flowers, our family would prefer that you donate the cost of the flowers to the Church's Foundation for the Poor instead. Now we ask you all to pray for God's help for our daughter."

When Kate and Betty got home, Betty said, "Thank God that's over."

Kate felt the same way herself.

"Mom, do we still have that brandy Dad drinks to toast holidays?" Betty asked.

"I don't think a little brandy will do us any harm. You sit down on the couch, and I'll get us both a glass," her mother said.

It wasn't long before the phone started ringing off the hook. Betty finished her glass of brandy and told Kate she was going up to take a nap. She looked ruefully at her mother as the phone rang again. Kate shrugged and answered the phone. Being the wife of the preacher carried its own burdens.

The telephone finally quieted down about the time Ray got home.

"Thank the Lord that is over," he said.

Kate laughed and said, "That's word for word what Betty said when she got home."

He smiled wryly at her. "Do we still have any of that brandy left?" he asked.

Kate laughed again. "Like father, like daughter," she said. "God, it feels good to laugh. I'll get us both a glass."

They sat on the sofa together and sipped their brandy.

"Some people just can't figure out how to talk to their minister at times like this, God bless them," he said.

The phone rang again.

"It must be some tail end Charlie who just got up the nerve to call," Ray said. "I'll answer it. You've already done your duty today."

"This is Reverend Anderson," he said.

"This is Don Walker. Mr. Anderson. Betty and I have a date later. I just called to see if she is up to it."

"Don, I think you can call me Ray now. Hang on and I will go up and check with Betty. She's taking a nap in her room." Ray gestured to Kate to take the phone.

"Hello, Don. We're all a little bushed after church service. How are you?" Kate asked.

"Hi, Mrs. Anderson, I'm fine. I had a few tiring days myself. I was training new navigators while we flew back from Oklahoma."

"Don, I heard Ray ask you to call him Ray, and I'd like you to call me Kate. We're all friends now," Kate said.

"Thank you, Kate. It's a privilege," Don said.

"Hi, big boy, are you trying to stand me up?" Betty asked, taking the phone from her mother.

"I'll be there at three o'clock with bells on," Don said.

"That I have to see. I'll be here. Bye for now."

"Goodbye, doll."

Betty went back to the couch and studied the jigsaw puzzle. She picked up another piece of the border and put it in place.

"We'll have this sucker done in no time," she said to her father.

The doorbell rang punctually at 3:00 p.m.

"See, Daddy, it pays to date a soldier. They're always on time," Betty said, and got up to answer the door. She put on her coat, hat, and muffler and opened the door. "Hi, GI, looking for a good time?" she asked.

"You bet! Let's go," Don said and laughed.

Betty smiled at him and went past him to Mike's Chevy. Don opened her door and then got in the driver's side.

"You said you wanted coffee. There's one of those aluminum diners that looks like a trailer not too far away."

"Perfect, lead on, Macduff, and get us a booth with some privacy," Betty said.

Don pulled up into a parking space in front of the Rocket Diner. It was Sunday afternoon and almost deserted.

"I don't think privacy will be an issue," Don said.

When they were seated on aqua-colored vinyl seat cushions in the last booth next to the wall, Don said, "Okay, what's going on?"

Betty ignored his question and picked up a menu and said, "They have milkshakes. I want a strawberry milkshake." She looked at him and asked, "Okay?"

Don signaled to a bosomy young waitress in a beige dress with an aqua apron and cap. When she came over to the booth, Don said, "We're going to have two strawberry shakes with a scoop of strawberry ice cream."

"The ice cream will cost you extra," the waitress said.

"This young lady is with the last of the big spenders. Go for it," Don said.

The waitress looked at Don and winked. She left with their order.

"I see I should have put more tissues in my bra," Betty said.

"I've seen what's in your bra. They don't need any help," Don said.

Betty smiled at him and started reading the inside cover of the menu. It had the history of the world-famous Rocket Diner on it.

"Did you know that Lucille Ball and Desi Arnaz ate here?"

"They were probably in this very booth. Italians like to have their backs against a wall," Don said.

Betty giggled. "Desi Arnaz is Cuban. He's not Italian."

"Same deal. Cubans like to have two walls behind them if they can."

Betty giggled again. "It also says Abbott and Costello ate here."

"I'll bet they didn't charge Abbott and Costello extra for the ice cream," Don said.

Betty laughed out loud. "Probably not," she said.

The waitress heard the last exchange as she came up with their milkshakes.

"If you're through being his straight man for a minute, I'll give you your milkshake," she said, giving them the shakes.

"Hey, only one comedian to a booth, sister," Don said.

The waitress picked up her tray, turned around, and wiggled her rear end at Don as she walked away.

"Crap, I don't think there are enough tissues in the world for me to beat that," Betty said.

"I've seen that too, and it doesn't need any help either," Don said and sipped his milkshake through his straw.

Betty smiled and took a sip through her straw.

"Are you going to fess up now?" Don asked.

She took another sip and then pushed away the glass. "I have leukemia," she said steadily, looking him in the eye.

He didn't move or look away from her for a minute or two. Then he took another sip of his shake and said, "Well, shit, if that's all that's wrong, I'll stop worrying."

Betty looked at him for a minute and laughed. "Damn, you're just what the doctor ordered," she said.

Don got up and slid in next to her. He put his arm around her and hugged her to him. She turned her face up, and he kissed her.

"Here's the plan. We suit up and show up. We fight with everything we got," Don said. "What do the doctors say is the next step?"

She kept her head on his shoulder and held his hand. "I go into St. Joseph's Hospital next Tuesday for treatment," she said.

"Okay, good. Eat your ice cream before it melts," he said. He took his spoon and dug out a bite of the strawberry ice cream floating on top of his milkshake.

She did the same. "This is the best meal I've had in a week. How did you find this gourmet restaurant?"

"Stick with me, kid, we're going places," Don said in his best Bogart impression.

Betty laughed and said, "Who was that? Jack Benny or Rochester?"

"Boy, this is a tough crowd," Don said.

The waitress came over with the check. "I thought his Bogie wasn't half bad," she said.

"Okay, you won him fair and square. He's yours," Betty said.

The waitress and Don both laughed.

"You keep him, honey. He didn't change seats for nothing. And you better treat this one right, buddy. She's a peach," the waitress said and left the tray with the check.

"She sure is," Don said and added a nice tip to the check. "Where do you want to go now?" Don asked and slid out of the booth. He helped Betty to her feet and waited for her to answer.

"Can you play gin?" she asked.

"Gin and poker and hearts, you name your game," Don said.

She looked up at him and said, "Take me home, and we'll see about that. I hope you brought plenty of money."

As they walked out the door, he said, "I do love a challenge."

He opened her passenger door.

Before she got in, she said, "You must, you're with me, aren't you?"

On the drive home, she slid next to Don and put her head on his shoulder. He put his arm around her and drove one-handed, except to change gears in the Chevy. They didn't say a thing. She won $3 off him playing gin rummy.

*****

When Mike reported to POW administration on Monday for another fun-filled day pushing paper, he was told to report to the S-1 office down the hall. He found a private first class clerk typing a form on the typewriter. He finished the box on the form he was typing and stopped and looked up at Mike.

"I'm Sergeant Thompson. I was told to report to the S-1 office," Mike said.

"Door on your left is T/Sgt. Michaels. Knock and go in," the private first class said.

Mike walked up to the left door and knocked.

"Come!" he heard through the door.

Mike opened the door and walked up to the desk of T/Sgt. Michaels.

"Sergeant, I'm Sergeant Thompson. I was told to report here."

"Pull up one of those chairs and sit down, Sergeant Thompson," T/Sgt. Michaels directed.

Mike got one of the two metal chairs against the wall and pulled it up to the desk and sat down.

"You are being discharged tomorrow. Here are copies of your discharge orders and the paperwork to clear the post. There is a pay envelope with your final pay and your unused leave. There is a travel voucher for travel to your home of record. The civilian transportation companies will usually honor it. If they don't, you can turn it in at the nearest base or post with a receipt for your ticket or tickets, and they will reimburse you the amount of the voucher. You have until Friday to clear all belongings out of your barracks. You may remain in your barracks through Thursday night. Turn in your key to the barracks sergeant when you leave. After you do the paperwork to clear the post, you may leave the camp any time after today. You are authorized to travel in uniform or in civilian clothes. You need to be in uniform if you want to use the travel voucher. Do you have any questions?" T/Sgt. Michaels asked.

"Where do I turn in the paperwork?" Mike asked.

"Give it to the S-1 clerk outside my office." T/Sgt. Michaels stood up. When Mike stood up, T/Sgt. Michaels shook his hand and said, "Thank you for your service, Sergeant, and good luck in your civilian career."

Mike knew he had just been dismissed. "Thanks, Sergeant."

He turned and left the office with his paperwork and orders. He stuffed the pay envelope in his front trousers pocket. It was satisfyingly thick. He was elated and let down all at the same time. Uncle Sam had told him what to do and where to go for almost four years. The Army had fed, clothed, and sheltered him. If it wasn't for June and their plans, he wouldn't know what to do at this minute. That thought put him back on track. *I've got to call June and Don.*

"The 562nd orderly room, Corporal Erickson speaking."

"This is Sergeant Thompson at Camp Crowder. I'm a friend of T/Sgt. Don Walker. Could I leave a message for him?" Mike put another quarter in the pay phone in his barracks to make sure he didn't get cut off.

"Sure. What's the message?" Corporal Erickson asked. He got a piece of paper and a pencil out of his desk.

"Meet me at the St. Joe train depot tomorrow night at 2000 hours," Mike said.

Corporal Erickson repeated back the message. "Is there a number where he can call if he can't make it?"

"No, tell him I'll take a cab to June's if he can't make it."

"Take a cab to June's," Corporal Erickson noted.

"Thanks for your help, Corporal," Mike said.

"Hey, T/Sgt. Walker is a celebrity here at the airfield. I'm happy to help."

*****

June got home shortly after 6:00 p.m. on Monday and flopped down on the love seat. It had been an exhausting day. On top of her regular work, she was writing the new SOP that Tim wanted. Tim's meeting with the production manager had gone well, and they had come up with the general description for the SOP. Now June had to fill in the details. She was excited her idea had gotten this far, but she was pooped. She went into the kitchen to heat up water for tea. She reached for the phone to order Chinese food from the little Chinese restaurant three blocks away.

The phone rang before she could pick it up.

"Hello," she said.

"Hello, honey, it's Mike. I have good news. I'm getting discharged tomorrow."

"Wow, that is good news. When are you coming here?" She turned down the heat under the teapot.

"I've made reservations on the train. I get into the St. Joe depot tomorrow night at eight. I left a message for Don to pick me up. I'll drop him back off at Rosecrans Field and come over to your place."

"I could pick you up, you know. I still have Betty's car," June said.

"Yeah, I thought of that. But I'm going to need my car to go job hunting. I'm getting married, you know."

June giggled and said, "Who to? Anyone I know?" She took down her tin of tea and measured out a teaspoon and put it in her teapot to steep.

"She's got big blue eyes, gorgeous red hair, and sexy legs. Do you know anyone like that?"

"If I did, I wouldn't tell you. She might take you away from me."

"I'm bringing a duffel bag and a big suitcase with me. I don't know where you're going to put them."

"Is that all your worldly goods?" June asked accusingly.

"Yeah, that and almost two hundred bucks final pay," he said.

"We're rich!" she said.

"And don't forget, I also have a luxury automobile."

"What was that ringing noise on the phone?" June asked. She poured a cup of tea.

"It was Julio's last quarter. I can't wait to see you, babe," he said.

*****

243

Kate checked Betty into the hospital and waited in her room to speak with Dr Leyland. Dr. Leyland came into her room with Dr. Friedman.

He introduced Dr. Friedman to them both and said, "Dr. Friedman will explain the treatment plan."

"We will administer a short series of chemotherapy. You will be given the medication orally, three doses per day for three days. I must warn you that it may make you nauseous or produce other unpleasant side effects. You must prepare yourself for that. I will monitor you closely, as will the nursing staff. If we encounter serious side effects, we will discontinue the treatment and try something else. This treatment has been successful in producing some remissions. It won't cure you. But it may buy us time, and you will feel a lot better if it works. I'll need your written permission to go ahead."

Betty looked at her mother questioningly.

"Honey, I can't decide this for you. You have to do that," Kate said.

Betty was quiet for three or four minutes. A determined expression came over her face.

"Don and I talked about this. He said we need to fight with everything we can. I agreed with him. Give me the form."

When the forms were signed, the two doctors went to the hospital cafeteria and got coffee.

When they were seated, Dr. Freidman said, "We're trying the arsenic compound in low concentrations the first day. If she tolerates that, we'll up the concentrations on the second and third day. It's nasty stuff, but it's had the most success. If it doesn't work or we need to discontinue it, we'll let her recover for a few days and then try X-rays. There's also been some success with folic acid. I'm hoping to hear from my colleague at John's Hopkins about another treatment Hopkins is investigating."

"This all depends on how much Betty can take before she gives up," Dr. Leyland said.

"You are absolutely correct, Doctor. That girl will need all the grit she can muster."

They drank their coffee and thought about the ordeal ahead of their patient.

*****

The tired old locomotive sent a trail of steam and coal particles onto the platform as Mike exited the antiquated passenger car at the St. Joseph depot, carrying his heavy duffle bag and a large suitcase. Mike had been lucky to catch the Southern Belle to Kansas City again, but then it was this old relic to St. Joe. He was in uniform, wearing his heavy overcoat and an overseas cap. He waved off a red-cap porter and carried his bags into the depot.

Don was sitting on one of the wooden benches in the open area of the depot. He got up from the bench along with a group of people who were there to meet their arriving friends and relatives. Don took Mike's duffle bag from him and said, "What the hell do you have in here, a load of rocks?" He hoisted the bag's strap onto his shoulder.

"Don't complain. I've got the heavy suitcase. Thanks for meeting me."

They walked out of the depot and down the street to Mike's Chevy.

When they had stowed the bags, Don handed Mike the car keys.

"So how does it feel to be a civilian again?" Don asked Mike.

"I'll tell you when I'm out of this uniform and into some civvies," Mike said.

He got into the driver's side and started the car.

Don settled into the passenger side of the bench seat and said, "Did you hear about Betty?"

"Yeah, June told me. I'm really sorry, buddy. What a rotten break." Mike pulled out into traffic. "Do you want to stop and have a drink someplace and talk?" Mike asked Don.

"Thanks, pal, I appreciate the offer. But I have a training flight early tomorrow morning. Just drop me off at Rosecrans. Maybe we can catch up with each other this weekend," Don said.

"Sure thing. Call me at June's and we'll set something up," Mike said.

*****

When June opened her door, Mike took one look at her and dropped his bags. He stepped into her apartment and picked her up and kissed her.

"God, it's good to see you!" he said.

"You better bring in your stuff before someone swipes it," she said.

He brought his duffle bag and his suitcase in and set them down in the living room.

"Tonight, you're not getting steak. You're getting hot dogs and chili. I don't want to spoil you," June said.

"Okay, but I'm going to need another kiss," he said.

She smiled and kissed him.

"I'm going to get out of this uniform. Should I change in your room?" he asked. Now that he was here in her apartment, he was suddenly unsure of how to act.

June saw his discomfiture and took his hand and said, "We're partners. What's mine is yours. We won't be using Betty's room. That's hers. Anything else is ours. This is our home for now. Go change your clothes."

13

"She's tolerated the arsenic solution better than I hoped," Dr. Friedman said to Dr. Leyland.

They were meeting in Dr. Friedman's office at St. Joseph Medical Center, studying Betty's chart.

"Her blood tests are improving, and the white cell count is coming down," Dr. Leyland said. It was the third day of Betty's treatment in the hospital. "Should we keep her on this regimen for a fourth day?"

"No, I don't think so. It's tempting since she's improving. But the literature says the toxic effects can accumulate. This is nasty stuff, and she has two more treatments today."

"When do you plan to send her home?" Dr. Leyland asked.

Dr. Friedman was smoking his favorite Meerschaum pipe. He took a puff from it and considered Dr. Leyland's question.

"If her blood tests are still good tonight, I think we can send her home tomorrow or Saturday, depending on her condition. Staying in the hospital won't benefit her if we truly have a remission. She's better off at home."

"Do you want to tell Betty and her parents the good news?" Dr. Leyland asked.

"No, I think you should do it. You're their family doctor. Save me, God help us, for the bad news when the remission fails and we have to move on to the next treatment regimen."

Dr. Leyland shook his head sadly and nodded his agreement.

*****

"Remission," Kate said. "That's another word for miracle." She was sitting close to Betty's hospital bed and studying her face. She reached out to touch Betty's forehead and push the strand of hair out of Betty's eyes.

Betty was still haggard from the arsenic, but she was cheerful with the news she would be going home tomorrow.

Dr. Leyland resisted the temptation to warn them not to be overly optimistic, that the remission might not last.

Let them be happy for as long as they can, he thought. He cautioned Betty to take it easy for a few days until she recovered from her treatment.

"But get some exercise and enjoy yourself, just don't overdo it," he said.

Kate and Ray thanked Dr. Leyland profusely and asked him to thank Dr. Friedman for them.

*****

June woke up to the smell of bacon cooking. She stretched and yawned. Then she realized she was naked under the covers. That brought back memories from the previous night. She smiled and threw off the covers. After she put on a pair of panties and her robe and slippers, she went out to see what Mike was up to. He had set two places at the breakfast table. There was a short stack of pancakes on each plate. The table held a saucer with butter and a small pitcher of syrup. She could smell coffee as well as the bacon Mike was taking out of the skillet and putting on a plate.

When Mike saw June, he said, "I hope you like pancakes. I found the pancake mix, so I thought you must."

"Now this is the way to wake up in the morning," she said and sat down at the table.

"You better enjoy it while you can. It might never happen again," Mike said, grinning at her. "On the other hand, if you always look this cute in the morning, I may reconsider."

"Oh, phooey, where's my coffee?" she asked.

He put the plate of bacon on the table and got them both a cup of coffee.

June buttered and added a generous covering of syrup to her pancakes and attacked them. She took bites of the bacon as she went through the pancakes.

"I'm really hungry this morning, for some reason," she said.

"You were pretty darn good yourself," Mike said and grinned at her. "I especially liked your choice of pajamas."

June blushed. *My God*, she thought, *I haven't blushed since the seventh grade*. "What are you doing today while I'm slaving away at good old Quaker Oats?" she asked, taking her last bite of pancakes and wiping her mouth with the napkin.

"I thought I'd go out to the college and ogle the coeds," he said.

"Don't expect me to bail you out after the campus cops bust you," she said.

"Okay, in that case, maybe I'll see about getting a job," he said.

June got up and went into the bathroom to shower and brush her teeth and get ready for work.

Mike cleared away the table and did the dishes.

It feels like we're married already, he thought. *I like it.*

June was thinking much the same thing.

*****

The surgical team in operating room two at Walter Reed Medical Center was working hard to keep their focus on the demanding procedure.

"How's he doing?" Major Reston asked the anesthetist who was keeping Ricky sedated.

"He's still doing fine, but we're running kind of long here," Dr. Connors, the anesthetist, said.

The surgical team agreed with Dr. Connors. They were all tiring.

"Keep me posted. I'm going for another ten minutes, and then we'll close," Major Reston said.

This was the second major surgery on Sergeant Taylor's left arm, and Major Reston was trying to make it the last one. He was pleased with the way it had gone. They were going to save the sergeant's arm. It was still an open question about how much function he would have in it. That would be up to the patient and his physical therapists. His Walter Reed surgical team had done all they could.

"Okay, let's get out of this kid's arm and close," Major Reston said after his ten minutes were up.

*****

The tanks of the Fourth Armored Division spent the month of January in pursuit of the remains of the German Army. M/Sgt. Lloyd Taylor's tank company skirmished with scattered German units as they rolled across France and into Luxembourg. A .30 caliber round ricocheted off his .50 caliber machine gun mount. A German sniper almost picked off M/Sgt. Taylor as he stood in his turret. They were passing a battered church in Luxembourg, and the sniper was holed up in the steeple. Lloyd shouted a command down to his driver to stop the tank, and he bailed down out of the turret and closed the hatch. His gunner rotated the turret until they had the main gun lined up on the steeple. It only took one HE round to finish off the sniper's perch.

"God will have to forgive us for that steeple," Lloyd said to his crew, and they resumed the pursuit down the road. "The silly bastards just don't know when to quit."

*****

"Hello," June answered her phone on Saturday morning. She was reading the newspaper and having coffee. The radio played the intro theme to the *Breakfast Club*. June never missed the show if she could help it.

"Hello, June, this is Don. Is Mike there?"

June put down the newspaper and said, "No, he went to the store for a few groceries."

"Wow, have you got him washing and ironing the clothes yet?" Don said and laughed.

"Just when I'm starting to like you a little, you talk like an ass," June said.

"The reason I'm calling is I spoke to Betty this morning at her mother's house. She came home from the hospital yesterday, and she's feeling better."

"That's great news. I was going to call her mother later this morning," June said.

"Anyway, Betty said she'd like to get out of the house and do something today. I'm thinking we all might go to the Saturday matinee at one of the movie houses."

"I like that idea if Betty is up to it. Why don't you call back in an hour and work it out with Mike?" June said.

Mike got back with the groceries shortly after Don called. June told him about Don's idea to go to the movies.

"Sure, honey, it sounds fine. Betty could probably use some fun after what she's been through. Why don't you check the newspaper listings and find us a good movie?"

Later, when Mike and June rang the Anderson's doorbell, Betty opened the door. She was dressed in a pleated gray skirt and a white sweater under a winter coat with a fur collar. Betty wore a pair of saddle loafers and white ankle sox. She looked like an Ivy League coed on her way to class. Her mother helped her do her hair.

Betty smiled at Mike and June. She turned her head and shouted over her shoulder, "Mike and June are here. We're leaving, Mom. Bye."

"Have a good time, dear!" Kate shouted back from the living room. She was happy Betty was feeling well enough to get out of the house, but she couldn't stop worrying about her. She kept her worries to herself. *There's no reason to spoil Betty's day out*, she thought.

When the three of them got to Mike's car, June said, "Betty and I will ride in the back seat."

"I don't have my chauffeur's hat," Mike kidded them.

"We can all fit in the front seat," Betty said.

"I want you all to myself for some girl talk," June said and opened the back door.

The girls settled into the back seat, and Mike pulled out onto the street. "I will expect a tip, you know," he said, glancing back at June and Betty.

"From what I hear, you're getting plenty of tips already," Betty said and winked at June, who smiled back at Betty.

Mike concentrated on his driving and left the girls to converse.

"So you're home from the hospital. How was it?" June asked.

"It was pretty crappy. But Dr. Friedman told me it would be," Betty said. "The important thing is it worked. I'm in remission. Do you know what that is?" Betty asked June.

"Yes, I do. I've been reading up on your illness in my medical books. I'm so happy to hear this, honey." June slid over and hugged Betty.

Betty hugged her back and said, "That's enough about me and my troubles. Let's just have a good time today, roomie."

During the drive to the theater, June and Betty talked about June's wedding. Betty said it was neat that June would wear her grandmother's wedding dress.

Mike parked the Chevy near the corner of Eleventh and Hickory. June had found a Humphrey Bogart movie at the Hickory Theater. Don liked *Casablanca*, so she thought he would like this one. It was called *To Have and Have Not*. It starred Bogart, Lauren Bacall, and Walter Brennan. Don was waiting for them at the ticket window.

"I have our tickets," he said. "You can buy the popcorn, Mike." Don got a lift into town with one of his buddies in the training squadron.

He gave them their tickets and said to Mike and June, "Betty and I are going to make out like teenagers. Don't say we didn't warn you," Don said and put his arm around Betty. Don continued, "You can sit with the other old married couples and look down your noses at us."

June stuck out her tongue at him. Then she planted a big smooch on Mike. "We'll see who shows who what!" June said. She took Mike's arm, and they sashayed into the theater.

They got their popcorn and drinks and sat halfway back on the left side, next to the aisle. Don thought Betty might want to talk to June during the movie, so he arranged for the two girls to sit together.

Betty turned to him and said, "Thanks, big guy, you think of everything." She kissed him and took a handful of popcorn.

June turned toward Betty and whispered, "Which was better, the kiss or the popcorn?"

They both giggled.

"The popcorn, but not by much," Betty said.

"I'll second that," Don said.

Betty poked him in the side with her elbow.

June turned to Mike and said, "Are you ready for the popcorn challenge, Mr. Thompson?"

"Bring it on, Mrs. Thompson," Mike said and planted a long, wet kiss on her waiting lips.

"I may just have to forget the popcorn," June said, coming up for air.

"Show-offs," Betty said.

Don laughed.

The theater lights dimmed, and the stage curtain opened. A newsreel logo appeared on the screen, followed by scenes of the war in Europe. Hundreds of Allied bombers devastated German cities. There were pictures of collapsed buildings and rubble. Allied ground forces advanced through Luxembourg and neared the Rhine River. The screen shifted focus to the war in the Pacific.

"General MacArthur is in command of all US ground forces in the Pacific. Admiral Nimitz commands all US naval forces as the Allies prepare for the invasion of the Japanese home islands."

Soldiers of the US Sixth Army waded ashore in the Lingayen Gulf on Luzon in the Philippines.

June thought about her brothers. Lloyd was still in the European theater of the war. She still hadn't told Betty about Ricky.

"Switching to the home front, the American Arsenal of Democracy is running full tilt, supplying our brave soldiers with the ammo they need to defeat the tyrants in Germany and Japan," the newsreader continued.

The cameras switched to scenes of automatic loading machines spitting out thousands of rounds of .50 caliber cartridges in an ordnance plant.

"This ordnance plant in Missouri is making four out of every ten .50 caliber rounds being fired by American troops worldwide," the announcer said.

"That looks like your plant here in St. Joe!" June whispered to Betty.

"I think it is our plant," Betty whispered back.

The newsreel ended, and the screen was filled with the Warner Brothers Studios logo, followed by the movie title and the credits. Mike and Don put their arms around the girls, who fed them popcorn while they all watched Humphrey Bogart get romantically entangled with the young Lauren Bacall.

"I'd kill for a husky, sexy voice like hers," Betty whispered to June.

"She was only nineteen years old when she did this movie," June replied.

"Shhh!" came from the seats behind them.

June put her finger to her lips. Betty giggled. They put their heads back on the guys' shoulders and watched the movie.

Occasionally, June would glance over at Betty. Betty looked like she was having a good time. June was happy for her friend. Impulsively, she kissed Mike on the cheek. He looked at her and lifted his eyebrows. She just smiled and settled back against his shoulder. She gave him the last bite of their popcorn.

After the movie, as they walked through the lobby of the theater, Betty stopped abruptly and fainted. Don caught her and helped her over to an upholstered bench along the wall and sat her down on the bench.

After a moment, Betty looked up at them and said, "I got a little dizzy for a minute."

Mike said, "Just rest for a little while, and then we'll take you home."

Color returned to Betty's face, and she said, "That was a good movie. Thank you for bringing me, guys. I should go home. The doctors told me to take it easy for a few days."

When they got to Mike's car, Betty said, "I'll ride in the back with Don."

Don opened the back door and helped Betty into the car. He followed her in and closed the door.

She leaned up against him and said, "Thanks for the movie, big guy." She turned to Mike, speaking over the back of the seat. "And thanks for the popcorn." She closed her eyes and went to sleep.

Her three friends talked about the movie on the way to Betty's parents' house. Mike pulled into the driveway and stopped. Betty was still asleep, so Don carried her to the door and rang the bell. Kate opened the door and saw Don holding Betty.

"What happened to her?" Kate asked, frightened.

"She's okay. She just got tired after the movie. Can you show me to her room?" Don asked. Don followed Kate up to Betty's room and laid her on her bed.

Kate took Betty's shoes off and covered her with the bedspread. "Did she have a good time?" Kate asked Don.

"She was fine. We all had a good time, Kate," Don said.

Kate walked out to the car with Don. "Thank you all for being Betty's friends," she said. A tear ran down her cheek.

They said goodbye, and Don got back into the Chevy. June and Mike took Don back to Rosecrans Field and went home to the apartment.

*****

On Sunday afternoon, June called her mother.

"How was church?" she asked Bess.

"I swear the reverend gets windier every year. But I suppose it's good for our souls," Bess said.

"Amen!" said Dee, who heard Bess's remarks. They were sharing the Sunday paper when June called.

"Mom, I've had some bad news. My friend Betty is very sick. She has leukemia."

"Oh, June, I'm so sorry to hear that. What can I do for you or your friend?" Bess asked.

June said, "Right now she is okay. Her doctors treated her in the hospital in St. Joe. She is in what they call remission. The disease is under control, but she's not cured. They don't actually have a cure for it."

"Then we are just going to have to pray they find one," Bess said. "How are you doing, honey?"

"I'm fine. Mike got out of the Army. They discharged him last Monday," June said.

Dee was reading the Sunday newspaper comics section but put it down on the table to listen to Bess's side of the conversation.

"That's wonderful news. Is he still down in Neosho?" Bess asked.

Ray asked, "Mike?"

Bess nodded her head yes.

"No, Mom. He took the train up here to St. Joe on Wednesday," June said.

"Where is he staying?" Bess asked.

Dee moved his chair closer to Bess. She held the phone between them so they both could hear June.

"Mom, he's staying with me," June said. She waited for her mother to chew on that.

Bess and Dee looked at each other. She put her hand over the mouthpiece of the phone and whispered to Dee, "Well, Dad, they are engaged after all." Bess took her hand away from the mouthpiece and said, "That's nice, dear. Let's talk about your wedding."

*****

Ricky was reading *Life* magazine when a woman walked in.

"My name is Lieutenant Wilkins," the woman told Ricky. "I'm your physical therapist. If you want that arm to work, you're going to have to hurt. The more you hurt, the faster that arm will heal."

Lieutenant Wilkins was a tall, well-proportioned blond with green eyes and nice legs. She wore a white hospital coat over a tunic with silver bars above the brass medical caduceus on her lapels. Her tunic and skirt were both dark green. The nice legs were encased in white hose and ended in a black pair of ugly Army shoes.

"I'm in love," Ricky said to himself.

Lieutenant Wilkins handed Ricky a small red rubber ball. "Put that ball in your left hand and try to squeeze it, gently at first."

Ricky put the ball in his left hand. His hand was sticking out of his cast. The ball fell out of his hand onto the bed. "I can't hold on to it," he said.

"Pick up the ball with your right hand and put it back in your left hand," she said.

The ball fell out again.

"This is stupid," he said.

"It's your arm. If you want to be a quitter, that's up to you. I have plenty of other patients," she said and left his room.

"Bitch!" he said when she was gone. He picked up the *Life* magazine he was reading before she came in. There was a pictorial spread of Bob Hope and Bing Crosby. He couldn't focus on the magazine. He picked up the ball and put it in his left hand. It rolled away again.

"Shit!" he said. "This is ridiculous."

By the next morning, he still couldn't squeeze the damn ball, but it wasn't rolling away all the time anymore. And his arm was starting to hurt.

We'll see who's a quitter, he thought.

*****

Betty was getting bored. *I guess even fear can't last forever*, she thought. She was working on the jigsaw puzzle, but most of it was done. The rest would be easy (and boring). Her dad was working, and her mother was shopping.

She called the ordnance plant and got through to Joe's office. A girl named Gail answered his phone.

"Can I please speak with Mr. Harding?" Betty asked Gail.

"One moment," Gail said and told Mr. Harding he had a call on line one.

"Joe Harding," he answered.

"Joe, it's Betty Anderson."

"Betty, my god, how are you? Where are you? I thought you were still in the hospital."

"I'm home. I'm feeling much better. I want to come back to work."

"When?" he asked. He put down the file he was studying and looked at his overflowing in-tray.

"Tomorrow, if that's all right," Betty said.

"Tomorrow is great," Joe said. "But is that going to be okay with your doctors?"

"Yes, they encouraged me to get back to normal activities, and I'm bored stiff here at home. But what about Gail?" she asked.

"Gail is a temp from the secretarial pool in the admin building. She'll go back there. She doesn't like the plant anyway."

"I'll see you tomorrow. Thanks, Joe."

On Tuesday night, Betty called June. She had told her mother and father she was going back to work. Ray was concerned but stayed quiet when Betty told them about it.

"Do you want me to bring your car back?" June asked.

"No, but I'll need a ride to work," Betty said.

"Hold on a minute," June said. She explained to Mike about Betty returning to work and needing a ride.

Mike said, "No problem. I'll take her. What time does she want me to pick her up?"

They worked out the details.

*****

Betty had forgotten how noisy the plant was. She flinched when she heard a .50-caliber test round being fired in the testing area. *What are they testing for?* she wondered. She still hadn't asked Joe about that.

There was no one at the desk she normally occupied when she arrived in Joe's reception area. She sat down at the desk and started sorting through the papers in her tray.

Gail walked in and said, "Great! You're here. Do you need me to bring you up to date?"

Betty could see from the documents she had perused that her system had collapsed.

"No, not unless you want to," she said tactfully.

"Not me. I'm going back to the admin building. Good luck, honey," Gail said.

Joe arrived an hour later and stopped at her desk. "How are you feeling?" he asked her.

"Okay. It's nice to be back."

She looked okay to Joe. She had three piles of memos and reports sorted out to go to him.

"When you get a chance, could you look at my in-tray? It's full."

Betty laughed and said, "I'll bet it is. Joe, I was curious. When the testing area fires all those test rounds, what are they testing for?"

"Mainly to make sure the misfire rates meet Department of the Army specifications. We also test muzzle velocity, range, and accuracy of the rounds. We disassemble some of the rounds and check the amount of powder, the weight of the bullet, and the dimensions of the shells."

"Why do you do that?" Betty asked.

"Government contracts come with very detailed specifications. We have to report our test results to the Department of the Army," said Mr. Harding.

"Do you ever fail the tests?" Betty asked.

"Not since I've been production manager. I don't know about before I came."

Betty had Joe's in tray caught up by the end of the day. She'd catch up on her desk tomorrow. She told Joe she couldn't work late as her friend's fiancée was picking her up.

"Betty, I am just happy to have you back. You take it easy," Joe said.

Though she was tired, Betty was happy. She had been immersed in her work, and the day had gone by quickly. She hadn't thought once about her illness.

*****

Mike invested some of his discharge money on civilian clothes. The clerk in the men's department at Sears and Roebuck had helped him pick out the outfit, and he now wore a tweed jacket, gray slacks, a white button-down collar shirt, and a figured dark-blue tie. He also wore a pair of shiny black wing-tipped shoes.

June said he looked swell. Betty said he looked like a million dollars. Mike hoped Kaufmann's Radio Sales and Service agreed with them. Kaufmann's was the largest radio and audio equipment store in town.

Mike presented himself to a salesclerk at one of the sales counters at 1:55 p.m.

"I have an appointment with Mister Cline at 2:00 p.m.," he told the clerk.

The clerk sent him to the back of the store to the offices, and a receptionist directed him to Mr. Cline's office. He knocked on the office door and went in.

A bald, middle-aged man wearing glasses sat behind a modest desk. He wore a white short-sleeved shirt with the collar open and a tie tugged down from the collar. He had a credenza on the wall behind him with pictures of his wife and children. There was a well-worn vinyl couch next to the wall.

"Mr. Cline, I'm Mike Thompson, here for my interview."

"Have a seat, Mr. Thompson," Mr. Cline said.

Mr. Cline picked up a file and opened it. He took out a paper and looked at it.

"You just got out of the Army?" he asked.

"Yes, sir, I was in the Signal Corps at Camp Crowder. The Army closed down my training unit and discharged the training cadre were who not career men."

"What are your plans now that you are a civilian?" Mr. Cline asked Mike.

"I have a great deal of experience in radio and electronics, both in the service and during high school. I want to get a job in that field and continue my education to be an electrical engineer."

"But first you want to sell radios?" Mr. Cline asked. He put the file down on his desk and studied Mike.

"If that's the only job you have for me, then I'll sell radios. But I hope you can use my skills in your service department. I need a job. I'm getting married in April."

Mr. Cline got up from his chair and came around his desk. "Come with me, Mr. Thompson."

He walked through his door, and Mike followed him. Mr. Cline walked out to the showroom floor and into a glass walled display room filled with console radios. He stopped in front of one and asked Mike, "What can you tell me about this radio?"

"It's a very nice radio. It's an Emerson DX model with an Ingraham wood cabinet. It's probably a six-tube or seven-tube with a super-het chassis. This model has a built-in loop antenna, which is convenient. It gets AM and shortwave. That's a beautiful veneer inlay cabinet."

Mr. Cline walked on and stopped in front of another radio. "What about this one?"

Mike studied the radio. "That's a Zenith Walton series seven-tube. It's got some nice options. It's got motorized tuning and an eye tube. This one looks like an older model."

"It's a 1938. The first year for the triangular dial," Mr. Cline said. "What do you know about the guts of this radio?"

"Everything," Mike said. "It has seven octal based vacuum tubes, electrolytic capacitors, resistors, and a lot of wires and circuits. If I have the parts, I can fix anything that goes wrong with it."

Mr. Cline turned and walked back to his office. Mike followed him.

When they were both seated, Mr. Cline asked, "Are you a leader or a follower?"

"Mr. Cline, I was an NCO in the United States Army for almost three years. Before that, I was a private. I can do both of those jobs."

Mr. Cline laughed. "Why don't you call me Bernie, everyone here does."

"Okay, Bernie. My friends call me Mike."

"Mike, I have an opening in our service department for a supervisor. The job pays $200 a month to start. It's yours if you want it."

"I definitely want it," Mike said. "When do I start?"

"Come in on Monday morning at eight. My secretary will give you some paperwork to take with you. Bring it in on Monday and see me. I'll get you started."

Bernie called in his secretary and told her what forms to give to Mike. Mike thanked Bernie and followed his secretary to her desk. When she gave him the forms and indicated where he needed to sign them, he asked her, "What is Mr. Cline's position with the company?"

"He's a vice president and Mr. Kaufmann's partner," she said.

Mike stared at her for a few seconds and whistled. "I think I'm going to like working here," he said.

*****

"I like my new boss, Bernie Cline," Mike told Betty as he drove her home from the ordnance plant. "He's a big shot at the store, but you'd never know it." He stood on the brakes to avoid a taxi that darted around him and cut him off. Mike held out his arm to keep Betty from getting thrown forward. He honked at the taxi and yelled, "Watch out, you stupid son of a bitch!" He looked over at Betty and asked anxiously, "Are you all right?"

Betty straightened up her hat and said, "I'm fine." She slid her rump back against her seat.

"I'm sorry about the language. I guess I'm not quite a civilian yet," Mike said.

"He was a stupid son of a bitch," Betty said and laughed.

Mike laughed with her and asked, "How was your first day back at work?"

"It was busy, but I was glad to get out of the house. My parents have been wonderful, but I was going stir crazy," Betty said. "I really like my boss too."

Mike pulled into the driveway at Betty's parents' house. "I'll pick you up in the morning," Mike said. He reached over and opened her car door.

"Won't you be late for your new job?" she asked, holding the door open.

"I don't start until next Monday," he told her. "I can take you in the rest of the week. We can work something out for next week. I'll talk to June."

"Thanks Mike. I'll see you in the morning." She got out of the car and closed the door. She went into the house and talked to her mother and father about her day. Then she took a nap before dinner.

Mike got Chinese takeout at the Chinese restaurant June told him about. He promised her he would do the cooking tonight. He stopped at a liquor store and got a bottle of wine. Tonight, they would celebrate his new job.

"What have you got in the sack?" June asked Mike when he came in the door of the apartment.

He hung up his coat and hat and answered, "Dinner!"

He put the food on the table and opened the bottle of wine. June came in from the living room and watched what he was doing.

"How was Betty tonight when you took her home?" June asked.

Mike got the plates and silverware and set the table. He poured them both a glass of the wine.

"She was fine. She said her day was busy, but she was happy she went to work. Dinner is served. Come and get it before we throw it out to the hogs."

June sat down at the table and started dishing up the fried rice and chicken chow mein. She picked up her wineglass and asked, "What are we celebrating?"

Mike picked up his glass of wine and said, "You are looking at the newest employee of Kaufmann's Radio Sales and Service Store."

June squealed and said, "You got a job!"

"I thought I just said that."

June tapped her glass against his and said, "Congratulations, honey. But I'm the farmer in this family. If anyone gets to talk about hogs, it's me."

They both sipped their wine.

"Now to the important stuff. How much do you think the pay is?" Mike asked.

"Well, to me, your scale varies from five cents to a million dollars, depending on the circumstances," June answered. "Right now, since you got dinner, it's on the high end of the scale." She ate some chow mein to demonstrate the point.

"Two hundred bucks a month," Mike said. "That's more than double what Uncle Sam was paying me." He waited for her reaction.

June yelled, "We're rich!" She jumped out of her chair and grabbed him and hugged him. "Mike, that's great. Good for you. Good for us!" He turned his head toward her, and she gave him a big kiss. She returned to her chair and took a big sip of her wine. "What are you going to be doing to earn all that money?"

"I'm going to be a supervisor in the repair department. I'm not exactly sure what that means," he said.

"When do you start work?" She dished up the fried rice and chow mein.

Mike topped off their wine glasses. "I start Monday morning at eight."

"Mike! How will we get Betty to work?"

Mike paused with a bite of chow mein on his fork and thought about that. "I guess it depends on whether or not she can drive herself. If she can, we just give her back her car. I can take us to work in my car."

"If she can't, I'll take her to work. I will have to leave earlier," June said. "You can't be late for your new job, Mike."

After they did the dishes, June sipped the last of her wine and said, "Now let's *really* celebrate." She took Mike's hand and led him into their bedroom.

As Mike was taking off his pants, he said, "I have to bring home Chinese more often."

June giggled and finished undressing.

*****

Lieutenant Wilkins pushed a rolling stand with an adjustable center rod into Ricky's hospital room. There was a short flat arm at the top of the rod, parallel to the floor. It looked like an IV stand. There was something hanging from the arm.

"Let me see you hold your rubber ball," she said.

Ricky reached under his pillow and took the ball in his right hand. He placed it in his left hand. His fingers closed over the ball.

"There's hope for you yet, Sergeant," she said to Ricky. "Now put the ball back under the pillow."

"Good morning to you too, Lieutenant," Ricky said. He put the ball back under the pillow.

Lieutenant Wilkins placed three fingers of her right hand across the palm of his left hand.

"Squeeze my fingers," she said.

"Now this looks like a more promising start to our romance," Ricky said. His hand closed on her fingers, and she felt a small pressure from his grip. Ricky tried to hold her fingers tighter. Sweat broke out on his forehead.

"Okay, that's enough," she said.

He let go of her fingers with a sigh of relief.

"That's not bad progress, Sergeant. From now on, squeeze the ball fifteen minutes every hour. Start on the hour and finish on the quarter hour. Don't miss any hour. Next week, I want you to squeeze hard enough to hurt me."

She positioned the cart with the flat arm of the upright over his left hand and adjusted the height.

"So now I have something to look forward to," Ricky said and smiled at her.

She took off the object hanging from the arm of the cart. It looked like two saddle stirrups connected by a flexible rope. She hooked one of the stirrups onto the flat arm. She placed his left hand on the other retainer.

265

"Hold out your right arm," she said.

Ricky held up and extended his right arm. He couldn't make heads or tails of what she was doing.

Lieutenant Wilkins extended her right arm and closed her hand. Then she bent her wrist toward the floor.

"Now you do it," she said.

He shrugged and bent his right wrist. "Now what?" he asked.

"Now you do the same thing with your left hand."

Ricky said, "Now I know you're crazy. How am I supposed to bend my wrist? You have my hand trapped."

"Use your right hand to help," she said.

Ricky pushed his left hand down. The rope stretched and his left wrist bent.

"Now you do it without helping your left hand."

Ricky strained to bend his wrist, but nothing moved, and his arm hurt.

"This is impossible," he said in frustration.

"So was holding that ball," she said and left the room.

"Sadistic bitch!" he grumbled.

*****

Betty was not up to driving yet, so June took her to work.

"You have to get up earlier to do this. I feel like I'm taking advantage of you," Betty said.

"Let's examine that for a minute," June said. "You've let me use your car for weeks now, saving me taking a slow, cold trolley ride both ways." She stopped at the entrance to the ordnance plant.

"Well, if you put it like that, I don't feel so bad. Thanks for the lift, roomie."

Betty got out and waved at June as she pulled away. She went in to work. Her desk was almost caught up, and Joe was smiling.

*****

266

Mike wasn't sure how a supervisor was supposed to dress. He compromised by wearing slacks and a white dress shirt with his new tie. He was ten minutes early, but Bernie's secretary was already at her desk. Mike gave Bernie's secretary the completed employment forms.

The secretary said, "Go on in. Bernie is expecting you. I'm Hilda."

Mike put out his hand and said, "I'm pleased to meet you, Hilda, I'm Mike."

Mike went into Bernie's office.

"Sit down, Mike. We'll have a chat, and then I'll introduce you to your team," Bernie said.

Hilda came in with two cups of coffee on a tray with cream and sugar.

"That was very nice of her," Mike said as they sipped their coffee.

"She's Sid's niece. Sid is my partner and president of the company. The first thing you need to know is that our service department is also one of our sales departments. We get a lot of our new customers because they bring in their old radios to repair. While they're here, they see the fancy new radios and they trade in their old radios for new ones. Or they take their old one home, and when they get an itch for a new one, naturally they come back to us." Bernie paused and took another drink of his coffee. He waited for Mike to respond.

"So you want the service department to help sell radios," Mike said.

"Yes, in a way. Our sales staff will sell them the new radios. What we want you and your people to do is treat them like customers and friends, not like problems to be dealt with." He paused again and waited for Mike to think about that.

"That's very smart. I'll bet other repair shops don't always do that," Mike said.

"Now you're catching on. Let's take a walk and meet your people."

Mike followed Bernie through a door that led to the back section of the building. They walked into a huge space. Most of it was taken up with racks of product, new radios, and audio equipment. The rest was filled with workstations and parts racks.

The racks were labeled with the name of the radio manufacturer and the manufacturer's descriptions and part numbers for the parts in the bins. There was a library of technical manuals. As they walked through the library, Mike saw *Most Often Needed Radio Diagrams 1944*, *Applied Electronics*, and the *Allied Radio Data Handbook* among other up-to-date manuals.

I'd love to sit in this library and read for a week, Mike thought.

The place was spotlessly neat and clean. Each work bench had its own tools, mounted on shadow drawings of the tools.

They don't have to search for a tool or lose many of them, Mike mused. *This place was as well organized as a military warehouse or maintenance shed.*

Bernie introduced Mike to his new staff as they walked into each section:

Console and armchair radios: Marvin Blake
Wood tabletop radios: Ben Donaldson
Wood refinishing: George Harris
Plastics tabletop radios: Dave Richie and Sam Wiseman
Parts: Ken Palmer
House calls and audio equipment: Tony Moreno

And finally, Bernie introduced Mike to Michelle Girard, the scheduler.

"Michelle is the brains of the outfit. Everything goes through her," Bernie said.

Michelle blushed and said, "Nice to meet you, Mike."

Bernie walked back to his office and told Mike to have a seat. Bernie sat down behind his desk and opened a drawer. He took out a big cigar, clipped off one end with a silver clipper, and lit it up. When he had it going to his satisfaction, he blew out a big cloud of smoke.

"Would you like a cigar?" he asked Mike.

"I'd love one. But my girl and I quit smoking at the same time. I'm going to marry her, so I guess I'll have to pass."

Bernie laughed and said, "You're a wise man." He took another puff on his cigar. "We really do need a supervisor for the service department. Michelle is overworked and reaching her limit. But that's not why I created the job." Bernie tapped the ash off into his ashtray.

Mike waited for Bernie to continue.

"We haven't gotten into this new thing, television. RCA has a stranglehold on patents for it. Televisions are not very good or reliable yet. But they will be the big ticket soon. Home radio is dead. It just doesn't know it. Jack Benny, Hope and Crosby, The Lone Ranger—they'll all be on television or they'll be gone. We will be too, if we don't get in on it."

Bernie picked up a thick file filled with brochures from television manufacturers. He handed them to Mike.

"Your main job is to help me sort out the wheat from the chaff. We sell high-quality radios and audio equipment. I want us to sell high-quality televisions when they are available. What do you think?"

Mike could hardly keep his seat; he was so excited. "I should pay you instead of the other way around. I can't wait to get started."

*****

June was busy in the kitchen when Mike got home. She had flour-coated pork chops frying in the skillet and peeled potatoes cooking in a pan of water. There was cooked broccoli on the table.

Mike came into the kitchen and said, "That smells good. I love pork chops." He gave her a quick kiss and sat down at the kitchen table.

June stuck a fork in a potato and decided they were ready to mash. She put them in a bowl with milk and butter and put the bowl on the table in front of Mike along with the potato masher. "This is why women need a big, strong man. Mash away!"

I'm back on KP duty, he reflected.

"How was your first day of work? You got home sort of late," she asked him.

"It was great. The service department is in great shape and the staff seemed to know what they were doing," Mike said. He started mashing the potatoes.

June took down two plates and ladled the pork chops out of the skillet and onto the plates. They were golden brown. She started making gravy with the grease from the pork chops.

"Then why do they need a supervisor?"

Mike paused mashing the potatoes. "The department is being run by a young woman named Michelle. She is the scheduler. My boss, Bernie, says she is swamped."

He set the bowl of mashed potatoes on the table.

"But the main reason Bernie is adding a supervisor is to get into the television business. Bernie wants someone like me to research the technical side to help him get into the right televisions."

"I didn't know you were a television expert," June said. She poured the brown gravy in a gravy boat and put it on the table.

"I'm not a television expert. But they use a lot of the same components as radios. The main thing I need to bone up on is the cathode ray tube. That's the heart of television sets. This job is a great opportunity for me."

"I'm so glad you found a job that winds your watch, honey," June said. "Dish up while it's hot."

Mike tried the pork chop and mashed potatoes and gravy. "Now this is what I call gourmet dining!" he said.

"I was thinking I might go out to the farm on Saturday. I'd like plan our wedding with Mom and my sisters." June said.

"That works for me. The reason I was late tonight is that I was studying technical manuals. While you are at your parents, I'll stay here to learn all I can about televisions. I really want to keep this job," Mike said.

"I'll call my mom and my sisters after dinner," June said.

When they finished dinner, she made her phone call.

When Bess answered, she said, "Mom, it's June. How are you and Dad doing?"

"We're fine, honey. How are you and Mike?" Bess had just walked in from the henhouse with a basket of eggs when the phone rang. She usually gathered them in the morning but put it off while she studied menus from caterers for the wedding.

"Mike got a good job with a big radio store in town. He starts next Monday," June said.

Bess set the basket of eggs down and sat at the kitchen table.

"That's great news. He doesn't let any grass grow under his feet, does he?"

"He sure doesn't. Mom, the reason I called is I'm thinking of coming out to the farm on Saturday to talk about wedding plans. Could you call Reverend Davis and check on getting the church on April 15?"

"Sure, I can do that. Is there anything else you want me to do?" Bess said.

"I'd like to have Emma Dee and Virginia Jane there Saturday if they don't have other plans," June said. "Could you call them and check?"

"Consider it done. Tell Mike congratulations from Dad and me on his new job. If there's nothing else, I just got the eggs out of the henhouse and I need to put them in the icebox."

"It's called a refrigerator, Mom. I wish I had one."

"I know, dear. Old habits die hard. You'll find that out some day. Goodbye, honey."

"Goodbye, Mom."

*****

Mike spent his first day of work at Kaufmann's between his office, next to Mr. Cline's office, and Michelle's office in the service department. Michelle walked him through her work order and scheduling procedures. Phone calls frequently interrupted them with customers asking when they would get their radios.

"Don't we give them a promise date when we get their radios?" Mike asked her.

Michelle's desk was littered with paperwork. "Sure, we do," she said.

"Then why are they all calling you?"

"It's after their promise date."

"Why are we late on their orders?"

"Because we promise them dates we don't meet," she said as though that was a reasonable thing to do.

Mike choked back an expletive trying to get out of his mouth. He took a deep breath and asked, "Why do we promise a customer a date we can't meet?" He had been standing beside her desk, but decided he'd better sit down. She had a battered metal chair next to her desk. He sat and waited for the answer.

"If I gave them a real promise date, they would be unhappy. They'd complain to Bernie and then I'd be in trouble."

The phone rang again. After making a new promise to the customer, she hung up.

"You have them complaining now, don't you?" *I sure as hell would*, he thought.

"Sometimes, but then it's the repairman who gets in trouble, not me," she said, as if that took care of the problem.

The phone rang again. Mike retreated to his office to study the television schematics Bernie gave him. He planned to talk to each of his staff tomorrow. He had to get to the bottom of this customer service problem.

On his second day at Kaufman's, he asked Marvin Blake, his console repairman, to come to his office. Marvin was a slim, pale-skinned, black-haired man in his forties.

Mike introduced himself and invited Marvin to sit down with him on the brown vinyl couch that matched the one in Bernie's office. He wanted his first meetings with his staff to be informal.

"How long have you worked for Kaufmann's?" Mike asked him.

"Ten years," Marvin answered.

If he's been here that long, he must like his job and be good at it. Console models were Kaufmann's top of the line products.

"On average, how long does it take you to repair a radio?" Mike asked.

"If it's only the innards, a couple of hours," Marvin said. "If I have to touch up the wood cabinet and refinish it, it could take all day."

"So if a customer brings in a radio to repair, he should get it back in a day or two," Mike said.

"Well, that depends on some other things. If it's a make we don't carry parts for, we'd have to order the parts. That could take up to two weeks if the radio is made by a small custom shop. Also, it depends on the backlog."

Mike thought about what he had seen in his walks. "I don't remember a lot of radios stacked up at anyone's bench."

Marvin explained that the radios waiting for repair were kept in the storeroom next to Michelle's office.

I need to see this storeroom, Mike thought. "How do you get the next radio when you have finished the one you were on?" Mike asked.

"Usually, I just take the one nearest the door," Marvin said.

Mike decided it was time for him to see the storeroom. Console models were in a line on one section of the floor. Table models were on racks. They all had repair tickets attached to them. He checked several of the tickets. They were in no particular order. The order numbers were out of sequence and the order dates were randomly distributed. Mike wondered how a place so well organized on the work floor could have such disorganized office systems.

His next priority was to investigate the television business for Mr. Cline. Mike was excited about this part of his new job. He agreed with Mr. Cline that television would be the next big thing.

Mike went to St. Joseph's main library after work and spent two hours researching television manufacturing and television broadcasting. He checked out reference manuals and technical articles. He'd study them on Saturday.

14

M/Sgt. Lloyd Taylor and the rest of the Twelfth Army Group under General Omar Bradley were sitting on their asses behind the Roer River, stalled in their march to the Rhineland in Germany. The Roer River had been turned into a lake by water released from two upstream dams still controlled by the Germans.

Bradley's Twelfth Army Group was supposed to have captured the German forces before that could happen. They didn't. So everyone was stopped, waiting for the Roer to recede so they could push on to the Rhine, where Hitler had ordered the remains of his army to stand and hold in place. The main British Army Group under Montgomery, including the Canadians and Americans attached to Monty, and the huge Twelfth Army group, which included the Third Army, was out of work. That included the Fourth Armored Division and M/Sgt. Lloyd Taylor's battalion.

Stopped by this overgrown puddle of water, Lloyd didn't know whether to laugh or cry. His tank crew could use the rest, but they had hoped to finish the Germans and have the war over with.

To make matters worse, Lloyd thought, *the damned Russians were gaining ground quickly and might beat the Americans to Berlin.*

*****

On Wednesday, Tony Moreno sat in Michelle's office and answered a customer query about their radio repair. Mike came into the office and asked him what he was doing.

"I'm taking calls for Michelle. She's expediting repair orders with the repairmen," Tony said.

"I thought you were the house-call guy?" Mike said. "Shouldn't you be making house calls?"

Tony was a muscular man in his midthirties with dark, curly hair. "I do make the house calls. When I'm all caught up, I try to help out Michelle."

Mike found that very interesting. *This guy could just be out in the field, sitting on his butt somewhere. Instead, he's here helping Michelle. I wonder why.*

"When Michelle comes back to her office, I'd like to talk with you, Tony. I'll be in my office."

"Sure, Mr. Thompson, whatever you say," Tony said.

The phone rang again, and Tony answered it.

Half an hour later, Mike was reading an article on television broadcasting when Tony came in. Mike waved him into his guest chair.

"How long have you worked here?" Mike asked.

Tony wondered why he was in trouble. He didn't relish being called in to see his new boss, who seemed unhappy about him answering Michelle's calls.

"Three years," Tony said. *He can't just fire me without giving me a warning.*

"What did you do before that?"

"I was a finish carpenter. I fixed radios on the side to earn extra money."

Now he wants to see if I can find a job elsewhere when he cans me, Tony worried.

"How did you avoid the service?" Mike asked, annoyed that this apparently fit man got out of fighting the war.

That's it! Tony thought. *He thinks I'm a shirker, and he's a veteran who doesn't want to work with a shirker.* "I tried to enlist in the Marines. They wouldn't take me. I went to the Army, and they turned me down too," Tony said.

"Why did they turn you down?" Mike asked. *Was Tony a conscientious objector or something worse?*

"I couldn't pass the physical. I have a heart murmur. Every time one of those doctors put a stethoscope on me, that was it. So now I'm 4F."

"So you have physical limitations? You can't lift heavy weights?" Mike asked.

Wow, he's looking for any excuse to let me go, Tony thought angrily. "Hell, no. I can do anything you can do, and I'll bet I can lift more than you can." *I don't have to put up with this crap,* Tony decided.

Mike grinned at Tony and said, "Take it easy. I was just asking. You have free time on your hands, do you?"

Now he's laughing at me! "Sometimes I'm busy, but usually there's some slack. Michelle is always buried under, so I try to help her out."

"Are you two more than just coworkers?" Mike asked.

"I wish. But she's got a regular boyfriend. I feel sorry for how hard she works. That's why I help," Tony said defensively.

"What if I can show you how to help her out and make our customers happier as well?" Mike asked him.

Tony was thoroughly confused. *Maybe I'm not getting fired,* he thought. "That would be good," he said cautiously.

Mike was completely unaware of Tony's unspoken fears. He liked Tony's responses and decided to enlist his help with the customer-service issues. Mike took Tony with him to the stockroom. He showed Tony how the radios waiting for repair were disorganized, and that generally the last repair orders were closest to the door and the oldest orders further from the door.

"We need to figure out how the first repair orders in are the first orders out. Now the last orders in get worked on first. This makes the first orders late when newer orders get ahead of them. That makes Michelle get a lot of unhappy customer phone calls. Then she has to run around trying to expedite the repair order for the unhappy customers."

Tony thought about what Mike had observed and said, "Why don't we just make the repair person check the repair tickets and take the oldest one first?"

"We could do that, but then we'll have them wasting a lot of time checking tickets. What we need is a physical staging system that puts the radios in the correct order, so the repairman just takes the first one in line. I'd like you to organize these rows and the racks in FIFO order."

"FIDO order? What do dogs have to do with this?" Tony asked, confused.

Mike laughed and said, "FIFO order—first in, first out. When you get the stockroom organized, show the repair team where to get the radio with the oldest date."

Tony caught on to the principle and started rearranging the radios. As he did this, he thought of a way to make it a lot easier to keep them in the right order.

Mike went to Michelle and asked her, "Is Tony scheduled to go out on a house call today?"

"He has one this afternoon."

"Call the customer and reschedule it for tomorrow if you can," Mike said. "I've got him working on a special project for me."

Mike then explained the FIFO concept to Michelle.

He had learned in the Army to give his subordinates a directive and a goal and then get out of their way. If they were competent, they would figure out the details. Mike planned to check back tomorrow and see how they were doing.

*****

Bernie Cline was in his office Saturday, looking over a sales report for the week. He often stopped by the store on Saturday to walk the sales floor. Saturday was the store's busiest day.

He looked up when there was a knock on his open office door. It was his partner, Sid Kaufmann.

Sid looked around Bernie's office and said for the dozenth time, "This place is a dump. Get some decent furniture in here."

Bernie smiled and said for the dozenth time, "You've got enough fancy furniture for both of us. What can I do for you, Sid?"

"You went ahead and hired a supervisor for service, didn't you?" Sid sat down on the aging vinyl couch next to the wall.

"I told you I would." Bernie got up and joined Sid on the couch, waiting for him to begin his tirade.

"It's wasted money. You could have hired a helper for Michelle for a third of the money," Sid said. He shifted his well-padded rear end around on the shabby couch, trying to get comfortable.

Sidney Kaufmann was a tall, overweight, fifty-five-year-old man with silver hair. He wore a gray three-piece glen plaid suit that was missing the suit coat he had left in his office. His silk tie was tight against his collar. His vest fit snugly over a generous stomach.

"A helper for Michelle wouldn't get us into the television business," Bernie said with a sigh. *Here we go again*, he thought.

Sid furrowed his brow and thought, *Not this television nonsense again*. "Television is a novelty. Have you seen the so-called pictures on them? The silent movies had better pictures. Who wants to watch silent movies again?"

"The pictures will get better. There's big money being spent on television technology. Ten years from now, the only person buying a radio will be a shortwave radio putz trying to talk to someone in Australia," Bernie said.

"So then we'll sell televisions," Sid answered reasonably.

He took out a cigar and handed one to Bernie. They clipped the ends and lit them. The two men had been partners for over twenty-five years. They were best man at each other's wedding.

"And be competing against every Tom, Dick, and Harry who got there ahead of us." Bernie took a puff of the cigar.

Sid bought good cigars.

"RCA, Zenith, Atwater Kent, Philco, and all the rest will have their franchisees already lined up and we'll be out in the cold trying to sell that putz a shortwave radio in a parquet wood cabinet," Bernie said.

"So who is this television genius you hired?" Sid asked, switching strategies. "I heard he's some sergeant who just got kicked out of the Army."

Bernie didn't take the bait. "If you're so worried about his salary, I'll pay it myself out of my own pocket."

"Oy vey, I give up. Just make sure he doesn't screw up the service department while he's chasing your televisions," Sid said and got up and left.

That went better than I thought it would, Bernie thought and went back to studying the sales report. He took another puff of Sid's cigar.

*****

June had left to go to the farm, and Mike was studying the technical manual he got from the library. It was starting to give him a headache.

June parked Betty's Ford in the yard of the farmhouse and walked past two other cars parked in the yard. She recognized Emma Dee's Studebaker Champion. The other car was a Ford Prefect she didn't recognize. She opened the front door and heard Emma Dee and Virginia Jane arguing about being her maid of honor.

She walked into the living room and saw her mother sitting next to Virginia Jane on the sofa. She was reading *McCall's* magazine and ignoring her daughters' argument. Virginia Jane was sitting on one of the upholstered armchairs and stopped in midsentence and said, "Here's the bride now. She can settle this."

"Hello, everyone," June said. "Where's Dad?" She sat down in the matching armchair.

"He's over at the old house, puttering around fixing something. I keep telling him he's wasting his time, but he won't let that old wreck go. Would you like some coffee, June? Emma Dee brought us her ration of coffee," Bess said.

"Sure, Mom," June said and followed her mother into the kitchen.

"Well, I guess we're just chopped liver," Emma Dee said. "She didn't even say hello to us."

Virginia Jane got up and joined her mother and sister in the kitchen. Emma Dee frowned and hesitated, then joined the others.

After they all had their coffee and were seated at the kitchen table, June said, "My friend Betty has cancer. I don't know if Mom told you about that," she said, looking from Emma Dee to Virginia Jane.

They both were dismayed.

"My goodness, June, that's just awful," Virginia Jane said.

Emma Dee reached out and took June's hand. "Can we do anything to help?" she asked June.

"She got treatment, and she's in remission. The doctors don't know how long that will last. But she's doing okay for now."

Emma Dee patted June's hand and sipped her coffee. "Thank God for that," Emma Dee said. "Good lord, Betty's very young to have such a terrible disease."

"I need to tell you that I have asked her to be my maid of honor and she has accepted," June said. "I hope that's okay with both of you."

Virginia Jane and Emma Dee looked at each other for a moment.

Emma Dee spoke first. "I couldn't be happier for her, June."

Virginia Jane was still digesting the implications of Betty's illness.

"Do you want to wait until April 15?" Virginia Jane asked. "Should we try to make it sooner for Betty?"

"I spoke with Reverend Davis. The earliest date the church was available is Saturday, April 14," Bess interjected.

June said, "That's fine with me. I think it will be okay with Mike. But let me call him and make sure." She went out to the living room and called her home number.

Mike answered on the third ring, "Hello."

"Hello. How is the studying going?" June asked.

"It's going pretty good. How's the hen party going?"

June ignored his male humor. "The reason I'm calling is my minister is asking if we can move our wedding up one day to Saturday the fourteenth instead of Sunday, the fifteenth."

"It's okay with me just as long as you don't get mad at me every year when I take you out to dinner on the fifteenth instead of the fourteenth. I'll never keep it straight now," Mike kidded her.

June laughed and said, "It's a done deal."

Bess, June, and her sisters spent the next three hours working out plans for her wedding and reception. Bess would take care of the invitations. Since her father was paying for the wedding, June insisted they keep it simple and not go overboard. She said she and her sisters could supply the food and appetizers for the reception. They didn't need a caterer.

Bess agreed with everything June said and ignored it while she mentally planned the wedding she wanted for June. She and Dee weren't paupers after all.

*****

June was setting up the packing line schedules for the week when she got a call from her boss, Tim, to come to his office. She opened the file drawer of her desk and took out a file folder labeled *SOP*.

She took it with her to Tim's office. "You wanted to see me, Tim?" she asked.

Tim turned toward her, and she saw that today's bow tie was vermillion, brighter red than June's hair. June stifled a laugh when she saw it.

"How's that SOP coming along? My boss and the production manager are asking me about it." He was eating a doughnut and drinking coffee.

You can tell the bosses to stop worrying about the SOP. Here it is," June said and handed him the file folder.

"Thanks, June. I'll read it later and then we'll discuss it." He finished his doughnut, drank a gulp of coffee, and said, "I've got to run to another meeting."

June went back to her office and resumed working on her schedules.

*****

Mike was writing a memo to his boss, Bernie Cline, about his investigation of the television industry when Tony knocked on his open door.

"Come on in, Tony, and have a seat," Mike said. He put down his pencil and asked, "What's up?"

Tony told Mike his proposal to convert the stockroom into a FIFO system.

"We put down roller conveyor tracks on the floor for the big consoles and install narrow roller conveyor tracks in the racks. The radios sit on plywood pallets, big ones for the consoles and small ones for the table models. The pallets ride on the tracks. As new radios come in, they start in the back end of the tracks and move forward. We could make it a lot fancier with powered conveyors, but I don't think it would be worth the money, and I doubt Mr. Kaufmann would go for it."

"Tony, it's a great idea. What's it going to cost?" Mike asked.

"We can use construction-grade 1/8 inch plywood for the small radios and 1/4 or 3/8 inch for the consoles. I can make the pallets myself. The only expensive part is the conveyors. I can buy salvage ones at a junk yard in town. I think we can do the whole thing for $400."

"Okay, I'll run it past Bernie. It sounds good to me. Great job, Tony."

"Thanks, boss." Tony got up off the couch to leave.

Mike stopped him. "How's it going now that you have organized the stockroom and instructed everyone in FIFO?" Mike asked.

Tony sat back down and scratched his head. "Michelle says we're doing better meeting promise dates and the customer complaint calls are down. The repair guys are being careful to get the oldest order to work on. The big problem is the receiving department. They still just put incoming radios wherever they can find room for them. That's why we need the conveyor system to make it easier for them."

Mike thought about that and said, "Yeah, I see the problem."

*****

Sgt. Richard Taylor was playing solitaire on his tray table when Major Reston came into his hospital room to see him.

"Hi, Doc," Ricky said and turned three cards off the deck.

"How are you feeling, Sergeant?" Major Reston asked. He walked up to Ricky's bed and examined the cast and Ricky's left hand.

"I'm just peachy, Doc, until I do those damned exercises your merciless therapist gives me," Ricky said. "What did you do, trade a couple of nurses and a draft choice to Hitler for her?"

Major Reston laughed and said, "I'll have to remember that one. I'll tell her how much you love her." He put three fingers of his hand into Ricky's left hand. "Squeeze."

Ricky grimaced as he squeezed as hard as he could.

"Okay, relax. That's coming along nicely," Major Reston said. "I think we can get the cast off now."

"Doc, that's the best news I've heard since I got here. You have no idea how much my arm itches, and I can't reach everywhere with the hanger."

Major Reston frowned. "The nurses were supposed to take that hanger away from you. I hope you didn't use it on your upper arm."

"Oops," Ricky said. "Forget I said that, Doc. And, no, I only use it on my lower arm. I don't want to mess up your good work."

"Well, it's too late for us to worry about infection now. That cast will be off by tomorrow. You'll still need to wear a sling. Lieutenant Wilkins will be by to help you with that. Lieutenant Wilkins is the finest physical therapist we have. You keep doing what she tells you, and you may be playing the violin yet."

"Great, I'll send her roses. She'll probably eat them," Ricky said.

Major Reston smiled, shook his head, and went back out into the hallway.

*****

Don had made friends with another cadre member in his barracks, S/Sgt. Harry Edwards. Harry was also a veteran of combat flights in the Pacific theater. He had been a navigator on supply and medical evacuation missions. He flew five missions on Gooney Birds into Guadalcanal to support the Marines that had taken a dirt air strip away from the Japanese and named it Henderson Field. The Japanese were trying to take it back. Japanese naval bombers and fighters made frequent raids. Japanese ground forces lobbed cannon and mortar fire onto the field, tearing up the linked metal runway. Using captured Japanese bulldozers and other heavy equipment, the Marines somehow kept Henderson Field open. Harry's twin engine C-47s brought in ammunition, food, medical supplies, and aviation fuel for the small force of Marine Wildcat and Buffalo fighters trying to stave off Japanese naval air squadrons. It was an unequal fight all the way around, but somehow, the Marines held out until they were reinforced.

Harry had a 1937 Buick on the base. Don liked the art déco styling and the car's flashy front grillwork.

Don asked him if he could borrow it to take his girl out on Saturday. He told Harry about Betty's illness, and Harry was happy to lend Don his car. Don called Betty Wednesday night.

Kate answered the phone and said Betty was resting after her workday, but she woke Betty and told her Don was on the phone.

"Hi, big guy. I was just taking a nap. What's up with you?" Betty asked.

"I've got a weekend pass, and my buddy is lending me his car. I thought we could get together on Saturday and do something," Don said.

"Doing something sounds like fun to me. What did you have in mind?" Betty asked.

"How about we have dinner and go to a club and dance?" Don suggested.

"As good as that sounds, how about we have lunch at Benny Magoons and go to my apartment afterward. I need to get a few things, and I miss my apartment," Betty said. "We might 'do something' while we're there," Betty said, talking softly so her parents couldn't hear.

"I like your idea better, but what about Mike and June?" Don asked.

"Leave that up to me. Pick me up here at eleven, okay?"

"Great. I'll see you Saturday morning, babe. Love you."

Betty called the apartment, and June answered the phone.

"June, it's me, Betty. I have a favor to ask you and Mike."

Mike was tutoring June on algebra. Math was not one of her strong suits, and it was sure to be on her entrance exam for the University of Missouri.

"Sure, Betty, what do you need?" June said to Betty.

"Don invited me on a date Saturday. We're going to have lunch at Benny Magoon's and then come over to the apartment afterward," Betty said.

"That's great. Mike and I would love to see you two."

"We'd like to see you both too, but maybe around 4:00 p.m. or 5:00 p.m.?" Betty asked.

June paused for a moment and laughed. "I think I see what favor you want. Sure, Mike and I can find something to do on Saturday afternoon. We'll even pick up dinner for all of us," June said.

Mike put down the algebra textbook and looked questioningly at June.

"Roomie, you're the best. We'll see you Saturday," Betty said.

"What was that all about?" Mike asked.

June joined him at the table and told Mike what Betty had asked.

"So, babe, what do you want to do while our friends are fooling around in the old homestead?" Mike asked her.

"Let's go downtown and go shopping. I need to get gifts for the maid of honor and my bridesmaids. Stop frowning at me. Being a husband carries certain obligations with it, you know."

"I didn't know they started before the wedding," he protested. Shopping in the lady's department was not high up on his list of things to do.

"Something else started before the wedding. Do you want to wait for that too?"

Mike ran up the white flag. He knew when he was whipped.

"Okay, okay, I give up. Shopping it is," Mike said and smiled ruefully at her.

*****

The next day June had a note on her desk from her supervisor, Tim. When she got to his office, he was on the phone and waved a hand to tell her to sit down. He finished the call and picked up a file on his desk.

"Your SOP is fine. Mr. Jamieson and Mr. Williams both reviewed it. Mr. Jamieson was the head of the scheduling department, and Mr. Williams was the packing department supervisor.

"They have made a few notes on your draft—nothing major. Please look over their suggestions and incorporate them into the SOP where you agree with them. If you don't agree with something, see me and we'll discuss it. Good job." He handed her the file.

June returned to her desk and reviewed the SOP when she had a spare minute. There were not many notes, and she didn't have a problem with them. But she was too busy to do the revisions.

I'll take them home with me tonight and turn in the revised SOP tomorrow, she planned.

*****

Mike was eager to present the FIFO project to his boss, Bernie Cline. He had a ten o'clock meeting with Bernie and arrived promptly at the scheduled time. Bernie invited him in and told him to have a seat in the guest chair.

"How are things going in the repair department?" Bernie asked.

"We're making progress, but we can do even better if you see your way clear to authorizing an improvement project Tony Moreno has proposed to me."

Bernie leaned back in his chair and looked at Mike.

"Tony Moreno has proposed a project, has he? He has never proposed any projects before. What's got into him, do you suppose?" Bernie asked, tongue in cheek.

"Tony and I discussed organizing the repair storeroom to implement a first-in, first-out system for the repair orders. He came up with his proposal to help me implement the new procedure," Mike said.

Bernie leaned back in his chair and studied Mike.

"Michelle told me that the repair department is having fewer late orders and that she is getting fewer customer complaints. I thought maybe someone was cracking the whip to get work done faster," Bernie said.

Mike shook his head and said, "The repair people are working just fine. It's a very good crew. The problem was that they were working on the orders in the wrong sequence, and that was due to the lack of a system in the stockroom.

"So the problem is solved?" Bernie asked.

"It's solved temporarily. But we need a physical system to stage the orders in the right sequence. That system is what Tony is proposing," Mike said.

"What is this new-fangled system?" Bernie asked. *And how much is it going to cost me?* he wondered.

"It's mainly roller conveyors and pallets for the radios to ride on. You put them in the back of the system, and they move forward in the correct sequence. It's called FIFO—first in, first out," Mike said.

Bernie asked the question that was foremost in his mind. "How much is this fancy new system going to cost?"

"Tony wrote up a bill of materials. Using low-cost plywood and salvage roller conveyors, Tony estimates it'll cost $400. We can do the labor in-house."

Bernie was surprised at the cost estimate. He thought it might be a few thousand dollars, not a few hundred.

"Well, happy customers are repeat customers. And Michelle said they're happier now. You've got your $400," Bernie said.

"Great! Thanks, Bernie. We'll start working on it right away," Mike said.

"Now what about televisions? Have you looked into that?" Bernie asked.

"Yes, I've studied the material you gave me and got technical manuals and books from the library about broadcasting. I'm still working through those. If you can give me another week, I should be ready to make some recommendations," Mike said.

Bernie took a cigar out of the humidor on his desk and rolled it around with his fingers.

This kid has figured out how to make customers happier and help Michelle and at the same time he's wading through all the television material, he thought. *And he's only been here a week. And he gets Tony to come up with this new FIFO thing in his spare time. Well, I know how to leave guys alone who are doing a good job.*

"Come back next week and tell me about television, Mike. Your parts guy has the authority to issue purchase orders for the FIFO stuff. If you need cash, see the accounting department. Now go away and let me enjoy my cigar."

*****

Tim, June's supervisor, called her to his office Friday morning to discuss the revised SOP she had turned in Thursday.

Tim said, "We have approved your SOP, and it will be effective Monday. You have been designated the point person to follow up on any questions or problems that come up. The production manager wants you to train his people on the SOP. I've arranged a training session for the schedulers."

"I'm going to be training people? I've never done that before," June asked. "And I'm still just a probationary scheduler."

Tim smiled and stood up. "Not anymore. You've been promoted to scheduler. You're off probation, and you're getting a 4 percent raise in salary. Congratulations."

June was pleased with her promotion but still nervous about having to train groups of people. She wasn't sure she could do it.

"Thanks for the raise, Tim, and the promotion. But I don't know about the training thing."

Tim had June figured out now. She always left herself a little elbow room in case a new assignment didn't work out. The trick was to agree with her and then stand back while she did it. But she might have a real issue with this. Tim sat back down in his chair and motioned for June to be seated.

"Are you afraid of public speaking, is that it?"

"Heck, no. But I know nothing about being a teacher," June answered. (She was a little nervous about the public speaking also.)

Tim thought for a minute and then said, "There's nothing to it. Write a lesson plan. Go through your SOP and make a list of topics you will talk about. You wrote the thing, so no one knows the material better than you."

"So I just read the SOP to them?" June asked.

"If you do that, they'll all be asleep before you're halfway through. They can read it themselves. Stick to your lesson plan. Explain why each topic is in the SOP and what it is supposed to do. Share your experience. Stop between topics for questions. That's all there is to it. When you have your lesson plan, see me and we'll go over it together. You'll do fine."

15

"Brave US Marines raise Old Glory on Iwo Jima," Mike read the headline Saturday morning at breakfast. There was an Associated Press photograph of an embattled small group of marines hoisting a tattered American flag. He read the accompanying story:

> "Casualties on both sides of this battle for a speck in the Pacific Ocean are appalling. Most of the Japanese refuse to surrender, and they must be dug out of every nook and cranny in the rocks of the volcanic island. The heroism of the Marines and the fanaticism of the Japanese soldiers resisting them are equally awe-inspiring. When this small group of Marines hoisted a battle-stained American flag on the rock pile called Mount Suribachi on Iwo Jima, an Associated Press photographer was there to capture the image."

Mike put the paper down on the table and took a minute to consider the gallantry of those Marines.

*****

M/Sgt. Lloyd Taylor and the Ninth Army finally saw the Roer River recede enough to resume their drive to the Rhine. Before daylight, Lloyd ordered the fire of his Sherman tank's main gun and joined the largest concentrated artillery barrage of the war. Two thousand artillery pieces and 1,400 tanks hammered the east bank of the Roer. They lit up the predawn sky.

By the time the engineers had laid bridging units for his tank to cross, German resistance was gone. It had been pounded to pieces. American losses were minimal. Thirty thousand Germans were captured.

Meanwhile, British bombers repaid the German town of Pforzheim for the London blitz. Three hundred and seventy-nine of them annihilated the town. Allied bombing raids were decimating other German cities, destroying German industrial capability. It was none too soon as Hitler was building a new generation of weapons. Advanced rockets and jet fighter planes might still save the German Army and snatch victory away from Lloyd's tankers and the rest of the Allied army.

*****

Don and Betty were seated in a booth at Benny Magoon's Deli. Don took a bite of his pastrami on rye sandwich. It took two hands to hold it, and the Russian dressing ran out over his hand. It was messy but delicious. Betty was having the matzo ball soup. Don put down his sandwich and wiped his hands on his napkin.

He told Betty about his friend Harry's service at Guadalcanal.

"Landing a Gooney Bird on that metal planking runway was hairy. A mortar fragment could have hit one of those links and left a nasty piece of metal sticking up, waiting to poke a nice hole in your tire. He was coming in between Jap attacks and the Marines didn't have time to check every metal link. A Wildcat pilot lost a tire on one and his fighter skidded off the runway into a bulldozer parked next to the runway. They got him out before the wreck caught on fire, but he was badly hurt. Harry's C-47 evacuated him along with other wounded Marines."

Betty took a spoonful of her soup. "Did Harry ever get wounded or hurt?"

"He flew twenty-five missions and not a scratch on him. He got back to base in a shot-up Gooney Bird more than once, but none of the rounds or flack got him, the lucky bastard," Don said and took another messy bite of his pastrami sandwich. It was falling apart, so he held it over his plate.

"It was nice of Mike and June to give us the apartment this afternoon," Betty said.

Don wiped his hands again and decided not to read too much into Betty's remark.

"It sure was. Do you miss your apartment?" he asked.

"Yes, but not as much as I miss some other things," Betty said and grinned at him.

Don grinned back. He finished his sandwich, cleaned his hands on another napkin, and drank the last of his iced tea.

Betty said, "I'm through with my soup. Let's go."

Don paid the check and escorted Betty out to Harry's Buick. She cuddled up to him on the way home to her apartment.

After they had hung up their coats and hats, Betty walked straight into her bedroom. Don followed her.

"Home sweet home," she said and started taking off her clothes.

Don wasn't sure what he should do.

"Get busy, big guy, before I run out of steam," Betty said. She lounged naked on the bed and waited for Don to finish undressing. "This is great. A strip show," she said.

Don laughed and did a bump and grind in his underwear.

They made love slowly, with a lot of pausing and kissing. Then their excitement worked them up into a frenzy. They were both panting when they finished. Betty laid her head on Don's chest and her leg over his. Neither one spoke. Then Betty started to cry.

"What's wrong, honey, did I hurt you?" Don asked.

Betty was sobbing now. She buried her face in his chest. Don didn't know what to do, so he just held her.

Finally, she looked up at him. Her face was covered in tears, and her eyes were red and swollen.

"I'm going to miss loving you," she said. "Heaven better be worth it."

The thought of losing her choked him up as well.

*****

Don was listening to the radio when Mike and June returned from their shopping trip. Betty was taking a nap. She had on a nightgown she had left in her room when she went to stay with her mother and father.

Mike said hello to Don and took an armload of food and shopping bags into June's room. He came out with the food bags.

June knocked on Betty's door. When there was no answer, she opened the door, went in, and closed it behind her. Betty woke up when June sat on the bed and stroked her forehead.

"Hi, roomie," Betty said and sat up. "Did you get all your shopping done?"

June thought Betty's eyes looked red and puffy, but she didn't comment on it.

"I sure did. How was your day?" June asked.

Betty looked forlorn for a moment, but then she smiled and said, "I can't complain. Don and I had a good time."

"I'm happy to hear it, honey. Do you want to get up and join us?"

Betty got out of bed to dress, so June left her to it and rejoined the boys in the living room. Mike set two paper bags on the kitchen table. One bag contained salad and spaghetti with meat sauce from a small Italian restaurant that did takeout. The other held a bottle of wine. June went to the hall closet and took out a folding table and four folding chairs.

Mike and Don set up the table and chairs in the living room. Mike uncorked the wine and put it on the table. June went to the kitchen and dished up the food. Mike carried the plates of food to the folding table. June got glasses and poured the wine.

"I smell garlic," Betty said as she came out of her bedroom.

The four of them sat down to eat. The food was good, and they talked and laughed while they ate.

June told them about her promotion at work. That was cause for a toast. Mike said his new job was going well, and he liked his boss. That was cause for another toast. Don said he and Betty had a good day together and thanked Mike and June for giving them the apartment for the afternoon. When the wine was gone and everyone had finished the spaghetti, Betty said she was pooped.

"I don't know how I could cope with this crap if I didn't have friends like you guys," she said.

Her remark brought the reality of Betty's illness back to them. Don got their coats and hats.

Shit, he thought, *suck it up. Don't start crying again.*

June felt like crying too, but she held it in also.

They all said goodnight, and Don and Betty left.

Mike sat down on the couch with June and put his arm around her.

"She's got grit, your friend Betty," he said.

"She sure does," June agreed and felt the tears she had held back earlier. "It's just not right, damn it," June said.

"It sure isn't," Mike agreed.

*****

On Monday morning, Bernie pondered the lengthy memo Mike had written on the status of the television industry.

"Tell me what this thing says, Mike," Bernie said.

"The long and the short of it is that here in Missouri, television is at least five years away from getting a start. The East Coast may be a couple of years closer, but I doubt it."

"Why do you say that?" Bernie asked.

Hilda came into Bernie's office with coffee.

Mike sipped his coffee and said, "There are two distinct developments that need to take place. One is technical improvement in the television sets. And the other is the establishment of broadcasting stations to send the signals to the sets. It's almost a chicken-and-egg situation as to which needs to come first. At present, there is very little connection between the two. RCA would like to control the first, as they have almost all the patents on television sets. The big radio networks want to control the second."

"Tell me about the first thing, the television sets," Bernie said.

Bernie was afraid that he was in for a long discussion.

"There are two categories of television sets, mechanical sets and electronic sets. But the mechanical sets will be gone shortly. They're obsolete technology. The electronic sets will get bigger and better all the time."

Mike was starting to get wound up in his presentation. He really liked the technical side.

"How do the electronic sets work? Keep it simple, Mike," Bernie said.

Mike answered, "An electronic television has two main components: a cathode ray tube or CRT and two or more anodes. The CRT is a vacuum tube with a heated filament inside it. The filament releases a beam of electrons into the tube. The electrons are negatively charged and are attracted to the positively charged anodes at the other end of the tube. Another word for the anodes is the TV screen, where you see the pictures. The inside of the screen is coated with phosphor. The electron beam paints the image on the screen, one line at a time. The more lines, the better the picture quality. The stream of electrons is fired and guided by two steering coils, which use magnets to steer the beam of electrons. One guides the stream up and down. The other one guides it from side to side."

Mike stopped talking and took a breath. He waited for Bernie to respond to his explanation.

"That's the simple version, huh?" Bernie asked.

Mike realized he had gotten a little carried away and thought about how to put the information in less technical terms.

"Think of it this way. You have a ray gun at one end of a glass tube. At the other end is a screen. The ray gun shoots a beam that draws a picture on the screen. When you look at the outside of the screen, you see the picture drawn by the ray gun," Mike said.

"Okay, that's better. What about the broadcasting side?" Bernie said. He hoped Mike would keep this simpler.

"There are a few stations on the East Coast who are broadcasting a signal that is received by television sets. The pictures are very poor quality. Until the sets are good enough to attract the public to purchase them, the radio networks or other major companies will not invest in television broadcasting stations. There are no television broadcasting stations in Missouri or surrounding states. And there are issues with the government. Broadcasters apply for assigned frequencies. Then they get approval for the strength of their broadcast signal, five hundred watts, for example. No one will go through this process until there are television sets that people want to buy. As I said, it's the chicken and the egg," Mike explained.

"My partner, Sid, is very negative about the future of television too," Bernie said.

"I'm not negative about it at all," Mike said. "I'm excited about it. It's going to be a gigantic business, just not tomorrow. It's still a few years away. But you are right to be ready for it when it comes," Mike said.

"What do we do in the meantime?" Bernie mused. He didn't expect an answer from Mike, but he got one.

"I think we could add a line of electric guitars. We already sell sound equipment—amplifiers and speakers. We would just have to match them up with the guitars."

"What do you know about guitars?" Bernie asked.

"I know a lot about them. I have played the guitar since junior high school. A friend in my band is a very talented guitar player."

This young man is just full of surprises.

"All right, put the television project on hold. Put a guitar proposal together, and I'll look at it. Don't say anything to anyone in the store about it for now. I don't want Sid to hear about it until we are ready to show it to him."

*****

Don strummed chords for his new song in his room in the barracks. He had the lyrics for the chorus. It was a blues song, and he was working on finding the right key. He played a few blues bent notes in different minor keys on his guitar to get a feeling for the song. Bent notes were commonly played by blues musicians. The guitar player bends the strings as he picks or strums them, creating a deeper, "bluesy" sound.

Don experimented with different progressions. He tried the usual blues twelve-bar progression and then an eight-bar progression. He even tried a sixteen-bar progression. A progression is a series of chords played in a defined order and repeated through the song. He knew what emotions were going into the song. And he knew he would recognize the right key and progression once he found it.

Then he could start working on the lyrics. The lyrics themselves were already asking to be heard. He jotted down bits and pieces of them as they came to him. This would be a song worth writing and singing. It was welling up from his soul.

*****

At Walter Reed, Ricky returned from his exercises with Lieutenant Wilkins and sat down on a chair next to his bed in the ward. He had been moved out of his room to make space for newly arrived surgical cases. Major Reston came into the ward and stopped at Ricky's bed.

"I just looked at the latest X-rays of your arm. It is coming along nicely.

Ricky shifted in the chair and adjusted his arm sling. He got up from the chair and Major Reston helped him back into his bed.

"I have good news for you. You're going home," Major Reston said.

"I'm being discharged from the Army?"

"No, you are not being discharged from the Army or from medical care. We are transferring you to the nearest hospital to your home of record. That hospital is in St. Joseph, Missouri. You will be going by air to St. Louis and then on to St. Joseph. You leave tomorrow."

"Why am I being transferred, Doc? Is the lieutenant trying to get rid of me?" Ricky asked.

The major laughed and said, "No, as a matter-of-fact, you're her star patient right now. She's very proud of your progress. We need the bed for other patients coming in. You'll do fine at St. Joseph's. I talked to the chief of physical therapy, and they are ready for you.

They have good orthopedic doctors to take care of your arm. And your family can visit you."

"When I was in Belgium in that evacuation hospital, I thought I would go home with only one arm. Thanks to you, I've still got both. How do I thank you for something like that?"

"Sergeant, you earned all the help we could give you with your service in Belgium. It has been a privilege to be part of your recovery. Go home, find a nice girl, and forget this damned war. That will be thanks enough."

Ricky held out his right hand to Major Reston, who shook it and walked on down the ward.

Ricky yelled to him, "Thank that cute Nazi lieutenant for me."

Major Reston smiled and waved an acknowledgment.

*****

June conducted her first SOP training session with the pack line schedulers in the Quaker Oats training room.

She knew most of the schedulers, so she was comfortable speaking in front of them. They asked questions and made suggestions about trimming down the presentation. It was a good learning experience for June. Afterward, she refined her lesson plan.

She felt more confident about her upcoming training session with the production supervisors.

*****

This was all too damn familiar, Ricky thought as the medics loaded him on a Dodge military ambulance for his trip to Bolling Field.

At Bolling Field, he was transferred aboard a Douglas C-54 Skymaster medical transport flight from DC to St. Louis, Missouri. Many of his fellow patients, like Ricky, would get transferred again to flights to fields nearest their home of record.

Ricky spent two hours at Lambert Field in St. Louis before being loaded on a C-47 Skytrain flight to St. Joseph. He was ambulatory, but his orders specified stretcher transport. After he saw the fold-down strap seating on the medical transports, he was happy to have his stretcher. He tried to sleep on both flights but declined morphine injections. Walter Reed had weaned him off morphine, and he didn't want to start it up again. He had seen too many wounded GIs hooked on it.

Ricky's flight landed at Rosecrans Field, where his buddy Don was stationed.

Another of the ubiquitous Army ambulances took him to the St. Joseph Medical Center. It was almost midnight when he got to his bed in one of the wards. His arm was hurting from the long trip. A night nurse on his ward gave him aspirin. He finally got to sleep for four hours before a nurse woke him at 6:00 a.m. to check his vital signs. She gave him more aspirin and said a doctor would see him later during rounds.

*****

On Saturday afternoon, Mike was tutoring June on algebra and listening to the radio when the phone rang.

"Hello," June said.

"Hello, June, honey, it's your mother calling."

"Hi, Mom, what's up?" June asked.

Mike checked the algebra problem June completed. She got it right. Mike gave her a thumbs-up.

"We got another telegram from the Army," Bess said.

Oh no, June thought.

"It said Ricky was transferred from Walter Reed to the St. Joseph Medical Center," Bess continued.

"That's wonderful news. He must be doing okay. Have you called St. Joseph's?" June asked.

Mike turned down the radio and sat down next to June.

"No, I called you first. I thought you might visit him."

"You bet we'll go. I'll call the hospital now.

"Is Betty back in the hospital?" Mike asked, overhearing that word.

299

"No, it's my brother Ricky. The Army transferred him from Walter Reed Army Medical Center to the St. Joseph Medical Center here. I'm going to call the hospital now."

The reception desk confirmed Ricky was on ward two in the hospital and could have visitors until 9:00 p.m.

On the way to the hospital, June told Mike that Ricky didn't know about their engagement.

Mike and June checked at the reception desk of the hospital and got directions to ward 2.

Ricky was in the third bed from the entry to the ward. The ward's thirty beds were only half occupied. He was sitting up in bed with his left arm in a sling. He was playing solitaire on his tray table. Ricky looked skinny and pale, but she was happy to see him holding the deck of cards in his left hand.

"Hi, little brother, welcome home," she said as she walked up to his bed and kissed him on the cheek.

Mike trailed after her.

"Hello, sis, who's that guy with you?" Ricky asked. He put the deck of cards on the tray table.

"Ricky, this is my fiancé, Mike. Mike, this is my brother Ricky," June introduced them.

Mike approached the bed and put out his hand.

"I'm very glad to meet you," Mike said.

Ricky shook Mike's hand and looked sternly at June. "I'm always the last to know about anything happening in this family."

"How's your arm doing?" Mike asked Ricky.

"It's probably going to mess up my golf game. But I'm damned glad I still have it," Ricky said.

"When can you go home?" June asked. "Our wedding is on April 14, and I want you there."

"They want me to come in twice a week for physical therapy after I'm released. But don't worry, big sister, I wouldn't miss your wedding for the world."

Mike fetched two visitor chairs for him and June to sit in.

"Have you been discharged from the Army?" Mike asked.

"No, I'm on medical leave. I stay on medical leave until the hospital discharges me. After that, it gets a little foggy. Either way my rehab is covered. Are you in the service, Mike?"

"I just got discharged. I was in the Signal Corps at Camp Crowder. They discharged the cadre in the training program, except the lifers," Mike said. "They call it being riffed. I just got a job in a big radio store here in St. Joe."

"So you have a place here in St. Joe? Maybe I could be your roommate while I'm in the physical therapy program. I'll spring for half the rent," Ricky said.

"He already has a roommate—me!" said June. "And my friend Betty, who's living with her parents right now." June told Ricky about Betty's leukemia.

"That's tough, June. I guess I should stop feeling sorry for myself. Your friend is the one with the big problem. She sounds like she's a real trooper."

June said, "Yes, she is. She's determined to be my maid of honor."

Ricky told them about running into Lloyd in Bastogne and Lloyd coming to see him in the hospital in Belgium. They laughed when he told them about Lieutenant Wilkin's treatments.

Finally, a nurse came to check Ricky's vital signs, and they said their goodbyes. June told Ricky she would bring their parents up to date on Ricky's status.

After Mike and June left, Ricky thought about June living with Mike. Mike seemed like a nice guy, and they *were* engaged. Still, he was surprised. He always thought June was a prude.

*****

In Dekalb, Bess and Dee were home from church service on Sunday and having lunch when June called.

"Hello, Mom, it's June. I went to see Ricky at St. Joseph's Medical Center yesterday. He's on ward 2 and can have visitors."

Bess was pleased they had visited Ricky.

"How is he? How's his arm doing?" Bess asked.

"He's pale and skinny, but he's happy they saved his arm. Ricky's doing physical therapy. He does a little more with his left hand every day, and that's a good sign."

Mike was studying guitar catalogues and listening to June's side of the conversation.

"When can he come home, did he say?" Bess asked.

"He thinks in a month or less. Then he will need to go to the hospital twice a week to get physical therapy. Can you or Dad drive him there?" June asked.

"He won't be able to drive?" Bess asked.

Dee was reading the Farmer's Almanac. He read it cover-to-cover every month.

"He won't be able to drive for a while. They want him to be very careful with his arm while the bones are knitting. Ricky said he could get an *X* gas ration sticker (unlimited) for your car," June said.

"Don't worry. I'll get him in for his treatments," Bess said. "Can you and Mike come to church with us next Sunday? Reverend Davis wants to see us after the service to talk about your wedding."

June put her hand over the phone and said to Mike, "We're going to church next Sunday with my folks, okay?"

"Don't you mean with *our* folks?" he asked with a grin.

"We'll be at the farm at 10:00 a.m. Sunday," June said and stuck out her tongue at Mike.

*****

Dee and Bess made the trip in from the farm to the St. Joseph Medical Center in their 1939 Buick Special sedan. Like June, Bess was dismayed at how frail Ricky looked. He was asleep when they came into his room.

He had been moved from the ward to a semiprivate room on the third floor. He and his roommate, a police sergeant Bruce Colson, had a window overlooking the parking lot. It gave them natural light in the afternoon. Sergeant Colson had a cast on his right ankle. It was broken when he and his partner were in pursuit of a bank robber and crashed their patrol car after it skidded on some ice on the road.

His partner was not seriously injured. A police roadblock captured the robber.

Bess kissed Ricky's forehead, and he woke up.

"Hi, Mom. Hi, Dad." Ricky wiggled himself up into a sitting position on the bed and adjusted his arm sling.

"How's that arm coming along?" Dee asked.

"It's still there, Dad. For a time, that was unlikely. And it's better each day. I just have to keep working on it," Ricky said.

Bess kissed his cheek and said, "You're home. That's enough for me, son."

"June told us about your Silver Star Medal. We are very proud of you," Dee said.

"Thanks, Dad. But I was just doing my job. Lots of guys did just as much as I did and didn't get any medals for it."

"I'm sorry they didn't get medals, but that doesn't change what you did."

"You're embarrassing him, Dad," Bess said.

Occasionally, a nurse or visitor walked past his room. Otherwise, the floor was quiet. Ricky thought about the chaos in the evac hospital in Belgium.

It sure is a different world here, he thought.

"So you're a big hero?" Sergeant Colson asked Ricky, eavesdropping on the Taylors.

"Now see what you did, Dad," Ricky said. "Cops never let up. He'll be ragging me all night."

Dee turned his attention to Ricky's roommate and said, "I read how you let those bank robbers get away."

Ricky laughed and said to Sergeant Colson, "That'll teach you to pick on a Taylor."

Bruce held up his hands. "I surrender. You've got me outnumbered."

"What did you think of your new brother-in-law?" Dee asked. He sat in one of the guest chairs, and Bess sat in the other one.

"I liked Mike. He must be a good guy if June picked him. She's always had a good head on her shoulders," Ricky said.

303

"He came out to the farm with June on Christmas Day and met Emma Dee and Virginia Jane. They both like him," Bess said.

They all talked a little longer until Dee said he didn't want to drive after dark.

When Ricky's parents had left, Bruce said, "Thank you for your service, Ricky, and congratulations on your decoration. You've got guts."

"Hey, a high-speed pursuit after those armed bank robbers ain't a walk in the park. You've got guts yourself," Ricky said.

"That was my job," Bruce said.

"So was mine," Ricky said.

*****

"Mr. Williams said you did a good job training his packing line supervisors."

June was meeting with Tim. Tim's requisite bow tie was a canary yellow accenting a black vest.

"Even Mr. Jennings?" June asked tongue-in-cheek.

Jennings was the supervisor who told June she was wasting his time when she talked to him about the new SOP.

June continued, "Tim, I've been thinking about the materials planners. We meet with them at a separate meeting every week to go over the new schedule. Wouldn't it make sense to include them in the meeting with the line supervisors? That way everyone could get on the same page in one meeting."

Tim sat back and mulled over June's latest idea. He liked it.

"I'm going to discuss this with my boss, Mr. Jamieson. If he approves, he'll recommend it to Mr. Fisher, the materials manager. You realize this would mean you have to amend your SOP?"

June smiled and said, "I'm way ahead of you, boss. There are a couple of other things I think should be added anyway."

"I'll get back to you when I hear from the big bosses," Tim said.

*****

Adolf Hitler ordered German forces between the Roer River and the Rhine River to hold in place. But after being smashed by the American Army advance from the Roer, the German Army retreated behind the Rhine River, and again, Hitler issued a hold-in-place order. The Germans destroyed all the bridges over the Rhine, except one. American troops got to the Ludendorff Bridge ahead of the German unit that was responsible for destroying it.

On Wednesday, March 7, eight thousand American soldiers crossed over into the Rhineland on the Ludendorff Bridge and secured the bridgehead.

M/Sgt. Lloyd Taylor's battalion was part of the huge American force poised to dash into the heart of Germany. M/Sgt. Taylor had been appointed first sergeant of Baker Company. His commanding officer let him keep his M46 and its crew when the company was engaged. He caught up his paperwork when they were off the line.

At the same time, the Russian army was advancing rapidly toward Berlin.

M/Sgt. Taylor couldn't believe it when General Eisenhower turned the Ninth American Army away from the Rhine toward the mountains of Austria.

"We're going to let those Russian bastards beat us to Berlin!" Lloyd complained to his company commander.

"Talk to General Patton. He's even madder than you are," said his CO.

"Why the hell are we going to Austria?" Lloyd asked.

"Intelligence thinks Hitler will make a last stand in the mountains. Eisenhower doesn't want him to have time to get set up there and drag out the war. And the Russians are our allies, you know."

"They were Hitler's allies too, until the German Army was outside Stalingrad," Lloyd said.

His CO just shook his head and said, "Mount up, First Sergeant. We're moving out."

*****

Thursday night, Mike and June listened to the radio as Perry Mason smoked out the murderer in the courtroom.

During a break in the program, June asked Mike, "How about asking Betty over here on Saturday for lunch and maybe we can play cards afterward?"

Mike turned down the radio and said, "Sure, that's fine. Maybe she can invite Don."

They listened to the rest of the *Perry Mason* show, and June called Betty.

Betty's mother, Kate, answered. Kate called Betty to the phone.

"Hi, June," Betty said. "We just finished listening to Perry Mason catch the killer."

June laughed and said, "So did we. You and I never miss *Perry Mason*."

"So what's up, roomie?" Betty asked.

"Mike and I thought you might like to have lunch with us here Saturday and then play some cards afterward. What do you think?"

"That sounds very nice. But I'll have to see if Mom can drive me and pick me up later," Betty said.

"Don't be silly. I'll pick you up, and we can have some girl talk in the car," June said. "If you hear from Don, invite him too."

"I'll do that. See you Saturday," Betty said.

*****

On the drive over to the apartment Saturday, Betty said, "I want to move back into our apartment. My parents have been great, but I'm feeling smothered there. Mike can stay until you guys are married and find your own place."

June maneuvered around a double-parked car.

"Honey, it's your apartment. You can move back whenever you want. But are you sure about Mike staying with us?" June stopped at the red light and looked over at Betty.

"I'm absolutely sure. I'll feel better with him there. I may need his help when I get sick again," Betty said.

June went through the traffic light and pulled over into a parking space and stopped the car. She turned off the engine.

"What do you mean, 'When you get sick again?'" June asked.

"This remission won't last. I'm not cured, and I could get sick again any time," Betty said. "I try not to think about it because I get really scared. I don't want to die." Betty started to cry.

June slid over on the car seat and put her arms around Betty and hugged her. June said, through her own tears, "You pack up your things at your mother's house. Mike and I are going to DeKalb tomorrow, but we'll come get you when we get back to St. Joe."

They held each other for a while and then Betty wiped away her tears and said, "Thanks, roomie, I can always count on you."

June started the car and pulled out into a gap in traffic. "Is Don coming today?"

"He said he'd be there after lunch."

*****

June told Mike about Betty moving back to the apartment.

"What do you think, Mike?" Betty asked. She was sitting in the chair in the living room.

Mike and June were sitting on the love seat.

Mike scratched his chin and said, "Let me see. Do I want to live with two gorgeous gals? Is this a trick question?"

Betty laughed, and June punched Mike in the arm.

"Get serious, buster," June said.

Mike rubbed his arm and said to Betty, "It's your apartment. If you get uncomfortable having me here, I'll move out."

The doorbell rang, and June opened the door to Don.

"How did you get here?" June asked as Don came in.

"I took a taxicab. I'll need a ride back to Rosecrans," Don said.

"June and I can take you home when you're ready," Mike said.

Betty got up from the loveseat when Don came in.

Don said, "Hi, good-looking," and kissed her.

"Let's play cards," Betty said.

The guys set up the card table, and June taught them all how to play pitch. It was Mike's second lesson, and June was a better teacher than her father. It was the guys against the girls. The girls skunked them.

Don said, "Let's change partners. I get June this time."

Betty said, "Okay, Mike, I think I'm catching on to this game. It's you and me, partner."

June made iced tea, and they drank it while June and Don narrowly won the second game. They spent the afternoon switching partners, laughing, and playing pitch. Betty told Don about moving back to the apartment with Mike and June.

"Is this where I get jealous, you lucky dog?" Don asked.

"I would if I were you," Mike said and grinned at Don.

June looked at Betty and said, "Ignore them or throw a bucket of water on them."

Betty laughed and said, "Where do you keep your bucket?"

Mike drove his Chevy into Betty's parents' driveway. Don walked Betty to her door, and they kissed.

"I'll call you next week," Don said.

"Thank you for sticking with me, Don. You're a good guy." She went into the house.

Mike drove to Rosecrans Field.

June leaned over the front seat and kissed Don's cheek. "You *are* one of the good guys, Don. I'm glad you're going to be Mike's best man."

Don smiled at her. "Thanks for the lift," he said to Mike and got out of the car.

June moved to the front seat, and Mike drove home to the apartment.

*****

The DeKalb Christian Church service was well attended. The church was a plain white clapboard building with a steeple and bell. Stone steps led up to the entrance. Carpeted aisles separated three rows of pews. Sunday school was conducted in the basement. To the left of the pulpit was the choir loft.

Reverend Davis's sermon on the Holy Bible's views on marriage and the duties of husbands and wives seemed to be directed mostly at Mike and June on Sunday. June agreed with most of the sermon, but she had reservations about the duties of wives, particularly the part about obeying her husband.

I'd like to see Mike try to order me around, she thought.

After the service, they joined Reverend Davis in the pastor's office. The carpeted office was not large, but it held the five of them comfortably. There were two brown couches at right angles to each other, facing the reverend's walnut desk. Walnut coffee tables fronted them. Reverend Davis was seated in his office chair behind the desk. He had christened June and seen her grow up into a fine young woman. He had been surprised at her brief courtship and engagement. He never thought June the impulsive type. And she came from an excellent Christian family. He hoped she knew what she was doing.

"I reserved the church for April 14. Who is your minister?" Reverend Davis asked June and Bess.

"We want you to conduct the wedding, of course," June said. "We'd like to start the service at 11:00 a.m. and end at 12:00 p.m. Could you arrange for the organist?"

"I'd be very pleased to officiate. I'm sure our organist, Mrs. Robbins, will be available. I'll arrange that for you," Reverend Davis said. "How many people do you expect to attend?"

"We expect about one hundred and fifty," said June.

Mrs. Davis entered the office with a tray of coffee service and sat it on one of the coffee tables. They all got their coffee and then continued the conversation.

"What about the reception?" the reverend asked.

"We booked the DeKalb town hall for that," Bess said.

Reverend Davis picked up a white padded catalogue and said, "We have wedding decorations for the church if you want to use them." He passed the catalogue to June to study.

Bess joined June on her couch.

June looked through the pictures in the catalogue and said to Bess, "I don't like the two angels, but the rest look good. What do you think, Mom?"

"This will do very nicely. I agree about the angels."

Bess handed the catalogue back to the reverend, who said delicately, "I offer marital counseling. Some couples find it helpful to discuss certain aspects of their new relationship before the wedding."

"It might be a little late for that," June said.

Mike blushed. Dee and Bess studied their shoes.

"I might have heard something about that from certain ladies in the congregation," the reverend said.

"I'll bet you have," June said.

"Reverend Davis, I realize people might think we are jumping the gun, but when you are lucky enough to find the right girl and she feels the same way, there's no reason to wait to start your life together," Mike said. "I've completed my service obligations and found a good job. June already has a good job, and both of us have plans for our future together."

Reverent Davis found it hard to disagree with Mike. *This is a sensible young man.*

"Well, I'll prepare a proposal for you. Who should I send it to?"

"Send it to me," Bess said firmly. She shook Reverend Davis's hand and thanked him.

The others followed suit. Mike and June left in the Ford to go back to St. Joseph. Bess and Dee drove to the farm in their car.

Mike and June stopped at the Anderson house to pick up Betty. Mike rang the doorbell, and Kate answered it.

"I'm not sure this is wise," Kate said to Mike about Betty's move back to her apartment.

"I'm not sure it is either, but it's what Betty asked us to do," Mike said.

"I know it is. And none of us can refuse her anything now. Just please take good care of her." Kate looked like she was about to cry.

Betty came out of the living room with her father who carried two suitcases. Betty kissed Ray and her mother goodbye and said to Mike, "Let's get this show on the road."

Mike picked up her suitcases and took them out to the car.

Ray put his arm around Kate's shoulder as they watched Betty get in the car and leave. Kate tried hard not to cry.

"I don't know how much more time we have with her, and she's leaving," she said to Ray.

*****

Tuesday morning, Tim asked June to sit down and told her about his meeting with the materials manager.

"Mr. Fisher liked the SOP and added another step. His materials planners meet regularly with his materials buyers to review the upcoming schedules. He said they could eliminate that extra meeting if the buyers were also included in your SOP procedure."

June chewed over that and said, "You know, what we are doing is forming a team. It's like a baseball team. Each player has his own area to cover. But they work together to win the game. Our new packing team has a player from each area—scheduling, production, materials planning, and materials buying."

Tim said, "You're absolutely right! But a team needs a captain. Who would be the captain?"

June was stymied. She hadn't thought of that.

"It's your SOP. You should be the captain," Tim said.

"Well, maybe not a captain, but I could be the moderator."

Tim agreed and asked her to include the moderator in the SOP.

"So far, we are only doing this with my three pack lines. What about the other lines? What about the other production areas?"

"I talked with the supervisors and managers about that. We agreed that your pack lines would be the test case. If it works well there, we will expand it to other areas," Tim said.

"In other words, we're the guinea pigs," June said.

Tim shook his head and said, "June, you're missing the point here."

"What is the point I'm missing?" She looked frustrated.

"This is a big opportunity for you. If you can pull this off with your lines, it will be expanded quickly to other areas. It will need a project manager to oversee it. You could be that project manager. It could be a big step up the ladder for you."

*****

Despite Mike's fear that the new living arrangements might be awkward, things worked out fine.

After work, they had dinner together and listened to their favorite radio shows. Betty tired quickly and went to bed after an hour or so. That left the remainder of the evening to Mike and June. Mike worked on his guitar proposal, and June crammed for her exam. Their lovemaking was quieter, but that didn't seem to bother either of them.

On Saturday, Don joined the three of them for a movie. He and Betty necked and ate popcorn during the film, while Mike and June smooched a little and ate their popcorn. After the movie, Mike and June offered to give Don and Betty the apartment for the afternoon. Betty thanked them, but said she was feeling tired and would like to take a nap. When they got to Rosecrans Field, Betty got out of the car and walked to the gate with Don.

"I hope you're not too disappointed with today, Don."

Don did not respond to her question. Instead, he held her and kissed her. He said, "I think I'm in love with you. I've never been in love with anyone before, so I'm not sure." He kissed her again. "Yeah, I'm sure."

"That's good because I've been sure about you for a while," Betty said. She kissed his cheek and turned away from him quickly so he wouldn't see the tears in her eyes. *He deserves a healthy girl to spend his life with*, she thought, *and that isn't me.*

*****

After the Methodist service on Sunday, Don joined the Andersons for dinner.

It had been some time since Don attended church, but he couldn't turn down Ray's invitation. Ray asked Betty to give thanks.

Betty bowed her head and said, "Thank you, Father, for the food we are about to receive and for my family and my friends. Amen."

Ray carved the roast, and they started passing around the potatoes, biscuits, and vegetables. The gravy bowl followed. Betty stopped eating and looked angrily at her father.

"Why is God letting this happen to me?" Betty questioned her father. "What did I do wrong to deserve this?"

The table was silent.

"You did nothing wrong, honey, and I don't think you deserve it either," Ray finally said. "Why do bad things happen to good people? It's one of the oldest questions people asked of God. I'm sorry, but I don't have an answer for you. Just don't turn your back on God when we need Him the most."

"Everyone, eat your dinner before it gets cold," Kate said.

They resumed passing around the food dishes.

Between bites, Betty looked at her father again and asked, "What do you think heaven is like?"

Everyone stopped eating and waited to hear his answer. He was the preacher at the table. If anyone knew the answer, it should be Ray.

"I believe that we receive our spirit or our soul, whichever word you like, when we are born. And when we die, that part of us goes back to God where it came from. That's heaven."

"Darn, I hoped I'd get to do a lot of fishing in heaven," Don said.

That broke up the somber mood, and they all laughed.

16

The radio called it the Nero Decree, because Hitler's order to destroy Germany to prevent the Allies from using it was like Emperor Nero who tried to burn Rome. Fortunately for the German people, much like German General von Choltitz ignored Hitler's order to demolish all Paris landmarks, including the Eiffel Tower, Hitler's subordinates ignored the order to destroy all factories, supply depots, transportation and communication facilities, and anything else of use to the Allies. Many of the top Nazis were busy stealing and smuggling their loot out of Germany and making their own plans to find safe havens for themselves, usually in South America.

*****

Joe Harding was coming out of his office when he saw Betty slide out of her office chair in a faint. Betty had just returned to her desk after lunch in the ordnance plant cafeteria when she started to feel dizzy. He barely reached her in time to catch her before she hit the floor. She was unconscious. He held her as he phoned the plant operator to call an ambulance and a security guard. When the guard arrived, Joe sent him to get a glass of water.

Joe carried Betty and laid her on the sofa in his office. He lightly slapped Betty's cheek and told her to wake up. Betty opened her eyes and looked groggily around her. The guard returned with the water, and Joe held the glass to Betty's lips. Her focus cleared, and she sipped it.

"What happened?" Betty asked Joe.

"You fainted," Joe said. "I carried you in here. Just take it easy. We called an ambulance."

Betty tried to sit up, but she was still very light-headed and lay back down.

"I don't need an ambulance," she protested.

Two ambulance attendants arrived with a stretcher moments later. They responded quickly to calls from the ordnance plant.

"She fainted," Joe told them. "She has cancer, but she's been in remission."

One attendant examined her eyes briefly and took her pulse. "She needs to go to the hospital," he said.

They slid her onto the stretcher and covered her with a blanket. Despite her weak protests that she was all right, they took her out to the ambulance.

Joe followed and said to Betty, "I'll call your parents and let them know what happened."

The emergency room doctor at the hospital checked Betty's vital signs. She had a temperature and was still weak. Her blood pressure was low. The admitting clerk brought the doctor her hospital records.

"She's a leukemia patient," he told the ER nurse. "We need to get a blood draw and get it to the lab. I'll put the orders in her chart. Also start an IV, just saline for now. I want to get her pressure up. Type and crossmatch her blood. We may want to start her on whole blood. I'll locate Dr. Friedman, who has been treating her leukemia. Her family doctor is Dr. Leyland, so I'll have the desk reach him as well. Let's admit her now."

When Dr. Friedman arrived, he looked at Betty's chart and the laboratory results.

Her white cell counts are back up, and she is anemic, he observed.

The remission was clearly over. He visited Betty in her room and examined her. He checked her abdomen. He didn't feel any enlargement of her liver or spleen. She was responsive to his questions, but lethargic. He scheduled a meeting with Dr. Leyland to discuss treatment later in the day.

"This is worse than the initial set of tests," Dr. Leyland said to Dr. Friedman, looking at Betty's blood tests results.

"Yes, I'm afraid it is," said Dr. Friedman. "I think we need to start treatment immediately. I want to try the arsenic again." He looked at Dr. Leyland, who just nodded.

"We need to watch her reaction very carefully. There could be a cumulative effect with the arsenic."

Dr. Friedman was worried about the same thing.

"We'll start her on a minimal dose. If she tolerates it, then we can slowly increase it," he said. "I'll put in the order, and we can start tomorrow morning."

*****

"She looks sicker than before," Kate whispered to Ray on Betty's second day in the hospital.

She wasn't allowed visitors on the first day, and now she was sleeping. Ray agreed with Kate about Betty's appearance. He looked haggard himself. Neither of them had slept very well the night before. Kate approached the bed and took Betty's hand. Betty stirred and opened her eyes.

"Hi, Mom. Hi, Dad," she said.

Kate held her hand and asked, "How are you feeling, honey?"

Betty sat up slowly. "They gave me something for my fever, and I feel a little better," Betty said. "I'm just tired."

Ray said, "Hello, honey."

He pulled up a chair for Kate, but she kept standing and holding Betty's hand. He sat down. There was no one in the other bed in Betty's semiprivate room. The blinds in the window were closed, and the room was dark. Kate released Betty's hand and opened the blinds, letting in the sunlight.

That's better, Kate thought.

"We visited with June's brother, Ricky," Ray said. "He's going to come up and see you tomorrow."

Betty looked at her father and then said, "I guess I am foggy headed. June told me he was in this hospital, but I forgot. I'd like to see him."

"The nurse said you passed out at work yesterday," Kate said.

"I guess so. I don't remember it," Betty said. "I guess the remission is over, isn't it?"

Kate bit her lip to keep from crying.

I need to be strong for her, she thought. "We'll just have to start another one, that's all," Kate said.

"That's my cue," said Dr. Friedman, entering Betty's room.

Ray got up and Kate and Betty turned toward the doctor.

"I met with Dr. Leyland, and we want to get you back in treatment tomorrow. We'll watch closely to see how you do," Dr. Friedman said to Betty. He explained the treatment plan to them and then warned them about the risk of arsenic buildup in Betty's system. "I want you all to know the whole picture. It's your decision, Betty."

"I need to get better again. I can't let June down. I'm her maid of honor," Betty said.

"All right, young lady, let's get you to your friend's wedding," Dr. Friedman said.

*****

The next day, when Betty saw a tall, pale young man in a hospital gown and wearing a sling on his left arm at the door to her room, she said, "You must be Ricky."

June had just finished breakfast. She had eaten some of the oatmeal and a bite or two of the scrambled eggs.

Ricky sat down next to her bed, adjusted his sling, and smiled at her. He had a nice smile.

"Guilty as charged. I'm pleased to meet you. How are you doing?"

"Not too good, but they start treatment today. It helped me before, and I hope it'll help me again," Betty said. She pushed away the serving tray and sat up straighter. "How's your arm?"

"It's coming along okay. The rehab is helping," Ricky said. He looked at her breakfast tray. "Do you want your orange juice?"

Betty passed him the glass of orange juice. "Was it really bad over there?"

"Normandy was bad. The airdrop scattered the division all over Normandy. Nobody was where they were supposed to be, and units were split up. Some of our guys landed right on top of a town held by the Germans and got slaughtered. It was a total snafu." He drank the rest of the orange juice and handed Betty the glass.

"What's a snafu?" Betty asked and put the empty juice glass on the tray.

Ricky laughed and said, "It means 'situation normal, all fouled up,' except the troops don't say 'fouled.'"

Betty laughed and said, "I'll bet they don't. June was terribly worried when the radio mentioned some town in Belgium."

"Oh yeah, that was Bastogne. Bastogne was bad. The Germans launched a big counterattack through the Ardennes Forrest. There were seven roads going in and out of the town. The Germans needed those roads for their panzers to take Antwerp. We were rushed up to be part of the defense, and we dug trenches all around the town. But a German panzer division cut off the roads to the south, and we were surrounded. Nothing could get through, not replacements, food, or ammunition."

"My goodness, what happened then?" Betty asked.

Ricky laughed and said, "My big brother showed up in his Sherman tank along with the Third Army."

"So your own brother saved you?" She was caught up in Ricky's story.

"We stalwart men of the 101st Airborne Division didn't need saving. That's our story, and we're sticking with it. Still, we were glad to see those 4th Armored Division Sherman tanks. Those poor bastards marched over 150 miles in a snowstorm in less than three days to relieve us. The rest of Patton's Third Army was right behind them."

"Did you see your brother after that?"

"I was sitting outside the shell of a bistro when his Sherman tank rumbled down the street. I saw the unit markers on his tank and recognized him. Lloyd was standing up in the turret of his tank, so I jumped up and waved at him. He had rolled a few yards past me before his tank stopped. When Lloyd jumped off and ran over to me, his CO saw us together and let Lloyd spend the night with me and my squad. We partied with some wine my buddies scrounged up."

"How did your arm get hurt?" Betty asked. She adjusted the pillows behind her back and drank her cold coffee.

"A sniper got me in an ambush in a small town north of Bastogne. That's enough about me. What's the story about you?"

"I have leukemia. There's no cure, but the doctors had me in remission for a few weeks. While I was in remission, my illness didn't seem real to me. It was like it was happening to someone else."

Ricky stood up and adjusted his sling again. He looked at Betty. "I'm very sorry about the leukemia. I hope the treatments help you. June said you want to go to her wedding."

"I have to go. I'm the maid of honor."

A nurse came in and said, "It's time for your first treatment. Your visitor has to go now."

Betty held out her hand and said, "It was a real pleasure meeting you, Ricky. Thanks for visiting with me."

Ricky shook her hand and said, "The pleasure was mine. Good luck, honey." He left her room.

*****

The night shift nurse came in to administer the third dose of Betty's treatment. She set down the tray with the medication and checked her patient. Betty was running a fever, and her breathing was labored. Her evening meal tray was untouched. She left the room and had the hospital operator page the night-shift doctor.

Dr. Price responded to the page and was directed to Betty's room. The nurse had awoken Betty, but she was woozy.

Dr. Price bent down close to her and asked, "How do you feel?"

Betty focused on the doctor and said, "I feel sick to my stomach, and I'm having a hard time breathing."

Dr. Price saw her dinner tray and asked her, "Did you eat any dinner?"

Betty wouldn't look at the tray. "Take it away. It makes me nauseous."

Dr. Price studied her chart. *She's on an arsenic regimen*, he observed. He turned to the nurse and said, "Don't give her anything. Stay here with her. I'm going to try to reach Dr. Friedman."

Dr. Price described Betty's symptoms to Dr. Friedman.

"Do you think she has gastroenteritis?" Dr. Friedman asked.

"That would make sense with her symptoms and the arsenic," Dr. Price said.

"I'm coming to the hospital. Don't give her the arsenic. Put her on oxygen. Treat her fever and get some fluids in her."

"Okay, Doctor. I'll watch her until you get here," Dr. Price said.

When Dr. Friedman had examined Betty and studied her chart, he added orders to treat her for inflammation of her stomach. He noted her dyspnea and ordered a continuation of the oxygen to help her with her breathing.

"You can take her off the oxygen if her breathing returns to normal," he told the nurse and put that in her chart. "Call me if she has severe distress," he told Dr. Price.

After she got the oxygen, Betty relaxed and went to sleep. Her temperature was still high but improving.

The next day, Dr. Friedman called Dr. Leyland and filled him in on Betty's reaction to the arsenic.

"How's she doing now?" Dr. Leyland asked.

"We have the inflammation under control and her fever is mild. The dyspnea is better, but I'm keeping oxygen available if it worsens. We're pretty much back to square one. The arsenic is off the table. We'll have to try something else soon. I'm thinking about trying X-rays."

"What about folic acid?" Dr. Leyland asked. "X-rays are usually directed at specific tumors. We'd have to radiate her entire trunk area to reach enough cancer cells to do any good. That would be risky."

"Hell, Doctor, it's all risky. I just don't want to stress her stomach again so soon with the folic acid. I'd like her to have two days to recover from the arsenic. Then we can add the folic acid. But I don't think we can just wait and do nothing. Her blood tests are bad. That leaves the X-rays for starters."

"Have you talked to Betty or her family about this?" Dr. Leyland asked.

"She has been too sick to make this kind of decision. But you're right, we need to talk to them as soon as she is up to it. We can do that tomorrow. Do you want to do it?"

"No, but I will. I'm her doctor. Will you be in the hospital tomorrow if I need to call you in to answer questions about the X-ray treatments?"

"I've got surgery in the morning. Have them come in midafternoon, I'll be available then," Dr. Friedman said.

The next afternoon, Dr. Leyland met with Betty's parents in her room. Betty was awake and coherent, and her breathing was normal. She was weak and appeared washed out.

Dr. Leyland explained why the arsenic treatment was discontinued.

"But we have other options," Dr. Leyland told them. "Dr. Friedman is recommending we start radiation treatment with X-rays. The idea is to kill the cancer cells without killing healthy cells. There has been some success in producing remissions with this method. The level of radiation required can make her sicker and even possibly produce damage to organs or other tissues. There are some guidelines from prior attempts, but we will still be experimenting with radiation levels and frequency of treatments."

Ray and Kate were horrified at this proposal.

Betty asked Dr. Leyland, "What happens if I don't do more treatments?"

"I'm afraid the prospects are grave. Your blood tests show high levels of affected white cells, and your red blood cells are dropping. We don't think the cancer has spread to any of your organs, but that is probable if we don't contain the cancer."

"In other words, I'm going to die. How soon?" Betty asked point blank.

Kate turned away from the bed, and Ray held her.

"No one can tell you that. But without treatment, the disease will progress rapidly," Dr. Leyland said. "I'm going to step out of the room while you all talk this over and then tell me what you decide."

Ray was the first to speak. "What do you think, honey?" he asked Betty.

Betty tried to concentrate on her father's question. "I'm not ready to give up. I want to see my friends get married." She might have said more, but that speech had exhausted her.

Ray looked at Kate and said, "Let's call Dr. Leyland back in."

Ray informed Dr. Leyland that Betty wanted to go ahead with the treatment. Dr. Leyland said Dr. Friedman would start the treatments tomorrow.

*****

General George Patton's Third Army joined other massive Allied forces crossing the Rhine River in the final push. The remnants of Hitler's once mighty army were being overwhelmed. Hitler's remain-in-place order prevented them from making orderly withdrawals.

In the meantime, 1st/Sgt. Lloyd Taylor sat idly in Austria waiting for a German effort that never materialized. There were no German divisions left to staff a last-ditch defense in the Alps. His battalion was out of work again. They were missing the big show, and Lloyd was mad as hell about it.

*****

It was Monday afternoon, and Dr. Friedman was reviewing Betty's latest blood tests. The X-rays weakened her, but her blood work showed improvement. The white cell count had come down, and her anemia was improving. He consulted with Dr. Leyland, and they decided to continue the X-ray treatment for another day. If tomorrow's test results continued to improve, they could discharge her Wednesday and treat her on an outpatient basis. She could come in daily for her radiation treatments.

"I think we should add folic acid tomorrow. Her stomach issues have cleared up," Dr. Freidman said.

"Okay, I agree," Dr. Leyland said. "If the folic acid helps, we might be able to lower the radiation level."

"Have you heard any more from your colleague at Johns Hopkins about his secret treatment?" Dr. Leyland asked.

"No, I'm haven't, I'm sorry to say."

Dr. Friedman's colleague was unable to help him.

The benefits of nitrogen mustard in the treatment of cancers were discovered while producing mustard gas as a weapon; Gilman and Phillips studied it in 1942 and made clinical observations about the benefits. Because of wartime restrictions on classified information, their findings were not published until 1946. Major medical research centers like Johns Hopkins University were under the same secrecy constraints.

"It's a hell of a situation," the colleague said to another doctor at Johns Hopkins.

*****

The same day her doctors discussed Betty's treatment, Mike was checking the stockroom at Kaufmann's Radio and Repair with Tony Moreno. Tony had installed his roller conveyor system for the console models and had most of the table model racks done as well. Mike checked the repair tickets on the radios and found they were all lined up in promise-date order, with the earliest promise dates first and the latest orders last. There was no more jumble of consoles on the floor, customer complaints were way down, and the volume of repair orders completed was up. More people were bringing in their radios to Kaufmann's and getting them back when promised.

"Tony, you've done a great job," Mike told him.

"It wasn't just me. The receiving department guys and the repairmen have caught on to the new system and got this stuff in the right order," Tony said.

Mike clapped him on the back. "I know you're right, and I'll thank them too. But none of it could have happened without your new roller system. And you came in under budget too."

*****

Kate and Ray waited nervously in Betty's hospital room for Dr. Leyland. He had arranged this Wednesday meeting with Betty's parents. He had reviewed her latest blood tests with Dr. Freidman, and they agreed Betty could be treated on an outpatient basis. Betty's hospital bed was raised so she could sit up, and Betty was awake and alert. Her parents stood up when Dr. Leyland entered the room. He asked them to relax and told them Betty's latest blood tests were encouraging. Betty's parents were heartened at this news.

"Her blood work has shown great improvement, but we aren't quite to a full remission yet. We added folic acid to the radiation treatment yesterday. So far, Betty, you seem to be tolerating it well. Do you have any more nausea or diarrhea?"

"No, I'm feeling better this week," Betty said. "I ate my lunch today."

"That's very good. The folic acid may allow us to lower the radiation level, but we will go slowly with that. How would you like to go home today?" he asked.

Betty perked up and said, "If you mean it, I think I'll kiss you!"

"I appreciate the thought, but I'm not sure your parents would approve," Dr. Leyland said with a smile. He turned to Kate and Ray. "She needs to come into the hospital every day for her radiation treatment. I've set up a schedule with the radiation department for her to be treated at ten each morning. Will that work for you?"

Ray said, "We are happy to have her home. We'll bring her in whenever the hospital wants."

"We'll continue both the radiation and the folic acid until we have a full remission," Dr. Leyland said. "The hospital is processing your discharge, and you can go home later this afternoon."

*****

Wednesday afternoon, Sid Kaufmann was having a drink with his business partner, Bernie Cline, in Sid's posh private office. The desk, chair, and credenza featured wood carvings with leather upholstery to match the sofa. The walls were covered in fox-hunt-pattern wallpaper, and even the baseboards and ceiling moldings were matching rosewood.

They sat on the leather sofa under the family oil painting Sid had commissioned when he made his first million dollars.

The two partners drank the imported Irish whiskey that Sid got through a business acquaintance.

"I've been checking up on your new repair department supervisor," Sid said to Bernie. "I talked to Michelle, and I walked through the storeroom. I was impressed with the new roller arrangement."

Bernie had done the same things himself, but he waited for Sid to finish his recital.

"I also talked to our floor salesmen," Sid went on. "I hate to admit it, but they all had good things to say about your young man."

"Are you talking about the guy the Army kicked out?" Bernie said, rubbing it in.

"Have your little laugh, Bernie. But the kid burst your television bubble, didn't he?" Bernie took another sip of his drink.

"He didn't burst it, he just postponed it for now. Anyway, what did you think of his guitar proposal?"

"I like it. I want to see what it'll cost to set up and stock his boutique. I think it might bring in some of the younger crowd. We could set up a window display and see if it draws customers in. Music is big now," Sid said.

"You surprise me, Sid. I thought you'd never go for it," Bernie said.

"I'm not such a big stick-in-the-mud as you think," Sid said. He handed Bernie a sales report.

Bernie looked it over. He had studied the same report before he came up to see Sid. The report showed that radio sales were up 15 percent from the week before. One week proved little. Still, it buttressed what the floor salesmen had told them both.

"I saw this report before I came up here," Bernie said. "Why are you showing it to me?"

Sid handed Bernie another report. This one showed the weekly income from repairs to customer-owned radios. There was an increase of 18 percent in revenues.

Sid took two cigars from his humidor and handed one to Bernie. When they both had their cigars going, Sid said, "Have our interior designer Hanna Morris meet your Mr. Thompson and do a preliminary design for the guitar boutique and window display. Hanna can give us her estimate on the costs. Ask your Mr. Thompson to give us a budget for the initial inventory investment.

"Mr. Thompson has been with us for almost two months. I think you should give him a review and a raise. This is an ambitious young man, and we need to hang on to him. If these results continue, we can promote him to manager of the repair department in a few months. What do you think?"

"A raise of 5 percent, do you think?" Bernie asked.

Sid raised his glass and nodded.

*****

The butterflies in June's stomach had butterflies. It was Friday, exam day. The proctor handed out the test pamphlets for the entrance exam to the University of Missouri. June squirmed on the hard wooden seat and prayed her math sessions with Mike would see her through. She felt confident about the rest of the exam subjects.

At the same time, the orthopedic resident at St. Joseph's Hospital, Dr. Eric Nelson, carefully examined Ricky's arm and chest. There were healing scratches and abrasions on Ricky's arm.

"It looks like someone was busy with a wire coat hanger," Dr. Nelson said to the nurse.

The nurse swabbed the areas with a disinfectant, and Ricky flinched.

"Well, it itched like crazy under that cast," Ricky said.

"It doesn't look like there is any infection," Dr. Nelson said. He removed the stitches from the mortar wounds on Ricky's trunk.

"The mortar wounds have healed nicely. Sergeant Taylor, I am going to manipulate your arm. If something hurts, tell me." Dr. Nelson tested rotation of the bones in his upper arm. "How did that feel?"

"My arm is sore, but it didn't hurt when you moved it," Ricky said.

Dr. Nelson held out his right fist to Ricky. "Grip my fist and squeeze it," he said.

Ricky squeezed the doctor's fist hard, and the doctor flinched.

"Good grip," Dr. Nelson said.

"I had a Nazi nurse at Walter Reed who gave me hell if I didn't squeeze a rubber ball all day," Ricky said.

"Just be glad she did," Dr. Nelson said. He put Ricky's arm back in his sling and said, "Your X-rays show the bones are fusing nicely. The docs at Walter Reed did a good job on the arm. But you need to continue with the sling and your physical therapy. Except for your therapy, don't try to use the arm for the next month. We'll check it then. You are being discharged this afternoon. Do you have someone picking you up?"

"Yes, my parents are coming in after lunch," Ricky said.

*****

Friday afternoon Mike was studying a report on the manufacturers' lead times for spare parts when Bernie came into his office.

Mike started to get up out of his chair, but Bernie said, "Keep your seat. This isn't the Army." Bernie sat in the visitor's chair in front of Mike's desk.

Mike sank back into his office chair and said, "What can I do for you, boss?"

"Consider this conversation your probationary review," Bernie said. "You're doing a fine job and you're getting a 5 percent raise."

"Wow, thanks, Bernie. I'm getting married next month, and we can use the money. I was going to ask you for a week off for our honeymoon. I know I haven't been here very long. And I guarantee I won't make a habit of asking for time off," Mike said.

"When's the wedding? I didn't get my invitation yet," Bernie chided him.

Mike blushed and said, "It's on Saturday, April 14. I'd like to get the next week off, if that's okay. Tony and Michelle can fill in for me."

"Speaking of Michelle, she thinks you walk on water. You can ignore me, but you better make sure she gets an invitation. You can have your week off with Sid's and my blessing."

"Thanks, Bernie. Was there anything else?" Mike asked.

Bernie handed Mike a business card. "This is Hanna Morris's business card. She does the designs for our floor and window displays. Set up a meeting with her."

Mike looked at the card and said, "Great! We're going ahead with the guitars?"

"Yes. I need you to put together an inventory stocking plan with a budget," Bernie said. "When you and Hanna have your ducks in a row, give me a date to introduce the boutique."

*****

"The *DeKalb Weekly* is sending over a photographer to the farm today," Dee said to the welcome-home party being held for Ricky. "They are doing a story about Ricky."

The family sat at the kitchen table, relaxing after their meal. Everyone had eaten a hearty country breakfast of smoked ham, eggs, biscuits, and white gravy. The ham came from one of their hogs they butchered in the fall and smoked in their smokehouse. The eggs came fresh from their henhouse. Bess had given an egg with the double yolk to Ricky, the guest of honor.

"When that reporter gets here, I'm hiding in the basement," Ricky said. He ate a bite of his third buttered biscuit and took a sip of his coffee.

Emma Dee glared at Ricky and said, "You will do no such thing. You will put on your uniform with all your decorations and do this family proud. It isn't every day one of us gets our picture on the front page of the *DeKalb Weekly*."

Ricky took another bite of his biscuit and adjusted his sling. "You just want something to shut up Wilma."

Wilma was a neighbor's daughter whose husband was a Marine. He got the Navy Cross in action on Guadalcanal. His picture was featured on the front page of the DeKalb newspaper, which Wilma brought out to display every chance she got. She and Emma Dee had been rivals in high school and still liked to one-up each other.

"You bet, and I'll break your other arm if you let me down," Emma Dee said.

Virginia Jane turned to June and said, "This quarrel started when they were in short pants, and it's still going on."

June agreed with Virginia Jane.

She turned to Ricky. "You know what DeKalb is like. If you don't go along with this, there will be gossip about what you are trying to hide."

"For crying out loud, stop ganging up on me. I'll let him take the damn picture," Ricky said. He got up and went to change into his uniform.

"Now let's talk about the important stuff—my wedding!" June joked.

"I got Betty's measurements for her maid-of-honor dress. And I have the sizes for Virginia Jane and my bridesmaid dresses," Emma Dee said. "They are all on order at a bridal shop in St. Joe and will be ready this Wednesday.

"They are peach colored, right?" June asked.

"Yes, they're peach, just like you wanted. The blue was prettier," Emma Dee said.

Mike and Dee looked at each other and silently withdrew to the kitchen. This was no time for the men to get caught up in a women's debate.

"What about the guys?" Virginia Jane asked. "Did you order their tuxedos?"

The guys settled down at the kitchen table, and Dee started a new pot of coffee. Ricky came into the kitchen wearing his uniform and decorations.

"That was a close call," Dee said. "We were almost trapped in the wedding planning."

"They don't want any opinions about that from us," Mike said.

"Maybe not, but we might get stuck with them wanting us to referee an argument between Emma Dee and June. No, thank you," Ricky said.

"Was it pretty rough over there, Ricky?" Dee asked. He turned down the burner under the coffeepot.

Ricky found the rest of the buttermilk biscuits on the counter and buttered one of them. Ricky loved Bess's biscuits and was determined to make up for the lack of them in France and Belgium.

"Not as rough as your trenches in WWI, but it was rough enough for me," Ricky answered.

Dee had been a doughboy in France near the French town of Rheims. The invention of the machine gun had turned mobile warfare into a stagnant misery of trenches and mud where thousands of men killed each other to take a few hundred yards of ground. Dee had survived the trenches with no worse damage than his share of rat bites and dysentery. Like most combat veterans, he never talked about it with anyone but other combat veterans.

In the living room, Emma Dee's dander was up after being quizzed by Virginia Jane.

"Yes, I ordered the tuxedos!" Emma Dee exclaimed.

"The invitations are going out on Monday," Bess said, diverting the sparring match between her daughters.

"Did you get Mike's friend on the invitation list, the one he added at the last minute?" June asked. "He's the one with the funny nickname Mike met on the train—Slats, that was it!"

"Of course, I did. Now about the tuxedos, Dee is picking up his, Ricky's, and John's tuxedos on Tuesday. John will have to take his chances on the fit. He isn't arriving until Friday before the wedding. Reverend Davis called me and scheduled your wedding rehearsal for Sunday, April 8, the week before the wedding at 2:00 p.m. after services. June, can you or Mike let Don know about the rehearsal?"

"The caterer is all set for the reception at the DeKalb town hall," Bess continued.

June was caught off guard by Bess's casual mention of a caterer. She protested, "I told you, my sisters and I will supply the food for the reception. I don't need a caterer!"

"What you need is to try on your grandmother's wedding dress so I can alter it if it needs altering," Bess said and ignored June's protest about the caterer. "I've laid it out on the bed. Come and try it on."

The two of them went into Bess's bedroom.

The front doorbell rang, and Emma Dee opened the door to the reporter for the *DeKalb Weekly*. He carried a large professional camera in one hand and a folded tripod in the other. A camera accessory bag hung on his right shoulder. He was a sandy-haired, freckle-faced, skinny young man who looked about fifteen years old.

"Come on in. Let me take some of that stuff," Emma Dee said to the overloaded photographer.

"I'm Jerry Campbell with the *DeKalb Weekly*," Jerry said as he stepped into the house. He set down his tripod and extended his hand to Emma Dee.

"I'm Emma Dee, Ricky's sister," she said and shook his hand. She picked up his tripod and led the way into the living room. She introduced Jerry to her sisters.

"You don't look old enough to be a reporter on a newspaper," Virginia Jane said. "You can set your things on this chair."

Jerry put his camera and bag on the chair and leaned the tripod against it.

"I'm twenty-one-years-old. I just graduated from the university with my journalism degree. Where is Sergeant Taylor?"

Emma Dee went to the kitchen and told Ricky the reporter had arrived and wanted to get started. They returned to the living room. Mike and Dee trailed along behind them.

Jerry introduced himself to the men.

"I'm pleased to meet you, Mr. Campbell. But I'd like to get this over with as quickly as possible," said Ricky.

Jerry turned to June and asked, "When is the wedding, Miss Taylor?"

"It's in two weeks on April 14," June answered.

Jerry took a notebook and pen out of his jacket pocket. "Could I please have the full name of the groom?"

Before June could answer, Bess interceded. "I gave your editor the details of June's wedding for the announcement in the next edition. Why do you want to know about June's wedding?"

"I'm going to take pictures of Ricky and of Ricky with his sister, June. The caption for the one with the two of them will be 'LOCAL HERO ATTENDS SISTER'S WEDDING.' It's great human interest stuff."

"I don't want to horn in on Ricky's ballyhoo," June said. "Leave me out of it."

Ricky stepped closer to June and whispered, "You are missing a bet here. Imagine how Wilma will react. She never got *her* picture on the front page of the *DeKalb Weekly* newspaper."

June considered that aspect of it, and it was a temptation. "Still, you should not have to share the limelight with anyone after what you did over there," she said.

Jerry eavesdropped on their conversation and said, "What about this? We'll put Ricky's picture by himself on page one with the lead story about him. Then we'll do a follow-up story about him attending the wedding on page 2 with the picture of both of you?"

"Hey, June, if you don't want to do it, I'll get in the picture with Ricky. 'LOCAL HERO WELCOMED HOME BY GORGEOUS SISTER,'" Emma Dee said and laughed.

"Never mind, I'll do it. I don't want you lording it over me," June said.

Jerry turned to Bess and asked if he could look around the rooms of the house.

"I need to find a good background for the pictures," Jerry said.

Bess said he could look wherever he wanted.

He returned shortly and said, "I'd like to use the beige wall in the master bedroom if that's okay?"

Bess said that would be fine.

Jerry took out his notebook and pen. "Is there somewhere I can sit with Ricky and talk?" He deliberately avoided the word *interview* as his experience was that subjects found the word intimidating. Also, he found that people were more forthcoming if they were alone with him.

"We can go into the kitchen. Dad just made some fresh coffee," Ricky said.

"Great! I'd like some coffee," Jerry said.

They settled at the kitchen table with their coffee.

"You were with the 101st Airborne Division. Was that the only unit you served with?" Jerry asked.

"Yep, the whole time I was over there," Ricky answered.

"Were you in the Normandy invasion?" Jerry sipped his coffee.

"I flew over it, and we parachuted behind it." Ricky got up and found the last biscuit on the counter.

"What was that like?" Jerry asked.

"It was a clusterfuck, pardon my French. We were nowhere near our drop zone, and my company ended up scattered all over." Ricky found some peach preserves in the refrigerator and spread it on his biscuit. "Several of the guys in my platoon joined up with guys from two other companies, and we tried to figure out what we were supposed to do. We ran across a lieutenant who took charge. Partisans had taken down the road signs to confuse the Germans. It sure confused us."

"So what did you do?" Jerry asked.

"We just headed toward the sound of the nearest battle," Ricky said. He sat back down at the table with his coffee and biscuit.

I think he just gave me the lead for my story, Jerry thought and wrote the answer down word for word, "We headed toward the nearest battle."

"Were you in any other big battles?"

"We were in Bastogne, what you press people called the Battle of the Bulge."

"Oh, yeah, that's where General Patton's Army rescued you all, right?"

A stormy expression came over Ricky's face. "Nobody rescued us. We didn't need rescuing. They did some mopping up. Not one single member of the 101st thinks Patton rescued us. If anyone did any rescuing, it was the Air Force dropping supplies and ammo to us when the damn weather finally cleared."

Jerry looked chagrined. "I'm sorry. That's my mistake."

Ricky finished his biscuit and drank his coffee.

"How did you get wounded?" Jerry asked as he flipped over a page in his notebook.

Ricky was tempted to give the kid a smart-ass answer like, "With a bullet, you dummy." But he just said, "My squad was ambushed in a small village. I got dinged with grenade fragments and then a sniper shot me in the arm."

"Was that when you got your Silver Star Medal?" Jerry asked.

Ricky finished his coffee and leaned back in his chair. He said nothing for a minute. Then he just said yeah.

Jerry studied Ricky for a few seconds and said, "I can get a copy of the citation from Army records, you know."

"Good, why don't you do that," Ricky said. He was getting hot under the collar again.

Jerry was starting to get annoyed. This would be the heart of his story. While it was true, he could get the record, it could take weeks. He didn't have weeks. The story would run in the next edition.

"Why don't I just ask your family for the story? I'll bet at least one of them knows what you did."

Ricky was annoying him too.

Now Ricky was really getting mad. He was wondering how much damage he might do to his left arm if he punched this asshole with his right hand.

Emma Dee entered the kitchen to get the coffeepot and to eavesdrop on the conversation when she noticed her brother's face.

"What are you getting all steamed up about, little brother?"

Ricky looked at her, and his anger evaporated. He grinned at her sheepishly. He turned back toward Jerry and said, "I was just doing my job. Thousands of guys did more and didn't get any damn medals for it."

"I'm sure you're right. And probably every soldier who got a Silver Star Medal feels just like you do," Jerry said. "But the people here at home need to know about you and the others who didn't get a medal. You need to represent them to the people of DeKalb. Otherwise, how will they know what you men did over there?"

"He's right, Ricky," Emma Dee said, pleased she had entered and saved the interview. "Ricky saved the life of one of his squad members who got wounded in the ambush. They were under fire from a machine gun, and Ricky went out and got his buddy and carried him to safety. Another man in his squad rescued a second wounded man. Ricky got shot in the arm, and the other man didn't. That's why Ricky was awarded his medal, and the other man wasn't. Did I get all that right, Ricky?"

"The other soldier was Pfc. Franklin, a black guy from Detroit. He did a better job than me. That's why he didn't get wounded," Ricky said.

"What is Pfc. Franklin's first name?" Jerry asked.

"Moses," Ricky said. "His family is Baptist."

"Why don't we go back to the living room and get your sister June so we can take the pictures and I can get out of your hair," Jerry suggested.

Ricky helped himself up with his right hand on the table and adjusted his sling. "Lead on, Macduff," he said.

June was in her mother's bedroom wearing her grandmother's wedding dress. Emma Dee and Bess checked the fit.

"I don't think we'll have to alter it a bit. It looks like it was made for you," Bess said.

June checked herself out in the full-length mirror next to the closet. She hardly recognized herself. The dress was a simple but elegant glory of strapless silk with a white satin neckline, waistband, and train. The cupped sleeves showed off her toned arms, and the dress tapered to her narrow waist and accented her slim hips.

"Most wedding dresses in my mother's time were heavily crocheted and high collared with long sleeves. But your grandmother liked silk and satin. Some of the women were scandalized by the strapless neckline. She didn't care," Bess said.

"It looks modern. Grandma was ahead of her time," Emma Dee said. "You are a knockout in that dress, sis. I'm so jealous I'm turning green."

Mike and Dee followed Jerry into the bedroom to watch the photography.

Mike was blown away when he saw June. "Wow! Is that all for me?" he exclaimed.

June smiled at him and said, "Count your blessings, Mr. Thompson."

"If I had known you were going to steal the scene like this, I'd never have agreed to let you get into my picture," Ricky teased her.

Jerry got good shots of Ricky in his uniform and decorations and took several shots of them together.

The pictures are going to be sensational, with June in her grandmother's dress next to the uniformed hero, Jerry thought.

He knew he would get practically the whole next edition with the two stories and photographs. He would see if the Associated Press was interested in the photos and stories.

*****

Mike and June said their goodbyes to the family and headed back to St. Joe. June was very pleased with the wedding plans and excited about her grandmother's dress.

Thinking about the dresses for the wedding reminded her of Betty. She needed to call Betty's mother when they got home and check on how Betty was doing with her treatments. She rang as soon as they got back to the apartment.

"Hello," Kate answered.

"Kate, this is June. I'm calling to see how Betty is doing."

Kate said Betty had been released from the hospital and was doing better, but not in remission yet. They had taken Betty to the hospital every day for her radiation treatments.

"We have an extension in her room if you want to speak with her," Kate said.

"Sure, unless she's asleep," June said.

Kate put down the phone and went up the stairs to Betty's room. Betty was sitting up in bed, reading the newspaper.

"Honey, June is on the phone," Kate said.

Betty laid down the newspaper and picked up the phone on her night table and said, "Hi, roomie, what's up?"

"Mike and I went out to the farm today. The folks had a coming-home party for Ricky who just got out of the hospital," June replied.

Mike was at the kitchen table, working on the inventory numbers and budget for the new guitar boutique. June sat on the love seat having a cup of tea.

"How's Ricky's arm? He visited me in the hospital when he was there too. If I didn't have Don, I would have snatched him right up. He's a cutie." Betty laughed.

June laughed and said, "I won't tell him that. He's got a big enough head as it is. There was a reporter from our small-town newspaper at the farm to take Ricky's picture and write a front-page article about him being a hero. He still has to wear the sling for another month, but he said his arm is getting stronger. But enough about the Taylors. How are you doing?"

"I'm out of the damn hospital. Don't get me wrong, the doctors and the nurses have been great, but hospitals are depressing." Betty shifted position in the bed and reached for her water glass. "Did you take your exam yet?'

"Yes, I took it last Friday, and I'm waiting to hear the results."

"You probably aced it. You've always been a brainiac."

"From your lips to God's ears. I felt like a matron among all those eighteen-year-old kids."

Betty laughed, picturing her friend in a gaggle of teenagers bent over their exam papers.

"How's did the wedding planning go?" Betty asked.

"It went great." June smiled and said, "That reminds me, your maid-of-honor dress will be ready this Wednesday at the Bridal Shoppe in St. Joe. I can pick it up for you, or if you feel up to it, you can go try it on."

"I wouldn't miss it. Mom can drive me over. She'll enjoy seeing it on me. Give me the phone number."

17

On April 1, 1ˢᵗ/Sgt. Lloyd Taylor walked into a hellish shed in Germany. Human bodies were stacked up like cordwood. It was one of many horrendous sights he'd seen that day. The Ohrdruf concentration camp reeked of burned and decaying bodies. The Fourth Armored Division liberated the first of what would be many concentration camps the Nazis called labor camps. Ahead of the approaching Americans, German SS troops had tried to empty the camp with forced death marches to the Buchenwald camp.

When the Fourth Armored Division got too close, they started shooting and burning the bodies of the remaining prisoners to destroy the evidence of the incredible cruelties that existed in their "labor camps."

The smells were overpowering, but Lloyd did not vomit when he entered the shed. He had already emptied his stomach when he passed the burned bodies lying on open ground. The tankers who sometimes wondered why they were fighting this war had their answer that April Fool's Day.

*****

This Monday, Tim's bow tie was navy blue with white polka dots under a white sweater vest. Tim told June the new SOP test was going well and there was talk of expanding it by the end of April.

"That's great," June said. "But I'm here to request a leave of absence for the week of April 16 to April 20. I'm going on a honeymoon with my new husband. We're getting married on the fourteenth."

"Congratulations. Am I invited?" Tim asked with a smile. He noted the event on the fourteenth on his desktop calendar. He checked the following week.

"You'll get your invitation this week," June said. "But the wedding is in DeKalb."

Tim finished his study of his calendar and said, "That week off will be fine. What the heck is DeKalb?"

"It's a small town in the sticks about thirty miles south of St. Joe. There are directions on the invitations."

"So it's like Dogpatch, USA? Will I meet Lil' Abner?" Tim teased her. "How about Daisy Mae? I'd like to meet her."

"You won't meet either of them, but you can meet my sister, Emma Dee. She isn't barefooted like Daisy Mae," June kidded him back. "But I warn you, she's a pip, and she has a boyfriend."

"Where are you going on your honeymoon?" Tim asked as he looked at his watch. He'd have to cut this short as he had a meeting with his boss in ten minutes.

"We're taking the train to St. Louis. Neither of us has seen the big city." June stood up and thanked Tim for giving her the week off.

*****

The headless chicken flopped frantically around the barnyard behind the Taylor farmhouse. June's mother, Bess, had just wrung its neck; and she waited for it to stop slinging blood all over the yard. After removing the feathers and cleaning it, Bess sent the fryer home with Mike and June. Chickens were scarce in the markets in St. Joe.

The apartment was filled with the aroma and the crackling sound of the chicken frying in deep fat in the black skillet. It made Mike's mouth water. Mike had never seen anyone wring the neck of a live chicken before and end up with the chicken's head in her hand. He'd turned a little green but kept his lunch, so he didn't disgrace himself entirely with June's family, who routinely raised and butchered their hogs and fryer chickens.

It sure smelled good frying, he thought. Mike had his customary job of mashing the potatoes.

"Did you get the train tickets?" June asked Mike as she turned over the golden pieces of chicken in the skillet.

"Yes, we go to Kansas City on an old coach and then we transfer to a streamliner to St. Louis. I got us a Pullman compartment on the streamliner. It is our honeymoon after all." He winked at her.

"I confirmed our reservation at the Union Station Hotel. We can get a trolley to the Forest Park Highlands Amusement Park."

June removed the fried chicken from the skillet and put it on a serving tray.

Studying the mouthwatering chicken on the tray, Mike laid his claim. "I get the gizzard."

June added flour and milk and some of her mother's favorite spices to the white gravy in the skillet.

"When do you get your exam results?" Mike asked.

June poured the gravy into a bowel and checked her biscuits in the oven. They were almost done. She turned off the burner under the broccoli and drained off the water and put it in a bowl. Broccoli was hard to get, but she'd got this batch at a farmer's stall on the road outside DeKalb. She would be happy when the rationing and shortages ended. She took the biscuits out of the oven.

"I'm not sure. They said within a month. I'd get a letter in the mail. Thanks for all your tutoring. It really helped with the math sections."

"My God, this is a feast. I knew there was a reason I was marrying you," Mike said, chewing on his drumstick. He'd already eaten his gizzard.

June ate the liver. She liked the liver better anyway. "Then you should be marrying my mother. She's the one with all the livestock and produce."

"Also, I'm nuts about you," Mike said.

"That's good, because I'm going to cost you a lot of money on this honeymoon. I want to take all the rides at Forest Park Highlands, and I want to see all the sights of the big city."

"Let her rip! I just got a raise, and I've still got Uncle Sam's discharge money. We're flush, baby," Mike said. "Let's have an adventure."

*****

Mike looked up from the guitar catalogue he was reading and saw a tall, willowy woman in a silk skirt suit with a colorful scarf around her neck.

"Hi, can I come in?" Hannah Morris asked Mike from his office doorway.

"Sure, make yourself at home," Mike said, getting to his feet. "I'm Mike Thompson."

"I'm Hannah Morris, and I'm here for our 9:00 a.m. meeting," she said, extending her hand to Mike.

Mike shook her hand and invited her to join him on the office couch.

"These are the catalogue pictures of the guitars and amplifiers for our new boutique," Mike said. "They are from three best manufacturers, Gibson, Gretsch, and C. F. Martin. The guitars are all top of the line."

Hanna started looking through the pictures. "Some of these don't look like electric guitars," Hanna said. She handed Mike two pictures of guitars.

"You are correct. These are high-end acoustic guitars without electrical pickups. We need acoustic guitars to round out our line."

"I thought the concept was to stay in the realm of electric guitars," Hanna objected.

Mike was having a little trouble concentrating on the conversation. Hannah's long, nylon-covered legs were very distracting. He tried to focus on her question and said, "The truth is that electric guitars are relatively new, and the technology is developing. The Gibson ES 150 and the Gretsch Electromagnetic Spanish 8165 are the most reliable electric guitars available, and we can get both. Charlie Christian plays the Gibson ES 150. Both companies are developing others and we will add them as they become available."

Hannah noticed Mike's glances at her legs, but she was used to male attention.

"Are we looking at a niche market of professional musicians?" Hanna asked.

Mike kept his eyes off her legs and answered, "We are definitely looking at the high-end market. The catalogue companies, Sears Roebuck, Wards, etc. cover the amateur market. There's no way to compete with them. But we will get some of the amateur market. There are many serious amateurs who want the same high-end guitars the professionals play. That is our market, along with the professionals, of course."

Hanna got up from the couch and said, "I'll need to take this file with me."

"Sure, it's your copy," Mike said. "What's our next step?"

"I meet with Bernie and walk the floor to see where we want to locate the boutique. I'll put together the preliminary design sketches for the boutique and the window display. Bernie can review them and finalize the design."

She said she would have the preliminary designs ready in three weeks.

They shook hands, and Hanna left. Mike couldn't resist a last peek at her legs.

*****

The Bridal Shoppe had a corner location two blocks down Felix Street from the Townsend and Wall Department Store. Professional offices occupied the upper floors. The Shoppe's display window featured a blond-haired mannequin wearing an elegant long-sleeved white wedding gown. The bride was accompanied by three bridesmaids in light-blue gowns. In the other display window was a groom in a white tuxedo with light-blue lapels and a light-blue bow tie. A best man and male attendants wore light-blue tuxedos.

On Wednesday morning, Kate and Betty entered the store, and a saleslady greeted them.

"Hello, ladies, welcome to the Bridal Shoppe. I'm Evelyn. How may I help you ladies today?"

Evelyn was a tall, buxom brunette in her midforties. She wore a calf-length black dress with a white collar and black high-heeled pumps.

"My name is Kate, and this is my daughter, Betty. Betty is the maid of honor at the Taylor wedding. She's here to try on her dress."

Betty's face was pale under her makeup. She was going for another radiation treatment after lunch. She insisted that Kate stop at the Bridal Shoppe first, so she could try on her dress.

"Certainly, please follow me to the back room, and I'll get her dress," Evelyn said.

Betty tried on the dress in the changing room.

"I don't wish to pry Kate, but is Betty all right?" Evelyn asked. "She looks a little peaked."

Kate hesitated to talk about Betty with a stranger.

"She is recovering from an illness, but she's feeling better," Kate said.

Betty came out of the changing room wearing the dress. She went to the mirror and looked at herself.

Evelyn came over and said, "It's a little loose at the waist, but otherwise, you look very pretty in it. We can take in the waist."

Kate stood up and said, "You look lovely, honey."

Betty turned and looked at her back in the mirror. "I just want to look nice for my friend's wedding."

Evelyn took in the waist and pinned it.

"That's better," she said. "You can take it off now."

While Betty was changing, Evelyn said to Kate, "It'll be ready Friday if you want to pick it up then."

Kate told her Friday would be fine as Betty came out of the changing room and handed Evelyn the dress. They thanked Evelyn and left.

When they got into the car, Betty said, "You know, I'm actually hungry. Can we go to Benny Magoons for lunch?"

Kate smiled at her and said, "You bet we can."

*****

After Betty's treatment that afternoon, she was directed to go to a consulting room to see Dr. Friedman. Dr. Friedman arrived shortly, carrying Betty's latest blood test results.

He laid the test report on the desk and sat in one of the chairs, facing Betty and Kate.

"How are you feeling today?" he asked Betty.

"I'm feeling better. I have more energy and my appetite has come back. Mom and I had lunch at Benny Magoon's today."

Dr. Friedman picked up the report and said, "That tallies with your blood test results. Your anemia is gone. Your red blood cell count is almost normal. That accounts for the improvements you are seeing. Your white cell counts are coming down, which is very good. I won't say we have a full remission yet, but we are close. For now, I'd like you to come in on Friday and next Monday for treatment. Then we'll see where we are."

Dr. Friedman leaned forward and said, "I want you both to feel free to ask any questions you have."

Betty stood up and waited for the doctor to do the same. When he did, she took his hand and said, "Today, I tried on the dress I am going to wear at my best friend's wedding. You did that for me. God bless you, Doctor." She kissed him on the cheek and walked out of the room.

Kate smiled at Dr. Friedman and wiped away a tear as she walked out of the consulting room after her daughter. Dr. Friedman was choked up himself.

*****

Don's Gooney Bird landed back at Rosecrans Field after a training flight with a new crop of navigator cadets. It was just a familiarization flight in the middle of their first week of training, which was mostly classroom. He gave each of them a half hour of hands-on instruction on the navigation equipment installed on the specially modified Douglas C-47 transport aircraft. The twin engine C-47 Skytrain transport was the most modified plane in the Army Air Force inventory. It had, at various times, been a fighter, a bomber, an amphibian, a tow plane for gliders, and itself a glider. It had even been a laundry, a hospital, a command post, and a chicken coop. This one was a classroom for navigators. Army pilots had nicknamed it the Gooney Bird after the albatross, a seabird with great endurance and the ability to fly long distances.

The phone rang in his barracks, and a sergeant answered who was walking by the phone. He yelled down the hallway, "Hey, Walker, there's a guy on the phone for you!"

Don put down the bottle of beer he'd just opened and went to the phone.

"This is Sergeant Walker," he said.

"Don, it's Mike. Can you get off duty this Saturday?" Mike asked, calling from the apartment. "We're taking Betty to get her dress for the wedding."

"Yeah, I'm good for Saturday," Don said. Then he put his hand over the phone and hollered, "Keep it down, you guys, I'm trying to talk on the phone."

There was a rowdy poker game in the game room.

June was halfheartedly studying a medical textbook. She was enjoying her job so much she was confused about her ambitions. If she got promoted again, she wasn't sure she wanted to quit and go to nursing school after she and Mike got married.

Oh well, I haven't passed that exam yet. Maybe I won't have a choice.

"Can you pick me up at the Rosecrans' main gate?" Don asked.

"Sure, what time?" Mike said. "Maybe we can get lunch before we go to the bridal shop." Mike poured an iced tea from the pitcher June had made for dinner.

"Let's make it noon. There's a drive-in near the base that has good burgers and malts," Don said. The poker game was getting noisy again. "I better sign off now. I'll see you Saturday."

"What time did you tell Betty we would pick her up on Saturday?" Mike asked June.

"I told her 11:00 a.m. I thought we'd have lunch before we went to the Bridal Shoppe," June answered.

"Great minds run in the same channels. I just told Don we'd pick him up at noon. He said there's a drive-in restaurant near the base that has good food. Are you okay with that?" Mike asked.

"You just want to flirt with the curb-service girls," June kidded him.

"Well, I'm not married yet. Besides, you'll be there to keep me honest," Mike teased her back.

"I haven't had a good chocolate milkshake for a while," June said. "I'm so glad Betty is feeling okay again. She sounded cheerful on the phone."

"She and Don don't get much time together. What if you and I go to the movies Saturday afternoon, and let them have the apartment to themselves?" Mike asked.

"That's a fine idea. Anything I can do to give Betty some fun is all right with me," June said.

*****

"Spend the afternoon alone with Don in the apartment? You bet!" Betty said to Mike and June after they picked her up Saturday morning. June made her the offer as Mike drove them to Rosecrans Field to pick up Don at the gate.

"That will be swell, but what are you and Mike going to do?" Betty asked June.

"We're going to the movies. We'll catch up with you at the apartment after the movie," June answered.

Mike pulled up at the main gate at Rosecrans Field. Don stepped out from the guard shack and got into the back seat of Mike's Chevy with Betty.

"Hi, cutie, how are you doing?" Don asked Betty.

She moved over on the seat and kissed Don. "I think I'm doing great. But you better give me another kiss to make sure," Betty said.

Don put his arms around Betty and kissed her soundly.

"Now I'm sure," Betty said, smiling at him.

"Hey, you two, that's not fair. If I tried that with Mike, we'd all end up wrapped around a tree," June teased them.

When the four of them entered the Bridal Shoppe, the shop owner, Mrs. Collins, greeted them. She was a trim, smartly dressed woman with a few streaks of silver in her black hair.

"June is the bride. Don is the best man, and I'm the maid of honor," Betty introduced them.

"I'm very pleased to meet you all," Mrs. Collins said. "I don't believe we have your wedding dress, dear, do we?" she asked June.

"No, I'm wearing my grandmother's wedding dress. I'm just here with my friends today. They are here for their fitting," June said.

"That's fine. We're happy to have you visit our shop. Let's get you all fitted."

Mrs. Collins led them back into the fitting room and retrieved Betty's dress from one of the wardrobes and handed it to her. She went into one of the changing cubicles and put on her dress. The dress had been loose in the waist the first time she tried it on, but it felt fine now. She came out and pirouetted in front of her friends.

"You're gorgeous! I told you peach was better than blue," June said.

Betty studied herself in the wraparound mirrors. "What do you think, best man?" she asked Don.

Don was thinking that for the first time in his life he wanted to marry someone, and she was standing in front of him in a peach dress.

"I think you're a peach. The dress is nice too," Don said.

Betty took a last turn in front of the mirrors and said, "Let's see how it looks next to Don's tux."

Don stepped out of the cubicle and struck a movie-star pose, doing his best imitation of Cary Grant in a white tuxedo with peach lapels, bow tie, and cummerbund. The peach accents didn't really fit his personality, but he was a striking figure.

"You look like a kumquat!" June said and laughed.

"Hey, you picked out this getup," Don protested. He walked over to the mirror and struck several poses. "It fits anyway," he said.

Betty came up and stood beside him in front of the mirrors. Suddenly, Don's tuxedo came to life next to Betty. It lost its garishness and blended beautifully with her peach dress.

"Wow," Mike said. "You two look great together."

"I've always thought so," Betty said and hugged Don.

"Let's see the groom now," Mrs. Collins said and got Mike's ensemble out of the wardrobe.

When he came out of the cubicle, Mrs. Collins got to work on him. She tied his bow tie and tugged at the waist of the trousers.

"My mother used to do that when I was a boy," Mike said.

When she finished with her adjustments, Mike went over to the mirror.

"Pretty spiffy, if I do say so myself," Mike said. "Betty, you and Don come back here and stand with me." He turned from the mirror and positioned Don on one side and Betty on the other. "What do you think, bride, will we do?" Mike asked June.

June tried to make a wisecrack, but the sight of her friends dressed up for her wedding brought tears to her eyes.

Betty saw her tears and said, "Heck, I didn't think we looked that bad." Betty's jibe broke the mood, and they all laughed.

Mrs. Collins said, "Mike, your alterations will be ready by next Wednesday. You can pick up everything then, unless your friends want to take theirs today?"

Betty and Don both agreed to wait if Mike didn't mind. June said they could all meet next Saturday morning at the farm and get their outfits.

They all thanked her Mrs. Collins and left the Bridal Shoppe. Mike dropped Don and Betty off at the apartment and went on to the movie with June.

Betty unlocked the door and let them inside. They hung up their coats and hats.

Betty turned to Don and said, "I'll all yours, big guy."

Don kissed her and hugged her tightly. He was still musing on his thoughts at the Bridal Shoppe. When he released her, she held his hand and led him into her bedroom. She started taking off her clothes.

Don said, "Are you feeling up to this?"

"Your first clue was me taking off my clothes," Betty said. "Are you going to catch up or what?"

Don had been with a lot of girls and had enjoyed sex with them, including Betty. But this time, he made love to her. He was amazed at the difference.

Afterward, Betty cuddled up to him and said, "Would you be offended if I took a little nap, honey?"

"Hell, no. You nap all you want," Don said.

"Wake me up in an hour," Betty requested and pulled up the covers and went to sleep.

Don went into the kitchen. He checked the icebox and saw four bottles of Schlitz. He started to take one but reconsidered and put it back.

"I'll just make us some coffee," he said to himself. He found the coffee and started the percolator on the stove. When the coffee was ready, he poured a cup and went into the living room. Setting down the coffee cup, Don went to the hall closet and took out Mike's acoustic guitar. He started playing and humming the new song he was working on.

After her nap, Betty came into the living room and said, "I like that song. What are the words?" She sat on the loveseat next to Don.

"I haven't finished the lyrics yet," Don said. "Want some coffee? I made a fresh pot?"

"Sure, that sounds good. With cream and sugar, please."

Don brought back her coffee and sat it on the table. He sat close to her on the loveseat.

"When we were all trying on our wedding clothes, I got an idea I want to talk to you about," Don said.

"Uh-oh, you sound serious, Don," Betty said.

"I was thinking we should get married," Don said.

Betty drank her coffee and said, "If that's a proposal, it's kind of lame. And haven't you heard that you don't need to buy the cow if you're already getting the milk?"

Don was taken aback at Betty's response.

Well, he thought, *that's the first time I ever asked a girl to marry me, and I fucked it up.* Don stood up, turned to face Betty, and stooped down on a bended knee. He took Betty's hand and looked her in the eye. "Betty Anderson, I love you, and I want to marry you. Will you marry me?"

Betty looked stricken. She burst out in tears and hung her head.

Don jumped to his feet and sat next to her and held her. "Honey, what's wrong? Did I do something wrong?" Don asked her.

Betty cried even harder. Don continued to hold her as she cried on his shoulder. Finally, the tears subsided. Don gave her his handkerchief, and she wiped her eyes.

She looked up at his face and said, "There's nothing I would rather do than marry you. But I will not marry you. I love you too much to do that to you."

"What do you mean?" he asked in frustration.

"You know what I mean, honey. If you love me, just hang in there for me. Pretend nothing's wrong. We started off being friends and lovers. Let's stay friends and lovers. Can you do that for me?"

Don picked up Mike's guitar and strummed the tune he was playing before. His emotions were in turmoil. Finally, he thought, *This is not about you. This is about her. If you let her down now, you're not much of a man.* "You bet I can, cutie," Don said. He played and sang the songs she requested.

Between songs, they cuddled on the love seat.

*****

Mike and June returned from their movie and heard Don playing and singing as June opened the door.

"That sounds like 'Don't Fence Me In,'" Mike said.

They hung up their winter gear and came into the living room.

Don finished playing Betty's request and asked Mike and June, "How was the movie?"

"It was hilarious. They played a double feature, Abbott and Costello in the first movie and the Three Stooges in the second one. The Stooges are silly, but they make me laugh," June said.

"Abbott and Costello did their 'Who's on First?' routine. It always cracks me up," Mike said. "How was your afternoon?" He sat in one of the living room chairs while June went into the kitchen.

"It was swell. Don's been serenading me," Betty said.

"I hope you don't mind me playing your Gibson arch top," Don said to Mike.

June checked the icebox and yelled, "We've got some beer. Who wants one?"

Everyone spoke up for a beer. June took down four glasses and poured the beer. She got a bag of pretzels from the pantry and poured them into a bowl.

Betty went into the kitchen to help June carry the glasses of beer.

Don followed her into the kitchen. "Can I help?" he asked.

"Sure, take these coasters and this bowl of pretzels," June said.

While they were setting up the refreshments, Mike went into June's bedroom and retrieved his electric guitar and amplifier and speaker and took them into the living room.

"Two can play at serenading the girls," he said. He hooked up the amplifier and speaker. He played a test cord on the guitar and turned down the volume on the amplifier.

Don and Mike sat together with their guitars on the love seat, and Don said, "Any requests from the audience?"

"I want to hear the song you guys played at the Frog Hop Ballroom," June said.

Don drank his beer and asked, "Which one?"

June sipped her beer and thought about the song title. "I can't remember the title, but it was about a girl with a gun."

Don looked at Mike and smiled. "A one, and a two, and a three!"

They played "Pistol Packin' Mama." Mike had the electric guitar, so he played guitar lead. Don played rhythm and sang the lead. Mike came in with him on the chorus. The girls whooped and applauded.

"I've got to get a gun to keep Don in line," Betty yelled to June. They cracked up.

"Don't forget, tomorrow is the wedding rehearsal in DeKalb," June reminded Don and Mike when they had finished jamming.

"Can you pick me up at the gate at Rosecrans tomorrow?" Don asked Mike.

"Sure, I'll bring the girls, and we'll be there at 1:00 p.m. That'll get us to DeKalb by 2:00 p.m. for the rehearsal," Mike said.

*****

Mike pulled up to the DeKalb Christian Church at 1:50 p.m. on Sunday with everyone on board. When the two couples got out of Mike's Chevy, Bess greeted them.

"Everyone's here except John, who is flying in from Washington, DC, next Saturday," Bess said.

Reverend Davis had the wedding party in the front pews with the ladies on one side of the aisle and the men on the other.

Ricky turned to Emma Dee across the aisles and said, "I guess we broke even on the bet."

Emma Dee laughed and said, "I guess we did."

June looked accusingly at Emma Dee and said, "What bet was that?"

Emma Dee and Ricky both laughed again.

Ricky said, "She bet $10 the groom wouldn't show up. I bet $10 the bride wouldn't show up. We both lost."

Don laughed, and Betty said, "You two are terrible."

June shrugged her shoulders and said, "I'm used to them."

Reverend Davis walked them all through the procession several times.

By that time, the wedding march had lost a lot of its luster for the wedding party. Ricky started mumbling and grumbling on the fifth time. He stopped when Emma Dee glared at him.

"I know this is a tedious process," Reverend Davis said. "But you'll be glad you practiced on the day of the wedding."

It was after four o'clock when the rehearsal was finally over.

Bess held the rehearsal party at the farm.

Don, Mike, and their band supplied the entertainment. They set up a bandstand in the roomy basement. The furniture was pushed to the far walls to make room for a dance floor. Additional folding chairs were added. A table with a punch bowl and soft drinks was set up in a corner. The Ping-Pong table and game table were put in the garage. Gaily colored bunting hung from the rafters and added a festive note. It didn't take long for a heated pitch game to start up in the living room.

Bess and her daughters set up a buffet in the kitchen with hors d'oeuvres and party sandwiches. After all the rehearsing, and since everyone had to work Monday, the party broke up early.

18

The day after the rehearsal, Betty was waiting with Kate at St. Joseph's Hospital for her treatment when Dr. Freidman came to see them. Betty clutched Kate's hand and waited for the news.

Dr. Freidman saw the anxiety on their faces and quickly said, "Please relax. It's very good news. Betty's blood test today was clear of cancer cells. She's in remission. I'm sorry if I frightened you." He sat in one of the chairs next to them. "After your treatment today, I want you to come in once a week for treatment and blood tests."

Betty still did not look reassured. "How long is it going to last this time?"

"I wish I could give you an answer, but I can't. That doesn't mean I'm pessimistic about your prognosis. You have responded remarkably well to new and unproven therapies. But we are breaking new ground, and I can't make you any promises."

"But I'm still not cured?" Betty asked.

"That's another question I cannot answer. The truth is that the only way we will know the answer is time. Cancer, this cancer, has never been cured. But someone must be the first. That's the best answer I can give you now. In the meantime, we will do all we can to keep you in remission. None of us knows how long we will live. The best we can do is make the most of the time we have."

"Thank you, Dr. Friedman. I know you are doing all you can for me. I'll try to keep up my end of the bargain," Betty said.

Kate marveled at her daughter's fortitude.

*****

Betty wanted to spend this week before the wedding with June to help with her last-minute wedding arrangements and asked Kate to take her back to her apartment after her treatment. Kate knew Betty would be happier returning to her apartment and being with her friends, but this going back and forth was hard on her and Ray. But it was only for a week this time.

June and Mike were still at work, so Kate stayed in the apartment with Betty until June got home.

June took the mail from her mailbox, stuffed it in her coat pocket, and went up to her apartment. She was surprised to see Betty and her mother.

Betty hugged her at the door and said, "I'm like a bad penny, roomie. I keep showing up."

"I'll be going on home now. I have to get dinner for your father," Kate said and briefly hugged Betty and June. She whispered in June's ear, "Betty had some good news today." Then she left.

"I'm going to make tea. Do you want some?" June asked Betty. She took the mail out of her pocket as she hung up her coat, dropped it on the kitchen table, and started the tea.

"Sure, that sounds good," Betty said. She followed June into the kitchen and sat at the table. "What's this envelope from the University of Missouri?" Betty asked.

"Ohmigod, it's my exam results!"

Betty handed her the envelope.

June clutched the envelope to her chest and closed her eyes. She wasn't sure what she was hoping for.

"Well, open it already," Betty said impatiently.

June slit open the envelope with a kitchen knife and carefully removed the letter inside. She didn't unfold and read it. What if she passed? What if she didn't?

"My God, you're driving me nuts!" Betty exclaimed. She stood up and waited anxiously for June to read the letter.

June unfolded it and read the crucial line. "I passed."

Betty hugged her boisterously and yelled, "Yippee!"

June hugged her back. *Whatever I'm going to do*, she thought. *I passed the darned exam.* She laughed along with her friend.

After they settled down, Betty said, "I saw Dr. Friedman today. He told me I'm in remission again."

June reached out and took Betty's hand. "That's wonderful news, honey."

"I hope you and Mike don't mind me coming back here this week. I wanted to help you with the wedding if I can."

The teapot whistled, so June got up and turned off the burner. She poured two cups of Earl Grey tea and put them on the table with the sugar bowl.

"Honey, I'm pleased as punch to have you here this week. I need a girlfriend to share the wedding with. Mike's great, but he's a guy. Guys don't get it when it comes to weddings. He won't admit it, but I think he'll be happy to get it over with," June said.

"I'll bet he's looking forward to the honeymoon though," Betty said and laughed.

"God, I hope the new hasn't worn off me yet!" June joked.

They both laughed.

The front door opened, and Mike came in.

"Hi, Betty. What's the joke?"

"It's just girl talk, Mike," Betty said from the kitchen. "June and I got great news today. I'm in remission again, and June passed her exam."

"That's outstanding! I'm tickled pink for you both." Mike kissed June and said, "Congratulations, honey. I knew you'd pass." He turned to Betty and asked, "Are you visiting or are you staying?"

"I'm staying until the wedding Saturday, and after the wedding, I'm going home with my folks," Betty said.

The phone rang, and June answered it. She turned to Mike and said, "It's Don. He wants to talk with you."

Mike took the phone from June and said, "Hi, best man, what's up?"

Don was calling from the barracks' phone. "The band is taking you out Friday night for your bachelor party."

Mike hadn't even thought about a bachelor party. He turned to June and said, "Don says the band wants to take me out Friday night for my bachelor party."

Don heard him and said, "What? You have to ask permission, and you're not even married yet." Don laughed.

Mike ignored Don's remark. "Who's going, and where are we going?"

"Danny and Sammy and I are taking you to the Burlesque Club. Why don't you tell June that too?" Don asked sarcastically.

"Don, Sammy, and Danny are taking me to the Burlesque Club to ogle almost-naked women," Mike said to June.

"Oh shit, I didn't think you'd really tell her!" Don said.

"Ogle away, Mr. Thompson. Get it out of your system. After Saturday, the only naked woman you'll be ogling will be your wife," June told him.

"We'll pick you up in Danny's Pontiac at 2000 hours. That's 8:00 p.m. to you, civilians," Don said hurriedly and hung up.

June turned to Betty and said, "We girls need to have our own party Friday night."

"Damn right!" Betty said. "Let's work on that."

June drank her tea and thought for a minute. "I'm calling Emma Dee. She'll know just what to do."

"Well, there goes the neighborhood," Mike said and laughed.

June raised an eyebrow at Mike and said, "So you have some objections to our girls' night out, do you?"

"Just as long as you're sober enough to say 'I do' on Saturday, you girls have a ball," Mike said.

June picked up the phone and dialed a number.

"Hi, sis, it's June," she said into the phone.

Emma Dee covered the receiver and said, "It's my sister, June, the one who's getting married Saturday."

Her boyfriend, Ed Benson, raised his glass of beer in acknowledgment.

"What's up, big sister? Did the groom get cold feet? Or did you?" Emma Dee asked.

"Not yet. Anyway," June said, "Mike just informed me his band buddies are throwing him a bachelor party on Friday night. Betty, and I figure what's sauce for the gander is sauce for the goose. We want to have a bachelorette party, and I thought you could organize it for us. What do you think?"

Emma Dee laughed. "Where do I sign up?"

June turned to Betty and said, "Emma Dee's in."

"Just what kind of bachelor party is Mike having?" Emma Dee asked.

"They are going to the Burlesque Club to leer at naked women," June answered.

"Oh, well now, that opens up the field of play," Emma Dee said. "You just leave everything to me. Virginia Jane and I will pick you and Betty up Friday at 8:30 p.m. Dress to kill."

June couldn't imagine Virginia Jane kicking up her heels at an Emma Dee-arranged shindig.

"How will you get Virginia Jane to go? I don't think her husband Jim would approve. Heck, I don't think Virginia Jane will approve."

Betty laughed at June's observation. She had met Virginia Jane.

"First, Jim is in Hawaii with his squadron. Second, you leave Virginia Jane to me," Emma Dee said. "How are you and Betty getting to DeKalb on Saturday?"

June said, "We're going with Mike and Don Saturday morning."

"Oh, sis, you can't do that. It's bad luck for Mike to see you before the wedding," Emma Dee said. "Why don't you and Betty pack your wedding clothes and toiletries, and I'll take you both with me to the farm after our shindig on Friday night?"

"Okay, that'll work. I'll see you Friday night," June said and hung up the phone. "The party's on," she said to Mike and Betty.

Mike was skeptical. "You're going to party with Emma Dee and Betty? Try to stay out of jail. I'd hate to have to bail you all out before the wedding."

June stuck out her tongue at him.

"Emma Dee will take us out to the farm after our party. Don can stay here, and you both can come out to the church Saturday morning," June said.

"Why don't we all just go together from here on Saturday morning?" Mike asked.

"That's what I said to Emma Dee. She said it's bad luck for the groom to see the bride before the wedding. Is that okay with you, Mike?"

"Sure, far be it from me to bring down a wedding curse on us," Mike joked.

Mike went to the Bridal Shoppe during his lunch break on Wednesday and tried on his tailored tuxedo. It fit perfectly, and he thanked Mrs. Collins.

He left with Don's tuxedo and the bridal party dresses and took them back to the apartment.

*****

On Thursday, April 12, Don was teaching a navigation class at Rosecrans Field when he heard an uproar in the hallway outside his classroom. He stopped his lecture and opened the classroom door. He stepped out and grabbed the arm of a corporal who was rushing down the hall.

"What's going on?" Don asked the corporal.

"The president's dead! It's on the radio!" the corporal said.

Don yelled, "Class dismissed!" into his classroom and ran up the hall behind the corporal.

The school office was crowded with airmen listening to the radio.

"To repeat, President Franklin Delano Roosevelt died today of a massive cerebral hemorrhage while vacationing in the Little White House at Warm Springs, Georgia," the radio announcer said.

Don was stunned. While President Roosevelt had suffered ill health, he had been president for all of Don's adult life. Mr. Roosevelt had just been inaugurated for his fourth term in office in January. The group of airmen around the radio all looked shocked at the news. It was almost as if the sun had forgotten to rise today. Mr. Roosevelt's presidency was a simple fact of everyday life, and suddenly, it wasn't.

"Oh shit! Do you realize this means that the clodhopper from Missouri will be our president?" a staff sergeant exclaimed.

It took Don a minute or two to understand what the staff sergeant meant. He couldn't even remember the name of the vice president.

"It's that communist, Henry Wallace," Don remembered. "My God, we have a communist for our president!" Don exclaimed.

The corporal that Don followed into the office said, "No, we don't. It's that new Truman character from some hick town in Missouri."

It started to dawn on the soldiers that the war wasn't over, and they had just lost their wartime leader. It was like losing your quarterback in the fourth quarter of the big game, and no one knew anything about the backup quarterback.

"Who will run the damn war now?" the staff sergeant asked.

Everyone started talking loudly over each other.

Don put two fingers in his mouth and whistled shrilly. Silence descended on the group and Don said, "We still have two guys named Eisenhower and MacArthur, and the Germans are almost whipped."

That settled everyone down.

Another sergeant said, "Quiet, there's more news on the radio."

The voice of the announcer continued. "Vice President Harry S. Truman has been notified of Mr. Roosevelt's death and arrangements are being made to swear in Mr. Truman as the thirty-third president of the United States in the White House later today."

A few hours later, Mr. Truman took the oath of office in the White House with Chief Justice Harlan Stone. Mr. Truman later told reporters, "I don't know if you fellas ever had a load of hay fall on you, but when they told me what happened yesterday, I felt like the moon, the stars and all the planets had fallen on me."

*****

June and Betty were in their rooms primping for their girls' night out. Mike was sitting on the love seat listening to the radio. The news commentator talked about the memorial arrangements for the dead president, Franklin Delano Roosevelt. His remains were being transported from the Little White House in Warm Springs,

Georgia, to Washington, DC, on the Ferdinand Magellan train on Saturday. His body would lie in state for several hours in the East Room of the White House and would be on view to the public. Flags were at half-staff all over the nation and in Allied countries.

June came out of her bedroom and said to Mike, "Do you think we should still go out partying tonight? It seems disrespectful somehow."

"I know what you mean. But life goes on. I don't want to disappoint Don and the guys in the band. They've gone to some trouble arranging my party."

"Yes, and so have my sisters. Betty is looking forward to some fun. God knows she can use it," June said and sat next to Mike on the love seat.

The doorbell rang, and June got up to open the door.

"Hi, kids, the band is waiting in the car," Don said and came in.

"Hi, yourself. I'm ready to go when you are," Mike said.

"I wanted to say hi to Betty, and then we can go. What's she doing?" Don asked.

"She's still getting ready for our night out," June said. "It's awful about Mr. Roosevelt, isn't it?"

"I didn't agree with some of his socialist ideas, but he sure did a good job running the war," Don said. "I hope this Truman guy has his head on straight. The war isn't over yet."

Betty came out of her room as Don made his remarks. "Hi, big guy," she said to Don. "It's like losing your father. I can hardly remember anyone else being president."

Don rose when Betty came out of her room and kissed her on the cheek.

"I feel funny going out to party tonight with Mr. Roosevelt's death and all," Betty said.

"Yeah, June and I were talking about that earlier," Mike said. "But life goes on for the rest of us. Our friends have taken the time and trouble to arrange this night's festivities. I think we should set aside our grief for tonight and tomorrow. I'm sorry this happened to Mr. Roosevelt, but it's too late to change our personal plans."

Don said, "Okay, enough about all that. Let's hit the road, Mike."

Mike followed Don to the door and said, "Have a good time, girls. Don't let Emma Dee drive you all home if she's had a few drinks."

June said, "Don't worry, I'm going to be the driver. I'll have my usual one drink."

Mike hesitated at the door and said, "Just think, honey, this time tomorrow night we'll be Mr. and Mrs. Thompson."

June gave him a big kiss and said, "Bear that in mind while you're ogling tonight."

Mike and Don left the apartment just as Danny, their drummer, honked the horn on his Pontiac.

June and Betty sat on the love seat in the living room and talked about President Roosevelt's death and his accomplishments while he was president.

"What I liked most about him were his fireside chats on the radio," Betty said. "I always felt he was like our father explaining things to us."

June agreed with Betty and said, "I hope Mr. Truman is a good man. Lloyd is still fighting, and he needs a strong leader to win this war and bring all our boys home."

"Where is your brother now?" Betty asked.

"I got a letter from Lloyd this week. The censors deleted most of his references to where his unit is fighting. But he's in Germany somewhere and says his division is doing well. They liberated some sort of German labor camp. I guess that was pretty awful."

"Well, at least your brother Ricky is out of the war now," Betty said.

"Yes, and I thank God for that," June said.

The doorbell rang.

"That must be Emma Dee," June said and opened the door.

"It's party time, ladies!" Emma Dee shouted and entered with Virginia Jane following quietly behind her.

After June had hugged and exchanged cheek kisses with both of her sisters, Betty got the same treatment. They settled down in the living room.

"Are you all ready to get wild and wooly tonight?" Emma Dee asked them.

"I'm sure you'll be wild and wooly enough for all of us," Virginia Jane said disdainfully.

"How on earth did she talk you into this?" June asked Virginia Jane.

"I threatened to let the skeletons out of her closet if she didn't come," Emma Dee said.

Ignoring Emma Dee's remark, Virginia Jane said, "I came along to drive you all home after this bacchanalia. I didn't want my little sister in the clink or in the hospital on her wedding day."

"I'm a great driver," Emma Dee said defensively.

"And she has the traffic tickets to prove it," Virginia Jane retorted.

June got up and asked, "If you two are through bickering, can we go now before the night is over?"

June retrieved Emma Dee and Virginia Jane's bridesmaid dresses from her closet and gave them each their dress to take to the car. Betty carried her maid-of-honor dress and a suitcase with her clothes for the reception. The dresses were still in their Bridal Shoppe slipover bags. June carried her suitcase. It was a tight fit, but they got everything in the car.

*****

The Burlesque Club had a battered oak bar along the wall to the left of the entrance. To the right of the entry, there were tables scattered around an open area facing a theatrical stage with a worn purple stage curtain. Despite the name of the club, there was only one stripper on the program. A chorus line of girls in tights and fishnet stockings were on stage when the guys found a table up front. The chorus line was showing off their fishnet stockings with choreographed high kicks. They were close enough to see tears in the stockings.

"You couldn't catch any fish in those nets," Danny said.

They laughed.

"A couple of them are old enough to be my mother," said Danny. "Hell, that *is* my mother!"

They all laughed.

A waiter took their drink orders.

The curtain fell on the chorus line, and the stage band took a break. The waiter brought their drinks.

Don leaned over and whispered to Mike, "I asked Betty to marry me, and she turned me down."

Mike drank his beer and slowly put the glass back down on the table.

"She's thinking of you, you know. She doesn't want to make you a widower before your thirtieth birthday," Mike said.

Don drank his scotch and soda and replied, "I know that, but I love her, and I want to spend every minute I can with her. If we're married, she can live on the base with me."

"Did you tell her that?" Mike asked Don between the hackneyed punch lines from the cornball comedian doing a doctor routine on stage.

Don took another drink and continued, "I'm not about to get into an argument with her over it. If she changes her mind, she'll tell me."

Danny and Sammy laughed at the doctor, taking a mallet to the head of his patient onstage.

Don said, "Mike, I apologize for the crappy taste of our bass player. He said this was a classy club."

"And you took the word of a guy who wears purple argyle socks and high-topped red basketball shoes?" Mike asked.

Everyone laughed, even Sammy.

"Yuck it up, you guys. But you just wait and see. The night's not over yet," Sammy said.

As the curtain opened, the band introduced an overweight brassy blond in a full-length gown. She did a Mae West imitation, sashaying around the stage, stripping off a pair of white gloves, one glove at a time.

"Shit, at this rate, she'll take all night getting down to her G-string," Danny said.

Mike turned away from Don and checked her out. The woman was blowsy, but she had a surprising grace to her movements. She might have been a talented dancer when she was younger. Mike couldn't take his eyes off her. He wasn't the only one. The mostly male audience quieted down and watched her peel off and toss aside her breakaway dress. She went into a hip thrust, bump-and-grind dance routine. Despite the love handles between the spangled bra and panties, the dance was genuinely erotic. The audience was mesmerized, and lewd shouts started coming from the tables. The stripper had style.

Mike could see that she was picking up energy from the audience, and she upped the ante by tearing off the bra and throwing it to a patron at one of the front tables.

The catcalls increased in number and volume as she paraded around in her pasties and panties. The band was playing louder and faster. Now the audience was pounding on the tabletops with beer glasses and fists.

"Take it all off, baby!" was the communal cry.

Suddenly, she stopped still in a provocative pose. The band went quiet. She stretched out the silence, not moving a muscle. The tension in the audience was palpable. She reached down to her waist and ripped off the tear-away panties and held them over her head as she resumed her pose. She gave the audience a few seconds to take in her body clad in pasties and a G-string, and then the stage lights went out and the curtain closed. The audience roared and clapped.

"See, I told you," Sammy said to his friends. "Now are you sorry you came?"

"That was a showstopper," Mike said. "No one will top that act. Drink up and let's go. I'm getting married in the morning. Thanks for a great bachelor party, guys."

*****

Over Virginia Jane's protest, Emma Dee drove the bachelor-ette party to the Top Hat Club. The four girls checked their coats and hats and looked the place over. The club was a few blocks from Rosecrans Field and always had a big contingent of airmen on the weekends. Tonight was no exception. Most of the airmen were in civvies, wearing coats and ties, but a few were in uniform. There was a separate bar in a room away from the dance floor and bandstand where couples could converse without yelling over the five-piece band. Band members were in top hats and tuxedos. But they didn't attempt big band music; instead, they played swing numbers and slow dance ballads. There was a generous dance floor surrounded by tables with candlelight. Seating was comfortable, and the tone of the club was sophisticated.

"Pretty classy, huh?" Emma Dee said as the waiter led them to a table away from the bandstand.

June had asked for a table where they could talk and hear each other. Emma Dee wore a red low-cut evening gown that accented her small, perky breasts. It had a wraparound skirt that flashed some leg when she moved in it. She caught the eye of every male they passed on the way to their table. Virginia Jane wore a gray formal evening dress with a high collar.

Betty's décolletage in her royal-blue gown stole some of the male attention from Emma Dee.

When they all were seated, Emma Dee said, "Big boobs do it every time. It's just not fair."

June wore her simple black cocktail dress. "Stuff some napkins in your bra when you get a chance," she said to Emma Dee.

They all laughed and gave their drink orders to the waiter, who wore a top hat and black jacket.

Soon, two uniformed airmen came up to their table. The tall blond-haired one asked Emma Dee to dance.

"Sure, anything for our boys in uniform," Emma Dee said.

"Anything, honey?" the soldier asked Emma Dee on the way to the dance floor.

"Start by showing me how good you can dance, and we'll see about anything else," Emma Dee said and laughed.

The other short, dark-haired airman surveyed the table. Betty was clearly out of his league. He considered June, but she shook her head, so he asked Virginia Jane. She looked like a nice girl. Virginia Jane got up and took his arm. They went out on the floor and joined the other swingers.

June was floored. "I can't believe Virginia Jane danced with that guy. She's already got one airman. She's married to her high school sweetheart, Jim. He's in the Army Air Corps."

Their waiter arrived with the drinks.

Betty reached for her purse, but the waiter said, "The girl in the red dress asked me to run a tab." Betty drank her cocktail and said, "Speaking of marriage, Don asked me to marry him."

June sipped her glass of beer and asked, "What did you say?"

"I asked him if we could just stay the way we are, friends and lovers," Betty replied. "He said okay."

June wanted to ask Betty why she turned Don down. But she didn't want to raise the subject of Betty's illness while they were trying to have a good time, so she said nothing.

Another soldier approached their table and asked Betty to dance. He was a tall, sandy-haired sergeant in uniform. He had a double row of ribbons on his tunic and a pair of wings above the ribbons.

"Are you stationed at Rosecrans Field?" Betty asked him.

The sergeant sat in one of the empty chairs and said, "Yes, I am. I'm Barry Mitchell. What are your names, ladies?"

"I'm Betty, and this is my friend, June. She's getting married tomorrow."

June said, "Hi, Barry. My girlfriends are throwing me a bachelorette party. Two of them are out on the floor dancing."

"Speaking of dancing, Betty, how about it?" Barry said.

The band was starting a hip-hop number.

"Okay, Barry, let's see what you've got."

They spun out on the floor. Barry was a good dancer, and so was Betty. June admired their style.

Emma Dee returned from her dance and thanked her partner. She sat down and took a healthy drink of her rum and Coke.

"He's a nice guy, but not much of a dancer," Emma Dee said. "He should have asked you, June."

June laughed and agreed she wasn't much of a dancer. Virginia Jane rejoined the table after thanking her dance partner.

"Virginia Jane Michaels, I'm surprised at you!" Emma Dee said, needling Virginia Jane. "You're already spoken for."

Virginia Jane drank her Virgin Mary cocktail and said, "I'm at a party. I'm not missing out on the fun. Besides, you're already spoken for too, and you're dancing."

"I'm not spoken for. I'm just dating. Ed's not my husband," Emma Dee said and spotted a good-looking blond man approaching the table. He was dressed in a gray tweed jacket and tan trousers. He wore an ascot around his neck. He walked with a military carriage. "This one's mine. I saw him first," she said to Betty and June.

The man looked around the table and asked, "Would one of you fine looking ladies like to dance?"

"Hey, Fred Astaire, I'm your Ginger Rogers," Emma Dee said and grabbed his arm and led him onto the dance floor.

"We won't see much of her tonight," June observed.

The girls turned down three more fellows, telling them, "We're resting, maybe later."

Betty turned to June and said, "I'd marry Don in a heartbeat if I had my health, but I don't. I don't have the energy to go through a wedding or a marriage. And I won't make Don responsible for taking care of me. He's already being a good friend and hanging in there with me. That's enough."

June couldn't argue with that. She had no idea how she would deal with Betty's situation if the tables were turned. Would she marry Mike?

"Let's talk about your wedding. How are you feeling on your last night as a single girl?" Betty asked June.

June sipped her beer and considered Betty's question. "I don't feel like a single girl. I feel like Mike and I are already married, and the wedding is just a formality. Don't get me wrong, I'm excited about the wedding. I think it will be great fun."

"I feel kind of the same way about Don. I'm excited about your wedding too. I'm so glad I'm able to stand with you tomorrow."

Emma Dee came off the dance floor with her handsome blond partner. "Girls, this is Capt. Malcolm J. Bridgestone. These are my sisters, June and Virginia Jane, and June's maid of honor, Betty."

"Please, just call me Corky, like all my friends do. I hope we will be friends," Malcolm said.

After the girls had introduced themselves, Emma Dee said to Malcolm, "Go grab another chair and join us." While Malcolm was retrieving a chair from a nearby table, Emma Dee said, "Is he a dreamboat, or what?"

June looked askance at her and replied, "Sure he is. Your boyfriend, Ed, is going to love him."

Emma Dee gave June a dirty look and said, "Don't be a party pooper. Get one of your own. There have been enough of them asking you to dance."

Malcolm returned with a chair.

Emma Dee said, "Make some room, girls," and slid her chair over toward June.

June and Betty both slid over to make room.

Malcolm sat down and said, "Emma tells me that this is a bachelorette party for June. I think that's splendid. How's it going so far, June?"

June was caught off balance. "I never heard anyone call my sister Emma before."

Malcolm said, "Emma and I made a deal. She gave me permission to call her Emma, and I told her she could call me Corky."

"Corky Bridgestone, I like it. It's quirky," Betty said.

Malcolm signaled to a waiter. "Please allow me to buy some champagne so we can toast the bride and her charming attendants." Malcolm had effortlessly won over the entire bachelorette party.

"If I didn't have Don, I'd arm wrestle you for this one," Betty said to Emma Dee.

"Are you an airman out at Rosecrans?" June asked.

"He's a pilot," Emma Dee said. "He flies those big planes."

The waiter and a busboy delivered the champagne and champagne glasses. The waiter opened the champagne and poured some into Malcolm's glass. Malcolm waved off the tasting and told the waiter to go ahead and serve everyone. When they all had glasses of champagne, Malcolm stood and held up his glass.

"To love and marriage," he toasted. "And to the lovely bride and her lucky groom."

"Hear, hear!" the table responded enthusiastically.

They all sipped their champagne, even Virginia Jane.

When the band struck up a slow dance number, Malcolm looked at June and said, "Surely the groom would not begrudge me one dance with the bride?"

June smiled at Malcolm and got up to dance. Emma Dee glared at her. She wanted the slow dance with Corky. When Malcolm looked away toward the dance floor, June stuck out her tongue at Emma Dee.

Virginia Jane's short, dark-haired dance partner from earlier in the night showed up at the table and said to her, "You promised me a slow dance, I believe."

Virginia Jane smiled at him and got up to slow dance. Emma Dee looked accusingly at her. She too stuck out her tongue at Emma Dee.

"Lighten up, honey, it's a party," Betty said to Emma Dee.

Sgt. Barry Mitchell, Betty's dance partner, arrived next. Betty shrugged her shoulders at Emma Dee and got up to dance.

"Well, if that doesn't take the cake, I don't know what does?" Emma Dee said to the empty table. Then she laughed at herself. Two more young men asked her to dance, but she turned them down. She was waiting for Corky to come back to her table. She would not let him get away again.

Malcolm and June came off the dance floor holding hands, and Malcolm escorted June to her seat. He bowed his head and kissed her hand.

"Thank you for the dance, June. I envy your fiancé."

"It was my pleasure, Malcolm. I'm not much of a dancer," June said.

The band started up a spirited swing number. Emma Dee jumped up and took Malcolm's hand.

"This dance is mine, Corky," she said.

Malcolm smiled at her and said, "I'm delighted, Emma."

They were swept up by the gyrating, high-stepping dancers.

Virginia Jane parted company with her dance partner and returned to their table. She sat down and lifted the champagne bottle out of the ice bucket and poured herself a glass. She held the bottle toward June inquiringly.

"Not for me, thanks. And aren't you supposed to be our sober driver?" June asked Virginia Jane.

"I guess you just took over the job. I love champagne," Virginia Jane said and giggled.

The band wrapped up the song and took a break.

Betty and Barry made their way back to the table. Barry thanked Betty for the dance and left to find his own table.

Betty sat down in relief and said, "That will do me for a while."

Virginia Jane picked up the champagne bottle and waved it at Betty. Betty held out her glass and Virginia Jane poured the last of the champagne into it. As they returned to the table, Malcolm and Emma Dee saw the champagne bottle being emptied, and Malcolm signaled to the waiter.

"Get us another bottle of champagne please," Malcolm said.

"Put that bottle on our tab," Emma Dee said to the waiter. "It's our turn to buy, Corky."

Malcolm gave in and pulled out Emma Dee's chair and seated her. He sat down next to her.

"My boyfriend is stationed at Rosecrans. He's a navigation trainer," Betty said to Malcolm.

"What's his name?" Malcolm asked her.

"His name is Don Walker. He's a tech sergeant."

"I know who he is. My buddy has flown some training flights with him. He said Sergeant Walker flew twenty-five combat missions in the Pacific. He's something of a hero to us at the base."

"He's a hero to me too," Betty said.

"Were you in combat, Corky?" Emma Dee asked.

The waiter showed up with their champagne, opened the bottle, and refilled their glasses. He put the bottle into a fresh ice bucket.

"I flew some supply and medical evacuation missions in Sicily and Italy," Malcolm said. "I don't know if I'd call that combat."

"Were they shooting at you?" Emma Dee asked.

"A few times they were. Mostly they were shooting it out with our fighter escorts."

"Sounds like combat to me," Emma Dee said.

"Is your fiancé in the service?" Malcolm asked June.

June told Malcolm about Mike's service in the Signal Corps.

Betty suggested that the hour was getting late, and they all had to drive to DeKalb tonight. Malcolm thanked them for including him in their bachelorette party.

As they all got up to leave, Emma Dee slipped Malcolm her name and phone number. Only Betty noticed.

"I'm driving home to the farm," June said firmly.

Emma Dee didn't argue with her.

*****

"I don't know why I'm so jittery this morning. I can't wait to make June my wife, so why should I be nervous about the wedding?"

He gave Don the wedding rings to hold for him.

"Stage fright, buddy," Don said. "But don't worry about it. No one will be looking at you. All eyes will be on the bride. Grooms are just supporting actors."

"We need to get going. I want to get to the rectory by 10:00 a.m. to change into my monkey suit," Mike said.

They carried their tuxedos out to Mike's Chevy.

Mike handed the car keys to Don and said, "You better drive. My head's spinning."

Mike directed Don as they drove to DeKalb.

*****

June was literally up with the chickens. She even heard the rooster crow. She put on her robe and slippers and went to the kitchen. Bess was up and making coffee.

"Did you girls have a good time last night?" Bess asked June.

"Yes, we did. We laughed and danced and drank champagne. Emma Dee may have found a new beau. Ed better watch out."

Bess poured coffee, and they sat at the table.

"Well, you are the first bride I ever heard of to have a bachelor-ette party," Bess said. "Mike didn't object to his future wife going out on the town?"

"He and his band buddies went to watch girls take their clothes off, so he didn't dare object." June drank her coffee.

"How are you feeling this morning?" Bess asked.

"I'm so excited I can hardly sit still," June said.

Dee came into the kitchen and went to the counter to get his coffee.

"Good morning, ladies. How are you both on this wedding morning?" Dee was dressed in his work clothes—overalls, denim shirt, and boots.

"Are you going to the wedding dressed like that, Dad?" June asked, joking with him.

"Wedding or no wedding, chores still need to be done, young lady. You've been a city girl too long and forgot that, I guess."

"Speaking of chores, I've got to go out and gather the eggs and feed the chickens," Bess said.

"I'll help you, Mom," June said and finished her coffee.

When June and Bess returned to the kitchen, Betty and Virginia Jane were having coffee.

Bess set the basket of fresh eggs on the counter and asked, "Who's ready for breakfast?"

The three girls all agreed they would love fresh eggs and farm-smoked ham. Before long, the kitchen had a team of cooks at work and was filled with mouthwatering aromas. Bess took egg orders and cracked eggshells. Betty cut ham steaks and gave them to June to fry. Virginia Jane made the toast. A fresh pot of coffee was perking on the stove.

Ricky came in from the living room wearing blue jeans and a white T-shirt under his arm sling.

"I see the carousing women made it back home in one piece," he said. "Make me a couple of scrambled eggs please, Mom."

Dee came in the back door and said, "Something sure smells good." He got a cup of coffee and sat at the table.

Bess cooked the eggs in the ham fat with a little lard as June set the plate of fried ham on the table, and Virginia Jane added her plate of buttered toast. June plated the eggs as Bess finished them and set the plates on the table.

Emma Dee came into the kitchen dressed in her pajamas and robe and said to Bess, "I'll have two eggs over easy, Mom."

"You'll have them the way I make them, young lady," Bess said. She was annoyed with Emma Dee about the way she was dressed with company in the house.

Emma Dee poured herself a cup of coffee and added cream and sugar. "I guess I'm going to have to sit on the floor," she said, looking at the full kitchen table.

"Get a folding chair out of the hall closet," Bess said.

"That's what you get for sleeping late with a hangover," Ricky kidded her.

Emma Dee retrieved the folding chair and told Virginia Jane to move over and let her in.

"First, you give Virginia Jane and me that lumpy foldaway bed in the basement, and now I have to sit on this card table chair," she grumbled.

Bess just shook her head and finished cooking Ricky and Emma Dee's eggs.

"I forgot how good fresh eggs taste," June said.

They all dove into breakfast.

"When are the guys going to get here?" Emma Dee asked June.

"They're going straight to the church," June answered. "Mike said he'd be there by 10:00 a.m. to change into his tux."

"After Mom and Dad, I claim bride's right to the first shower," June said. "Betty is our guest, so she gets second. You three can fight over the last two showers."

"I took mine last night, so that just leaves you and Virginia Jane," Ricky said to Emma Dee.

Dee wiped his mouth with his napkin and said, "I'm going to take mine right now." He got up and left to take his shower.

"June said you found a new beau, Emma Dee?" Bess asked.

"That remains to be seen, but I have hopes," Emma Dee said. She started clearing the table and taking the dirty dishes to the sink. "I'll wash and you can dry, Virginia Jane," she said.

"I can dry," Betty said, getting up.

"Not on your life," said Emma Dee. "The bride and the maid of honor need to take their showers and start getting ready for the big day."

Virginia Jane joined Emma Dee at the sink. Ricky had a second cup of coffee and finished his eggs. June and Betty went into the living room and sat together on the couch and sipped their coffee.

"What's it like, being the bride on your wedding day?" Betty asked June.

"It's like being the leading lady in the senior play in high school. I'm excited and skittish at the same time," June said. "I hope I can remember my lines and I don't trip going down the aisle."

"Last night was fun, wasn't it?" Betty said.

"It sure was. I hope the boys had as much fun as we did," June said.

"Are you a little sorry you won't be a footloose single girl after today?" Betty asked.

"Not a bit. I plan to be a footloose married lady. Mike and I will have adventures together. Besides, when you've found what you want, why keep looking?" June said. "I'm so happy you're sharing this day with me."

Betty reached over and patted June's hand. "I wouldn't have missed it for the world, roomie."

Bess came into the living room and said, "The shower's all yours, girls."

Emma Dee and Virginia Jane finished the breakfast dishes.

"I'm going up to the guest bathroom and take a bath and get ready," Emma Dee said.

"I'll wait for the shower," Virginia Jane said. She refilled her coffee cup and sat down at the kitchen table with Bess and Ricky.

"Did Emma Dee really meet a new man last night, or are you all teasing me?" Bess asked Virginia Jane.

"His name is Malcolm. He's a hunk—tall, blond-haired, and very charming," Virginia Jane said.

"How many guys did you girls pick up last night?" Ricky asked, needling her.

The front doorbell rang, and Virginia Jane said, "I'll get that, Mom."

Her brother, John, was at the door holding his suitcase in one hand and a folding suit bag over the other arm. "Hi, sis," he said and came in and set down his suitcase.

Virginia Jane said, "Hi, John. How was your flight?"

"The first one was okay. It was a TWA flight on a Constellation. Then I changed planes in St. Louis and got on a puddle jumper. I hate small planes, they scare me. But I'm here in time for the wedding. Where is everyone?"

"They're getting ready. Ricky and Mom are in the kitchen."

John laid his suit bag over his suitcase and followed Virginia Jane into the kitchen.

"Well, look what the cat dragged in. Hi, brother," Ricky said.

Bess got up and hugged John.

"It's good to see you, son. I'm so happy you could be here for June's wedding. Help yourself to some coffee, I just made a new pot."

"Thanks, Mom, I could use a cup. It was a long trip," John said. "How's the arm doing, Ricky?"

"A lot better than the last time you saw me in DC," Ricky responded. "I'm supposed to get out of this sling in a couple of weeks."

"Have you met June's fiancé?" John asked Ricky. He got his cup of coffee and sat down across from Ricky at the table.

"He came to see me at the hospital in St. Joe. I think sis has got a keeper. I like him."

"What does he do for a living?" John asked.

Bess got up from the table and said, "I think I'll check on the girls and see if they need any help getting ready."

"He's working at Kaufmann's Radio Sales and Service store in St. Joe. He was a radioman in the Signal Corps. He just got riffed a couple of months ago. He was a trainer at Camp Crowder."

"He sounds like a go-getter," John said."

"What do you think of our new president, this Truman fellow?" Ricky asked.

"He did a good job clearing out some of the crooks in the military supply chain, both the Army G-4 types and the civilian contractors they were in bed with," John said. "I think he'll do okay."

"It seems strange to think that FDR is not our president anymore," Ricky said.

"He's lying in state at the White House today. The radio says thousands of Americans are lined up to pay their respects," John said. "I hope this doesn't put a damper on June's wedding."

"Well, it didn't put a damper on her bachelorette party," Ricky said.

"What do you mean? What's a bachelorette party?" John asked.

"Mike's friends threw him a bachelor party last night, so our sisters and her maid of honor decided June should have a bachelorette party, and they gave her one."

"What did they do at this party?" John asked.

Emma Dee came into the kitchen and said, "We raised hell, let our hair down, and scandalized DeKalb, big brother."

John got up and hugged Emma Dee. "I'll bet you did," John said. "Where did this rumpus take place?"

"At the Top Hat Club in St. Joe. The place was packed with horny servicemen looking for loose women," Emma Dee said.

"It sounds like your kind of place, Emma Dee," Ricky said.

Emma Dee sat down next to John and said, "The peanut gallery has been heard from." She turned to Ricky and said, "Children should be seen and not heard, you know."

"I guess I better try on my monkey suit. Where is it?" John asked.

"Check with Dad. He picked up the tuxedos," Ricky said. "I think he's in his bedroom getting dressed."

John went in search of Dee and his tuxedo. He saw June sitting on the couch in the living room with an attractive blond girl.

When he approached them, June said, "Hi, big brother. I didn't know you were here. How was your trip?"

"Long and tiring. But I'm glad to be home," John said.

The girls stood up, and June said, "John, this is my best friend and maid of honor, Betty. Betty, this is my brother, John. He just got here from Washington."

"I'm glad to know you," Betty said.

"I'm very pleased to meet you, Betty," John said. "If you ladies will excuse me, I'm looking for Dad."

"He's in his bedroom getting dressed," June said.

Dee looked up from tying his tie as John came into the bedroom. He was already in his tuxedo.

"John, I'm glad to see you made it all right. Have you seen Ricky yet?"

John replied, "Yes, he's in the kitchen."

"Go get him. We need to get you both dressed for the wedding."

Bess started rounding up the bridal party. She had Emma Dee and Virginia Jane in tow and took them into the living room with June and Betty. The girls were wearing their clothes for the reception.

"Emma Dee, can you take Betty and your sisters in your car?"

Emma Dee said, "Sure, Mom."

The girls went to round up their bridesmaids' clothes.

"What about Dad, John, and Ricky?" June asked.

"They're getting dressed right now. I'm going with them. Your trousseau will be at the rectory with me. How's your friend Betty feeling?" Bess asked.

"She's doing fine so far. I think she'll be all right. She's excited about being the maid of honor."

"God bless her," Bess said.

The men appeared in their tuxedos.

John was looking skeptically at his ensemble. "June, are you responsible for this costume?"

Ricky laughed.

Ricky said, "I look great in mine. I've even got a sling to match."

Dee said, "Let's get this show on the road."

They followed him out to his car. Dee helped Bess carry June's trousseau as they all got in Dee's car.

Meanwhile, Emma Dee was organizing the women to go with her in her Studebaker.

"Let's go see if the groom shows up," Emma Dee said and locked the house as they left.

*****

Don pulled into the driveway next to the rectory of the DeKalb Christian Church. He turned off the Chevy's engine and set the hand brake.

"Does the condemned man have any last words?" he asked, looking at Mike.

"Yeah, he does. Thanks for being my best man, buddy. As General Lee said at the South's surrender at Appomattox, 'I'd rather face a thousand deaths. Can't I just skip to the honeymoon?'"

Don laughed and got out of the car. He got his tuxedo from the back seat and handed Mike his.

"Cheer up," Don said. "Maybe the bride will get cold feet."

When they knocked on the front door of the rectory, the minister's wife, Mrs. Davis, opened the door and invited them inside. She led them back into one of the bedrooms and said, "This is your changing room, gentlemen. The bride has the room down the hall. She hasn't arrived yet."

"See, there's hope for you yet," Don said.

After Mrs. Davis closed the bedroom door, they started changing into their wedding clothes.

19

"Are you nervous, June?" Betty asked, as Emma Dee drove to the rectory.

"A little bit, but mostly I'm excited. How are you feeling?" June asked Betty.

"I feel like I've run a marathon and I'm on the last mile and I can see the finish line ahead. I'm tired but happy," Betty said and smiled at June.

June was suddenly overwhelmed with sadness for her friend. A tear rolled down her cheek.

"Hey, sis, knock off the tears. This is the happiest day of your life. Besides, you'll spoil your makeup and have red eyes. Not a good look for the bride," Emma Dee said.

June hugged Betty and said, "Thanks, sweetie. It wouldn't have been the same without you."

"I hope the groom and the best man aren't getting as sappy as you two," Emma Dee said.

Count on Emma Dee to lighten the mood, June thought.

Reverend Davis came into the groom's changing room and saw Mike and Don were both dressed and ready.

"The bride will be here soon. Let's all go over to the church and leave the rectory to the bride's party." He led them into the church office and said, "Just relax and I'll come get you when it's time.

He left to greet arriving guests.

"I saw a back door in the church. You can still make a run for it," Don teased Mike.

"You know, right now I have a dandy feeling that I am in exactly the right place, doing exactly the right thing. It's how I felt when I proposed to June," Mike said.

Don could see Mike was serious. "In that case, you're a very lucky man, my friend."

Bess helped June into her grandmother's wedding dress, while Betty and her sisters changed in one of the other bedrooms in the rectory. Bess finished zipping up June's wedding dress and stepped back to look at her.

"Your grandmother would be very proud of you."

June looked at herself in the full-length mirror in the bedroom. The strapless décolletage showed off her strong shoulders and freckled bosom. The calf-length hemline was perfect for her shapely legs.

"Not too bad for a farm girl from DeKalb," she said. "Thank you for my wedding, Mom." June hugged Bess and kissed her on the cheek.

"Dad and I are happy to do it. You are getting a very good young man. He's a fine addition to our family."

June studied herself in the mirror and said, "I don't know who that lucky girl is, but I'm sure happy to be her today."

Emma Dee was also studying her reflection in the mirror. "Peach does absolutely nothing for me. It clashes with my red hair." She looked at Betty, who had just finished putting on her dress. "Can I borrow your blond hair and boobs until after the ceremony?" she asked.

Betty laughed and said, "You look fine. Besides, we're all going to blend in together anyway."

Virginia Jane said, "I like the peach. It matches my shape."

Emma Dee and Betty both laughed.

"You know, I think she's right," Emma Dee said. "She does look like a peach."

Now they all laughed.

Mrs. Davis came into the bedroom and said, "Fifteen minutes, girls. Then we have to head for the church."

"Has anyone seen the groom?" Emma Dee asked.

"Of course, we have. He and the best man are over at the church," Mrs. Davis said.

"Just checking," Emma Dee said.

Virginia Jane giggled, and Betty smiled.

*****

Reverend Davis was very pleased with the ornamentation of the church. The pulpit and the aisles were all draped in white bunting. The bride's family contributed colorful flower arrangements.

Reverend Davis was extremely gratified with the turnout for the wedding. Most of DeKalb was in attendance, as expected. But a significant representation of St. Joseph was showing up as well. The groom's employer, Mr. Bernie Kline, a partner in Kaufmann's Radio Sales and Service store, arrived with several of the groom's coworkers. And the bride's supervisor, a Mr. Tim Sullivan, was effusive in his admiration of the bride. Accompanying Tim was June's packing line friend Wendy and scheduling trainer, Cheryl. Three airmen who were fellow cadre at Rosecrans Field had been invited by the bride at Sergeant Walker's request. Gratifyingly, they arrived in uniform and added a patriotic air to the proceedings.

The maid of honor's father and mother were there. Reverend Davis chatted with the reverend and Mrs. Anderson and was sad to learn of their daughter's illness but impressed to hear how she had been determined to stand with her best friend at her wedding. While he was talking with the Andersons, a Packard Phaeton sedan pulled up to the church. The driver was in livery and opened the rear door for his passengers. The other partner in Kaufmann's Radio Sales and Service store, a Mr. Sidney Kaufmann and his wife, exited the Packard.

Mrs. Davis escorted Bess over to the church, where the usher took her to her seat in the front pew.

"Okay, gentlemen, you're up, just like we rehearsed," Reverend Davis said to Mike, Don, Ricky, and John.

As they made their way forward to the altar, the buzz of conversation in the church died down.

"It's too late to back out now," Don whispered to Mike.

Mike gaped at the crowd and was too befuddled to respond to Don's kidding.

Don looked at Mike's pale face and jabbed him in the ribs. "Look alive, buddy. Your bride will be coming down the aisle any minute," he whispered.

The wedding march started the procession down the main aisle. The cute little blond-haired scamp leading the procession was Kathy, one of Mrs. Davis' granddaughters. She obviously liked the limelight and scattered flowers with abandon. Some of them ended up in the laps of the spectators. There was some scattered laughter at her performance. Solemnity went out the window.

Betty, Emma Dee, and Virginia Jane restored order with their dignified march down the aisle just as they practiced. They lined up in their places at the altar. Don winked at Betty as she stepped up onto the platform. She smiled back at him. The organist switched to the "Bridal Chorus."

All eyes turned to the back of the church, where Dee escorted his daughter down the aisle. When Mike saw his bride, his nervousness vanished, and his heart filled with emotion. The first of these was amazement.

Can this beautiful woman really be marrying me? he wondered.

Don whispered to Mike, "You are one lucky son-of-a-gun, pal."

June was walking on air. She felt like a queen on the way to her coronation. There was an air of unreality to it all. It was like a fairy tale. All the faces blended in a smiling mass. Halfway down the aisle, she gazed at Mike and smiled at him. He smiled back and appreciated the fact that he was marrying the love of his life.

Dee was grateful for the practice at the rehearsal. When he stopped at the front pew, and Reverend Davis asked him, "Who gives this woman in marriage to this man?" he knew to say firmly, "Her mother and I do!" He then sat down next to Bess, glad his job was done.

June stepped up to the altar with Mike. Reverend Davis extolled on the institution of marriage and the obligations of the couple. When he asked Mike for his affirmation of his vows, Mike looked at June and said, "I sure do." Don handed Mike June's ring, and Mike put it on her finger.

As Reverend Davis recited June's vows, Betty suddenly saw red. Anger and self-pity overwhelmed her.

"Why am I not the one getting married? Why am I the one who's sick! It's not fair!" She struggled to keep the words from flying out of her mouth.

Emma Dee saw Betty turn scarlet and look like she was going to explode. With the rest of the chapel focused on the bride, Emma Dee surreptitiously reached over and squeezed Betty's hand. She kept smiling at the crowd as she did it. Betty felt the firm squeeze of Emma Dee's hand, and her rage faded away. It was like coming out of a trance. She glanced at Emma Dee and nodded. Emma Dee released her hand just as Reverend Davis said, "I now pronounce you man and wife. You may kiss the bride."

Mike looked into his wife's eyes and said, "I'll love you the rest of my life." Then he kissed her.

The church erupted in cheers.

Reverend Davis announced, "The reception is in the town hall across the square. I believe refreshments are being served now."

The church started emptying fast.

*****

While the new husband and wife were posing for the photographer, Betty turned and hurried to the office in the back of the church. She slammed the office door and burst into tears. She was mortified. She had come within a hairsbreadth of spoiling her best friend's crowning moment. There was a knock on the office door.

"Please go away," Betty said and sobbed.

The door cracked open, and Emma Dee peered in at her.

"Please leave me alone," Betty said to her.

"Not on your tintype, honey," Emma Dee said. She came in the office. "Let's take a load off, doll." She steered Betty to the couch in front of the desk. She put her arm around Betty as they sat down. Emma Dee gently held Betty. Betty wiped her eyes with a tissue she found in a tissue box on the end table next to the couch.

"I feel like a complete jerk. I almost spoiled June's wedding," Betty said.

"Gee, I thought you swallowed a bug," Emma Dee said.

Betty looked at her for a long moment and laughed.

"That's more like it! Now clean up your face, put on a little powder and lipstick, and let's go see if we can get lucky at the reception," Emma Dee said.

"You're a pip, Emma Dee," Betty said.

"Ain't it the truth?" Emma Dee replied. She linked arms with Betty and led her to the ladies' room to repair her face.

Bess rounded up the bridal party for the photographer.

June had pleaded with Bess to limit the photographs to the bare minimum. June refused the garter shot.

"Mike has already seen my leg, and no one else needs to," she said.

The happy couple walked over to the rectory.

At the back door, June said, "One kiss isn't going to do it, Mr. Thompson," and kissed Mike firmly on the lips.

"If you keep that up, the honeymoon's going to start early, Mrs. Thompson," Mike said. "And we'll be late to our reception."

June laughed and went into the rectory. "I'll see you after we get changed."

She went into the changing room and started getting out of her wedding dress. There was a knock on the door.

"Who's there?" June asked loudly.

The door opened a crack and Betty said, "It's Betty, are you decent?"

June was standing in her underwear, holding her wedding dress. "I'm decent enough for you, roomie. Come on in."

Betty entered the room and closed the door.

June went to the closet and pulled out her reception dress.

"I am so happy that you are here to share this day with me," June said.

"June, honey, I have a confession to make to you," Betty said.

June stopped pulling up the zipper on her dress and looked at Betty. "What do you mean? What confession?"

Betty's expression remained sober. "I had some terrible thoughts about you during the ceremony. I was angry with you, and for a second, I hated you." Betty's eyes filled with tears. "I thought it should be me being so happy, not being the one who is dying."

June finished zipping her dress and walked over to Betty and held her.

"I'm so ashamed of myself, June. I let you down, and I let myself down."

June stepped back but kept her hands on Betty's shoulders. "You let no one down. You're the bravest person I know. You're even braver than my brother, Ricky."

"I was so jealous of you I almost shouted those awful things in the middle of your vows," Betty said.

June turned and sat down on a divan that was next to the wall.

"Come over here and sit with me," she said to Betty.

Betty sat down reluctantly.

"If I had to deal with what you are dealing with, I'd be howling at the moon. I'd hate everyone around me, not just you. 'How dare you all be healthy when I'm so sick? Why me?' I can't believe you kept a lid on this long. I'd have raised hell a lot sooner."

"So you forgive me?" Betty asked.

"There is nothing to forgive. I love you, and I'm glad you're here with me," June said.

*****

The DeKalb Town Hall was decked out with gold, silver, and white bunting. The rows of spectator chairs had been moved to the basement and the hall set up with chairs and folding tables with gleaming white tablecloths. Each table had a floral centerpiece. The town council podium was replaced with two head tables separated by a four-piece quartet to provide the music. The space in front of the podium was left open for a dance floor. There were two empty seats at the left table. The best man, the maid of honor, and the bridesmaids occupied the other four seats. The right-hand table was for the father and mother of the bride, the father and mother of the maid of honor, and the two groomsmen.

The St. Joseph caterers Bess hired set up an open bar in the rear of the hall. The bartender offered a small selection of cocktails. Champagne and beer bottles were in ice buckets. Punch and soft drinks were also available. The bar was doing a land-office business. The band played soft background music while the guests were being seated. It was a full house.

The band stopped playing, and the bandleader stepped up to the microphone. He was also the master of ceremonies for the reception. He nodded a signal to a side door that had opened and announced to the crowd, "Ladies and gentlemen, for the first time anywhere, I'm honored to introduce, Mr. and Mrs. Michael Thompson."

Mike and June stepped out of the side door and joined the bandleader at the microphone on the small podium. The crowd erupted in cheers.

"Thank you all for joining our celebration," Mike said. "Now let's eat!"

There was another cheer.

Mike and June joined their table. Waiters started taking orders. The choices were roast beef or chicken.

After all the tables had been served, the master of ceremonies introduced Don to make the best man toast. The room quieted down.

Don had a serious demeanor. "Before I begin my toast, I would like to ask for a moment of silence to honor our fallen president, Mr. Franklin D. Roosevelt."

Amidst the gaiety of the party, the gathering had forgotten about the president lying in state in the White House.

After the tribute to the president, Don continued in a different tone. "Mike, my best friend, you are one lucky galoot! You were a long shot to prevail against the field, but by gosh, you came home a winner."

Mike held up his clasped hands in victory, and everyone laughed.

"So to maintain your lead, I offer two pieces of advice—when you are wrong, admit it, and when you are right, keep it to yourself!"

The audience laughed again.

"To the happy couple!" Don held up his glass, and the audience joined him in the toast.

"To the happy couple!" the guests responded.

The master of ceremonies then introduced Betty. There were cheers and catcalls to welcome the maid of honor.

"Before I offer a toast to the groom and to my best friend, the bride, I'll leave you all with a single piece of advice—don't marry anyone unless you absolutely can't stand the thought of not marrying them."

The crowd laughed and applauded.

"To Mr. and Mrs. Thompson!" she toasted.

"To Mr. and Mrs. Thompson!" the crowd toasted.

The MC regained the microphone and called on the groom.

"My thanks to my best man, Don, who talked his lady friend, Betty, into inviting her best friend, June, to go to the Frog Hop Ballroom. People say there is no such thing as love at first sight. I was one of those people until it happened to me. June is still one of those people."

The audience laughed.

"Thank you for your toast, Betty, and thank you for twisting June's arm to go to the Frog Hop."

There was applause for Betty.

"Thank you all for being here. You St. Joe city slickers had to brave the wilds of DeKalb."

Laughter.

"You DeKalb people had watch out for these crazy city drivers."

Laughter.

"I want to thank Bess and Dee Taylor, my new in-laws, for putting on this swell wedding and celebration. Let's give them a hand!"

Applause.

"They are not the only new in-laws I want to thank. Emma Dee and Virginia Jane, please stand up. John and Ricky, you stand up too. Ladies and gentlemen, our bridesmaids and groomsmen."

He led the applause for them.

"Our minister and his extraordinarily patient wife put the wedding party through six rehearsals of the procession to get it right."

Mike pointed to his right foot and said, "This is your right foot, Emma Dee."

Big laugh.

When the room settled down, Mike went on, "And finally, to the girl who won my heart at the Frog Hop Ballroom, my wife and my best friend for life. Here's to June!"

All glasses were raised. "To June!"

Mike sat down to applause and cheers.

Sid Kaufman and his wife were seated at a table with Bernie Cline and his wife.

Sid leaned over to speak to Bernie, "That young man certainly carries himself well."

"Not too bad for a military reject, is he?" Bernie said sardonically.

After the room quieted, the MC said, "Let's hear from the lady herself. Ladies and gentlemen, I give you, the bride!"

June stood at the podium with her champagne glass and looked around the room. Her experience as a trainer at Quaker Oats had cured her of her fear of public speaking. But this was different somehow, and she was nervous. She glanced over to her table and saw Mike smiling and giving her a thumbs up.

"Talk about a tough act to follow. Thanks, Mike."

Laughter.

"Mike mentioned the family and friends who made this day possible for us. So I won't repeat his thanks to you all. But I would like to recognize two very special and brave people who are here with us today. The first is my best friend, Betty Anderson. Betty made a commitment to me to be my maid of honor. She kept her commitment even though she is waging a battle with a dreadful illness." June held up her glass and said, "To our maid of honor, Betty Anderson!"

The room echoed the heartfelt toast.

"The second person is my brother, Ricky Taylor, who is a symbol of all of our brave fighting men. Ricky won the Silver Star Medal and a Purple Heart in combat in Europe. Here's to Ricky Taylor!"

The entire room stood up for this toast and then cheered.

Bernie leaned toward Sid and said, "Mike has pretty good taste in women, doesn't he? She's a dandy."

"She'll keep him on the straight and narrow, all right. I'm pleased to see him settling down and starting his family. He'll go far. I hope we can keep him."

When the crowd quieted down, June continued, "Lastly, please join me in a toast to my new lifetime partner and friend, my new husband, Mike."

After another thundering response to her toast, Don turned to Mike at the table and said, "Don't ever let her get away. You'll never find another one like her."

The MC regained the microphone and said, "Let's give our speakers a big hand, folks. Weren't they great?" After the applause subsided, he said, "Let's get our newlyweds out on the floor. The bride requested the recent number one hit on the hit parade, "I'll Be Seeing You," by Mr. Bing Crosby." The MC picked up a saxophone and played a soft background melody while the electric guitar player sang the lyrics. He wasn't Bing Crosby, but he did a passable job.

Mike escorted June out onto the dance floor, and they swayed slowly to the tender love ballad.

June whispered to Mike, "Enjoy this dance. It may be the last time you get me on a dance floor."

Mike held her closer and whispered, "Just think of it as a long hug."

The MC traded his saxophone for a trumpet. He announced, "Let's have the best man and the maid of honor show us a little swing."

Don took Betty's hand and led her onto the floor. The quartet fired up "Boogie Woogie Bugle Boy from Company B." They were both good dancers, and the crowd reacted with cheers and applause. The open bar was having its effect.

After a minute, the MC said, "Bridesmaids and groomsmen, please take the floor."

John danced with Virginia Jane, and Emma Dee took charge of Ricky, being careful of his arm in the sling. Soon, Emma Dee signaled to the rest of the guests to join in.

After the dance, Mike and June circulated among their guests, thanking them for coming.

Mike stopped abruptly at one table and said to one of the men, "I didn't think you could come."

The man stood up. "I told you I had to meet this enchantress who stole your heart the first time you met her," Slats said. "It is a great pleasure to meet you, Mrs. Thompson. Congratulations and best wishes to you both."

Mike turned to June and said, "This fellow is Mr. Warren Nelson, or Slats to his friends."

June held out her hand and said, "It's nice to meet you, Slats."

"Come up to our table after June and I make the tour of our guests, Slats," Mike said.

He and June moved on.

"Is he one of your Army buddies?" June asked Mike.

Mike laughed. "Not hardly," Mike said. "It's a long story. Wait until he joins us at our table."

June stopped at the Quaker Oats table. Mr. Jamieson, her scheduling department manager, introduced his wife and thanked June for inviting them to the wedding.

"Mrs. Thompson, I've been telling my wife about your astonishing progress in our department. I'm very pleased to have you on my team."

Mrs. Jamieson said, "It has been a lovely wedding, my dear, and I'm glad to meet you."

June next chatted with her scheduling trainer, Cheryl, and her supervisor, Tim Sullivan.

"Does Mike have any brothers?" Wendy asked June.

"No, but I have a couple of them. That's my brother, Ricky, in the arm sling."

"Ricky is kind of cute. Does he have a girlfriend?" Wendy asked.

Mike came up to their table in time to hear the exchange between June and Wendy. "I'll tell him you asked. Now I must borrow June for a minute," Mike said to Wendy.

Wendy blushed and took another sip of her champagne.

"I want to introduce you to my bosses at Kaufmann's," Mike said as he led June away from the Quaker Oats table.

"June, these are the owners of Kaufmann's Radio Sales and Service store, Mr. Sid Kaufmann and my boss, Mr. Bernie Kline," Mike said when they reached the Kaufmann table.

Mr. Kaufmann and Mr. Cline had both stood up when Mike and June approached the table. Sid shook June's hand and said, "I'm very pleased to know you, June. This is my wife, Margaret."

Margaret offered June her hand and said, "I liked your toast, dear. I'm sorry about your friend's illness."

"Thank you, Mrs. Kaufmann. Betty has been struggling with leukemia for several weeks. She's in remission now."

"Honey, this is my boss, Bernie Cline."

Bernie shook hands with June and said, "Mike is a very fortunate young man to have found the right woman so early in life." Bernie introduced his wife, Sarah, to Mike and June.

"I think it's just terrible about your best friend," Sarah said.

Mike and June finished their tour of the guest tables and joined Don and Betty at their head table. When they were seated, Slats came up to their table.

Mike made the introductions and told Slats to sit down with them.

"I met Slats on the train out of Kansas City. He kept me from sitting on my duffel bag in the aisle all the way to Joplin," Mike said.

"Well, Mike told me about falling for this lovely young lady and getting her to consent to marriage in record time. I couldn't leave a guy like that sitting in the middle of the aisle, could I?" Slats said.

Mike and Slats shared the story, and everyone laughed at Mike's run-in with the surly master sergeant and Slat's description of the girl that passed Mike in the aisle. Slats told amusing stories about himself and his well-to-do but quirky family.

"It's about time for your grand exit, isn't it, buddy?" Don asked Mike when there was a pause in the conversation.

"Yeah, I guess so," Mike replied. "How are you and Betty getting back to St. Joe?"

"My parents are taking us home," Betty said. "They'll take us to the apartment tomorrow. Then I'll take Don back to Rosecrans in my car tomorrow night and go home to my parents' house for the week. Don't worry about us. Just have a fabulous honeymoon, roomie."

"That's the plan," Mike said. "We're going to shoot the moon."

June stood up from the table and Mike joined her. Betty and Don also stood up. Slats took his leave and went back to his table.

June and Betty hugged, and June said, "My wedding wouldn't have been as special with any other maid of honor. I'll never forget that you were here for me."

"Oh heck," Betty said. "Go on and get out of here before you make me cry. Live it up on your honeymoon."

Mike signaled to the MC, who announced, "Ladies and gentlemen, please leave the hall for the exit of the bride and groom!"

Betty and Don joined the rest of the guests outside the hall.

As the couple exited the church, they were bombarded with rice and a few ribald remarks. June tossed her bridal bouquet to the crowd. Virginia Jane ducked it; and it was Cheryl, June's scheduling trainer at Quaker Oats, who grabbed it. Mike and June ducked into Mike's Chevy under the customary hail of rice.

The getaway Chevy was festooned with "Just Married" whitewash on the back window. There were peach and white bows on the door handles. The rear bumper trailed strings of peach and white pom-poms and a string of round Quaker Oats boxes painted a peach color. Wendy and Tim had organized this touch.

Don yelled honeymoon advice to Mike as the Chevy sped away.

Once they departed, the crowd dispersed and left for home.

When they reached the edge of DeKalb, Mike stopped the car. He gathered up the trailing strings of pom-poms and oatmeal boxes that were tied to the rear bumper to keep them from littering the road to St. Joe. He left the bows on the doors and the "Just Married" in the rear window.

He and June had enjoyed the good-natured honks and salacious remarks the car had been eliciting from pedestrians and passing cars.

"I always thought this car thing was kind of corny," June said to Mike.

"I think it's great fun." Mike smiled at his new wife and said, "It's like being a one-car parade."

June kissed Mike's cheek and asked, "How does it feel to be an old married man?"

Mike thought about that and said, "I'll let you know after the wedding night."

June laughed and said, "Okay, I'll second that." She put her head on his shoulder and her hand on his leg the rest of the drive home.

*****

Later that night, June again had her head on his shoulder and her hand on his bare leg.

"You know, that was different, somehow," June said.

"Uh-oh," Mike responded. "It seemed to go pretty good to me. Did I forget to do something?"

June poked him in the ribs. "Don't be silly."

"Well, I'd hate to think I shortchanged you on your wedding night," Mike kidded her. He cupped her bare breast with his hand.

She relaxed and enjoyed his attentions to her breast.

After a few minutes of quiet cuddling, Mike asked her, "How was it different?"

June propped herself up on her elbow and said, "It was legal." Then she laughed.

Mike laughed with her and asked, "What was it before then, illegal?"

"Not illegal exactly, just a little naughty."

"I thought you liked naughty," Mike protested.

"I do. But now I know that legal is not so bad either."

Mike smiled at her and said, "I'm glad that's all cleared up. We have an early train ride tomorrow so we might want to get some legal sleep, Mrs. Thompson."

"Well, if once is all you're up to, I guess we better go to sleep, Mr. Thompson," June said impishly.

Mike couldn't let that remark go unchallenged.

20

M/Sgt. Lloyd Taylor observed the Elbe River from the turret of his new M26 Pershing tank, only fifty miles from Berlin. The recently introduced Pershing heavy tank was just getting to units in the field. It mounted a 90mm main gun, bringing it into the same class with the heavy German Tiger tank. It had the latest torsion bar suspension and heavier armor than the 76mm Sherman tank that M/Sgt. Taylor commanded earlier in the war. Its only flaw was that it still had the same slightly underpowered engine that was in the Sherman. This improved firepower did not improve M/Sgt. Taylor's mood. General Eisenhower had done it to him again. M/Sgt. Taylor's unit was part of the Ninth US Army. At General Eisenhower's orders, the Ninth Army was now halted at the Elbe. Lloyd was sure that this halt guaranteed that a Russian tank would be in the streets of the German capital before his M26.

Then the damn Russians would control postwar Germany and as much of postwar Europe as we let them get away with, Lloyd thought.

*****

Mike turned in his cramped wooden seat and grumbled to June, "I warned you that the first leg of our train ride would be on this old relic."

"I don't care. This is the first train I've ridden, and it's exciting," June retorted. "I've never even been to Kansas City before."

Mike looked at June incredulously. "I keep forgetting what a small-town farm girl I married," he said.

"Well, it's too late to trade me in now. You're stuck with me," June told him.

"It could be worse, I suppose. I could have got Emma Dee," he said, and they both laughed. "I'm going to take a nap while you watch Missouri go by. For some reason, I didn't get a lot of sleep last night."

"Go ahead and nap. You might not get much sleep tonight either," June said.

"There is something to be said for you red-blooded farm girls," Mike said and closed his eyes.

*****

June wanted to get a sandwich when they arrived at the bustling Kansas City train station, but Mike talked her out of it.

"Wait until we get on the streamliner. We can have a proper lunch in the dining car. You'll be glad you waited, I guarantee it," Mike said.

He watched the hurrying passengers rushing to the various train platforms. They were seated on an oak bench near the concession stands.

Mike caved in and said, "Okay, have your sandwich, but don't complain to me when I'm having my elegant luncheon and you're not hungry."

June laughed at Mike and said, "I just won our first marital quarrel. But, okay, I'll wait."

Mike grinned at her capitulation and said, "We probably should be heading to our platform."

June marveled at the gleaming silver, bullet-shaped locomotive and matching passenger cars that made up the streamliner. It looked like something out of an H. G. Wells fantasy.

"Wow," she said to Mike. "I've seen pictures of it, but they didn't do it justice."

"Wait until you see inside it. It is fancier than most hotels," Mike told her.

Porters started ushering the passengers into the passenger cars from the packed platform. The redcap with their bags helped clear a space for Mike and June to step up to their car. At the aisle, the redcap turned left, directed by a sign with an arrow toward the group of compartments with their number. The aisle was carpeted in a rich maroon color with the railroad logo woven into it. The hall wallpaper had a light-gray background with tiny silver streamliners in the pattern. The compartment doors were dark-red mahogany with brass handles and hinges.

The redcap opened the door to their compartment and put away the luggage. Mike tipped him as he left to exit the train. June admired the furnishings in their compartment. Two bench seats faced each other and opened to the view from their large window. The seats and backs were plush and upholstered in dark-green velvet. There were overhead compartments where the redcap had stowed their luggage.

"This is not a full sleeper compartment, but the bench seats can be converted into a bed," Mike said.

"Isn't that interesting?" June observed. "But first you need to show me that dining car you've been touting."

"They won't be serving until we are out of the station, but it's a good idea to get a seat early. Hold the handrails when we walk down the aisle. Let's go."

Halfway to the dining car, the streamliner started moving. The acceleration was much smoother than the first train, but June followed Mike's advice and kept one hand on the handrail. They made their way through two open seating cars with stairs to observation decks.

The dining car was nearly empty when they walked into it. June thought it looked like a miniature dining room in a swank hotel. It was elegant. The tables were covered in white linen. The seats were individual hardwood chairs with comfortable seats and backs upholstered in the same velvet used in the compartments. Brass lamps with green lampshades hung from the ceilings. The maroon carpet continued from the hall throughout the dining car.

Mike seated them at the table next to the bulkhead. They sat side by side, facing forward to see the passing landscape in the window. Some people get nauseous facing backward to the travel of the train. Mike wasn't taking any chances with June. He gave her the window seat and took the aisle seat for himself. He didn't like facing backward himself.

As soon as the train was up to cruising speed, a waiter appeared at their table. He handed them lunch menus. He set a linen napkin folded around the silverware in front of each of them.

"What would you like to drink, folks?" he asked.

June asked, "Do you have lemonade? I'd like a glass of lemonade."

Mike said, "I'll have coffee with cream and sugar."

The waiter left with their drink orders. A server set a glass of water in front of each of them and left.

June studied the menu. "It seems like lunch will be soup and sandwiches."

Mike checked his menu and said, "I'll have the corned beef on rye with potato salad. I don't need any soup."

Their waiter brought their drinks and asked them for their lunch orders.

"I'm hungry. How's the beef stew?" June asked the waiter.

"It's very good, madam," the waiter answered.

"In that case, I'll have a bowl of the stew and a chicken salad sandwich," June ordered.

"The stew is very hearty, madam," the waiter questioned her order of both dishes.

"Good!" said June.

Mike laughed and ordered his sandwich with the potato salad.

June sipped her lemonade and said, "That's real lemonade with fresh squeezed lemons. It's almost as good as my mom makes."

Mike sipped his coffee and said, "The coffee's excellent too."

June looked out the window and said, "That must be the Missouri River over there."

Mike looked over her shoulder and said, "That's the muddy Mo all right. The train track runs along the Missouri River valley most of the way to St. Louis. You're going to see a lot of that old river."

A tugboat towed four barges downstream. A stream of small powerboats going both directions stayed clear of the tugboat and barges.

Mike continued his tour-guide speech while June watched the river traffic.

"When we decided to honeymoon in St. Louis, I went to the library and read up on the trip. Did you know that both Ulysses S. Grant and Daniel Boone had homes near St. Louis? We can go see them while we're there if you want to."

"Nobody likes a know-it-all," June chided him.

Mike just smiled back at her. She stuck out her tongue at him just as their waiter arrived with their food and saw her do it. The waiter struggled to keep a straight face, and June's face turned red.

As the waiter served their food, Mike told him, "Don't be concerned about my wife. She just took an oath to love, honor, and cherish me and to stick out her tongue at me whenever possible."

That did it. The waiter laughed and said, "I can always tell the newlyweds, sir."

June ignored them and said, "That stew smells really good. Could you bring me another lemonade?"

"The server will be right over, madam," their waiter said.

The server brought her lemonade and topped off Mike's coffee cup.

Mike picked up his corned beef sandwich with both hands. As he brought it to his mouth, he noticed the gold ring on the third finger of his left hand.

"I'll be damned," he said. "I really am married."

"There was some doubt in your mind about that?" June asked as she tried her stew.

Mike swallowed his bite of sandwich and said, "I guess it hadn't really soaked in until I saw the ring on my finger."

June looked at her ring and said, "I've been wearing mine for a while now, so it seems natural to me. But I know what you mean about feeling married. It happened to me last night, you may recall." June smiled.

Mike looked at his ring and declared, "This ring is never coming off my finger. You'll have to bury me with it."

June put down her soup spoon and stared at him. Her eyes filled with tears.

"Darn it, you're not supposed to make me cry on our honeymoon." She wiped her eyes with her napkin.

After their lunch, they made their way back to one of the observation cars and found seats on the upper deck under the glass dome. The view was spectacular. They could see the full span of the wide Missouri River with the parade of boats going up and down the river. The hills on the far side of the river had spouted their spring grass and were a rich green color. Trees were just beginning to leaf out. The bright sun shone through a patchwork of blue sky and fluffy white clouds.

June said, "This is wonderful. You did well, Mr. Thompson."

"Well, I had to wait in line to order the weather, but it was worth it," Mike said.

They enjoyed the passing scenery, and Mike told her more about the attractions of St. Louis and some towns they were passing through.

June said, "Let's go back and explore the comforts of that fancy compartment you got for us."

Mike smiled at her and said, "Are there any comforts in particular you have in mind?"

"I'm sure we scandalized the porter," June said later, "asking him to make up the bed in the middle of the afternoon."

"Scandalized or not, he didn't turn down the five bucks I tipped him," Mike retorted. "Anyway, we couldn't pass up making love on a fast train, could we?"

June laughed and said, "I guess not. It's something to tell our grandkids."

"I hate to say this. It's like telling the Louvre to cover up the Mona Lisa, but you better get dressed. We'll be coming into St. Louis shortly," Mike said, putting on his underwear.

June struck a provocative pose on the bed and said, "Are you sure? If we get up, the porter has to make this bed back into a seat. You could save five bucks."

Mike laughed and picked up her panties from the floor and tossed them to her.

"Spoilsport," she said, and got dressed.

*****

Union Station in St. Louis looked like a large medieval castle with rounded corner walls (to repel cannon balls) and a tall square tower. The walls were yellow stone, and the steep roofs were covered with red tiles. Red dunce caps topped the lone tower and the round corners. A narrow block-long fountain fronted the building. Water spray fountains and statuary stood in the center of the fountain and marble railings bordered it. The cavernous Grand Hall was filled with tony shops and concessions. At the end of the hall was the luxurious Union Station Hotel.

June and Mike followed their redcap through the spectacular Grand Hall. June kept stopping to rubberneck at the elegant archways and decor and to window-shop the high-end merchandise on display in the boutiques. When they reached the hotel, June stood in wonder and looked around the enormous lobby.

"Are we actually staying in this palace?" she asked Mike.

He was awed himself. "I sure hope so," Mike said. "They have our deposit."

Their porter took their luggage to the reception desk, and Mike gave him a generous tip for being their tour guide through the building. After checking in, a uniformed bellhop took their luggage and escorted them to their room on the fourth floor.

June entered their room first and squealed, "I love it!"

The room belonged in a gay nineties' hotel of the past century. There was a huge bed with brass footboard and headboard. The brightly colored patchwork quilt looked handsewn, and the bed stands were antique oak with gaslight lamps converted to electric. The figured wallpaper looked like the wallpaper in the old Taylor farmhouse, and the lacquered hardwood floor was accented with woven oval throw rugs.

The bellboy smiled at June's reaction and said, "These old-timey rooms are very popular." He put their luggage in the closet, and Mike tipped him when he left.

"When I made the reservations, I asked about these rooms, and they had this one available. I thought it would remind you of home," Mike said.

June sat on the soft bed and looked at a large print hanging on the wall. It was a foxhunt with the riders dressed in red hunting costumes, tall black boots, and black caps, mounted on thoroughbred horses. They were in hot pursuit of a pack of dogs and a lone fox. The first rider and horse were in a full jump over a white wooden fence.

"It's perfect," June said. "You've done well again, hubby."

"Do you want to unpack first or go for a walk around the Grand Hall?" Mike asked her.

June walked into the bathroom and admired the white porcelain wash bowls with brass faucets with white porcelain handles. The lavatory was an old-fashioned toilet with a pull chain flush and an oak box above the bowl. There was a roomy tall-sided oval bathtub with claw feet. It too had brass faucets with porcelain handles.

"Let's go explore!" June said. "We can unpack later."

Mike peered over June's shoulder into the bathroom and said, "You know, that tub is built for two."

"That's bold talk from a man who has had the workout you've had last night and today on a fast train," June said.

"Hey, I'm just talking about a bath. I don't know what you're talking about," Mike joshed her.

June laughed and said, "Okay, then let's go shopping!"

They walked the promenade down the Grand Hall and passed through the Grand Hall Lounge with its high-arched ceilings and frescoed walls with gold-leaf trim. The lounge was already busy with cocktail-hour patrons. They passed other inviting eateries named the Train Shed Restaurant and the Station Grille.

June said, "Look, there's a soda fountain. Let's stop and get an ice cream soda."

"You'll spoil your appetite for dinner. I made reservations at the Train Shed Restaurant," Mike warned her.

"I'll risk it," June replied.

They got seats on the revolving bar stools at the counter.

"I'm going to have a root beer float," Mike said.

The soda jerk came over and stood across the counter from them. He asked, "What'll ya have, folks?" He wore a white shirt with red piping and a white paper campaign-style hat with red piping. His name tag identified him as Bill.

"I'll have a strawberry ice cream soda," June responded. "He's having a root beer float."

Bill asked, "One scoop of ice cream or two in those drinks?"

"I want two scoops of strawberry ice cream in mine," June said.

"Just give me one scoop of vanilla in my float. I will not spoil *my* dinner," Mike said sanctimoniously.

They sat and watched Bill dip the metal scoop into the ice cream containers and drop the scoops of ice cream into the fluted soda glass and into Mike's root-beer mug. He pulled the long handles on the soda water and root beer feeds to fill the glasses. Then he topped both off with a dollop of whipped cream and straws and set them in front of Mike and June.

Mike removed his straw and sipped his root beer and watched June spoon a bite of her strawberry ice cream out of her soda.

June ate her ice cream, looked at Mike, and laughed.

"You've got a mustache," she said.

Mike's tongue licked off the whipped cream on his upper lip.

June sipped her soda through her straw.

"You make a swell strawberry soda," June said to Bill.

"Thanks, miss," Bill said.

"You just lost your tip, Bill. She's a Mrs., not a Miss," Mike said.

June held up her hand and showed Bill her ring.

"My mistake, madam."

After their stop at the soda fountain, they continued their stroll through the Grand Hall. June stopped in front of the glass display window at an upscale dress shop. Small tasteful signs proclaimed the dresses to be the latest Paris fashions. After the liberation of Paris by the French and American armies, Paris fashion houses started shipping toned-down versions of their creations to America and Great Britain. Unlike the utilitarian boxy-style dresses imposed by austerity war measures, these gowns were full-length evening dresses with cinched waists, side bows, and back yokes. A light-blue one with a medium-blue waist cinch and a full flowing skirt entranced June. The plunging neckline was ruffled in a medium-blue color. The mannequin wore matching fabric French-heel platform shoes. Since the start of the war, in the US all shoe leather had been strictly limited to the making of shoes and boots for the troops. Fabric composition dress shoes took the place of leather.

"So do you like that dress?" Mike asked June.

"What's not to like? It's gorgeous. But it must be horribly expensive."

"Why don't we go in and ask them?" Mike suggested.

"Oh, Mike, we're already spending a fortune on this trip. We need to start being practical with our money," June said, frowning at him.

Mike smiled at her and said, "Okay. It's a deal. We'll start being tightfisted penny pinchers, right after we buy that dress and the shoes to go with it."

"They probably don't have my size anyway," June grumbled.

"Yeah, probably not, with your freakishly distorted figure," Mike teased her.

June breezed through the shop door ahead of Mike.

A trim middle-aged woman in a black calf-length dress with bloused white sleeves welcomed them into the shop. Her light pancake makeup was eclipsed by the blood-red lipstick in vogue now.

"How may I help you?" she asked Mike and June.

"Do you have the blue dress in your window in a size six?" June asked, half hoping the answer would be no.

"Allow me to check for you, madam," the saleslady said. She went through an open archway into the back section of the shop.

June perused the hat and glove display while she waited for the saleslady. Mike found a chair in the shoe section and sat down. June tried on a beige pillbox hat and examined herself in the small mirror mounted on the counter. Mike studied a poster displaying women's shapely legs, wearing shoes made by a French company. He wondered if the rest of them looked as good as their legs.

The saleslady returned and said to June, "It happens that the only size six is the one on display in our window. I can order it for you."

"We're here on our honeymoon. We won't be staying long enough to wait for that," June said.

Mike joined June when he saw the saleslady come back. "How about selling us the one in the window?" Mike asked.

"Let me ask my manager. She rarely likes to sell the display dresses."

The saleslady walked to the rear counter and talked with an older woman who was showing another customer some scarves.

The older woman returned with the saleslady and said, "My name is Mrs. Hampton. I own the shop. I understand you wish to purchase a dress on display in the front window?"

"I'm June Thompson, and this is my husband, Mike," June said. "Yes, the blue one. But I'd have to try it on first."

"Of course, you would. This is the reason I don't sell display dresses. My help must disrobe the mannequin for you to try on. Then if you don't take it, they must redress the mannequin. That sounds simple, but I assure you it is not. In the meantime, I have an incomplete display window," Mrs. Hampton said. "We can order it in your size and have it shipped to your home."

June responded, "You're very kind, but I have two problems with that. I still wouldn't have tried on the dress, and I want to wear it here on my honeymoon."

Mrs. Hampton considered what June said. "So you two are newlyweds? Where are you from?"

"We're from St. Joe," Mike answered.

Mrs. Hampton said, "Well, for fellow Show-Me staters... all right, Libby, let's get that size six out of the window for Mrs. Thompson to try on."

June admired her reflection in the mirror. The blue dress fits perfectly.

"I should have asked this before," June said, "but how much is this dress?"

Mrs. Hampton told her and said, "However, since the dress has been used for display, there is a discount of fifteen percent. But there is a no-return policy on display merchandise."

June still hesitated on the price, but Mike said, "We'll take it! Thank you for accommodating us, Mrs. Hampton." Mike turned to June and asked, "How about the shoes to go with it?"

June looked at Mike like he had two heads and said, "My white heels be just fine with it."

Mike paid for the dress and the saleslady, Libby, wrapped it carefully for June.

Out in the Grand Hall, June said, "Thank you for my wedding present, Mr. Thompson. I really love this dress."

"It looks terrific on you."

*****

A miniature steam locomotive sat on a turntable in the center of the dining room in The Train Shed restaurant. Every hour on the hour, the turntable rotated the locomotive 180 degrees. Railroad lanterns hung over the dining tables and railroad signs adorned the walls. The entrance to the bar had a RR Crossing sign over it. Patrons in the booths in the dining room sat on antique hardwood bench seats softened by upholstered seat cushions.

Mike and June sat in their booth and studied their menus.

"What looks good to you?" June asked.

Mike peered at her over the top of his menu and said, "That new dress with you in it."

June couldn't wait to wear her new dress out in public.

She smiled at him and said, "Flattery will get you everywhere with me."

"I may have to test that statement later," Mike replied.

Their waiter walked through the tables in the center section of the main dining room to their booth. He was dressed as a porter with a dark-red button-front jacket and a red pillbox hat. His brass name tag read "Cameron."

He said, "Welcome aboard, folks, can I have your tickets?"

When Mike had checked in at the arrival station, the headwaiter gave them each a train ticket to take to their table. Mike thought it was a souvenir. Cameron took their tickets, tore them in half, and handed half of the ticket back.

"What do we do with these?" June asked Cameron.

"The tickets are numbered. Every hour a ticket is drawn. The winning ticket entitles the winner to get either a free round of drinks or a dessert of his or her choice. At the 9:00 p.m. drawing, you get two free meals."

"That sounds like great fun," June said. "What do we do if we have a winner?"

"Just shout out, and I'll come get your ticket and take it up to the engineer to verify it. Then I'll come back with your prize coupons," Cameron said. "It's nearing the hour. Let me put your tickets in the draw, and then I'll be back to take your order."

Cameron walked to the locomotive and handed their ticket stubs to the engineer in the cabin of the locomotive. The engineer was dressed in light-gray pinstriped overalls and wore an engineer's cap and a bright red handkerchief around his neck. He put the ticket stubs into a glass jar and mixed them in with the others.

Cameron returned to their table and took out his order pad.

"What will you have, madam?" he asked June.

"I'm still thinking. Ask my husband," June said.

"I'll have the porterhouse steak, medium rare, with a baked potato and salad with blue cheese dressing," Mike ordered.

June said, "I'll have the New York strip steak, very rare. Tell the chef to grill it for one minute on each side, no more."

Cameron looked aghast. "But, madam, the meat will still be bloody!"

June looked sternly at Cameron and said, "It better be."

"May I suggest a wine with your meal?" Cameron inquired hesitantly.

"Sure, suggest away," Mike said.

Cameron thought an expensive French Bordeaux would not suit this couple.

"I recommend our pinot noir from a very good, small California vineyard."

Mike said, "That's fine with me. June?"

June replied, "I'm sure Cameron picked something nice for us."

Cameron said, "You're very kind, madam. I admire your dress."

June preened at the compliment. "It was a wedding present from my new husband. I'm glad you like it."

"It's very becoming on you, madam. Congratulations to you both on your nuptials." He left with their order.

"What a nice fellow," June said.

"You ate medium-rare steak at the Pioneer Room, didn't you?" Mike reminded her.

"I didn't have a choice. It was a meal for two."

There was a loud burst from the locomotive steam whistle, and the turntable started to move. The locomotive completed its turn and blew its whistle again. The patrons cheered, and the engineer pulled his red handkerchief over his eyes and reached into the glass bowel. After mixing the tickets, he pulled one out and handed it to an attractive young woman standing next to his train window.

She walked over to a podium and announced into a microphone, "Number 15671."

June looked at her ticket and said, "Rats, that's not even close to my number."

Mike started to tear up his ticket.

June grabbed his arm and said, "Hey! There are more drawings. Keep your ticket."

Mike sheepishly put his ticket in his jacket pocket. There was a cheer from one of the tables when a man discovered he had the winning ticket. There were groans from the other patrons. They had hoped the winner had left the restaurant and another ticket would be drawn.

"It's kind of like Bingo," Mike said. "The winner yells 'Bingo!' The losers yell, 'Oh, crap!'"

June laughed. "It's fun though."

While they waited for their meal, Mike asked June if she was excited about going to nursing school now that she passed her exam.

"I'm not sure. I've wanted to be a nurse since grade school. But my new job at Quaker is interesting and challenging. Oh well, I still have a month to confirm my reservation for the fall semester."

"It's a big decision, honey," Mike said. "I'll have your back, whatever you decide."

Cameron brought their salads and said he would be back with the wine.

"What about you? Do you still want to go to engineering school?" June asked.

"Yes, I do. I like my job at Kaufmann's, and I'm enjoying being in management, even if I'm only on the bottom rung."

Cameron returned with their wine and pulled the cork. He poured a sample for Mike.

Mike sipped and said, "That's very tasty. You're the bee's knees, Cameron. You can pick all our wine."

"I'd glad you approve, sir. We strive to satisfy in the Train Shed. Your food will be coming out soon." He poured them a glass of the wine and set the bottle on their table and left.

"Cameron's a cool waiter," Mike said.

"Who do you think is better, Cameron or Claude at the Pioneer Room?" June asked.

"Claude was funnier. They're both classy," Mike said.

"We haven't given Cameron a chance yet. He may catch up," June said.

They laughed.

June tried her salad and said, "I want you to do whatever you think is best for you. If you want to go to school full time, that's okay with me. I can support us until you graduate. I think it will be a good investment for our future."

Mike stopped eating his salad and looked at June. "We're going to be a great team."

"So, Mr. Tour Guide, what are we doing tomorrow?"

"You need to get your rest tonight, honey. Tomorrow we go to the Forest Park Highlands Amusement Park. We can catch a trolley from our hotel."

June clapped her hands and said, "We have to go on all the rides, especially the Comet."

Cameron brought their entrees and looked askance as he set down June's bloody steak.

"The chef refused to cook your steak. I had to have one of the sous chefs grill it," he told June. "He followed your instructions exactly. I hope you like it."

June cut through her steak with her steak knife and studied it. The outside was seared, and the inside was almost blue. Blood seeped out of the cut.

"It's perfect, Cameron. Thank the sous chef for me," June said.

Mike said, "I married a barbarian." He cut a piece off his steak and looked at it on his fork. "Nice and pink in the middle. That's perfect, Cameron."

"Shoe leather," June rebutted and hungrily attacked her steak.

"How do you know about the Comet?" Mike asked and cut off another piece of steak. He dipped it in the house steak sauce and ate it with a smile.

"You weren't the only one who did some research. The Comet has a main hill eighty feet high, and a bunch of stomach twisting hills and turns. I can't wait to try it!"

"I think I'll stick to the merry-go-round," Mike said. "They have a big dance hall too. I know how much you love to dance."

"I'll make a deal with you, honey. If you ride the Comet with me, I'll go dancing with you," June proposed.

Mike sipped his wine and replied, "They say the best marriages are based on compromise, so I guess you've got a deal. But if I upchuck in your lap, don't blame me."

"That's great dinner conversation, Mike," June said. She finished the last bite of her rare steak.

"It hasn't slowed you down any, honey," Mike retorted. "How did you get started eating raw meat?"

June finished her mashed potatoes and answered, "It was my uncle Jim who started me on it. He always raised a few head of beef and butchered one or two every year. He taught me to ride when I was three years old. While I was out riding, he butchered one of his beeves. I came in from riding just as he was hanging up a side of beef in his slaughter shed. I went over to see what he was doing. He cut off a slice of loin and ate it raw. Then he cut off a small slice and offered it to me. I ate it and asked for more. I've never liked steak cooked very much ever since."

"Now I'm sorry I asked," Mike said. "So barbarism runs in your family?"

Cameron came to their booth just as the locomotive whistle blew again. He handed them dessert menus. The turntable started moving.

The menus featured an assortment of pies and cake. They both chose pie. The train whistle sounded again as the locomotive completed the turn. The engineer pulled another ticket out of the jar and handed it to the young lady. She stepped up to the microphone and announced, "The winning number is 15709!"

June looked at her ticket and said, "Poop! Mine is 15708. I missed it by only one number."

Mike took his ticket stub out of his pocket and said, "That's because you picked the wrong ticket." He stood up and put two fingers in his mouth and whistled. He held up the winning ticket.

Cameron applauded when Mike handed him the ticket. He took it up to the young lady who checked it and announced, "We have a winner, folks!"

Cameron returned to the booth and said, "You folks won the 9:00 p.m. drawing, so you get the big prize." He handed Mike two coupons for a free dinner.

Mike and June finished their dessert and went back to the hotel and up to their room.

"If you're going to make me ride that roller coaster tomorrow, I better get to bed," Mike said.

It had been a long day, and June was tired as well.

"I guess we'll have to try out that bathtub tomorrow," she said.

Mike got under the sheet and patchwork quilt with June and kissed her.

"Good night, honey," he said and turned out the light on the nightstand.

June was still for a minute, and then she said, "I hope Betty is still doing okay."

"Amen to that, honey," Mike said and turned over and went to sleep.

21

Monday dawned bright and early in the Anderson household. Kate was in her kitchen mixing batter for waffles. Ray and Betty both liked waffles. Ray had a morning meeting with his parish board. After lunch, he was meeting with a group of church women to organize another paper drive. His congregation was proud of their dedication to saving newspapers and other paper products to contribute to the war effort. Kate poured batter into her waffle iron and turned down the burner under the coffeepot. Betty came into the kitchen dressed in her pajamas, robe, and slippers.

"Can I help you with anything, Mom?" she asked Kate.

"You can set the table, honey," Kate told her.

Ray joined the women in the kitchen and said, "Waffles! Great!" He sat at the table wearing his suit and tie.

Kate handed him two napkins to protect his good clothes from the heavy maple syrup he used to drown his waffles. He tucked one napkin into his collar and spread the other one in his lap.

"How are you girls this morning?" he asked.

"I'm just fine," Kate answered and set the butter dish and syrup bottle on the table.

Betty poured coffee for them. She sat across from Ray and put sugar and cream in her coffee.

Ray repeated his question to Betty, "How are you this fine morning, honey?"

Betty drank her coffee and considered his question. "I feel like a bird's egg in an empty nest. Everything's all right now, but that could change any minute."

Kate took the waffles out of the waffle iron and served Ray and Betty. While she poured more batter into the waffle iron, she said to Betty, "You're not in an empty nest, honey."

"I know, Mom, but I feel as fragile as that egg."

*****

The trolley car was a third full when Mike and June caught it at the trolley stop outside their hotel. The early morning commuters had come and gone by the time Mike and June had finished a late breakfast and got to the trolley stop at nine. It was a one-hour trolley ride to the park. There was still a nip in the air as spring hadn't firmly established itself yet.

They were dressed casually for their day on the rides in the amusement park. Mike wore jeans and a flannel shirt under his jacket. June wore dark-green wool trousers and a white cable-knit sweater under her windbreaker. She had a canvas drawstring bag hanging from her right shoulder and was as excited as a ten-year-old girl at her first county fair. She had never ridden a big roller coaster before.

Mike hadn't either, and he wasn't looking forward to it. He wasn't kidding June about what his stomach might do on the Comet. He had gotten sick once on a tilt-a-whirl ride. June explained that it was the spinning motion that made him sick and that the Comet didn't spin. Mike was still dubious.

An ornate gateway used to be the gateway to a temple in Japan, and now was the entry to the park. The St. Louis World's Fair brought it to Missouri in 1904 to be the entry to the Fair. After the World's Fair, the amusement park owners bought it and had it transferred to the amusement park along with other World's Fair attractions.

Mike paid their ten cent admissions, and they walked through the oriental gateway. The first hill of the Comet and the Ferris wheel towered over the rest of the park. It was still an hour until lunchtime, and the park was not busy.

Mike and June strolled hand in hand past a huge swimming pool. A few hardy bathers were in the pool. A double-deck enclosure and changing rooms partially surrounded it. There were food concessions on the lower level and a sun deck on the upper level with open air tables for eating or just relaxing and watching the bathers.

Continuing their stroll, they stopped to look at the Highlands carousel. The carousel was the first ride added by the Highlands Cottage Restaurant in 1897 to attract patrons to the restaurant and started the conversion of a beer garden to an amusement park. The carousel was still one of the most popular attractions and sported a variety of animal figures, the most popular being the four deer.

"Well, there's your ride, you daredevil," June said to Mike.

"I'll have to fight off the kids to get a deer," Mike said. "That'll be hazardous enough for me."

June laughed. They continued past a theater with billboards featuring the Sunflower Girls.

"They don't go onstage until 6:00 p.m.," Mike read on the billboard. "We'll have to get back by 5:30 p.m. to get a good seat." He looked questioningly at June.

"I would have thought you ogled enough scantily-clad women at your bachelor party," June observed.

Mike turned back to the playbill. "They're supposed to be very funny and entertaining," Mike said. "They're like an old-fashioned miner show."

"We'll see how you do on the Comet. If you don't embarrass me, maybe we'll check out the Sunflower Girls," June said. "Hey, there's another ride for you." She pointed at the Cuddle Up next to the theater.

"You bet," Mike agreed. "If you won't ride it, maybe I can get one of the Sunflower Girls to go on it with me."

June laughed and said, "Good luck with that, Romeo."

"Here's your favorite part of the park, honey," Mike said as they passed the dance hall.

June looked at the notice board and replied, "It doesn't open until 7:30 p.m. We can ride the Comet four or five times by then."

Mike studiously ignored her remark.

The Comet was at the far end of the park from the entrance. The Park designers knew it would be the biggest draw, so they placed it where the patrons would pass other attractions on the way and spend extra cash at the booths in the midway. Mike looked warily at the eighty-foot hill when they got to the Comet.

June was even somewhat daunted but said, "Shoot, that big hill levels off at the top before you go down the other side. That's not scary."

Mike saw the section she was talking about and said, "I don't know. It gives you longer to worry about the drop-off."

June saw the ticket booth and said, "Come on, there's not much of a line yet. Let's get our tickets. We can get in our first ride on the Comet before lunch."

June got in line to buy their tickets while Mike protested, "What do you mean by our *first* ride?"

The Comet attendant buckled their lap straps and dropped the safety bar. They were in the first car. June cuddled close to Mike as they started the long, slow climb up the big hill. June was thrilled as they gained height and she could see the whole park. Mike had his eyes closed, and his white knuckles gripped the bar. The car reached the top of the hill and rolled along the flat section they talked about.

Mike opened his eyes just in time to see the drop on the other side. "Oh, shit!" he said and closed his eyes again.

As they careened down the back side, June shrieked along with the girls in the other cars. Their car clattered and banged through the succession of dips and turns. Mike had given up closing his eyes. That only made it worse. The car rocketed up another hill and made a sharp turn at the top. Mike was sure it would jump off the tracks. The turn tossed June against him, and she wrapped her arms around him and screamed. When the car came to a sudden stop, Mike thought it had run into something. The attendant bent over, raised the safety bar, and unbuckled their belts. Mike dazedly wondered why the attendant was yelling at him. June grabbed his arm and helped the attendant pull him up out of the car.

June stood aside and let the other riders go past them down the ramp.

"Wow! Was that great or what!" she said.

Mike took her arm and tottered down the ramp. "*Or what works for me,*" he said. "It was exciting though," Mike admitted. "I liked the part where you grabbed hold of me and hung on."

June laughed and said, "I sort of liked that part myself."

"Let's go back to the swimming pool and have some lunch," Mike said.

They walked past the midway booths with their rigged games of chance and smelled the hot popcorn and cotton candy machines. The voices of the barkers rang out from the booths as they passed, cajoling Mike to try his hand at throwing softballs at fuzzy-fringed, weighted-bottom dolls or darts at balloons or coins in clear glass dishes—all to win stuffed animals or kewpie dolls for his girl. Maybe he'd give it a try later.

*****

The swimming pool was busier, and there were a few girls flaunting convention by wearing daring two-piece swimming costumes and showing bare midriffs.

Mike studiously avoided staring at any of them. His appetite had returned since he was no longer facing the dreaded Comet. He had a cheeseburger and a large order of fries. June went for a Coke and a Coney Island hot dog with chili.

While they were eating, June pointed at the pool and said, "Look at that blond in the two-piece suit."

Mike ignored her pointing finger and said, "Is this a test or something?"

June looked surprised, then she laughed and said, "No, I was just calling your attention to someone interesting."

"I thought you didn't want me ogling other women," Mike protested.

"I don't want you ogling them, but I don't expect you to spend the rest of your life never looking at other women. That would be ridiculous."

Mike looked down at the pool and saw the blond June was talking about. "She is interesting, I have to admit," Mike said with a grin.

"Okay, now you're ogling," June said. "But I can't blame you. She's got the goods."

Mike turned back to June and said, "I'm having lunch with the girl who's got the goods."

June smiled and ate her chili dog.

After lunch, Mike said, "Okay, now it's your turn to go on my ride."

June took the last drink of her Coke and replied, "Which one, the carousel or the Cuddle Up?"

Mike got up from their table, glancing down at the pool.

"She went into the bathhouse a few minutes ago," June said.

Mike ignored her jibe and said, "We're going on the Ferris wheel."

The lines to the major attractions had grown. Several servicemen and their dates were in line for the Ferris wheel. June took their place in line while Mike bought their tickets. The ride was in the loading phase of operation. The operator cycled the swinging seats and loaded each one with a couple, or in one case a father, mother, and their exuberant six-year-old son. It was evident to June that she and Mike would not get on during this cycle. The last three seats came down to the loading platform. When they had been off loaded and new riders put in their place, the operator started the wheel revolving. The soldiers and airmen put their arms around their girls, who snuggled up to them. One couple had barely cleared the loading platform when they locked lips in a prolonged kiss.

"Now that is the way to ride a Ferris wheel," Mike said, coming up to June with their tickets.

"Only if you think kissing is a spectator sport," June disagreed.

June noticed that the Ferris wheel was taller than the first hill of the Comet. The riders all seemed to be having a good time, and the smooching had caught on with other couples. They kept breaking into laughter and spoiling their effort to outkiss each other. The first couple still held the record. They had maintained their kiss for a full revolution of the wheel.

"The Ferris wheel at the 1904 World's Fair was twice as big as this one. It had thirty-six enclosed wooden cars that could hold up to sixty people each," Mike told June. "Eighty couples actually got married inside the cars, one of them on horseback. Car number 19 was the wedding car. It had a piano inside."

"You're making that up," June accused him.

"I keep telling you I did my research. Look it up if you don't believe me."

"What happened to it?" June asked.

The Ferris wheel was starting to slow down.

"The owners tried to sell it, but there were no takers. So finally, it was blown up with dynamite, and the parts salvaged for scrap."

The operator started recycling passengers and the line was moving.

"That's a sad story," June said.

Their turn came, and June was seated first. Mike followed, and the operator lowered the restraining bar. Mike started to kiss June but stopped when she glared at him. That was okay. He had an ace up his sleeve.

They rose higher step by step, and June saw the traffic passing the park on US Highway 40. At each stop, the car swiveled forward and back. It was an unsettling sensation. The higher they got, the more threatening it felt. June found herself gripping the restraining bar as tightly as Mike had gripped the one on the Comet. The forward tipping motion made her feel like she was falling out of the car. They were finally the topmost car on the wheel when Mike played his ace in the hole. As the car stopped and tilted forward, he leaned forward with the motion and rocked the car forward and down. June saw the ground coming up at them and screamed. She turned and wrapped both arms around Mike and buried her head in his shoulder. The car settled down, and June raised her head into perfect position for Mike to kiss her, and he did.

"Don't do that again!" June ordered him.

The wheel made another move into the next position and rocked their car. Mike repeated his move, and June slugged him.

"It'll cost you another kiss if you want me to stop," Mike said.

June had the stubborn look on her face that Mike was learning to recognize. At the next stop, she lunged forward and rocked the car more than Mike had done. He gasped, and she laughed and said, "Two can play that game."

This time he felt like he was falling out of the car.

"Now we're even," she said.

The operator boarded the next couple in line in the last empty car and started the wheel, turning smoothly.

When their car got to the top again, June pointed and said, "Hey, there's the Missouri River again."

Mike looked where she was pointing and said, "Sorry, honey, but that's not the Missouri, that's the Mississippi."

"Where's the Missouri then?" June asked.

"It's north of us. It joins the Mississippi up north," Mike said.

Their car went over the top of the wheel and swung down the other side. They had a great view of the amusement park and the crowds in the midway. They completed two more turns of the wheel, and then the operator started taking the riders off again. Mike and June were the fourth ones off, so they didn't get to linger near the top of the wheel.

"What do you want to do next?" June asked Mike.

"Let's ride the Comet," he said.

"No, really, you did your duty. You don't have to do it again," June said.

"Yes, really. I want to try it again. I had my eyes closed the first time," Mike said.

They walked to the back of the park where the Comet lured in the paying customers.

June angled toward the line for the ride, expecting Mike to join the line buying tickets. But he came over and stood in line with her. She gave him a questioning look.

"I knew you would want to ride it again, and I didn't want to stand in line again, so I bought us four tickets." He gave her a ticket.

The line moved steadily, and when they reached the platform, June got into the leading car. Mike joined her. They got strapped in, and the safety bar came down. Other couples filled the cars behind them. Then they were on their way up the big hill.

The slow climb is designed to scare you, Mike thought. *Well, it's working.*

Mike looked around the park and the surrounding hills to distract himself.

June waved and yelled out to the crowd below them, "Geronimo!" Mike looked at her quizzically, and she shrugged and said, "I heard the paratroopers say it in a war movie." At the top of the hill, she yelled it again. Then she joined the rest of the girls, who screamed their way down the back side of the big hill.

By the time they hit the bottom of the hill, Mike was yelling too. Adrenalin rushed through his veins. When they reached the abrupt stop at the end of the ride, they were both flushed and grinning like fools.

"I wish I'd bought six tickets," Mike said as they walked down the ramp. "That's a riot!"

June couldn't agree more.

Mike spent five dimes before breaking enough balloons at the dart throw to win a prize. This heroic effort won June a small teddy bear with a pink ribbon around its neck.

"I'm going to name her VJ for Virginia Jane. She's roly-poly and cute, like my sister," June said.

Mike laughed and said, "Let's go on the merry-go-round next."

June put VJ away in her bag and said, "Why, do you want to grab the brass ring?"

"No. I grabbed the brass ring yesterday in DeKalb."

Mike and June were the only adults riding the carousel. They rode side by side on horses and secured ones that went up and down. The quicker kids had each grabbed one of the four deer. As Mike's horse went up, June's horse went down. They tried to grab kisses in the middle of the cycle. The kids near them made fun of them. Two older boys made rude remarks and mocked them with exaggerated air kisses. June laughed at them. Mike saw an overweight middle-aged woman glaring at them in disapproval each time they came around.

The third time around, he stuck out his tongue at her. June laughed so hard she almost fell off her horse. The woman stuck her nose in the air and marched off in a huff. When the carousel stopped, Mike dug two nickels out of his pocket and gave them to the rowdy boys and said, "Have a cotton candy on us, boys."

"Gee, thanks, mister," one boy said, and they ran off to get their treats.

"Why did you give money to those two ruffians?" June asked him.

"Because they made you laugh."

June smiled at him and said, "Better not make a habit of it, lots of people make me laugh."

*****

June looked at her reflection in the funhouse mirror and said to Mike, "Now VJ and I both look like my sister."

Mike stood in front of the mirror next to June's. "Not me. I look like Stan Laurel," referring to the skinny member of the Laurel and Hardy comedy team.

"I guess that makes me Oliver Hardy," June said.

They stumbled across the tilting floor and ran through the revolving barrel.

When they left the funhouse, it was dusk. They walked back to the pool area and found an empty table on the sun deck.

"What's on the program for tonight?" June asked Mike.

"I can offer madam two choices. First, we can have dinner here, go watch the Sunflower Girls in the theater, and then go dancing. Or we can go back to our hotel, try out that two-person bathtub, and use our free dinner tickets. What is your pleasure, Mrs. Thompson?"

"How can I deprive you of the Sunflower Girls? So how about this? We go to the first showing at the theater. You take me for a night ride on the Comet. We skip the dance hall and go back to the hotel. We use the free dinner tickets and wind up the evening in the tub."

"Sounds like a plan, honey. We need to hurry to make that first show."

The theater was a plain wooden building with a stage. Pine benches provided the seating. The entry was decorated with show posters of the acts that played there. The color was provided by the Sunflower Girls. They were fresh-looking young women in flashy dresses with layers of brightly colored petticoats and bloomers. Their dance routines were energetic and showed plenty of bloomers. The comedy tended toward the risqué side with a liberal dose of double entendres. June thought they were a hoot. Mike couldn't stop laughing at them. They had a slapstick quality that cracked him up.

After sunset, the Park lit up with a festival of colored lights. The lines to the Comet were double the afternoon lines. Mike and June split up, with Mike going to the line to the ticket booth and June joining the line to the ride. Even with this strategy, it was twenty minutes before June got to the steps of the platform. She let three other couples go ahead of her before Mike finally showed up with their tickets. The slow climb up the first hill seemed twice as intimidating in the dark. Even June had an attack of nerves. By the time their car reached the top, she had goose bumps on her arms. The steep drop from the first hill was like being swallowed by a black hole. Half the riders were too scared to scream. The other half made up for them.

This time Mike absolutely knew their car would go flying off the tracks when it hit the sharp bends. He kept his eyes slammed shut during those sections of the ride. June was exhilarated. Flying through the night on the Comet was a different experience from riding it in daylight. When her car came to the sudden stop at the end, she didn't want to get out of the car. She felt like she could ride it all night. The attendant tried to get her out of the car. June had a death grip on the safety bar. The attendant was rapidly running out of time to load the new riders, so he stopped trying to disembark Mike and June and loaded the seats behind them.

Before Mike knew what was happening, he was headed up the big hill again. June was ecstatic. Mike thought she had flipped her wig. She laughed and yelled the entire ride. This time, the attendant had recruited help to make sure they got off at the platform. A large, hairy-shouldered man in a sleeveless undershirt released the safety bar and seized June's hand. She meekly came out of the car. Mike hastily followed.

Mike said to the big man, "I'll pay you for the extra ride."

The man said, "Just get your girlfriend off my platform, and we'll call it even, buddy."

"I'm not his girlfriend, I'm his wife," June said.

"My condolences to you both. Now get your asses off my platform," the man said.

"What just happened back there?" Mike asked as they walked through the midway.

"I guess I got carried away," June said. "But wasn't it amazing!"

"You're lucky the hairy guy in the undershirt didn't have you arrested," Mike said.

"I'm starving!" June said. "Let's get the trolley back to the hotel and go to the Train Shed. I'm going to have Cameron get me the biggest, bloodiest piece of meat they have."

Mike shook his head ruefully and said, "Life with you won't be boring, that's for sure."

June just laughed and took his arm.

When they got back to the Union Station Hotel, Mike put their name on the list for a table at the Train Shed. June went up to their room to change clothes. She looked longingly at the big tub with the shiny brass fittings. But hunger won out, and she settled for washing her face and hands. She had just changed into her black cocktail dress when Mike came into their room.

"That tub is sure inviting," he said.

"Me too," June replied. "Hold that thought until after you feed me."

Mike changed his clothes and did it a quick wash up. "Our table should be ready in fifteen minutes," he told June.

"Don't forget our free meal tickets," June reminded him.

They went downstairs and stopped at the host station in the Train Shed to check in. Mike had requested a booth in Cameron's section, and one was reserved for them. The host checked them off on his seating chart and picked up two menus. He escorted Mike and June to their booth and handed them menus and two train tickets. A busser brought glasses of water and their silverware wrapped in red napkins. June looked up from her menu when she saw Cameron approaching their booth.

"Welcome, folks, I'm happy to see that you have returned. What can I get for you this evening?" Cameron said.

Mike asked, "How's the meatloaf?" He didn't want to eat steak again tonight.

Cameron assured him that he would enjoy the meatloaf.

Mike said, "Okay, let's go with that."

Cameron turned to June.

"I'm starving, Cameron. What's the biggest steak you have?" June asked him.

"We have the Cattleman's steak, a sixteen-ounce rib eye, but that's a lot of steak."

"Perfect! I'll have that. Do you remember how I like my steaks, Cameron?" June asked him.

"How would I possibly forget, madam? Unconscionably rare, as I recall."

"You bet!" June said, "And please instruct the chef to cut off a sample piece of raw steak for me before he cooks the rest."

Cameron winced and turned to Mike and said, "Your wife is just teasing me now, isn't she, sir?"

"I wouldn't count on it, Cameron," Mike corrected him. "She's pretty serious about her steaks."

Cameron turned back to June, who just smiled and nodded.

Mike handed Cameron their train tickets. He distractedly tore off the bottom sections and returned them to Mike. He left the booth and deposited the top sections in the drawing bowl in the locomotive. *How can I present this order to the chef?* he wondered.

June was eating her salad and sharing it with Mike, whose meat-loaf did not come with salad, when a tall man in a white apron and chef's hat came up to their booth. He was carrying a wood carving block with a sixteen-ounce rib eye steak and a carving knife on the block.

The chef scowled at June and asked, "Are you the woman who wants to eat raw meat?"

Cameron lingered in the background, having pointed June out to the chef.

June said, "That would be me."

The chef set the board on the table in front of June and asked, "How much raw steak do you want?"

June picked up the carving knife and cut off a four-ounce piece. "That much," she said to the chef, "and don't overcook the rest, please. One minute on each side will do it."

The chef shook his head, then turned to Mike and asked, "You just married her, is that right?"

"I sure did," Mike confirmed.

"Well, if I were you, I wouldn't let her get too hungry before bedtime. You might wake up with something missing."

Mike laughed. The chef picked up the cutting board with the steak and the knife and went back to the kitchen.

"I think he likes me," June said and laughed.

Cameron came forward and asked if they would like wine with their meal.

Mike said, "Sure, bring us a bottle of that wine we had last night. That was good." Mike noticed three men peering around the swinging door leading into the kitchen. They wore white aprons and chef's hats and were pointing toward his booth and holding a spirited conversation.

"I think you are a celebrity," Mike said to June, pointing out the three sous chefs.

"Goodness, you'd think nobody had ever ordered a rare steak before," June said.

When Cameron brought their dinner plates, June's plate held her rare steak and the four-ounce slice of raw steak she cut off. Cameron handed June a small white envelope.

"What's this?" June asked him.

"It's from the chef."

June removed the note from the envelope, read it, giggled, and handed it to Mike.

Mike read the note and laughed.

The note said,

> *Bon appétit, madam.*
> *Bon chance, monsieur*
> *Chef Henri.*

Mike stopped watching after she took her first bite of raw steak.

June said, "I promise not to eat raw steak in a restaurant again. I only did it because they were being stuffy about the way I wanted it cooked."

"Do you really like it that way?" Mike asked.

"It's actually much tastier raw than it is cooked," June said. "Do you want to try the last piece?"

"I'll take your word for it, honey," Mike replied.

Dessert was included with their free meal coupons, and they both tried the carrot cake. June had ice cream on hers.

She eats like a horse and doesn't gain a pound, Mike observed enviously. He gave Cameron their meal coupons.

"The wine is not included in your coupon," Cameron said. "But it's on the house, a wedding present from the kitchen."

"See, I told you he liked me," June said.

Mike left a generous tip for Cameron.

*****

They took a walk around the Grand Hall to settle their dinners.

"I really loved riding the Comet at night," June said.

"Yeah, I noticed," Mike said. "Hell, half the park noticed."

June stopped at a men's hat shop and looked at the hat display in the front window.

"You bought me a dress. I want to buy you a hat," June told Mike.

"Okay, but I want a summer hat, not a winter hat," Mike said.

He looked around the store until he spotted the straw boater with a snazzy hatband. He asked the salesclerk if they had it in a size 7.

June looked doubtfully at his choice. "It's kind of flashy, isn't it?" she asked Mike.

"That's what I like about it," Mike said.

The clerk returned with the 7.

Mike put it on and tilted it at a racy angle. He looked at it in the mirror on the counter and said, "I like it. It's me."

June laughed and said, "No, it's not, it's Bing Crosby. If you get that hat, you'll have to buy saddle shoes and white duck pants to go with it and maybe an ascot." She laughed again.

Mike reluctantly took off the boater and gave it back to the clerk.

"Wet blanket," he said to June.

She smiled and took his arm and steered him away from the straw hats. She stopped in front of another hat display and pointed to one of the hats.

"How about that one?" she asked. It was a gray felt dress hat with a black silk headband.

"It looks like the hat Bogie wore in *Casablanca*," Mike protested.

"Try it on," June said.

The clerk handed Mike the hat, and he tried it on. It fit comfortably.

He looked in the counter mirror and said, "I look like Sam Spade, private eye."

June stepped back and told Mike to turn around. She studied the hat carefully and said, "No, you look like an up-and-coming young manager in Kaufmann's Radio Sales and Repair store."

Mike turned back to the mirror and tilted his head forward and back and side to side. "Damn, I think you're right."

"I'll take it," June told the salesclerk. "How much is it?" She opened her purse.

The clerk was surprised. Usually, the man handled the money transactions. He turned to Mike inquiringly.

"I'd just take her money if I were you," Mike advised him.

428

The clerk took her money and placed the hat in a hatbox and tied a ribbon around the box.

*****

Mike was naked as he added bubble bath to the steaming water in the roomy bathtub. He stepped into the tub and sat down with his back against the end of the tub, away from the porcelain faucet handles. A few errant soap bubbles landed on his nose.

June laughed at them as she slipped into the tub and nestled up against him. Mike pushed her down under the pad of floating bubbles, and she emerged with bubbles covering her face and head. Mike laughed. She rolled over on her stomach and grabbed Mike's head with both hands and dunked him under the soapy water. He came up with his face obscured by bubbles. That started the horseplay that resulted in soapy water being splashed all over the tile floor.

It ended with June on top of Mike and kissing him through the soap bubbles.

That kiss started a different kind of play as June made some adjustments in her position to line up the relevant body parts. The layer of soap bubbles started moving gently. Before long, the tile floor was splashed again.

When the splashing ceased, June returned to her original position, reclining contentedly against Mike. She reached and took a washcloth off the sink stand next to the tub. She turned her head toward Mike and said, "I'll wash you if you'll wash me."

"If you wash me, there won't be much water left in this tub," Mike said.

June laughed and handed him the washcloth, "Go to work, husband."

*****

"Thanks for the hat, honey," Mike said.

They were under the covers on the big brass bed. Mike had his arm around her, and she was yawning.

"You're welcome, honey. Now let's get some sleep."

"Tomorrow we see the Old State Capitol building," Mike said.

"Whoopee," June said peevishly. "Good night, hubby."

*****

Mike and June caught the 10:00 a.m. bus from the stop outside their hotel and rode northwest through St. Louis. The bus crossed the Daniel Boone Bridge into St. Charles. They purchased a tourist map from a gift shop on South Main Street, an old-fashioned brick street with nineteenth-century buildings lining both sides for ten blocks. June reluctantly admitted that St. Charles was cool. Following their map, they located the Lewis and Clark Boat House.

St. Charles was the town where Meriwether Lewis joined Captain William Clark to set off on their expedition of discovery of the newly acquired Louisiana Territory, purchased from Napoleon by President Thomas Jefferson.

They walked into the ancient wood sided boathouse, and Mike started reading the informational panels inside.

"The famous Lewis and Clark expedition launched their three boats up the Missouri River from the small town of St. Charles. The small fleet consisted of a keelboat and two large pirogues which took them to their winter camp in present day North Dakota." Mike was surprised to learn how large those boats were.

June walked through the building, out on a dock at the back of the boathouse, and looked out at the Missouri River.

Mike read another panel.

"The pirogues were propelled by a sailing mast and oars. In some conditions the boats had to be poled along or even dragged upstream with ropes from the banks."

That sounds like a lot of fun, Mike doubted.

He looked around for June but didn't see her, so he walked through the boathouse and found her out on the dock. She was watching the boat traffic go by on the river. He joined her at the end of the dock and said, "I guess Lewis and Clark didn't ring your bell, huh?"

"Well, reading about them didn't. But I would have liked going with them," June said. "Imagine it—a whole unexplored half of a continent that no civilized man had ever set foot on. What an adventure!"

"Let's make a deal. We'll explore the world and have our own adventures," Mike said.

June shook his hand and said, "It's a deal."

They had lunch at a small sidewalk café on South Main Street. The café featured St. Charles-style barbecue sandwiches on sour-dough buns with a big garlic pickle. They each had a glass of wine from the local vineyards. June topped off her lunch with five small pieces of dark chocolate she bought at a chocolate shop down the street.

Mike said, "Wine and chocolate?"

"Don't knock it until you try it," June said and gave him one piece of her chocolate.

Mike bit off half of the piece of chocolate and sipped his wine.

"Damn, that's not half bad," he admitted and ate the other half.

"Give me time," June said, "and I'll have you eating your steak the right way too."

Mike laughed and said, "Don't hold your breath on that one." He studied their tourist map and said, "Next stop is the original Missouri state Capitol building."

June grimaced and said, "Great, more history."

"It's just down South Main Street toward the river. It won't take long to see it," Mike urged.

"It's sure not much to look at," June said when they had wandered down to the long two-story faded red-brick building. It was a utilitarian building with no architectural features.

"It was built in 1821, what do you expect? It's amazing it's still standing," Mike rebutted. "I'm sure it was considered very modern in 1821. A lot of Missouri resided in log cabins with dirt floors at the time."

"We don't have to go inside, do we?" June pleaded.

"Why don't you walk on down the street and look at those old Victorian houses, and I'll glance inside for a few minutes," Mike suggested.

When Mike came out of the Old Capitol building, June was sitting on a bench waiting for him.

"Mike, we can catch a bus from the St. Charles bus stop that goes to Laclede's Landing on the Mississippi."

"What is Laclede's Landing?" Mike asked.

"It's the oldest section of the city with a collection of original nineteenth-century warehouse buildings fronting on the water. They have been converted into shops and restaurants. It sounds like an interesting area. The landing was a busy riverfront back in the paddleboat days."

"See, you do like history," Mike said.

June ignored his remark. "There's a three thirty bus. If we hurry, we can catch it," June said.

After their bus ride, Mike and June walked along the riverfront and looked out at the Mississippi River.

"It sure is a big river, isn't it?" June asked Mike.

"Yeah, the biggest one in America," Mike replied. "There's a concession at the Landing where we can get on a boat and go out on the river. What do you think?"

"I think I've seen enough old buildings for one day," June answered. "Let's take a boat ride."

When they got to Laclede's Landing, they found the boat ride booth.

"At six o'clock there's a twilight boat ride on a paddle wheeler with dinner included," the clerk at the booth told them.

"Sold!" Mike told the clerk after getting the nod from June.

"It'll be here and start boarding in half an hour," the clerk said, taking Mike's money and handing him their tickets.

"Where does it go?" June asked.

What difference does that make? Your husband already bought the tickets, the clerk thought. But he said, "It goes upriver to the bridge. Then it goes across to a landing on the Illinois side and comes back here around 9:00 p.m."

"I've never been to Illinois," June remarked.

"Me neither," Mike said.

The surly clerk said, "You're not going to see much of it, and what you do see looks the same as here."

Mike and June walked away with their tickets.

"I don't care what that sourpuss said," June declared. "I want to see Illinois for myself. Emma Dee will be so jealous when I tell her we went to Illinois in a riverboat."

Mike laughed and said, "I'm sure you're right."

*****

The *River Queen* was a smaller three-deck replica of the paddlewheel steamboats that plied the mighty river when Mark Twain was a cabin boy. It was splendid in its white paint with the red-and-blue trim. The double-fluted black smokestacks emitted plumes of white smoke, with the boilers idling at the dock. The decks and passageways gleamed with varnished mahogany rails and brass fittings.

The upper two decks held dining rooms. The second deck also featured a bandstand and a dance floor. Mike and June climbed the stairs to the third deck.

The smokestacks belched out a cloud of white smoke mixed with black, and the ponderous stern paddlewheel started, turning its wide wooden paddles. The heavy craft moved slowly away from the dock, helped by dock hands that fended it off from the dock with long poles. As the *River Queen* cleared the pier and entered the river, the paddlewheel picked up speed to gain steerageway in the strong current. The crowd on the upper deck cheered as the *Queen* turned upriver.

June said to Mike, "I thought this was a big boat until we got out on this river. Now it seems a lot smaller."

"Yeah, it's a long way across to Illinois, isn't it?" Mike agreed.

The captain blew the steam whistle, alerting river traffic he was entering the river channel. Mike and June stood at the stern railing and watched the big paddlewheel churn up the brown water. After a few minutes, they moved to the port side railing and watched St. Louis go by them.

"This is a lark!" June said. "It's not as exciting as a night ride on the Comet, but it's fun."

As night came on, the temperature dropped, and they moved down to the second-deck salon and got a window table where they could see the city passing by.

A white-jacketed waiter brought water glasses and took their drink orders. *River Queen* was embroidered above his jacket pocket. Their waiter brought Mike his cocktail and June her glass of Anheuser-Busch beer brewed in St. Louis.

"For dinner tonight we have New Orleans Cajun-style catfish or Creole shrimp with dirty rice."

"The cook puts dirt in the rice?" June asked.

The waiter laughed and said, "No, they call it that because of the spices that turn it brown. It's hot, but it's tasty."

June said, "I like spicy." She ordered the shrimp.

Mike said, "I'll stick with the catfish."

"Tomorrow morning, I want to call Betty and see how she's doing," June told Mike once they had placed their orders.

"Okay, we can go back to our room after breakfast, and you can call her," Mike replied. He sipped his scotch and soda while June sipped her beer. "There's a dance floor on this deck," Mike said. "You still owe me a dance since we skipped the dance hall at the amusement park."

"I've decided about nursing school," June said.

Mike listened attentively.

"I'm going to start the fall semester at the university, but I'm going to major in business administration, not nursing. I love my job now, and I want to be a manager."

"I think that's great, honey. You need to follow your heart."

When their meals arrived, Mike said, "I've never had Cajun catfish before. What's that black stuff all over it?"

The waiter was used to tourists from the sticks. "That's a rub," he said.

"The cook rubs it and bruises it?" Mike asked.

The waiter laughed again. "A rub is a layer of spices that the cook rubs into the fish. It's called blackening because the spice turns black when it is cooked."

"Oh, go ahead and try it, Mike. Expand your horizons," June told him. She took a bite of her shrimp with some of the dirty rice. "That's really tasty," she said.

Mike hesitantly cut off a piece of the catfish and tried a bite. "That's not half bad."

They exchanged samples of their dishes.

"The shrimp's pretty good," Mike commented. "But I'm not a fan of the dirty rice."

June tasted the catfish sample and said, "It's okay, but I like my shrimp better."

When they finished their meal, they went out to the bow and watched the boat approach the Illinois landing.

Like Laclede's Landing, there were old warehouse buildings mixed with souvenir shops and eateries. The *River Queen* docked long enough to load and unload passengers and allow forty-five minutes to explore Illinois. Mike and June entered one of the souvenir shops and perused the overpriced trinkets on sale to the tourists. June picked up a pewter beer mug engraved with the name of a local brewery and "East St. Louis, Illinois."

"You aren't seriously thinking of buying that sleazy beer mug, are you?" Mike asked her.

"It's either that or one of those chintzy ashtrays. I need something to prove to Emma Dee we were in Illinois."

"In that case, buy the mug. Those ashtrays are worse."

The paddleboat steam whistle sounded to call the riders back onboard.

June hastily paid for her purchase, and they went back to the gangway.

Once the paddlewheel was up to speed and the bow was headed south toward Laclede's Landing, Mike and June joined the dancers on the second deck dance floor. The band was playing "I'll Be Seeing You," a Billie Holiday ballad. It was a perfect slow dance tune for

June. Mike softly sang the lyrics in June's ear as they danced cheek to cheek. Mike could feel June's firm breasts against his chest.

Hip-hop is fun, Mike thought, *but this slow dancing has its points.*

The band finished with Billie Holiday and segued into the "Beer Barrel Polka." Tables emptied of polka dancers, and Mike and June found an empty table near the window. Soon the room was echoing with the chorus, "Roll out the barrel, we'll have a barrel of fun…" Everyone at the tables was clapping and singing, including Mike and June. In the spirit of the song, they each ordered glasses of beer. The room shouted and applauded the band at the end of the polka.

"I think the *River Queen* has already rolled out a lot of barrels of beer," June said, laughing.

"Yeah, it's a rowdy crowd all right," Mike agreed.

The band played a waltz, and Mike cajoled June into dancing again. Halfway around the dance floor, Mike said, "Hey, you know how to waltz!"

"Blame eighth-grade coed gym class. For part of every hour, Mr. Brown taught us how to dance," June admitted. "Oops, I'm sorry I told you that."

"You can't unring that bell. Now I know that you can dance."

"I never said I couldn't dance. I just said I didn't like to dance," June objected.

At the end of the waltz, Mike and June went outside and stood at the rail. The *River Queen* was nearing the pier at Laclede's landing.

"This was fun, honey. Thanks for thinking of it." She kissed him on the cheek.

They caught a trolley car back to Union Station.

When they got up to their room, June asked Mike, "What are we doing tomorrow?"

"I thought we'd shop Cherokee Street and visit the Anheuser-Busch Brewery," Mike suggested. "You'll like it. There are a lot of shops on Cherokee Street."

June gave Mike a suspicious look and said, "You just want to tour the brewery and sample all the beer."

"Maybe not all the beer. Besides, we can see the Clydesdale horses and the Dalmatians," Mike protested.

June smiled and said sarcastically, "That's right. I forgot what a big animal lover you are." She cuddled up to Mike. "Please remind me to call Betty in the morning. I want to find out how she's doing."

Mike kissed her and said, "Sure thing, sweetheart."

"The boat ride was fun," June said and yawned.

"Yeah, it was. I'm still not sure about the blackened fish, but I liked waltzing with you," Mike said.

June laughed and said, "Good night, hubby." She turned off the light on her nightstand, rolled over, and went to sleep.

Mike was right behind her. It had been a busy day.

22

"Is this an urgent call?" the long-distance operator challenged June.

After breakfast, Mike and June had returned to their room, and June was trying to place a call to Betty. Wartime policy restricted long-distance lines to military and government business and urgent personal calls.

"Yes, it is, operator. My sister has leukemia, and I'm calling to check on her condition."

Mike looked askance at June's fib to the long-distance operator.

"I'm sorry to hear about your sister. Please hang up, and I'll call you back when we get your party on the line," the operator said.

June hung up the phone.

Mike said, "You just lied to the long-distance operator. Why did you say Betty was your sister?"

June shrugged and said, "Unless it's about a family member, some fussbudget operators won't place the call."

"Next time, let me make the call," Mike said. "They always put through calls for servicemen. I'd hate to visit you in the federal clink."

The phone in their room rang, and June answered it. "Your party is on the line," the operator said to June. "Go ahead."

"Hello," June said. "This is June."

"Hello, June. This is Kate."

"Hello, Kate. Can I speak to Betty?"

Kate put her hand over the receiver for a moment and composed herself. "I'm afraid Betty's not here. We took her to the hospital today. She's had a relapse."

Mike saw June's smile collapse, and her knuckles whitened on the phone.

"Oh no," June said. "When did it happen?"

Mike came over and stood next to June. "Betty?" he asked her quietly.

June nodded.

Kate sat down on the chair next to her phone stand. "She woke me up early this morning. She had a high fever and nausea. We drove her to the hospital, and they checked her in. Dr. Friedman will see her this afternoon. I just came home to get a few things for her when the phone rang. Her father is still at the hospital with her."

June sat on the bed. "Can she take phone calls at the hospital when she feels better?"

"I don't think so, at least not for a while," Kate answered.

"Can I call you back tonight and see how she's doing?" June asked.

"June, sweetie, you're on your honeymoon. You can go see her when you get home. You and Mike need to enjoy this time in your life. It won't come again."

"Yes, but…" June's voice broke, and she sobbed and handed the phone to Mike.

"This is Mike. June can't talk for a minute. Who am I speaking to?"

"This is Kate, Betty's mother. You need to talk sense to June. Betty will be in the hospital getting treatments, at least for the rest of the week. She won't be able to have visitors for a few days. The last thing she would want is to spoil June's honeymoon. Please go on and have a good time."

Mike held out the phone to June, but she shook her head.

"Mrs. Anderson, please tell Betty we asked about her and we will see her as soon as we get back. We'll pray for her to get better again," Mike said.

"I'll tell her, and you thank June for being a good friend to my little girl. Goodbye now," Kate said and hung up.

Mike hung up and took June into his arms.

"Thank you, honey, for taking over for me," June told him.

"Kate said Betty would be in treatment and couldn't have visitors this week."

"I'm so scared for her," June said. "I don't know what to do."

"I know, sweetheart. I'm scared for her too. If you want, I can have the concierge call and get us tickets on the train today."

June looked into Mike's eyes and said, "I told Betty once you were a keeper. I couldn't love you more if you were twins. Betty's mom is right. We have a honeymoon to finish."

"I might need to be twins to keep up with you."

*****

"We won't know what's happening until we get the blood work tomorrow," Dr. Friedman said to Betty's parents in his office at St. Joseph Hospital. "Right now, we are treating her fever and nausea. My physical examination showed a possible enlargement of her liver. We are testing for liver function and for the spleen. I don't mean to frighten you, but you need to be informed. If there is organ involvement, we can treat it with the same treatment we used before, primarily radiation. Actually, with organs we can focus the radiation more accurately than with the blood."

"Can we see her?" Ray asked.

Kate was silent as she tried to cope with this latest development.

"Not today. She won't be responsive until we get her fever under control. She needs rest."

Kate asked, "When will you start her treatments again?"

"After we get the blood test results, I'll consult with Dr. Leyland, and we'll formulate the treatment plan. We'll get it started tomorrow."

*****

On Wednesday night, Kate and Ray were having dinner when the phone rang.

Ray said, "I'll get that, honey." Ray answered the phone. "Hello."

"Hello, this is Don Walker. Can I speak with Betty?"

"I'm sorry to have to tell you this, Don, but Betty has had a relapse and is back in the hospital."

"Oh no! She was doing so well. How bad is it?" Don asked.

"She woke up early this morning with a high fever and nausea. They are treating her for that. They won't know what to do until they get her tests tomorrow."

"Can she have visitors?" Don asked.

"No, not now, and she probably can't for a few days. Check with us on Friday," Ray said.

"Okay, Mr. Anderson. I'll very sorry to hear this. Do Mike and June know about it?"

"Yes, June called us this morning from their hotel in St. Louis. We told them not to interrupt their trip because Betty couldn't see them even if they were here."

"Okay, I'll check back with you on Friday."

Ray thanked Don for his concern and hung up the phone.

"That was Don Walker on the phone," Ray said as he sat down to finish dinner.

Kate put down her fork. "When I first met him, I thought he was just a playboy guitar picker with a girl in every little town his band played," Kate said. "And I think I might have been right too. But there's more to Don than I thought. He's really been a stout friend to Betty since she's been sick."

"I think she's pretty stuck on him too," Ray said. "It's all just too damn bad."

"Oh, Ray, I don't remember you ever cussing before," Kate said. "But I agree with you. It is too damn bad. We're going to lose our little girl." She started crying.

Betty drifted in and out of a disturbed sleep. Her fever was down but not gone. Her stomach had settled down, but she had no appetite. The worst thing was the terrible tiredness she felt. It was all so familiar now. She wanted it to be over. She lapsed back into sleep.

*****

Dr. Friedman and Dr. Leyland went over Betty Anderson's test results in Dr. Friedman's office Thursday morning.

"Well, it's a full relapse," Dr. Friedman said.

"Yes, and it looks like her liver is involved now," Dr. Leyland said.

"When I examined her yesterday, I thought I could feel some enlargement in her liver."

"What treatment plan do you recommend, Doctor?" Dr. Leyland asked.

"If we do anything beyond comfort care, I'd go back to the radiation and extend treatment to her liver as well as her blood." Doctor Leyland put down the test report he was holding and looked at his colleague.

"That was a big 'if' you just threw in there, Joel," Dr. Leyland observed.

Dr. Friedman nodded his head in agreement. "We always knew the prognosis was gloomy. I don't know how much more we want to put this poor girl through," he said.

"That's kind of up to the patient, isn't it?" Dr. Leyland asked.

"Yes, Doctor, I guess it is."

*****

Dr. Friedman met Betty's parents in Betty's hospital room.

"I know you are not feeling like much conversation, Betty. But you need to know what's happening with your care."

"Betty just got over her fever. I don't know if she is up to this. Maybe we should wait until tomorrow," Kate said.

"Let's hear what Dr. Friedman has to say, Mom," Betty said in a tired voice.

"Your tests are not good. The white cell counts are way up, and your anemia is back. And we are afraid your liver is being affected. We can resume your radiation therapy and the medication you were on last time. If we do, the sooner we start the better."

"Do you think it will make me better again?" Betty asked.

"I fear I am in the same position as last time. There simply is no way to predict outcomes. I wish I could give you a better answer, but I can't."

"I'm so very tired, Doctor. And I'm tired of being tired. I don't know if I can put up with much more of this," Betty said. "Last night I just wanted it all to be over."

Dr. Friedman said, "I understand completely. You've been awfully brave through this. Why don't you talk it over with your parents and let me know what you want to do? If you decide against the treatments, we will do all we can to keep you comfortable." Dr. Friedman left the room.

When he had gone, Kate said tearfully, "Oh, honey, I just don't know what to tell you except that your dad and I love you. We will do whatever you want us to do."

Ray put his arm around Kate's shoulder and said to Betty, "I won't try to tell you what to decide. But if you don't mind, I could make a suggestion?"

"Oh, please, Daddy, help me if you can," Betty said. Her throat was dry, and she sipped some water.

"My suggestion is this—try the treatments for four days. If they don't help, then we will take you home with us."

Betty looked at her father and said, "That's a good idea, Dad. Would you and Mom talk to the doctor about it?"

"We sure will, honey. Now you get some rest," Ray said.

Betty closed her eyes, and her parents went to find Dr. Friedman.

Dr. Friedman was in his office, waiting to hear Betty's decision. Ray explained what they had decided.

"Is that okay with you, Dr. Friedman?" Ray asked.

"I think it's very sensible. We start her treatments tomorrow morning. If she responds badly, we can discontinue them at any time," Dr. Friedman said. "I will advise Dr. Leyland about this decision."

Kate took Dr. Friedman's hand and said, "We will always be grateful to you for the extra time with our daughter. It was so important to her to be at her friend's wedding. God bless you, Doctor."

"Thank you, Mrs. Anderson, Mr. Anderson. I have great admiration for Betty, and it has been a privilege working with her. We will do all we can for her."

*****

"It seems like we just got off the train from Kansas City five minutes ago. How did this week go so fast?" June said as she ate her omelet.

Their bags were packed and waiting in their room when Mike and June went down to breakfast on Friday morning.

"I know what you mean. But I think we did St. Louis justice. Thank you for going to the museums with me. I know you would rather have ridden the Comet again," said Mike as he ate his eggs and sausage.

"I liked the airport museum. It was cool seeing those old planes," June said. "Anyway, this was the best honeymoon anyone ever had, and I've got an Illinois mug to prove it."

Mike laughed and said, "Don't forget your dress and my new Sam Spade hat."

"I'm awfully worried about Betty, honey. I have to see her tomorrow," June told him.

Mike said, "We'll both go. But we better get moving if we are going to catch the 9:00 a.m. train."

When they got up to their room, Mike looked in the bathroom and said, "I'll really miss that big old tub. When we buy a house, I want to get one just like it."

June laughed and said, "It's a deal. Now please close the door and let me pee."

Mike carried their bags down to the lobby, and they checked out of the hotel.

The concierge had a redcap porter waiting to take their bags and escort them through the Grand Hall to their landing. The redcap handed their bags up to the porter on their train car. Mike tipped him, and they followed the porter to their compartment, who put their bags in the overhead compartment. Mike tipped him as well.

When he left, Mike said, "I've tipped more people on this trip than I have the rest of my life. I never dreamed so many people got tips."

"In our future adventures, Mr. Rockefeller, we may have to drop down a few stars on our accommodations and do more for ourselves. But it sure was nice seeing how the other half lives," June said. "Thanks for a great honeymoon, hubby." She kissed him.

*****

Don cut short his lecture to his current crop of trainees on Friday afternoon. He was anxious to find out about Betty's condition. When he returned to his barracks, he called Betty's parents.

Kate answered the phone.

"Hello, Mrs. Anderson, this is Don. I was calling to see how Betty is doing."

Kate had just got home from the hospital.

"She's not doing very well, I'm afraid. But today was her first day of treatment. We hope she will be better tomorrow."

"I'm sorry to hear that. Can she have visitors?" Don asked.

"Not yet. Only her dad and I are permitted, and they don't like us to stay very long. Maybe by Sunday she'll be better, and you could see her. You can check with me tomorrow."

"Thank you, Mrs. Anderson. I'll do that. Please tell her I asked about her," Don said.

"I certainly will. Thank you for calling."

In the evening, the Anderson phone rang again.

"Hello, this is Mrs. Anderson speaking," Kate answered.

"Kate, it's June. Mike and I just got back from St. Louis. How is Betty?"

Kate filled June in on Betty's condition and the treatment plan.

"Mike and I would like to see her tomorrow. Can she have visitors?"

Kate repeated what she told Don about visitation. "How was your honeymoon trip?"

"It was great. We stayed at the Union Station Hotel. It's a fabulous place with a giant Grand Hall with shops and restaurants."

Kate laughed and said, "My goodness, it sounds wonderful. And you two rode the train to get there, didn't you?"

"We sure did. We followed the Missouri River from Kansas City to St. Louis. We were on a streamliner, and it had a dining car and an observation car. We traveled like rich folks. I'd never been on a train before," June said.

"I'm green with envy, dear. It sounds like you two are off to a good start. Remember that if things get a little rocky later. It'll help you both hang on to each other when you may not want to, temporarily," Kate said.

"Did you and Ray have rocky times?" June asked.

Kate laughed and said, "Every married couple has rocky times, honey. Sometimes the grass looks greener somewhere else. Don't you believe that. Hang on to what you have. And that's the end of my sage marital advice."

"Thank you, Kate. I'll try to remember it when Mike and I get in a fuss with each other," June said. "I'll call you again tomorrow night about visiting Betty, if that's okay?"

"Of course, it's all right," Kate said. "Betty needs the support of her friends."

*****

Betty's condition had not improved after her second day of radiation therapy. The attending physician and nursing staff were struggling to keep her fever down and her nausea under control. Dr. Friedman was unhappy to see the appearance of petechiae, red spots under her skin, a new symptom of her blood disorder. She had no appetite and hadn't eaten solid food since entering the hospital. Dr. Friedman placed her on intravenous feeding and hydration. He ordered mild sedation to keep her more comfortable, and she slept most of the day. His reservations about continuing the experimental treatment were growing.

He was glad the patient had placed limits on him. He would see where they were after two more days.

*****

Kate stopped by the hospital after Ray's sermon at the Sunday service. Ray had a meeting with the church elders. Betty had received her radiation treatment that morning and was sleeping when Kate entered her room. A nurse was changing one of her IV bottles.

"How's she doing today?" Kate asked the nurse.

"She's a little better. Her fever is gone, but she still has no appetite. Do you want me to call the ward doctor?"

"No, I'll just sit with her for a while," Kate said. "Can she have other visitors?"

The nurse checked Betty's chart. "Her chart says she can have brief visits."

"What time are the visiting hours today?" Kate asked the nurse.

The nurse double checked the IV connection to the new bottle of saline. "Visiting is from two to five o'clock and then from seven to nine o'clock tonight."

Kate sat in the visitor chair next to Betty's bed and said, "Thank you. Her friends would like to see her. I'll call them."

*****

Betty opened her eyes when Mike and June came into her hospital room. Her nurse had just helped her drink water and orange juice, and Betty had gone back to sleep.

"Hi, roomie," Betty said and tried to sit up in bed.

Mike hurried to her bed and helped her sit up. He adjusted her pillows until she was comfortable.

"How are you feeling?" June asked her.

"I'm better just seeing you two. How was the honeymoon?" Betty asked.

"It was wonderful. Mike was such a good sport. He rode the Comet roller coaster with me at the Forest Park Highlands Amusement Park. We went on a paddleboat ride on the Mississippi River. I felt like Huckleberry Finn."

Betty smiled tiredly and said, "You two really lived it up. I'm glad."

Mike smiled and said, "She ran me ragged and almost got us arrested on the Comet."

Betty laughed weakly and asked, "How did she do that?"

June sat next to Betty's bed and replied, "It was after dark, and the amusement park was all lit up. We rode the Comet earlier in the afternoon, but I wanted to ride it at night. It was amazing. At the end of the ride, I was all atingle. I just had to ride it again, so I wouldn't get out of the car. Poor Mike was trying to help me out, and I wouldn't move. The attendant had to get the car moving, so he gave up on getting me out of the car. The second ride was as good as the first. I'd probably still be on it if they'd let me."

"When we got to the end of the ride the second time, there was a big, beefy guy waiting to throw us off," Mike said.

Betty sipped water and said, "That's my roomie, all right. I'm sorry I missed that."

"What did you miss?" asked Don, who entered Betty's room and overheard her remark.

"It's kind of a long story, Don," Mike said. "June got us kicked off a roller coaster in St. Louis."

Don leaned over Betty's bed and kissed her on the cheek. "How's tricks, cutie?" Don asked her.

Betty's face wore a serious expression. "Big guy, I'm worn out this time. I think I'm ready to move on."

Don protested. "Your mother said they were going to give you more of your treatments. They worked before."

"Yes, they did, and I'm very grateful for the extra time they gave me. There was time for me to be maid of honor for my best friend and to get a proposal of marriage from you," Betty said quietly. "But I'm ready to go home. I want to meet heaven at home, not in this hospital bed."

Don's eyes watered, and Mike and June were stunned into silence.

Betty saw Don's tears and said, "Don't weep for me, honey. I'll give these doctors two more innings, then I'm going home. My dad works for God. He'll put in a good word for me. I'll be fine."

June fought back her tears. She took Betty's hand and said, "I don't know very much about God. But I'm sure that He has a sense of humor, and I'm also sure you have made Him laugh. And I think heaven can use all the laughter it can get. I love you, Betty."

"Thanks, roomie. I love you too," Betty said.

A nurse came in from the hallway and said, "Sorry, folks, but we need to let Miss Anderson rest now."

June kissed Betty's forehead and left with Mike.

Don lingered at her bedside and held her hand. "I love you, and I'm going to keep rooting for you to get well," Don said and kissed her on the lips.

Betty smiled at him and let go of his hand. "Goodbye, big guy," she said and turned away before he could see her cry.

*****

On Monday morning, Mike's repairmen congratulated him on his marriage and ragged him with an assortment of risqué remarks about his honeymoon. Michelle laughed when Mike told her about June and the Comet.

"I was so pleased to meet her at your wedding," Michelle said. "She's a peach."

Mike had a 9:00 a.m. meeting in his office with Tony Moreno.

Tony asked Mike about his trip. "It was a ball. It put a big dent in my mustering-out pay, but it was worth every penny. Say, let me show you something," Mike said.

He got up and walked to the coat rack in his office and took down the new felt hat hanging there. He put it on and tilted it at a jaunty angle.

"What do you think?" Mike asked Tony.

"That's some snazzy hat, boss," Tony answered. "You look like Humphrey Bogart."

Mike laughed and said, "My new Mrs. bought it for me in a hat shop in the Grand Hall of the Union Station Hotel." He took it off and hung it back on the coat rack. "So what have you got to show me on our new guitar repair station?" Mike had assigned Tony the project when the guitar boutique was a go.

Tony gave Mike a memo that outlined his manning plans and budget for adding guitar repair to their repair department. Mike looked it over and asked Tony a few questions. Mike was ready to meet with Bernie.

*****

It was almost 6:00 p.m. on Monday when Dr. Leyland and Dr. Friedman met to discuss Betty's latest blood tests the lab had just delivered them.

"Our four days of treatment are up, and we got nowhere. In fact, she's worse now. What do you think, Joel?" Dr. Leyland asked.

"What I think doesn't matter, Doctor. Betty has decided to go home. And I can't think of a good reason why she shouldn't. With proper nursing care, she will do just as well at home as she is doing here. And she will be happier."

Dr. Leyland put down the test reports. "It won't be for very long anyway, will it?" he asked, dispirited.

"No, I'm afraid it won't. The cancer has spread to her liver and possibly her spleen. There will be more discomfort. We'll need to mitigate it with pain medication," Dr. Friedman said. He opened the cabinet in his office and took out a bottle of scotch. "I'm going to have a highball, Miles. Would you like one?"

Dr. Leyland replied, "Sure, with water, please."

Dr. Friedman made their drinks and handed one to Dr. Leyland. He raised his glass and said, "Here's to medical science. God help us."

Dr. Leyland raised his glass to the toast and then took a drink. "Do you think we were wrong to get this all started in the first place?"

Joel set his glass on his desk and looked at Miles. "Our patient doesn't think so. Her parents don't think so. It's easy to second guess ourselves at the end when it's not to our liking. I've discussed this case with my friend at the Mayo Clinic. He's agreed to coauthor a paper with me. We did have two remissions with our regimen. Maybe that will lead other researchers to a cure."

"What will you do with your paper?" Miles asked. He took another drink of his highball.

"That's where my friend comes in. He and his colleagues know the right places to submit our paper and have the contacts to get it published. I would like to include you as my associate in our paper."

"That's very generous of you, Joel, but I didn't do much."

"You guided the patient and her family through their ordeal. That may have been critical to our successes. It's important to note that in the paper."

Miles poured another drink for each of them. He handed Joel his glass and repeated Joel's toast.

"To medical science. God help us."

*****

Dr. Leyland met Betty's parents in her room Tuesday morning. Betty was awake, and her temperature was normal. But she was starting to suffer pain, and she was extremely fatigued.

"Betty wants to go home now," her mother said.

Betty was sitting up in bed, supported by pillows.

"Please, Dr. Leyland, let me go home," Betty pleaded with him.

"Don't distress yourself, Betty. You're being discharged today," Dr. Leyland told her. Then he asked Kate, "I understand you and Ray have arranged for a private nurse for Betty?"

"Yes, we have. Ray and I met her this morning."

Dr. Leyland approached Betty's bed and said, "I have some instructions for you, young lady."

Betty responded, "You should probably give them to my mother. I'm not very alert."

"I have separate instructions for her and for your father, but these are for you. If you are in any pain, tell your nurse or your mother immediately. I'm prescribing medication to deal with pain, and I don't want you to try to be a hero. Let someone know, and they can give you the medication."

"I'm not feeling very heroic, Doctor. I'll take the medicine. Now you can help me. How long do I have?" Betty asked. "Tell me the truth, please."

"Not very long, I'm afraid," Dr. Leyland said. "It'll be a matter of days."

"Good," Betty replied. "I just want to get it over with."

Kate shuddered and turned to Ray. He held her to him for a few moments.

"Can you give me anything to help me with the fatigue? Betty asked him. "I don't want to spend my last days as a vegetable."

Dr. Leyland considered her request. Ordinarily, a combination of painkillers and stimulants would be very unwise. In this case, he felt it was indicated. "We'll see what we can do for that," he said. He added a note to her chart with specific instructions for the stimulant.

The exchange with Dr. Leyland had exhausted Betty, and she closed her eyes and went to sleep. The others quietly left her room. She went home that afternoon.

*****

Mike and Bernie sat in Bernie's office at Kaufmann's Radio Sales and Service store and looked over the drawings of the new guitar boutique. Hanna, the designer, was reviewing her proposed budget for this addition to their sales floor.

Bernie set down the drawings and said, "Another excellent job, my dear Hanna. The instruments are attractively displayed, and you've stayed inside the footage allowed. What do you think, Mike?"

"It's fine except there is no demo station," Mike said.

"What is a demo station?" Bernie and Hanna echoed each other.

"It's a station for our guitar player to demonstrate the instrument by playing it. It can also serve as a try-out setup for customers to play the instruments. Our customers will be professionals or very talented amateurs. They will insist on trying the instruments before buying," Mike explained.

"What will this station require?" Hanna asked.

"It's nothing very elaborate—two seats, two guitar stands, an amplifier and two speakers, and electrical outlets. I can set one up for you by tomorrow," Mike said.

"That will be fine. We should be able to work that into the layout," Hanna said. She turned to Bernie. "I can get you revised plans in two weeks."

"I'm sorry I didn't mention this before," Mike said. "It didn't occur to me until I saw your drawings."

Hanna laughed and said, "Don't sweat it. There are always changes to plans. I'll see you tomorrow afternoon."

*****

Saturday was a cheerful spring day with bright sunshine. Fluffy white cumulous clouds drifted across bluebird skies. Kate opened the curtains in Betty's room and cracked open her window to let in the light and fresh air. Betty woke and asked Kate to help her to the bathroom in the hall. She didn't like using the bedpan. Her nurse wasn't due for another two hours. Kate helped Betty to her feet and gave her a shoulder to lean on. Betty's lethargy made walking a mental ordeal, but it hadn't affected the strength in her legs. Her fever was mild, and she hadn't taken pain medication this morning. After using the bathroom, she was more alert, and she sat in the upholstered chair in her room. Kate gave her two aspirin for her fever and helped her drink water with the aspirin. Betty looked out her window and saw a robin in the big oak tree in their front yard.

"Mom, there's a robin in our tree," Betty said.

Kate looked out the window and saw the robin skip to another branch.

"I see him, honey. Spring's here for sure," Kate said.

"It's a good day to go to heaven, Mom," Betty said. "Could you call June and ask her to come see me? I'd like to say goodbye to her." This was the first time since Betty came home that she had talked about dying.

Kate stifled her tears and said, "I'll call her right now, honey." As Kate was leaving her room Betty said, "I'd like some hot tea too, Mom."

Mike and June were finishing breakfast when their telephone rang. They still wore their pajamas and robes. June put down her coffee cup and went to answer it.

"Hello," she said.

"Hello, this is Kate, Betty's mother," Kate said. "Betty asked me to call you and see if you could come see her today."

"Sure, I can come. Is there any special reason she asked?" June asked.

There was silence on the other end of the phone.

"She said she wants to say goodbye to you," Kate finally said in a choked voice.

June was momentarily stupefied. "Is she doing worse?"

"No, she's not any worse than the rest of this week. But she seems convinced she's dying today. She's very resigned to it. I frankly don't know what to think."

"Would it be okay for Mike to come with me?" June asked.

"Yes, of course it would. Please bring him if he wants to come," Kate said.

"We'll be there shortly," June said. "Goodbye, Kate."

"What was that all about?" Mike asked June when she sat down again.

"Betty's mother said Betty wants to say goodbye," June said. "Betty thinks she's dying."

"I'm going with you," Mike said.

"Thank you, honey," June said. "We need to leave now."

When Kate hung up, she went back up to Betty.

"Your friends are coming soon, honey," Kate said to Betty.

"Please help me get dressed, Mom," Betty said and swung her legs off the bed and sat up. "I want to go downstairs to the living room."

Kate helped Betty dress and assisted her down the stairs to the living room sofa. They just got seated when the front doorbell rang. Kate opened the door to Betty's nurse, Mrs. Higgins, who entered and followed her into the living room with her medical bag. She joined Betty on the sofa. Kate sat in one of the living room chairs.

Mrs. Higgins put a thermometer under Betty's tongue and felt her forehead. She checked the thermometer and said, "It is 99.5 degrees, not too bad."

"Mom gave me aspirin," Betty informed Mrs. Higgins. "I want you to give me one of my pep pills. I need to be alert to visit with my friends when they arrive."

"How is your pain?" Mrs. Higgins asked. "Do you need your pain medicine?"

"I'm okay for now. It makes me groggy, and I want to be clear-headed for my friends."

Mrs. Higgins asked Kate to fetch a glass of water. When she had done so, the nurse gave one of the stimulant pills to Betty. Betty swallowed it with the water. Mrs. Higgins closed her bag and got up from the sofa.

"I'll be back this afternoon to check on you, dear," she told Betty and left the house.

"Where's Dad?" Betty asked Kate.

"He had a meeting with the church ladies to organize the charity food drive. He'll be back for lunch."

"Did you tell him what I said this morning?" Betty asked.

"Yes, I did. That's why he's coming home right after his meeting. I'll get you the tea you asked me for. Could you eat some toast with it?"

"I'll try, Mom," Betty said. "Could you please turn on the radio while we wait for my friends?"

Kate turned on the radio and left to make Betty's breakfast. She didn't know what to make of Betty's demeanor. She returned with Betty's tea and toast on a tray and set it down next to her on the sofa.

Betty sipped her tea and said, "Thanks, Mom. Two sugars, just as I like it."

"Honey, after what you said this morning, I don't know what you're thinking or what you want to do with your friends when they arrive," Kate said.

Betty nibbled her toast and sipped the tea. The stimulant was working, and she felt more awake and alert.

"Mom, please don't worry about me. I just want to talk with June and hear about their honeymoon. Everything's going to be fine. I'm not scared anymore."

*****

The doorbell rang again, and Kate went to answer it. She invited Mike and June to come in and took them into the living room.

"Betty's having tea and toast. Can I get you two tea or coffee?"

Mike said, "I'll go with you while June and Betty have a girl talk."

June sat on the couch next to Betty and asked, "How are you doing, honey?"

"I'm all aces, roomie. Tell me more about your honeymoon," Betty said. "Don't leave out the racy stuff!"

June laughed despite herself. "Well, there was this big cast-iron bathtub in our room at the Union Station Hotel that came in handy. And our compartment on the train had seats that could be made into a bed. Mike believes the old saying 'waste not, want not.' You can probably take it from there."

"Like hell, I want details, girl," Betty said and laughed.

June sipped Betty's tea and frowned at the sugar. "Okay, if it's details you want, here goes nothing. In the case of the bathtub, the maid had to mop up a lot of bubble bath. In the case of the compartment, it was love at sixty miles an hour with my heart keeping up with the clickety-clack of the tracks."

Betty and June both laughed.

"You're lucky they didn't kick you both out of your room and off the train," Betty said.

"Well, they did kick us off the Comet," June said.

Kate made coffee and gave Mike a cup. She looked haggard and worn out with worry. She poured one for herself and sat at the kitchen table with him.

"How's Betty doing?" Mike asked.

"I don't really know. This morning she talked like she thought she would die soon and was resigned to it. Now she acts like every-

456

thing is fine, so I just don't know what to think. Her doctors say she hasn't long to live."

Mike drank his coffee. He didn't know how to respond.

"What else did you do? Tell me all," Betty said to June in the living room.

"Mike bought me a new dress at one of the fancy stores in the Grand Hall at the Union Station, and I bought him a new felt hat," June said with a smile. "They were our wedding presents to each other."

"You and Mike are the real deal together, aren't you?" Betty asked. "Hand-in-hand, off-into-the-sunset stuff."

"I guess we are. But I'm sure there will be bumps in the road along the way to the sunset," June laughed. "I'm not that easy to get along with."

"What's it like, being a married woman?" Betty asked. She wrinkled her brow as a pain spasm hit her.

June saw her distress and asked, "Are you okay? Should I call your mother back?"

Betty waited for the pain to pass and said, "You didn't answer my question. What's it like to be married?"

"I can only answer for me. It's like from now on I have a best friend, and so does he. We can count on each other no matter what happens to us."

"That sounds wonderful, roomie. Good for you," Betty said.

"Well, it may be wonderful, but it isn't always easy. We're both stubborn people, and we can't get our own way all the time. We have to compromise sometimes."

"I want to ask you for a favor, roomie."

"Sure, whatever you want, honey," June answered.

"I want you to tell Don goodbye for me. Tell him I wish I could have married him. Tell him I loved him." Another pain seized her abdomen. She grimaced and moved around on the sofa to relieve her spasm.

June was alarmed. "I'm going to go get your mother," she said.

Betty grabbed June's arm and held it until the pain passed.

"Not yet, sweetie," Betty said. "I need to say goodbye to you first."

June's eyes filled with tears. She covered Betty's hand with her own.

"Don't cry for me, roomie. I'm going to be in heaven soon, and there's no pain in heaven," Betty said and held June's hand in both of hers. "Thank you for being my friend and for including me in your wedding. Goodbye now. Please go get Mom." She released June's hand.

June hugged her fiercely as her tears ran down her face. "Goodbye, honey. I love you."

June walked shakily to the kitchen. Kate and Mike both stood up quickly when they saw her face.

"What's wrong? What's happened?" Kate asked.

"Betty sent me to get you, Kate," June said.

Kate rushed out of the kitchen as June sat down heavily in a kitchen chair.

"What happened in there?" Mike asked and handed June his handkerchief.

She wiped her eyes and looked at Mike. "She told me goodbye. She said she's going to heaven."

"Maybe it's the pain medication she's on that is talking," Mike said.

June shook her head sadly and said, "No, it's not that. She's in a lot of pain right now, and she hasn't taken the medication this morning."

Kate hurried to the sofa and sat down next to Betty. Betty had her eyes closed.

"I'm here, honey. June said you needed me."

Betty opened her eyes. "I'd like to go back to bed, Mom. And I think I'm ready for my pain pill. Thank Mike and June for coming," Betty said.

Kate assisted Betty up the stairs and helped her change into a nightgown.

Betty took the pain pill that Kate gave her and got into bed. She closed her eyes and said, "Goodbye, Mom. I love you."

Kate pulled up her covers and kissed her forehead. She went back downstairs to the kitchen, where June and Mike were waiting.

"How is she?" June asked.

"She went back to bed," Kate said. "I gave her one of her pain pills, and she went to sleep. She told me to thank you for coming to see her." Kate went to the counter and made herself a cup of coffee. She asked Mike and June if they wanted a cup.

They both declined, and June said, "Are you okay, Kate?"

Kate sat down and stared at her coffee. "I don't know if I'll ever be okay," she said. She looked as weary as Betty. "My little girl is dying." She burst into tears and pounded her fists on the table. "It's just not fair. It's not right!" Her coffee cup jumped up and spilled her coffee.

Mike was flabbergasted. Mrs. Anderson had always been so composed. Now she was falling apart in front of them. June pulled a chair up close to Kate and put her arm around Kate's shoulder.

"You're right, Kate," June said. "There's nothing right about it at all."

Kate let June hold her until she finished crying. "We can stay until Ray comes home," June told Kate.

Kate shook her head no and said, "I'm okay now. Ray will be home shortly. You two go on. Thank you for coming."

*****

Kate wiped up the spilled coffee and washed the cups and saucers. She was putting them away when Ray came home from his meeting.

"How's Betty doing? Did her friends come over?" Ray asked her.

"Yes, they did. Betty came downstairs and sat and talked with June while I entertained Mike in the kitchen. Betty wanted to be alone with June."

"Where is she now?" Ray asked.

"She went back to bed when her friends left. She asked me for a pain pill, so I gave her one."

Ray checked the coffeepot and turned on the burner to heat up the remaining coffee.

"I'm afraid I threw a fit in front of her friends," Kate said.

"What happened?" Ray asked incredulously. He sat down to wait for the coffee to heat up.

"Betty told June goodbye, and that's what she said to me when she went to sleep. She told me goodbye and said she loved me. When I got to the kitchen with her friends, it hit me like a ton of bricks. My little girl was dying, and she knew it. It made me so mad I wanted to hit somebody, anybody. So I hit the table instead, and then I just bawled."

Ray hugged her and said, "I think I'll go up and check on her." He entered the bedroom and saw the still form of his daughter under the covers. He bent over and kissed her forehead. It was cold. He took her arm from under the covers and felt her wrist. It too was cold, and there was no spark of life.

"Goodbye, my precious child," he said.

He got down on his knees and held her hand. His tears ran down his face and dripped onto her hand.

"Father, please keep her spirit safe with you in heaven. I ask this in the name of your Son, Jesus Christ, amen."

He got up and put her arm gently back under the covers. He said, "You are with the angels now and out of harm's way, honey."

Kate saw Ray's expression when he came into the kitchen.

"Oh my God, no!" she said and ran past him up the stairs to Betty's room. She threw herself on the bed and clutched Betty to her.

"I should have been with you. I should have been with you," she kept repeating over and over. "You told me you were going. I should have stayed with you. I should have stayed with you." She held the body of her child and rocked back and forth.

Ray looked in the open door and listened to his wife chant the same thing over and over while she held her daughter tightly to her. He walked up to the bed and put his hand on Kate's shoulder and said, "We have to let her go, Kate."

Kate was lost in her grief. She didn't even know Ray was in the room.

Ray went back downstairs and phoned Dr. Leyland. After hearing what Ray had to tell him, he said he would come right over. Ray unlocked the front door of the house and went back upstairs. He sat in the easy chair in Betty's room while Kate held Betty and kept repeating her apologies to her dead child.

It wasn't long before Dr. Leyland arrived with an ambulance and two attendants.

He directed the ambulance attendants to wait until he had called for them to enter the house. He opened the front door and went up the stairs to Betty's room. Ray got up from the easy chair and just pointed toward Kate, who was still holding her daughter.

Dr. Leyland leaned over Kate's shoulder and peered into her unseeing eyes. "Kate!" he said loudly and shook her.

She didn't respond.

He told Ray to bring up the ambulance attendants with a stretcher. Ray returned with the attendants.

Dr. Leyland told them, "I believe she's in shock. I'll give her a sedative. When she releases Betty, put Kate on the stretcher and take her into the other bedroom and put her on the bed. I'll lay Betty back in position on the bed and then I'll come attend to Mrs. Anderson." He opened his bag and brought out a hypodermic needle. He swabbed Kate's arm with disinfectant and administered the sedative. She paid no attention to him. When the sedative took effect, the attendants caught Kate as she slumped forward and placed her on the stretcher. Ray led them into the master bedroom, and they laid her on the bed. After Dr. Leyland eased Betty back down on her bed, he went to the master bedroom and checked Kate for shock. Then he went to talk with Ray.

"Ray, these men are here to take Betty to the mortuary. They need your permission," Dr. Leyland told Ray.

Ray said, "Yes, of course. That would be best, I suppose."

Dr. Leyland nodded at the attendants to proceed. They left the room and placed Betty's body on the stretcher. Dr. Leyland and Ray heard Kate stir in the other bedroom.

Dr. Leyland went back to her.

Kate opened her eyes and looked wildly around the room. "Where's Betty? What have you done with Betty?"

Dr. Leyland held her down and administered another dose of sedative. "I gave her enough to keep her out until this evening. I'll be back later to check on her. Are you going to be all right, Ray?"

"I don't know, Doctor. I just don't know," Ray answered.

*****

"What's wrong, honey?" Mike asked June, putting down his newspaper.

June hung up the phone, stared at Mike, and said, "Betty died yesterday after we went to see her. That was her father on the phone."

Mike got up and hugged June. "You told me she said goodbye to you. I guess she knew somehow," Mike said.

June leaned her head on Mike's chest and tried to come to grips with the news about Betty.

"I didn't believe her. She was so cheerful, like her old self," June said. "But she was in a lot of pain. I guess it was for the best." June took a napkin off the table and dried her eyes. "Her father said the mortuary is sending her home to lie in state at her house until the funeral on Tuesday. He is announcing Betty's passing in his church this morning."

"How's her mom doing?" Mike asked.

June picked up the breakfast dishes and put them in the sink with the skillet. "Mr. Anderson didn't say. He just told me the bare facts and hung up. He sounded depressed." She started washing the dishes.

"Do you want me to dry?" Mike asked.

"No, thanks, honey. I need to be doing something right now. Read your paper."

Mike picked up the paper and turned to the war news. "It looks like the Germans are just about whipped. The Allies are almost in Berlin and the Army Air Force bombing raids are leveling German cities," Mike said. "Maybe your brother Lloyd will be home soon."

June dried the dishes. "I'm going over to the Andersons' home to pay my respects this afternoon."

"I'll go with you, honey," Mike said.

"Thanks, Mike," June replied. "I can't believe she's really gone."

*****

The custom of lying-in-view in the home was fading away, but Mrs. Anderson had grimly insisted on it.

Reverend Anderson greeted mourners as they arrived at his home. Mrs. Anderson was seated in the downstairs bedroom next to the open casket that held her daughter.

She had not moved since the mortuary attendants had set the casket in place in the bedroom. She wore a full-length black dress, black stockings, and a round black hat with a black veil. She hadn't said a word to anyone who came in to pay their respects. The dining room was set up for buffet service, and the table was filled with casserole dishes of food brought by the ladies of the church. Most of the mourners avoided the bedroom and focused their condolences on Reverend Anderson. The rigid figure of Mrs. Anderson and her silence discouraged viewings of the girl in the casket. June and Mike located Reverend Anderson in the living room and waited for an opening to speak with him.

"I'm awfully sorry about Betty, Mr. Anderson," June said. "It's hard to believe she's really gone. I miss her dreadfully."

Ray took June's hand in both of his and said, "Thank you, June. You were very special to her."

June looked around the room for Kate.

Ray saw June searching the room and said, "Kate's in the bedroom with Betty. She's taking this very hard. She hasn't spoken a word to anyone except the mortuary since Betty died."

June left Mike and Ray and went to the bedroom. Mike offered his condolences to Ray. June looked in the door of the bedroom and saw Kate next to the casket. There was no one else in the room. June went up to the open casket and looked down at her friend. She looked asleep, and June felt she could wake up at any moment.

June unconsciously reached her hand in and touched Betty's face. "Wake up, roomie, we've got things to do," she whispered.

Kate stirred and raised her veil. "I wasn't with her when she died. I should have been with her."

June came out of her trance when Kate spoke to her. She kneeled down next to Kate, held her hand, and said, "You were with her when she was born. You were with her when she grew up. You were with her when she got sick. You were with her through all her treatments. God was with her when she died. I think everyone did their job, Kate."

Kate got out of the chair and stood, looking down at her daughter. "She took my heart with her," Kate said. "There's just a big hole there now."

June joined her at the casket. "I know what you mean, Kate. That's how I feel too."

The two women, the mother and the best friend, hugged each other and wept.

*****

Ray saw Don come in the front door and went to meet him.

"Thank you for inviting me here," Don said to Ray. "I can't tell you how sorry I am things turned out like this. I kept hoping and praying she would be okay."

"We all did, Don. Thank you for coming," Ray said.

He was about to say something else to Don when Kate and Betty came out of the hall bathroom together.

Kate had taken off the hat and veil and looked like she had just washed her face. June looked the same. They came over to Ray and Don.

Kate said, "Welcome to Betty's memorial. She would be very pleased that you came, Don. Would you like to see her?"

Don said, "Hello, June. Thank you, Mrs. Anderson. I would very much like to see her."

Ray was amazed at Kate's composure. Whatever June had said or done had brought her back to reality. Kate escorted Don to the bedroom and left him there to visit Betty.

Mike said, "Maybe I should go and check on Don?"

June said, "That's a good idea."

Don had seen men die in shot-up airplanes, his buddies and comrades-in-arms. This wasn't the same. It wasn't real. There was no blood or screaming. It was like someone had made a Betty doll and placed it on display in a fancy box. He couldn't get his mind to wrap around it. This artificial being had no connection to the girl he loved and wanted to marry.

"Are you okay, buddy?" he heard someone ask him.

He turned and looked at Mike standing in the doorway. "Oh, hi, Mike," he said. He had to get out of this room. He walked out past Mike and didn't look back.

"Let's get some fresh air," Mike said to Don.

Outside on the front stoop, Don lit a cigarette. He took a heavy drag on his Camel and said to Mike, "That was really weird. I can't believe Betty is dead, and I don't know what I saw in that bedroom, but it wasn't Betty."

"Let's go sit in my Chevy for a while," Mike suggested.

Don followed him down the block, and they both got in the Chevy. Don offered Mike a cigarette from his pack.

"Hey, I quit, remember," Mike said. "You really have a screw loose today."

Don sat and smoked his cigarette. Finally, he said, "People keep telling me Betty is dead, and I'm sure they are right. But my brain just won't accept it. I keep thinking I'm going to see her again."

"You poor bastard, you've really had it bad for her, haven't you?" Mike asked. "I'd feel the same way if it had been June instead of Betty."

"I just finished my new song. It's about Betty. Now she'll never get to hear it, will she?"

Mike thought about his answer. "I don't know. Maybe she will if you play it for her."

That did it. The dam burst, and Don started sobbing. His grief overwhelmed Mike, and tears came to his eyes as well.

"Well, shit," Mike said. "I haven't cried this way since my dog died when I was seven years old. But you go on ahead and let it all out, buddy. She was a hell of a girl."

23

The ruler of the thousand-year Reich sat in a concrete underground bunker and looked at his new wife and longtime lover, Eva Braun, lying on the floor, dead from the cyanide capsule she had swallowed. He placed the gun barrel of his service pistol to his head and pulled the trigger in case his own cyanide capsule didn't do the job.

It was years too late for the millions of people who had died for his warped dreams of glory. Adolf Hitler, the Austrian corporal, went to his Maker to account for his crimes against the people of the world. He was unwilling to share the fate of his fellow dictator, Benito Mussolini, who had, two days earlier, been shot by a firing squad and hung up by his heels in a square in Milan, Italy. Hitler's own SS would do much worse if they turned against him.

*****

Reverend Anderson sat with his wife, Kate, in the front pew of the First Methodist Church. His colleague, Rev. James White of St. Joseph's Methodist Church, was conducting the memorial service for their deceased daughter, Betty. Reverend Anderson feared his grief might unman him if he attempted to conduct the service himself. He could not risk disgracing his family or dishonoring her memory. He needed to support Kate, who was still distraught. Betty's body lay in her closed casket in front of the pulpit. There had been a short period before the service when the casket was opened for viewing. Most of the mourners were church members or friends who had visited the Anderson house on Sunday and had not viewed her then. This period accommodated others like her coworkers at the ordnance plant. Her supervisor, Joe Harding, came with her trainer, Marlene. The director of personnel, Mr. Winston Matthews, his wife, and his secretary, Gladys Smythe, were in attendance. They had all come to know and admire Betty in the short time she had worked at the ordnance plant.

Betty's best friend and roommate, June Thompson, sat in the second row behind Betty's parents. She was with her new husband, Mike, and her family. Her mother and father had driven in from DeKalb with their son, Ricky, and their daughters, Emma Dee and Virginia Jane. Ricky had discarded his sling and was doing well with the recovery of his wounded arm. The church was filled with Reverend Anderson's congregation. He was a popular minister. Betty's free-spirited childhood had caused some tongue wagging, but she was well liked by them, and many tears would be shed at her service.

Reverend White offered the invocation to begin the service. The choir sang "Amazing Grace." Reverend White delivered his sermon with the theme of the resurrection and hope of eternal life.

June listened to Reverend White's sermon and thought about Betty's conviction she was going to heaven.

It was like she was planning a trip, June thought. *She even arranged to say goodbye to her family and to me. She seemed to know it was time to go. I'm glad she is free of her suffering. But I miss her dreadfully.*

Kate appreciated Reverend White's message. But she had difficulty containing her anger and depression at losing her only child.

Ray thought Reverend White was doing a splendid job with his sermon and was very grateful to him. He doubted he would have been able to carry such a hopeful message. His grief was too deep for that.

On the way to the funeral, Don told Mike, "I have a hole in me that you could drive a truck through."

Mike had replied, "Like you always tell me, we have to suit up and show up, buddy."

Don sat next to Betty's parents and hoped he would give a good account of himself with his contribution to Betty's service. He listened to Reverend White wrap up the sermon, and then to the choir who sang "Abide with Me."

After they had finished, Reverend White resumed the pulpit and said, "Betty's friend, Mrs. June Thompson, will now share a few words with us."

June came forward and assumed the pulpit. She was determined not to cry.

"I was privileged to call Betty Anderson my best friend. She was true blue and honest all the way through. I loved her like a sister. We lived together and shared everything. Betty loved life, and she made you love it with her. She was a livewire, and she had class. I never saw her do a mean thing to anyone. When she found out about her illness, she decided to make a fight of it. And she did. With the help of her doctors, she achieved two remissions contending with unpleasant and trying treatments. As a result, she lived long enough to be the maid of honor at my wedding. She's the bravest person I've ever known. She was one of a kind, and I'll always miss her."

June rejoined Mike in the second pew. Mike took her hand and held it for a moment. Reverend White then introduced Don.

Don picked up the guitar next to him on the pew and walked up to the podium. He adjusted the microphone. "I am a fellow who always had good luck with the ladies. I've liked a lot of women, but Betty's the only woman I've ever loved. I asked Betty to be my wife after she became ill. She turned me down because she loved me. I wrote this song for her." He played a few introductory bars and began singing out his own blues.

> *Her heart was warm as the noonday sun*
> *Her eyes were blue as a tropical sea.*
>
> *Her hair was a golden shock of wheat.*
> *I don't know what she saw in me.*
>
> *My sweet Betty. My sweet Betty.*
> *You were all the world to me.*
>
> *Love and laughter were her gifts*
> *with joy she gave to me.*

I wish I could have had her love
for all eternity.

My sweet Betty. My sweet Betty.
You were all the world to me.

She lived her life up to the hilt
She was wild and free.
Now that she has gone
I'm left with her haunting memory.

My sweet Betty. My sweet Betty.
You were all the world to me.

She's a bright new angel
And she's mine no more.
My lonely heart is broken
But she walks on heaven's shore.
Yes, she walks on heaven's shore.

My sweet Betty. My sweet Betty.
You were all the world to me.

When he finished his song, Kate and June were both crying. They weren't the only ones. He took his guitar and sat back down next to Ray.

"Thank you, son," Ray said.

Reverend Wilson said the closing prayer. Don, Ray, Mike, and the other pallbearers lifted up the coffin and marched out of the church while the choir sang "A Closer Walk with Thee."

Don lit a Camel cigarette outside and then rode with Mike out to the cemetery.

"That's a great song, buddy," Mike said. "You should record it."

"I finished it when Betty came home from the hospital and the doctors gave up on her treatments. I asked Mr. Anderson if I could sing it at her service, and he agreed."

"Well, it's a dandy song. I think you should talk to our manager about it," Mike said.

Don smoked his cigarette and said, "Maybe I will. Right now I'm down in the dumps, and I can't seem to get out of them."

"Listen, pal, after this shindig is over, let's you and I go get good and drunk," Mike said.

"Yeah, June would really appreciate you coming home bombed," Don warned him.

"Okay, then let's just go hoist a couple for Betty. She'd like that," Mike said.

"It's a deal, buddy," Don said.

They parked with other cars near the canopy over the burial site.

"That was a swell service," Emma Dee said to her sisters as they rode in their parents' car.

"It sure was," Virginia Jane agreed.

"I think Betty would have liked it," June said. "I cried when Don sang his song. It was so sad. Don and Betty were like peanut butter and jelly. They went together."

Dee pulled the car into the cemetery grounds and up to the burial site.

Reverend Anderson presided at the burial of his daughter. Then he set aside his Bible and said, "I know Betty is in heaven. God must have had an urgent task for her to have taken her so young. Or maybe He just needed the company of my Betty to cheer Him up in the face of so much evil in the world. Thank you all for coming to honor and remember her."

24

Shortly after the suicide of Adolf Hitler on April 30, the Germans surrendered, and the War in Europe was finally over.

*****

Don Walker's song, "My Sweet Betty," was a hit and made the top 40, rising to number 2 on the Hit Parade. He never recorded another hit record. He was a successful songwriter, and several of his songs made the top 40 recorded by other artists. And he was a sought-after studio musician. He was married three times and divorced twice. He always said it took him three tries to find another Betty. The truth was that he couldn't get over losing her. His third wife, Ruth, finally helped him with that.

June got her business degree, and then Mike got his degree in electrical engineering. He and June founded an engineering firm. Warren Nelson (Slats) invested in the Thompsons' company, and they expanded into television manufacturing. Their timing was perfect. The company went public ten years later. June was company CEO (chief executive officer) until the birth of their daughter, Betty. Betty had all the gumption of her namesake, June's best friend.

On their fortieth anniversary, June made Mike ride the biggest roller coaster at Six Flags Park in Texas with her. They rode it twice, once in the daytime and once at night. Mike made her promise to get off the ride when it finished. She did.

The End

About the Author

Darrell Wyatt was a WWII war baby whose mother was a nurse and his father a musician who served in the Pacific theater in the Army Air Corps. The author served in the US Army for three years and worked in factories the rest of his career. His interest in American war history and the contribution of women in those efforts inspired this book. Some of the characters and locations in this story are based on his experiences and encounters in the St. Joseph, Missouri, area. His grandparents were tobacco farmers near DeKalb, Missouri.

CPSIA information can be obtained
at www.ICGtesting.com
Printed in the USA
LVHW040224280123
737897LV00001B/19